THE BREATH OF GOD

Tor Books by Harry Turtledove

The Two Georges (by Richard Dreyfuss and Harry Turtledove)
Household Gods (by Judith Tarr and Harry Turtledove)
The First Heroes (edited by Harry Turtledove and Noreen Doyle)
Between the Rivers
Into the Darkness
Darkness Descending
Through the Darkness
Rulers of the Darkness
Jaws of Darkness
Out of the Darkness
Conan of Venarium
Gunpowder Empire
Curious Notions
In High Places
The Disunited States of America
Beyond the Gap
The Valley Westside War
The Breath of God

(Writing as H. N. Turteltaub)

Justinian
Over the Wine-Dark Sea
The Gryphon's Skull
The Sacred Land

THE BREATH
OF GOD

HARRY TURTLEDOVE

TOR®

A Tom Doherty Associates Book
New York

THE BREATH OF GOD

Copyright © 2008 by Harry Turtledove

A Tor Book
Published by Tom Doherty Associates, LLC
175 Fifth Avenue
New York, NY 10010

www.tor-forge.com

Tor® is a registered trademark of Tom Doherty Associates, LLC.

Library of Congress Cataloging-in-Publication Data

Turtledove, Harry.
    The breath of God / Harry Turtledove.—1st ed.
        p.   cm.—
    "A Tom Doherty Associates book."
    ISBN-13: 978-0-7653-1711-7
    ISBN-10: 0-7653-1711-7
    1. Prehistoric peoples—Fiction.   2. Bronze age—Fiction.   I. Title.
    PS3570.U76 B74 2008
    813'.54 dc22

                                                2008034074

First Edition: December 2008

Printed in the United States of America

0   9   8   7   6   5   4   3   2   1

THE BREATH OF GOD

1

THE BREATH OF God blew down hard from the north. Here in the Bizogot country near the Glacier, the wind off the great ice sheet blew hard all winter long. Hamnet Thyssen's own breath smoked as if he were puffing on a pipe. He wished he were, though Ulric Skakki liked tobacco better than he did. Unless Raumsdalian traders had brought a little up from the south, there was none for hundreds of miles.

Count Hamnet was a Raumsdalian himself. He was large and dark and dour, with a black beard that had a streak of white above a scar and some scatterings of gray elsewhere—and that looked whiter now than it really was, what with all the rime and snow caught in it. He wore Bizogot-style furs and leather, with the stout felt boots that were the best footgear ever made for fighting cold. In spite of hooded jacket and furred trousers, he felt the frigid weather like an icepick in his bones.

Ulric was up from the south, too, though Hamnet wasn't sure the foxy-faced adventurer had been born inside the borders of the Raumsdalian Empire. Whether he had or not, he spoke Raumsdalian perfectly these days. Pitching his voice to carry through the shrieking wind, he said, "Things could be worse."

"How?" Hamnet asked. "We could have frozen to death already?"

"Oh, you don't freeze to death up here, not if you're careful. You just wish you could," Ulric said, which was true. "That's not what I meant. A couple of thousand years ago, we could have enjoyed this lovely weather down near Nidaros."

Sigvat II, the Raumsdalian Emperor, ruled from Nidaros these days. Two thousand years earlier, the great city was no more than a hunting camp on the edge of Hevring Lake. The meltwater filling the lake came from the Glacier, which in those days lay just to the north. The glaciers had fallen back all this way in the years since. Nidaros was almost temperate these days; barley grew there most years, and wheat in the warmer ones. Hevring Lake was long gone. When the ice dam that corked it melted through, it poured out to the west in a great flood that carved out the badlands still scarring that terrain.

Despite the warming weather in the south—or rather, because of it— Hamnet Thyssen bared his teeth in a mirthless grin. "Better that, some ways, than this."

"What?" Ulric mocked without mercy. "I thought you always wanted to go beyond the Glacier."

"Not always. I didn't used to think there *was* anything beyond the Glacier," Hamnet answered. "And even after I found out there was, I didn't want what lived beyond the Glacier coming here, curse it."

"Life is full of surprises," Ulric Skakki said, which would have been funny if only it were funny.

For some time now, the Glacier had been melting back towards the northwest and northeast, leaving a corridor of open land—the Gap— between the two great frozen sheets. Now at last the Gap had melted through, allowing travelers from the south to discover what lay on the far side of the Glacier.

Up until that finally happened, Hamnet Thyssen had always thought the northern glaciers went on forever. So had most Raumsdalians—and most of the nomadic Bizogots who lived north of them. The Golden Shrine? As far as Count Hamnet was concerned, the Golden Shrine was only a myth.

He knew better now. Oh, not about the Golden Shrine, which might still be mythical for all he could prove. But he'd gone beyond the Glacier himself. He'd seen the striped cats called tigers, which preyed there in place of the lions and sabertooths he knew. He'd seen the great brown bears that scooped salmon from streams unfrozen in summer. He'd seen vast herds of deer with both stags and does bearing blunt-tined antlers.

And he'd seen the folk who rode those deer as men on this side of the Glacier rode horses. The Rulers, they called themselves. They not only herded woolly mammoths, as the Bizogots had for centuries uncounted, but rode them to war, with lancers and men with long, long lances on the beasts' shaggy backs.

The Rulers seemed convinced any folk not of their blood were animals, to be tamed like mammoths or hunted and killed like wolves and tigers. They were not warriors to be despised, and their sorcerers had strength neither Raumsdalian wizards nor Bizogot shamans could easily withstand.

Trasamund rode up to Hamnet and Ulric. He too looked north. "Any thing?" he asked, doing his best not to sound worried. He was a big, burly man, bigger than Hamnet Thyssen, with piercing blue eyes and a thick, curly red-gold beard almost like a pelt.

"Hard to tell with this snow, Your Ferocity, but I don't think so." Hamnet gave the jarl of the Three Tusk clan his proper title of respect, even if the Rulers, pouring down through the Gap, had shattered the clan and left him a jarl with only a remnant of a folk to rule. Trasamund's pride remained grand as ever—grander, maybe, to help compensate for all he'd lost.

"A couple of men from the Red Dire Wolves are right behind me," Trasamund said. "You southerners can ride for the tents now. I know you're feeling the weather worse than a man born to it would."

"It gets this cold down in the Empire," Ulric Skakki said. "It just doesn't stay this cold from fall through the start of spring."

"Well, go in anyway. Warm yourselves. Get some food. You need more when it does stay like this." Trasamund was right about that; Count Hamnet had seen as much. He ate like a dire wolf to keep from freezing, and didn't gain an ounce. The Bizogot paused, an anxious look flitting across his face. "You *can* find your way back to the tents by yourselves in this weather?"

It wasn't an idle question. With snow and wind wiping out tracks almost as fast as they were made, with visibility short, someone who didn't know how to make his way across the frozen steppe could wander till he froze to death.

All the same, both Hamnet Thyssen and Ulric Skakki smiled. They weren't Bizogots, born to the northern plains, but they could manage. Smiling still, Ulric said, "Yes, Mother dear."

Trasamund's snort birthed a young fogbank. "Scoff all you please," he said. "Any Bizogot clan will tell you about Raumsdalian traders who ended up stiff clean through because they thought they knew more about this country than they really did."

"We'll get there," Hamnet Thyssen said. He wheeled his horse. The beast seemed glad to face away from the Breath of God. Hamnet and Ulric rode south, towards the encampment housing the remnants of the Three Tusk clan and the Red Dire Wolves, who guested them and who, reluctantly, joined them in the war against the Rulers.

ONE STRETCH OF snowy, windswept ground really did look a lot like another. Count Hamnet was starting to wonder whether he and Ulric had bragged too soon when the Bizogots' mammoth-hide tents appeared in the distance. The mammoths' thick skins and the long, shaggy dark brown hair on them offered a barrier formidable even to the fiercest gales.

All the same, entrances invariably faced south. They did down in the Empire, too. Hamnet Thyssen and Ulric Skakki tethered their horses behind a snow-block wall that shielded the animals from the worst of the wind. They'd bought the horses in Nidaros, but the animals were of the small, shaggy Bizogot breed, better suited to the harsh northern weather than other horses.

Hamnet ducked into the tent belonging to Totila, the jarl of the Red Dire Wolves. He needed a moment to get used to the gloom inside. A couple of bone lamps burning butter made from the milk of musk oxen and mammoths gave only a dim, flickering light. A brazier that burned dried dung added a little heat, but not much.

The brazier and lamps did contribute to the pungency. Hamnet Thyssen knew his nose would soon get used to it, but it was fierce when he'd just come in from the fresh if frigid steppe. Chamber pots of leather and wickerwork had tight lids, and people emptied them often, but their reek hung in the air. So did that of unwashed bodies, Hamnet's own among them. Bathing in winter in the Bizogot country was asking for anything from chest fever to frostbite.

"Anything, Raumsdalian?" Totila asked. The Red Dire Wolves' jarl sounded worried, for which Count Hamnet could hardly blame him. Now his clan, along with what was left of Trasamund's, stood on the front line against the Rulers. Any blow that fell would probably fall on him.

He relaxed—a little—when Hamnet Thyssen shook his head and said, "No." Hamnet let his hood drop down off his head and undid the top toggle on his fur jacket. It *was* warmer inside the tent, though more from the body heat of the people it sheltered than from the brazier's feeble little fire.

"I sense nothing amiss—nothing close, anyhow." Liv was the shaman from the Three Tusk clan. She was close to thirty, with golden hair (short and greasy and dirty, as the Bizogots' hair commonly was), cheekbones as

proud and sharp and angular as the Glacier, and eyes of the deepest blue
Count Hamnet had ever seen.

He'd studied those eyes from very close range indeed. He and Liv were
lovers. She was the only woman he'd met since Gudrid left him who made
him . . . oh, not forget his former wife, but remember she wasn't the only fish
in the sea. And if that wasn't a miracle, Hamnet Thyssen had never met one.

Totila went right on worrying. "Would you?" he asked. "Or could their
magic mask their moves so you wouldn't know till they got right on top of us?"

"It could," Liv said seriously, at which the jarl gnawed on his lower lip.
Hamnet understood how he felt. He himself had fretted over the way things
went in his county down in the southeastern part of the Empire. And his
domain never faced danger close to that which hovered above the Red Dire
Wolves like a teratorn soaring through the air in search of a fresh corpse to
gnaw.

"What good are your precious senses, then?" Totila snapped.

Liv didn't rise to his anger and fear. "Maybe no good," she answered,
"but I don't think so. Masking movement on that scale isn't easy for us or
for the Rulers. And we have sentries out." She nodded towards Hamnet.
"Even if my spells do fail, sharp eyes shouldn't."

"They'd better not," the jarl said. He too nodded towards Hamnet, though
his expression was gruff, not fond. "Feed yourself. We have meat, and you
need to stoke your fire."

"I know." The Raumsdalian took off his mittens.

The meat came from a mammoth liver. Hamnet Thyssen impaled a
chunk on a long bone skewer and started toasting it over the dung-fueled
brazier. Through most of the year, the Bizogots didn't have to worry about
salting meat or smoking it to keep it edible. They had the biggest ice chest
in the world right outside their tents.

They also had peculiar tastes—or so it seemed to a man from farther
south. Listen to a Bizogot and he'd tell you meat cooked with wood lacked
flavor. They were used to what dung fires did, and they liked it. Count Hamnet was getting used to it, too. He had to, or eat his meat raw, or starve.
Whether he would ever like it was a different question.

Mammoth liver would have been strong-flavored stuff no matter what it
was cooked over. Hamnet stolidly ate. He had to get used to being as carniv-
orous as a sabertooth, too. No grain up here—no bread, no porridge. No
potatoes or turnips or even onions. In summer, the Bizogots varied their

diet with the small, sweet berries that quickly ripened and then were gone. Those in the southern part of the frozen steppe gathered honey from the few hardy bees that buzzed about when the weather warmed and flowers blossomed frantically. They were fond of mushrooms. But for that, they ate meat, and occasionally fish.

"Nothing wrong to the north? You're sure?" Liv said.

He shook his head. "There's plenty wrong to the north, and we both know it. But I didn't see any sign that the Rulers were about to swoop down on the Red Dire Wolves."

"That's what I meant," Liv said. "But I don't think they'll wait much longer."

Hamnet Thyssen liked the flavor of that even less than he liked the flavor of dung-cooked mammoth liver. "Is that your feeling?" he asked. "Or is it what your magic tells you?"

"Not mine. Audun Gilli's," the shaman answered. "His seems better at piercing the wards the Rulers use than mine does." She didn't sound jealous, merely matter-of-fact.

"Where is Audun, anyway?" Hamnet asked. The Raumsdalian wizard usually stayed in the jarl's tent, too. He'd never learned much of the Bizogot tongue, and needed another Raumsdalian or Liv or Trasamund to translate for him.

"He's with Theudechild, in the tent where she stays," Liv said.

"Oh." Hamnet left it there. He wondered what the Bizogot woman saw in Audun Gilli, who was short and slight and unprepossessing and could hardly talk to her. Whatever it was, she doted on him. And Audun seemed to like her well enough. He'd lost his family some years earlier, and lived in a drunken stupor till Ulric Skakki plucked him from the gutter—literally— and made him dry out.

Getting drunk among the Bizogots took dedication. Except for beer and wine brought up from the south, their only tipple was smetyn—fermented musk-ox or mammoth milk. It was sour and not very strong. The mammoth-herders poured it down, though.

Something else occurred to Hamnet. "He's with Theudechild? The lamps are still lit."

"So what?" Liv said. "People look the other way. They pretend not to hear. When you live in crowded tents most of the year, you have to do things like that. I've seen your *houses* with all their *rooms*." She dropped in a couple of Raumsdalian words for things the Bizogots didn't have and didn't need to name. "You can get away from one another whenever you please. All we have are blankets—and the sense not to look when it's none of our business."

Not many Raumsdalians had that kind of sense. Maybe they didn't need it so much. On the other hand, maybe they would have got along better if they had more of it. Hamnet said, "Well, it's good to see Audun happy, too."

Was it good to see himself happy? He had to think about that. He wasn't used to thinking of himself as happy. After what Gudrid did to him—and after the way he spent years brooding and agonizing about what she did to him—he was much more used to thinking of himself as miserable. But he wasn't, not any more.

"So it is," Liv said. Did she know how happy she made him? If she didn't, it wasn't because he didn't try to show her. And was that a twinkle in her eye, or only a flicker from one of those odorous lamps? Whatever it was, she asked, "Are you Bizogot enough to think blankets and the sense not to look are enough?"

"I'm not a Bizogot at all, and I never will be." Count Hamnet paused, but not for long. "I don't suppose that means I can't act like one, though. I *am* here, after all. . . ." Not much later, he did his very best to pretend he and Liv had all the privacy in the world. By the small sounds she made even when trying to keep discreetly silent, his best seemed good enough.

MUSK OXEN WERE made for the frozen plains the Bizogots roamed. Their shaggy outer coats and the thick, soft hair that grew closer to the hide warded them against the worst the Breath of God could do. They knew how to scrape snow away with their hooves to uncover plants frozen under the snow. When danger threatened, they formed protective circles, with the formidably horned bulls and larger cows on the outside and the smaller females and calves within. Dire wolves and lions took stragglers now and again, but they had to be desperately hungry to attack one of those circular formations.

The Bizogots hadn't fully domesticated the musk oxen they herded, but the beasts were used to having men around. The herders helped protect them from predators . . . and preyed on the musk oxen themselves.

Despite the threat from the Rulers, the Red Dire Wolf Bizogots had to follow the herds. If they lost them, they would starve. And the survivors from the Three Tusk clan and the Raumsdalians up from the south took their turn tending the musk oxen, too. The Three Tusk Bizogots knew just

what to do; all across the northern steppe, the Bizogots tended their animals in much the same way. Hamnet Thyssen and Ulric Skakki did their
best, and seemed to pick up what they needed to know fast enough to suit
the Red Dire Wolves. Audun Gilli also did his best. Not even the Bizogots
said anything else. How good that best was . . .

"Careful, Audun!" Count Hamnet pitched his voice to carry through the
howling wind. "If you get too close, you'll spook them."

"If I stay this far away, though, I have trouble seeing the front part of the
herd," the wizard answered.

Patiently, Hamnet said, "Other riders are up there. We're not doing this
by ourselves, you know. We worry about the beasts close to us, they worry
about the ones close to them, and when we put everything together the job
gets done."

"I suppose so." Audun Gilli sounded distinctly dubious. "Better one person should be able to take care of everything."

That was a wizard's way of looking at the world. Wizards had as much
trouble cooperating as cats did, and used weapons sharper and deadlier
than fangs and talons. Working together meant sharing power and secrets,
and power and secrets didn't like to be shared. Audun and Liv had teamed
up a couple of times against sorcery from the Rulers, but it wasn't easy or
natural for them.

"One person would need to use magic to take care of a whole herd of
musk oxen," Hamnet Thyssen said. "Do you want to try?"

Audun thought about that. It didn't take a whole lot of thought. "Well,
no," he admitted, shaking his head.

"Good," Hamnet said. "If you'd told me yes, I would have thought you
were as arrogant as one of the Rulers."

"I hope not!" Audun exclaimed. "The worst thing about them is, they
have the strength to back up their arrogance. That makes them think they
have some natural right to it, the way they think they have the right to lord
it over all the folk they can reach."

"No," Count Hamnet said. "The worst thing about the Rulers is, they can
reach folk on this side of the Glacier because of the Gap."

"I think we said the same thing," Audun Gilli replied.

"Well, maybe we did." Hamnet looked north, towards the Gap that had
finally melted through the great Glacier and towards the two enormous ice
sheets that remained, one to the northwest, the other to the northeast. He

couldn't have seen the opening in the Gap anyway; it lay much too far north. Swirling clouds and blowing snow kept him from getting even a glimpse of the southern edge of the Glacier now. When the weather was clear, those frozen cliffs bestrode the steppe like the edge of any other mountains, but steeper and more abrupt.

He'd had an odd thought not long before. There were mountains in the west. They ran north and north, till the Glacier swallowed them. Did any of their peaks stick out above the surface of the ice? Did life persist on those islands in the icebound sea? Were there even, could there be, men up there? No one had ever seen fires burning on the Glacier, but no one had ever gone up there to look at close range, either.

This time, his shiver had nothing to do with the frigid weather. Trasamund had told him once that Bizogots had tried to scale the Glacier to see if they could reach the top. It had to be at least a mile—maybe two or three— almost straight up. The mammoth-herders hadn't managed it. They were probably lucky they hadn't killed themselves. One mistake on that unfor- giving climb would likely be your last. You might have too long to regret it as you fell, though.

Hamnet Thyssen imagined men roaming from one unfrozen mountain refuge to another. He imagined them trying to come down to the Bizogot country, stepping off the edge of the Glacier as if off the edge of the world. Descending might be even harder than reaching the top of the Glacier. Down near the bottom, you had at least some margin for error. Up above, the tiniest mischance would kill you, sure as sure.

He suddenly realized Audun Gilli had said something to him. "I'm sorry. What was that?" he said. "You caught me woolgathering."

Above the woven wool that muffled his mouth and nose, the wizard's eyes were amused. "I must have. You seemed as far away as if someone had dropped you on top of the Glacier."

That made Hamnet shiver again. Wizards . . . knew things. Sometimes they didn't know how they knew or even that they knew, but know they did. "Well, ask me again," Hamnet said. "I'm here now."

"How lucky for you." Audun still seemed to think it was funny. "I said, what do we do when the Rulers strike the Red Dire Wolves?"

"The best we can. What else is there?" Hamnet answered bleakly. "How good is the Red Dire Wolves' shaman? How much help can he give you and Liv?"

"Old Odovacar?" Audun Gilli rolled his eyes. "Liv's got more brains in her little finger than he does in his head. He turned them all into beard."

Audun wasn't far wrong about the shaman's beard; it reached almost to his crotch. Even so, Count Hamnet said, "Are you sure? You can talk with Liv now—she's learned Raumsdalian." *And why haven't you learned more of the Bizogots' tongue?* But that was an argument for another day. Hamnet went on, "Odovacar might be clever enough with spells in his own language."

"Yes, he might be, but he isn't," Audun said. "I've talked with him through Liv. He has one spell down solid—he can take the shape of a dire wolf. But even when he's in man's form, he hasn't got any more sense than a dire wolf. I'm surprised nobody's caught him sitting on his haunches licking his bal-locks."

That started a laugh out of Hamnet. Even so, he said, "Odovacar must be able to do more than that. Shamans can't be shamans on so little. Whoever he learned from surely taught him other things, too."

"Oh, I suppose he can find lost needles and read the weather and do some other little tricks that won't help us against the Rulers at all," Audun said. "But the one thing the shaman of the Red Dire Wolves *has* to do is commune with dire wolves, and by God Odovacar can do that. And since he can, they forgive him for all the things he cursed well *can't* do, starting with learning anything he didn't get from his teacher a thousand years ago."

"Don't exaggerate." Mock severity filled Hamnet Thyssen's voice. "Odovacar can't be a day over eight hundred."

"Ha!" The Raumsdalian wizard laughed for politeness' sake alone, be-cause he plainly didn't find it funny. "However old he is, he's outlived his usefulness. If you don't believe me, talk to your lady love. She's as fed up with him as I am."

Talk to your lady love. Audun Gilli had lost his wife, too, in circumstances more harrowing than Hamnet's. But he didn't seem jealous that the other Raumsdalian had won Liv's love. Hamnet was glad he wasn't. Audun might have made a rival, since he and Liv had sorcery in common. *If I thought she cheated on me the way Gudrid used to, I'd worry about Audun now.* Hamnet shook his head. If you let thoughts like that grow, they would poison whatever good you'd found in your life.

When he pulled his mind away from that notion, it lit on a different one. "Odovacar communes with real dire wolves, you say?"

"Well, he doesn't smoke a pipe with them or anything like that, but he goes out wandering when he wears wolf shape," Audun Gilli answered. "He must meet real dire wolves when he does, and they haven't eaten his scrawny old carcass yet."

"That's what I'm driving at," Hamnet Thyssen said. "Do you suppose he could go out as a dire wolf and rally the real ones against the Rulers?"

Audun started to shake his head, but then caught himself. "I don't know," he said slowly. "It might be worth a try. The Rulers wouldn't like packs harrying their riding deer, would they? Harrying them, too, come to that, if Odovacar can bring it off. And if he goes out in a wolfskin and doesn't come back, the Red Dire Wolves might be better off."

"Are you sure *you're* not wearing Ulric Skakki's skin?" Hamnet asked; the adventurer was more likely to come out with something that cynically frank.

Audun pulled off a mitten and lifted his cuff. "Nothing up my sleeve but me," he said, and thought for a little while. "You know, Your Grace, that could work. The Rulers wouldn't like dire wolves worrying at their animals—or at them."

"Who would?" Count Hamnet said. "The other nice thing about this is, they may have a harder time returning the favor."

"Why?" Audun Gilli frowned. Then his face cleared. "Oh, I see what you mean. No dire wolves on the far side of the Glacier, just those smaller, skinnier beasts."

"That's what I meant," Hamnet Thyssen agreed. "Maybe the dire wolves would be friendly to a wizard in the hide of one of those other wolves. But maybe they'd have him for supper instead. That's how I'd bet."

"Well, we'll see what Odovacar thinks." Audun frowned again. "For that matter, we'll see *if* Odovacar thinks."

Like every other Bizogot shaman Count Hamnet had seen, Odovacar wore a ceremonial costume full of fringes and tufts. His were all made from the hides and furs of dire wolves. Some were dyed red with berry juice, others left their natural brown and gray and cream. Even old and bent and thin, he was a big man; he must have been enormous, and enormously strong, when in his prime.

Getting anything across to him wasn't easy, for he'd grown almost deaf as he aged. He used a hearing trumpet made from a musk-ox horn, but it didn't help much. Audun Gilli, with his problems with the Bizogot language, didn't try to talk to the shaman—he left that to Hamnet and to Liv.

She bawled into the hearing trumpet while Hamnet Thyssen shouted into Odovacar's other ear. The racket they made surely disturbed some of the other Red Dire Wolf Bizogots, but it bothered Odovacar very little because he heard very little of it.

"A wolf? Yes, of course I can shape myself into a wolf," he said. Many old men's teeth were worn down almost flat against their gums. Not his—they were still long and sharp and white, suggesting his ties to the Red Dire Wolves' fetish animal.

Getting him to understand what to do after he went into dire wolf's shape took the best—or maybe the worst—part of an afternoon. It wasn't that Odovacar was stupid. Hamnet Thyssen didn't think it was, anyhow. But he heard so little that getting anything across to him was an ordeal.

With Audun Gilli or another Raumsdalian wizard, Count Hamnet could have written down what he wanted. Nothing was wrong with Odovacar's eyes, but writing didn't help him, for the Bizogots had no written language. Hamnet and Liv had to keep shouting over and over again till, one word at a time, one thought at a time, they tunneled through the wall deafness built between Odovacar and the folk around him.

"Ah," he said at last, his own voice too loud because he wanted to have some chance of hearing himself. "You want me to lead the dire wolves against the invaders from the north."

"Yes." Hamnet Thyssen hoped it was yes. Or did Odovacar think he and Liv meant they wanted him to take command of the Red Dire Wolves' human warriors? By then, nothing would have surprised Hamnet overmuch.

But Odovacar had it right. "I can do it," he said in that loud, cracked, quavering old man's voice. He began to sway back and forth, chanting a song that sounded as if it was in the Bizogot language but that Hamnet couldn't follow. Liv's nod said she could.

He slowly rose and started to dance, there inside his tent. At first, the dance seemed little more than swaying back and forth while on his feet, more or less in rhythm to the song he chanted. But it got more vigorous as the song went on. The chant grew more vigorous, too. Hamnet still couldn't understand it, but growls and snarls began replacing some of the sounds that seemed like Bizogot words. The tune, though, stayed the same.

Odovacar's fringes shook. His long white beard whipped back and forth. In the lamplight, his eyes blazed yellow.

Yellow? Hamnet Thyssen rubbed at his own eyes. Like almost all Bizogots, Odovacar had ice-blue eyes. But was this still Odovacar the man? Hamnet shook his head. No, not wholly, not any more.

Liv was nodding in understanding and, Hamnet thought, in admiration as she watched the change sweep over the other shaman. She was used to seeing such things. She'd probably shifted shape herself, though Count Hamnet didn't think she'd done it since he'd known her. She might take it for granted, but it raised the Raumsdalian's hackles.

Odovacar dropped down onto all fours. His wolfskin jacket and trousers and his own beard all seemed to turn into pelt. His teeth, already long and white, grew whiter and much longer while his tongue lolled from his mouth. His nose lengthened into a snout. His ears grew pointed and stood away from his head. He wore a wolf's tail attached to the seat of his trousers. As the spell took hold, it was still a wolf's tail—it was *his* tail, attached to him as any beast's tail was attached to it. As if to prove as much, it lashed back and forth.

"Can you hear me?" Hamnet Thyssen asked in a small voice. Odovacar the dire wolf was doubtless still old, but seemed much less decrepit than Odovacar the man. And he swung his fierce head towards Hamnet and nodded somewhat as a dog might nod, but also somewhat as a man might. Shapeshifters kept some of their human intelligence in beast form. How much? Hamnet wasn't sure even they could answer that question once they returned to human shape.

"You know what you are to do?" Liv sounded far more respectful of the shaman as a dire wolf than she had of him as a man.

Odovacar nodded again. A sound that wasn't a word but was agreement burst from his throat. Hamnet Thyssen had heard an owl that was also a wizard use human speech, but that was under the influence of the magic Liv used to capture it, not through the spell the wizard used to transform himself.

"Good," Liv said. "Go, then, and God go with you."

One more nod from Odovacar, who bounded out through the south-facing tent flap. He made another sound once he was out in the open air, a canine cry of joy pure and unalloyed. To a dire wolf's senses, the inside of the tent had to be cramped and smelly. Unlike people, wolves weren't made to be confined in such places. Hamnet Thyssen stuck his head out into the cold. Odovacar trotted purposefully off to the west, wagging his tail as he went. Yes, he was glad to get away.

"He seems happier as a dire wolf," Hamnet said.

"I suppose he is," Liv answered. "But he will die sooner if he keeps that hide and not the one he was born with. He knows that. Even as a wolf, he knows it. He will do what needs doing—what he can recall of it in beast shape. And we will see how much good it does us."

"Quite a bit, I hope." Hamnet Thyssen stuck his head out into the cold again. Like Odovacar, he was sometimes glad to get free of the Bizogot tents himself. Living through the long northern winters in the enforced close company of the mammoth-herders wasn't easy for a man of his basically solitary temperament. If he weren't in love with Liv, he wondered if he could have done it.

"Don't get frostbite," she told him—in this climate, an even more serious warning than it would have been down in the Empire.

"I won't." He wanted to twist around so he could look north towards the Gap, north towards the grazing grounds of the Three Tusk clan, the grazing grounds the Rulers had stolen. In his mind's eye, he saw swarms of dire wolves raiding those grounds, feasting on the Rulers' riding deer, dragging down musk oxen that couldn't keep up with the herds, maybe even killing mammoth calves if they wandered away from their mothers. And he saw something else, even if it wasn't so clear as he wished it were.

When he ducked back into the big black tent again, some of what he imagined he'd seen must have shown on his face, for Liv said, "What is it? What's wrong?"

"I don't know," he answered. "But we've thought a lot about how we can hit back at the Rulers. What have they been thinking about all this time? I don't know that, either, and I wish I did. Whatever it is, I don't think we're going to like it."

THE SUN HAD turned in the sky. Days were still short, shorter than they ever got in Nidaros, but they were getting longer. Each day, the sun rose a little farther north and east of due south, swinging away from the tiny arc it made in the southern sky around the solstice. Each day, it set a little farther north and west of due south. And each day became more of a *day*, not just a brief splash of light punctuating the long hours of darkness.

Hamnet Thyssen would have hoped the longer daylight hours meant warmer weather. In that, he was disappointed but not much surprised. Down in the Empire, the worst blizzards usually came after the turning of the year, but before longer days finally led to the spring thaw. Those blizzards started here, when the Breath of God howled down off the Glacier. Spring would take longer to get here, and would have a looser grip when it finally did.

Odovacar returned to the Red Dire Wolves' tents. Hamnet Thyssen saw him ambling in, still in dire-wolf shape. He was heavier than he had been when he set out, but he walked with a limp. A long, half-healed gash scored his left hind leg.

For a moment, the shaman didn't seem to know Count Hamnet. Lips lifted away from those formidable fangs. A growl sounded deep in the Odovacar-wolf's throat. The Bizogots told of shamans who turned beast so fully, they couldn't come back to man's shape again.

But Odovacar hadn't gone that far. With a human-sounding sigh, he went into the tent that had been his. A moment later, Totila joined him. Word must have spread like lightning, for Liv and Audun Gilli ducked in together inside of another couple of minutes.

By then, Odovacar the dire wolf was already swaying back and forth in a beast's version of the dance the shaman had used to change shape. The growls and barks and whines that came from the animal had something of the same rhythm as the song Odovacar had used when he was a man.

And he became a man again. His muzzle shortened. His beard grew out on his cheeks and chin—he *had* a chin again. His ears shrank; the light of reason came back to his eyes. The hair on his back and flanks was a pelt no more, but fringed and tufted wolfskin jacket and trousers. His dire wolf's tail now plainly had been taken from a wolf, and was a part of him no more.

He let out a long, weary sigh—more regret than relief, if Hamnet Thyssen was any judge. "Well, I'm back," he said, his voice as rusty as a sword blade left out in the rain. "I'm back," he repeated, as if he needed to convince himself. After so long in beast shape, chances were he did.

"Have you harried the foe?" Totila asked. "Can you do it again at need?"

"We have . . . done what we could," Odovacar answered slowly. Speech still seemed to come hard for him. "It is less than I hoped, better than nothing." He shrugged stooped shoulders—yes, he was old. "Such is life. And the Rulers . . . The Rulers are very strong, and very fierce, and they are gathering. They are mustering. The time is coming, and coming soon." His eyes—blue again, not wolf-amber—found first Liv and then Count Hamnet. "Well, you were right, the two of you. I wish you were wrong, but you were right. They are a danger. They are a deadly danger."

"What did you do . . . when you were a dire wolf?" Hamnet asked in a low voice.

Odovacar heard him without trouble; maybe some of the dire wolf's sharper senses stayed with him for a little while. "Hunted. Killed. Mated.

Slept. Ran. Those are the things a dire wolf does," he said. "Harried the Rulers' herds. Fled when they hit back at us. I told you—they *are* strong and fierce. I smelled—watched, too, but scent matters more—too many wolf-brothers die. I was still man enough inside the dire wolf's head to sorrow, not just to fear. And I watched the foe gather, and I smelled their muster, and I came back. And it might be better had I stayed a wolf." A tear ran down his cheek.

II

B Y G O D, I will do this thing, or I will die trying," Trasamund said. The mammoth from the Red Dire Wolves' herd pawed at the ground with a broad, hairy forefoot, looking for whatever forage it could find under the snow. The hump on the mammoth's back was far flatter than it would have been in warm weather; the beast had burned through most of the fat reserve it carried from the good times. It couldn't understand what the Three Tusk Bizogots' jarl was saying, which was just as well.

Hamnet Thyssen and Ulric Skakki looked at each other. Hamnet had trouble putting what he wanted to say into words. Ulric, as usual, didn't. "Do you have to do this thing *right now*, Your Ferocity?" he asked.

"And why not?" Trasamund demanded.

"Because we'll need you for the fight against the Rulers." Now Count Hamnet found the words he needed. "Because if you kill yourself it will be the same as if they won a great battle."

"They ride woolly mammoths to war," Trasamund said. "I swore *I* would do the same. I will ride this beast. You shall not stop me."

Maybe Hamnet and Ulric could have tackled him and sat on him. But, even if he didn't try to draw his great two-handed sword and kill them both, what good would that do? He would only come out and try to ride a mammoth while they weren't around. If he fell, if he was thrown clear, they might be able to save him before the beast crushed the life out of him. Hamnet didn't believe it, but it was possible.

"Now," Trasamund said, and advanced on the mammoth. Its hairy ears flapped—what was this man-thing up to? Trasamund was a big man, but seemed tiny beside the cow mammoth.

When he took hold of two big handfuls of mammoth hair and started scrambling up the the beast's side, Hamnet thought he *would* die, and about as unpleasantly as a man could. The mammoth's trunk flew up into the air and blared out a startled note. The animal could have used the trunk to pluck off Trasamund and throw him down to the snow-covered ground. One of its great feet descending on his head or his chest, and that would be that.

"If I were mad enough to try to ride a mammoth, I wouldn't be mad enough to try it that way," Ulric Skakki said. "By God, I hope I wouldn't, anyhow."

"I don't think there's enough gold in the world to get me up on a mammoth's back," Count Hamnet agreed. "Not unless I'm up there with somebody who knows what he's doing, I mean. And since the Rulers are the only ones who ride mammoths . . . Well, there you are."

"No, there Trasamund is," Ulric said. "I'm here where I belong—on the ground, and far enough away from that shaggy monster."

But in spite of trumpeting in surprise and alarm, the mammoth didn't dash Trasamund to the ground and trample him. The Red Dire Wolf Bizogots said they'd chosen the gentlest animal in their herd, and they seemed to mean it. Count Hamnet wouldn't have let a cat climb him. That had to be what it was like for the mammoth.

With a shout of triumph, the jarl straddled the beast's broad back. "I'm here!" he roared. "I really am up here! Look at me!" He let out a loud, wordless whoop almost as discordant as the mammoth's trumpeting.

"By God, I don't think I got that excited the first time I went into a woman," Ulric said. "Of course, if you'd seen the woman I did it with the first time, you wouldn't have got very excited, either."

Hamnet Thyssen had a hard time not laughing. "What did she think of you?"

"She thought I'd paid her, and she was right." Ulric raised his voice to a shout. "Now that you're up there, Your Ferocity, how do you make the mammoth go?"

"You think I haven't got an answer," Trasamund yelled back. "Shows what you know." He pulled a stick from his belt. "The Rulers use a goad to make the beasts obey, and I can do the same." He thwacked the mammoth's right side. "Get moving!"

"The Rulers probably start training their mammoths when they're calves," Hamnet said. "The animals know what the signals are supposed to mean. This mammoth's never run into them before. What will it do?"

"You can see that, and I can see that, but do you really expect a Bizogot to see that?" Ulric Skakki answered. "Well, the beast's hair is thick. Maybe it won't think he's hitting it hard enough to be really annoying. He'd better hope it doesn't, because otherwise the last thing he'll ever say is 'Oops!' "

After Trasamund belabored the mammoth for a bit, it did start to walk. He whooped again—too soon. The mammoth was going where it wanted to go, not where he wanted it to go. And it was going there faster and faster, too, first at a trot, then at what had to be a bone-shaking gallop. Trasamund had no saddle and no reins. All he could do was hang on to handfuls of mammoth hair for dear life—and he did.

Ulric and Hamnet mounted their horses and rode after the mammoth. They made sure not to come too close. Spooking it might mean killing Trasamund. It might also mean getting killed themselves. Discretion seemed the better choice.

Even now, the woolly mammoth didn't try to pull the obstreperous human off its back. It *was* a good-natured beast; the Red Dire Wolves had chosen well. And Trasamund, to Hamnet Thyssen's surprise, had the sense not to be *too* obstreperous. After goading the mammoth into running, he let it go till it wore itself out, without trying to urge it on any more. When it finally stopped, breath smoking and great shaggy flanks heaving, Trasamund slid down and off over its tail, nimble as one of the monkeys that sometimes came up in trade from lands in the distant south.

Monkeys never lasted long in Nidaros; when the weather turned cold, chest fever carried them away. Hamnet hadn't thought Trasamund would last long on the mammoth's back, either. He was glad to find himself wrong. The Bizogot trotted away from his enormous mount before it could decide to turn on him for revenge.

"Bravely done—you idiot," Ulric Skakki said.

"Call me whatever you please. I don't care." Trasamund's grin was as wide and foolish and wondering as if he *were* just coming away from his first woman. "But you can't call me an oathbreaker, by God. I swore I would do this, and I cursed well did. And I'll do it again, too."

"I have a question for you," Count Hamnet said.

"What was it like?" Trasamund said. "I'll tell you what it was like. It—"

But Hamnet shook his head. "No, that wasn't what I wanted to ask."

Trasamund glowered at him; it was what the Bizogot jarl wanted to talk about. Pretending not to notice, Hamnet Thyssen went on, "You might have done better—smoother—if you'd asked one of our captives from the Rulers how they ride their mammoths. Why didn't you? That's what I want to know."

Trasamund went from scowling to flabbergasted in the blink of an eye. "I never thought of it. I wanted to find out for myself."

"Is that a Bizogot, or is that a Bizogot?" Ulric Skakki said, not loud enough for Trasamund to hear. Hamnet Thyssen nodded.

"Do you think the captives would give good advice or bad?" Trasamund asked. "They might want to see anyone from this side of the Glacier who gets on a mammoth die. If we have mammoth-riders, too, that gives us a better chance against their brethren."

"If we were talking about Bizogots or Raumsdalians, I'd say you were right," Hamnet answered. "But if the Rulers get captured, they're disgraced. They're cast out from their own folk. They can never go back—the sin, or whatever they think it is, clings to them."

"That's why a lot of them try to kill themselves," Ulric added.

"It is," Hamnet agreed. "But it's also why I think you can rely on what they tell you. In their eyes, they aren't of the Rulers any more, because they know their own folk don't want them back and won't take them back. If they're going to live any kind of life at all, they have to do it with us."

"They're queer birds, all right," Trasamund said. "Well, maybe I will talk to them, then. If I like what they say, I'll try it. And if I think they *are* lying to me, they'll die, but not so fast as they'd want to."

The cow mammoth lifted her trunk, bugled once more, and strode off with an air of affronted dignity. *You got away with that, but if you think I'm happy about it you'd better think again*—every line of her body told how she felt. She might have been a frumpy matron down in Nidaros offended because her soup was cold.

"I'm just glad the Rulers have held off from hitting us as long as they have," Ulric Skakki said. "If they'd come after the Red Dire Wolves right after they hit the Three Tusk Bizogots, I don't know how we could have stopped them."

"My guess is, my brave clan hurt them badly even in defeat," Trasamund said. "They haven't pressed farther south because they can't."

"It could be." Hamnet Thyssen doubted it was, but he was willing to let the Three Tusk jarl keep as much pride as he could. "But it could also be that they're building strength up there, bringing men and mammoths and riding deer down through the Gap and getting ready for a big campaign." If he were a chieftain of the Rulers, that was what he would have done.

"Makes sense to me," Ulric said. "I wish we'd had more luck getting the Bizogots to fight as one army and not by clans. If they're not careful, they'll all go down separately, one clan at a time."

"Getting Bizogots to do anything together with other Bizogots is like herding mosquitoes," Trasamund said. "They fly where they want, they bite where they want, and if they feel like biting the herder, they do that, too."

"And the swifts and the swallows swoop down and eat them as they please," Hamnet said. Trasamund sent him a sour stare, but couldn't very well claim he was wrong. "We need more spies up at the edge of the country the Rulers hold," Hamnet went on. "I wish Odovacar's wolves could tell us more, because it's hard to get men up there without letting the Rulers know."

"Maybe magic would serve where spies can't," Ulric said.

"It had better, by God," Trasamund said. "Liv and Audun Gilli have been going on for a while now about how their toenails itch, and that means the Rulers have a hangover. Let's see what they can do when they set their minds to it, and when old Odovacar tosses in whatever he can."

"If the Rulers' wizards catch them spying, it may do us more harm than good," Hamnet Thyssen said. Did he fear what the Rulers' wizards might do to Liv if they caught her working magic against them? He knew he did.

By the glint in Ulric Skakki's eye, he knew the same thing. "A goldpiece is no good if it sits in your belt pouch. You've got to spend it," he said. "A soldier is no good if he sits in a tavern pinching the barmaids. He's got to go out into the field and fight. A wizard's not worth much if he can't work magic."

"That's all true, every word of it," Trasamund said. "Let's see what our shamans can do."

Count Hamnet wanted to hate both of them. They aimed to send his beloved into danger. But he found he couldn't, for he knew they were right. And he knew Liv would say the same thing when anyone got around to putting the question to her. And so he nodded heavily, and hated himself instead.

AUDUN GILLI LOOKED worried, which would have alarmed Hamnet Thyssen more if Audun didn't look worried so much of the time. Liv looked serious, which again was nothing out of the ordinary. Odovacar looked like a man who wanted a skin of smetyn. But, as far as Hamnet could tell, the Red Dire Wolves' shaman was sober.

Deciding what the three of them wanted to do hadn't been easy. Audun Gilli still knew much less of the Bizogot language than Hamnet wished he did. Liv's temper frayed with translating for him and for Odovacar. And the Red Dire Wolves' shaman's deafness meant she had to shout the same thing over and over, which did nothing to make her any happier.

After a lot of shouting—not all of it having to do with Odovacar's bad ears, by any means—the three sorcerers decided to send a spirit animal to what had been the Three Tusk Bizogots' lands to see what the Rulers were doing there. Liv's spirit would make the spearhead of the magic; Audun Gilli and Odovacar would lend her strength and help ward her against anything the invaders tried.

"What can go wrong?" Hamnet Thyssen asked Liv the night before they tried the spell.

She shrugged. "All kinds of things. Shamanry is not a certain business, especially when the enemy's shamans fight against what you do."

That much the Raumsdalian noble knew for himself. "What's the worst that can happen?" he asked.

"Maybe they can kill me," Liv answered. "Maybe they can kill my spirit and leave my body alive without it. Which is worse, do you think?" She sounded as if it were an interesting abstract question, one with nothing to do with the rest of her life—however long that turned out to be.

"Should you go on with this, then?" Yes, Hamnet feared for her.

"Warriors go into battle knowing they may not see the sun rise again," Liv said. "You have done this yourself. You know it is so. We need to find out what the Rulers are doing. I'm best suited to look out over the lands that were my clan's—that *are* my clan's, by God—and see what the Rulers are doing there. It will be all right, Hamnet. Or if it isn't, it will be the way it is."

It will be the way it is. The hard life the Bizogots led made them into fatalists. Most of the time, Hamnet Thyssen admired that. Now it terrified him. "I don't want to lose you!" he exclaimed.

"I don't want to lose you, either," Liv said. "You asked for the worst, and I told you. I do not think it will come to that. We are working on our home ground, with spells we know. I may not learn everything I want to, but I should be able to get away again afterward. Does that make you feel better?" She sounded like a mother comforting a little boy who'd had a nightmare.

The way they chose to comfort each other a little later had nothing to do with little boys, though there was some small chance it might have made Liv the mother of one. Afterward, if the old jokes were true, Count Hamnet should have rolled over and gone to sleep. He didn't. He lay awake a long time, staring up at the darkness inside the mammoth-hide tent. Liv was the one who slipped quickly into slumber. He supposed that was all to the good; she would need to be fresh when morning came.

At last, he did sleep. He wished he hadn't—his dreams were confused and troubled. He hoped that didn't mean anything. He was no wizard, no foreteller. All the same, he wished they were better.

Liv broke her fast on meat and marrow. Through the winter, the Bizogots ate little else. She showed a good appetite. Hamnet Thyssen had to force his food down. "It will be all right," she said again.

"Of course it will," he answered, and hoped he wasn't lying.

The weather should have cheered him. It was bright and sunny, and not far below freezing—after what they'd been through, it felt like spring. The equinox couldn't be far away; the sun spent more time above the horizon every day. But even after winter formally died, the Breath of God would go on blowing for another month, maybe even six weeks. Only then would the snow melt, the land turn to puddles, mosquitoes and midges start breeding in mad and maddening profusion, and the landscape go from white to flower-splashed green.

Breathing didn't feel as if Hamnet were inhaling knives. Getting out of the stuffy, smelly tent was a relief to the nose, too. If any air was fresher and cleaner than that which came down off the Glacier, the Raumsdalian couldn't imagine what it might be.

He looked north. There stood the Glacier, tall as any other formidable mountains. He wished the Gap had never melted through. Then the Rulers would still be walled off from the Bizogot country—and from the Raumsdalian Empire to the south.

But if the Gap hadn't melted through, Trasamund wouldn't have come south to Nidaros looking for help exploring the land beyond the Glacier. Hamnet wouldn't have come north with him, which meant he wouldn't have met Liv.

He started to ask her if she thought the opening of the Gap was worth it to her, if their meeting made everything else worthwhile. He started to, yes, but he wasn't fool enough to finish the question. Of course she would say no, and she would have good reason to. Because the Gap had melted through, the Rulers had crushed her clan. Her kinsfolk and friends, the folk she'd known all her life, were dead or exiled or living under the heel of the invaders.

No, she wouldn't think that was worth it. She might have found love among her fellow Bizogots. Even if she hadn't, they would still roam their grazing grounds as free men and women. Nothing right now meant more to Hamnet Thyssen than she did. As a Raumsdalian, he naturally thought nothing should mean more to her than he did. But Raumsdalians were, and could afford to be, more individualistic than Bizogots. To Liv, the clan mattered far more than the Empire did to Hamnet—and he was, by the standards of his folk, a duty-filled man.

Here came Audun Gilli, a somber look on his thin, scraggly-bearded face. And here came Odovacar, in his tufted and fringed shaman's costume. He carried a drum—a frame made of mammoth bone, with a musk-ox-hide drumhead. Tufts of dire-wolf fur and sparkling crystals attached with red-dyed yarn dangled from it.

"Are we ready?" he asked.

"If we aren't, what are we doing here?" Liv replied. Audun Gilli had picked up enough of the Bizogot tongue to understand the simple question, if not her reply. He nodded to Odovacar.

"Good. Good. Then let us begin." The Red Dire Wolves' shaman tapped the drum—once, twice, three times. The tone was deeper and richer than Hamnet Thyssen had expected. The rhythm, to his surprise, didn't put him in mind of a dire wolf's howl. It was shorter and sharper; it might have been bird tracks in the snow.

Odovacar started to dance. However old and stooped he was, he moved with surprising grace and ease. Liv began dancing, too. Her steps perfectly fit the beat of the drum. Count Hamnet was almost taken aback that she left ordinary footprints in the snow, not marks with three toes forward and one behind. Her arms flapped as if she were a bird.

Audun Gilli set semiprecious stones in a circle around the two Bizogot shamans. He murmured his chant so as not to interfere with the drum. "Ward spell," he told Hamnet, who nodded.

Liv suddenly sat down in the snow. Her arms went on flapping. "I fly," she said in the Bizogot language. "Like the snowy owl, I fly." Her eyes seemed wider and more unwinking than they had any business being. They didn't go yellow, as Odovacar's had when he took wolf shape, nor did she sprout feathers and fly in the flesh. All the same, she gave an overwhelming impression of owlishness.

"Fly north, hunting owl," Odovacar sang in a loud, unmelodious voice. He thumped the drum. "Fly north, fly north. Spy out our foes." He went on dancing, as Liv went on flapping. If she was the arrow, he was the bow that loosed her.

Audun Gilli stood ready just inside the ward circle. He was still completely human, and completely alert, too. If Liv was arrow and Odovacar bow, he was the shield protecting them both. *The shield that's supposed to protect them, anyhow,* Hamnet Thyssen thought uneasily. Audun had been the first to admit that the Rulers' magic was stronger than any known on this side of the Glacier.

"I fly," Liv said again. "Like the snowy owl, I fly."

"Fly north, hunting owl. Spy out our foes," Odovacar sang to her. "What do you see, hunting owl? Tell us what you see."

"I see the lands of the Three Tusk clan, the grandest grazing and hunting lands in all the Bizogot country," Liv answered. In calling them that, owl-Liv saw with her heart, not with her head. The lands hard by the Glacier were poor even by the sorry standards of the frozen steppe.

"Tell us more, tell us more," Odovacar sang. "Spy out our foes. Fly north, fly north. Spy out our foes."

"I see herds." Liv sounded dreamlike, or perhaps owllike, as her spirit soared far from her body. "I see herds of musk oxen. I see herds of mammoths. The herds seem large. I see herds of . . . deer?" All at once, doubt came into her voice. Those riding deer had traveled down through the Gap with the Rulers. They weren't native to the Bizogot country.

"You begin to find the foe," Odovacar assured her. "Tell us what you see, before the foe finds you."

"I see an encampment," Liv said. "It is wide. It is broad. All the tents are laid out in square array." That surely marked it for a camp of the Rulers. The Bizogots were not an orderly folk. They scattered their tents every which way across the ground. The Rulers, as Count Hamnet had seen beyond the Glacier, had far more discipline.

"Tell us more, tell us more, before the foe finds you." Even if they understood Odovacar in a Raumsdalian tavern, they would have thrown things at him. But he wasn't singing to entertain; he worked with the charm to remind Liv what to do.

"I see men of the Rulers tending to mammoths. Some of the mammoths must be theirs. Some are stolen from the Bizogots." Though her spirit had flown far, anger still fired her voice. She went on, "I see women of the Rulers. They are ugly bitches." That wasn't anger—it was scorn.

"Does the foe ride to war? Does he mount mammoths and ride to war?" Odovacar sounded more urgent now. He probably couldn't hear her answers, but he was bound to know others could.

"I see . . . I see . . . I think I see . . ." For the first time, Liv hesitated. Were the Rulers' wizards working to thwart her? Her arms flapped faster, as if she was flying away from the encampment. Her eyes widened. "I do see them. By God, I do! They ready their host! Mammoths and deer without number. Soon they will sweep down on the Red Dire Wolves! How did they bring so much through the Gap?"

"Tell us more!" Odovacar sang. "More! We must hear more!" He thumped the drum harder, as if to pull words from Liv.

"They are in a place we always called the Four Breasts because of the big frost heaves there," she said. "That is a fine place to move south from—the forage is always good there. Even horses have no trouble finding grass under the snow in winter. It is easy for mammoths and musk oxen—and I see it is easy for the riding deer the Rulers use, too."

Then she gasped. Her body twisted. She might have been banking in flight. She let out an angry cry, a cry that might have burst from a true owl's throat. Her hands stretched into what were plainly meant for talons, visible even through her mittens.

Audun Gilli gasped at the same time. "Spirit hawks!" he said in Raumsdalian, and then, "Drum her home, Odovacar! Quick!"

The Red Dire Wolves' shaman spoke no Raumsdalian. Even if he had, he wouldn't have been able to hear Audun. But he too could sense what needed doing. The rhythm of his drumming changed. So did his chant. "Back to safety!" he sang. "Back to the tents of your folk! Evade all evil! Back to the tents you know so well!"

How well did Liv know the Red Dire Wolves' tents? Well enough to home on them? Hamnet Thyssen watched in an agony of suspense, that being the only thing he could do. Liv twisted again, as if sliding away from something. Spirit hawks, Audun called whatever the Rulers were mustering against her. What did that mean? No wizard himself, Hamnet didn't know.

Then, without warning, Liv reached out and grabbed with the claws that were really fingers. "Ha!" she cried. "That one will trouble me no more!"

Audun Gilli's face twisted in pain. Whatever she'd done, he felt it. "They might as well slay that wizard's carcass, for his soul is dead," he said somberly. Hamnet remembered what he'd asked Liv before her spirit flew. One of the things she'd feared most for herself, she'd just visited upon the Rulers. *Good,* Hamnet thought. *Do it again!*

But, by the way she moved, she went back to trying to escape. How many enemy sorcerers were flying against her, riding the winds of the world and whatever equivalents the spirit world knew? Defeating one might be— was—bold and brave, but a shaman flying alone surely couldn't hope to outfly and outfight a flock of foes.

"Here is the circle! Come back to the circle!" Audun, for once, had the sense to speak the Bizogot language, not his own. Odovacar's drumming also— Count Hamnet hoped—helped guide Liv's spirit back towards her body.

"Fly like the Breath of God," Hamnet whispered harshly. "Fly straight, fly hard, fly fast. Oh, fly fast!"

And then Liv came back to her body once more. No more than a couple of heartbeats after she sprang to her feet, reason on her face once more and all owlishness banished from it, two of the wardstones in Audun's circle flared to brilliant life. Liv winced, but stood steady. Odovacar lurched in his dance, though he also stayed on his feet. Audun Gilli grunted as if he'd taken a punch in the belly. But the circle held.

"I saw—enough," Liv said, panting as if she'd run—or flown—a long way.

"Can they strike you even with your spirit back in your body?" Count Hamnet asked, still anxious for her.

"I don't see how," she answered. "I know we couldn't. They were trying to hold my body and spirit apart. Now that I've returned to myself, they've failed."

No sooner were the words out of her mouth than she staggered. Odovacar cried out and dropped to one knee. Audun Gilli shouted, too, in what seemed to Hamnet mixed pain and surprise. Liv's left hand shaped a Bizogot gesture against evil. Audun pulled out an amulet he wore under his fur jacket and brandished it like a sword.

Hamnet Thyssen did draw his sword. He slashed the air all around Liv, hoping to cut any influence lingering close by. He had no idea whether that did any good. He didn't see how it could hurt, though.

"Begone!" Liv said, and her hand twisted into that sign again. "*Begone,* by God!" She sounded fierce and frightened at the same time. Hamnet had heard a lot of soldiers going into battle sound the same way.

Odovacar barked and snarled and bared his teeth. They always seemed long and sharp for a mere man's. Now they looked more than halfway wolfly. Hamnet Thyssen didn't think he was imagining that.

He was sure he wasn't imagining things when the tension broke, as quickly and cleanly as if he had severed it with his sword. Odovacar nodded and grinned, and his teeth went back to normal again, or as normal as they ever were. Audun Gilli breathed a noisy sigh of relief. He returned the amulet to its hiding place.

Liv sighed, too, and shook her head. "Every time I say what the Rulers can't do, I turn out to be wrong. I won't say anything like that anymore."

"They did strike you, then—the, uh, spirit hawks?" Hamnet asked.

"Oh, yes." Now she nodded, shakily. "They chased me here, and they struck me—they struck me hard. I don't know how they did, but I do know I came off lucky to get away with nothing worse than scrapes and scratches on my spirit." She paused, visibly reconsidering that. "No, not just lucky. I had good friends and comrades who came to my aid." She bowed to Odovacar, to Audun, and to Hamnet. "I thank you all."

"I don't think I did anything to be thanked for." Hamnet wished he knew more of magic. Loving a shaman made him feel foolish and ignorant.

But Liv squeezed him hard enough to make the air leave his lungs in a startled *Oof!* "You did! You did!" she said, and her eyes glowed. "Couldn't you feel your blade cutting through the links between me and my pursuers? What wise shaman taught you to do that?"

"I couldn't feel anything. Nobody taught me. I didn't even know if I was helping," he answered honestly. "I wanted to do *something,* that's all."

She kissed him. "You were wonderful!" Then she smiled at Audun Gilli and Odovacar. "And so were you, both of you."

You were wonderful. Had Gudrid ever said anything like that to him, in all the time they spent together? If she had, he couldn't remember it. That made him wonder why he'd loved her so fiercely, and why he'd felt so lost and damned when she played him false. Only one thing occurred to him: *I was a fool, and I didn't know any better.*

"Now—what I saw," Liv said in tones that brooked no argument. Hamnet Thyssen saluted her with clenched fist over his heart, as if she were a Raumsdalian general. He wasn't sure she understood precisely the honor he was giving her, but she did understand it was an honor. With a smile aimed his way, she went on, "The Rulers muster for war. They have a host of mammoths and those riding deer they used gathered together at the place we call the Four Breasts."

"Yes, you said so as you, uh, flew," Hamnet reminded her. He wondered how she'd recognized it before the thaw set in and exposed the landscape beneath the blanket of snow. He supposed Bizogots marveled that Raumsdalians could find their way through Nidaros' winding streets and alleys. *All what you're used to,* he thought.

"The Four Breasts aren't far north of the Red Dire Wolves' grazing grounds," Liv said. To Hamnet and Audun, she added, "We went almost that far before we found out the Rulers had set on the Three Tusk clan. So it seems likely they plan to come south, and the Red Dire Wolves stand in their way."

"What's that?" Odovacar asked. Liv repeated it louder, then louder still. At last, the shaman nodded, though Count Hamnet still wasn't sure he understood.

"How many warriors do the Rulers have?" Hamnet asked. "A Bizogot clan's worth? Three? Ten? Could you tell?"

Liv frowned. "I'm not sure, not when you put it like that. They had many mammoths and many deer—more, I think, than we could keep in one place for very long."

"Did they have men there, too, to move straight to the attack?" Hamnet persisted.

"Some, at least," Liv replied. "I'm not sure how many. Their magic tried to keep me from seeing anything at all, but it failed, it failed. That is my land, and it knew me." Pride filled her voice, and with reason—she'd defied the enemy and got away with it.

"What do we do now?" Audun Gilli asked.

"Talk to Totila." That wasn't Liv—it was Odovacar. Somehow or other, he'd understood Audun just fine. And he seemed to have found the right answer, too.

THE JARL OF the Red Dire Wolves plucked at his graying beard. "They muster in great numbers, you say?" Totila asked Liv.

"They do, Your Ferocity," she said.

"We have no great numbers here. How could we?" Totila said. "The Red Dire Wolves are what we are—one clan. We also have some of your Three Tusk Bizogots, but not many—and even those we have trouble feeding.

How can we hope to stand against a great host of foes, with strong magic? Would we not be wiser to move aside and let these enemies pass through?"

"This is a coward's counsel!" Trasamund cried.

Totila eyed him. "You are in a poor position to tell me what is best for my clan when you think on what happened to yours."

Trasamund turned red. "We were taken unawares. We would not have been if I were with the clansfolk and not down in the Empire."

"And whose fault was that? Did someone steal you and drag you down to Nidaros?" Totila could be as sarcastic as a Raumsdalian.

To Hamnet Thyssen's mind, though, the Red Dire Wolves' jarl asked the wrong question. The right one was, *Even if you were there, even if the Three Tusk Bizogots were alert, how much difference would it have made?* Hamnet feared he knew the answer, which wouldn't have gladdened Trasamund's heart. *Not much. Not much at all.*

"I was trying to get help for us," Trasamund said. "I did my best to bring the Bizogots together and warn them there was danger coming down out of the north. We stopped here on our way to the southlands, by God. Did you want to listen?" He laughed. "Not likely!"

"Well, who would have listened to a mad, wild tale like the one you were spinning?" Totila retorted. "I thought you were lying through your teeth. Anybody else in his right mind would have, too."

"And he would have been wrong, and he would have paid for it," Trasamund said. "And you were wrong, and you are wrong, and you cursed well will pay for it. So what the demon is being in your right mind worth?"

They scowled at each other. They both squared off into positions from which they could easily grab for their swords. With Bizogots, quarrels often ended in blood, not words. A fight here, though, would throw the Red Dire Wolves against what was left of the Three Tusk Bizogots and the Raumsdalians who'd ridden north to help them. Neither Trasamund nor Totila seemed to care.

"Have they both gone crazy?" Ulric Skakki whispered to Count Hamnet. "Crazier, I mean? They sure act like it."

"They do," Hamnet agreed. Then he raised his voice to a shout: "Hold, both of you! I can tell this is the Rulers' deviltry, not your own will. This is one of the things they try to do. They pit our leaders against each other, and then swarm through after our quarrels leave no one who can stand up against them."

"By God, he's right," Liv said. "Despite all we can do, their wizards must be working on you. Why else would you fight when danger to both of you and to all your folk builds just to the north?"

Ulric translated in a low voice for Audun Gilli. The Raumsdalian wizard said, "I feel no enemy magic." Ulric kicked him in the ankle. For a wonder, Audun caught on. Hastily, he continued, "That only proves how subtle the spell is. Will you let it seduce you?"

Trasamund and Totila looked at each other. Then they both looked shamefaced, and a shamefaced Bizogot was as rare as a white woolly mammoth. "No!" they said loudly. Trasamund drew his sword, but only to brandish it in the direction of the Rulers. Totila shook his big, hard fist towards the north.

"We fight together!" he cried.

"Side by side, till we slay them all!" Trasamund roared. They embraced each other like brothers. All the watching Bizogots cheered. They too aimed weapons and clenched fists at the invaders from beyond the Glacier.

In a low voice, Ulric Skakki said, "You're sneakier than I gave you credit for, Thyssen."

"Nothing sneaky about it," Hamnet answered. "For all I know, I was telling the truth. Even for Bizogots, that fight between Trasamund and Totila was stupid."

"Even for Bizogots." An ironic smile played across Ulric's lips. "Well, you said it—I didn't. But don't expect me to tell you you're wrong."

"I'm just glad Liv and Audun went along with me," Count Hamnet said. "And thanks for giving Audun a hand—er, a foot. I saw, even if neither jarl did."

"Sometimes he's too innocent for his own good. I helped him along a little," Ulric said. "And now all we have to do is beat the Rulers. Should be easy, right?" He laughed. So did Hamnet Thyssen. A moment later, he wondered why.

III

THE SUN SHONE warm in a bright blue sky—not merely above freezing, but *warm.* Just as the Breath of God could reach past Nidaros in the wintertime, southerly breezes came up onto the Bizogot steppe, even up to the edge of the Glacier itself, when days lengthened. After only a few hours of such weather, the snow started looking threadbare. Drips and puddles were everywhere.

"Mosquitoes any day now," Ulric Skakki said mournfully. "We go straight from the scratching season to the slapping season. Isn't it grand?"

"Maybe, but maybe not," Hamnet Thyssen said. "There'll be another blizzard or two before winter says good-bye for the year. And the birds are coming north to eat the bugs."

He was right about that. Even so early in the season, the air was murmurous with the sound of fluttering wings. Birds of every size, from larkspurs and flycatchers up to swans, came to the Bizogot plains to breed and to feast upon the brief bounty they offered when they thawed out.

Ulric Skakki only shrugged. "They don't eat all the bugs. They don't even eat enough of them. Plenty of bloodsuckers left alive. Anybody who comes up here when the sun shines has reason to know about that." He mimed smacking at himself.

Count Hamnet nodded. "Not just bloodsuckers on the plains these days," he said. "We've got bloodspillers, too." As usual, his gaze turned to the north.

"We've done everything we could," Ulric said. "We've got scouts out. They'll warn us when the Rulers move. The Red Dire Wolves are as ready to fight as they ever will be. And we've sent messengers to the clans close by. Maybe we'll get reinforcements."

"Yes, maybe we will." Hamnet didn't sound as if he believed it. And he didn't. "We can't *make* the other Bizogots join us. Since we can't, chances are they won't."

"Well, why should they?" As it often did, acid rode Ulric Skakki's voice. "They're free. If you don't believe me, just ask them. They can do whatever they choose, whatever they please—no matter how idiotic it is."

They spoke Raumsdalian, which kept most of the mammoth-herders around them from following what they said. Trasamund, though, was an exception. "You don't understand my folk," he told Ulric.

"By God, Your Ferocity, I hope I don't," the adventurer answered.

"You Raumsdalians are a servile people. You need people to tell you what to do," said the jarl of the Three Tusk clan.

Both Ulric and Hamnet Thyssen burst out laughing. Trasamund scowled first at one, then at the other, then at both of them together. "Oh, yes, Your Ferocity, I obey orders like any other slave," Hamnet said. "When Sigvat commanded me to come back to Nidaros, I turned around and went. That's why I'm sleeping in silk sheets on a feather bed in the capital now, instead of up here getting ready to fight the Rulers."

"And everyone down in Raumsdalia told me how smart I was to come north again," Ulric Skakki added. "Everyone there knows how important this fight is. Everyone cheered me on."

Trasamund's scowl darkened. "You make fun of me."

"Wouldn't you say that's the chance you take when you come out with something funny?" Ulric said.

"But you are not like most of your folk," the Bizogot said.

"Then why talk about us as if we were?" Hamnet Thyssen asked.

They might have gone on bickering, but someone at the northern edge of the encampment raised a shout: "Scout coming in!"

Hamnet Thyssen tensed. He could think of only one reason a scout would come back to the Red Dire Wolves' camp—to warn that the Rulers were on the move at last. He hurried forward, wondering what the man would say. Several Bizogots waved to the scout. "Is it war?" they cried.

"It's war!" the scout yelled back, and hope and fear went to war inside Count Hamnet. The rider went on, "Where are the others? Haven't you heard before me? I'm the third one who set out with the news."

"You're the first who got here," Totila said, and Hamnet's fear jeered at his hope. What had the Rulers done to the other scouts? Reached out with their dark magic? He couldn't think of anything else likely. Totila, meanwhile, continued, "You have seen the Rulers face-to-face. What do you make of them?"

"What we heard before from the strangers and foreigners seems to be true, Your Ferocity," the scout replied. "They have lancers and archers on mammoths. The rest of their warriors ride deer. They keep in straight lines where we would ride in groups."

Discipline, Hamnet Thyssen thought, not for the first time. The Rulers had it—had, perhaps, even more of it than the Empire's soldiers. The Bizogots? The Bizogots didn't even have a word for it, and had to talk around it when they saw it.

But the Bizogots were fierce. Totila shook his fist. "Straight lines, is it? Well, we'll put some kinks in them, by God! See if we don't!" His clansmen bawled their approval. "To horse!" he roared, and they ran for their mounts.

Liv asked the scout, "Did you see anything of their magics? Did you feel as if something passed close to you but didn't strike?"

"No, lady shaman." The man touched his right fist to his forehead in token of respect. "But may the teratorns take me if I know what happened to the other two men who rode south with the news."

"How lucky are we that even one got through?" Ulric Skakki murmured to Count Hamnet. "And what will we be riding into when we go against those devils?"

"We beat them once, up in Three Tusk country," Hamnet said.

"Yes? And so? A raid. And we caught them by surprise," Ulric said. "This time, they'll know we're coming. And they'll be ready."

"If you don't think we have a chance, maybe you'd better not come along," Hamnet said.

"Oh, no. I might be wrong. I don't think so, but I might." Ulric grinned a crooked grin. "And if admitting that doesn't prove I'm no Bizogot, demons take me if I know what would."

"Well, we'll know pretty soon," Hamnet said. "Sometimes finding out is better than waiting."

"So it is. And sometimes it's worse, too," Ulric said, which, unfortunately, was also true. Instead of answering, Hamnet went to mount. So did Ulric Skakki. The smile on the adventurer's face might have meant anything.

Most of the Red Dire Wolves and all the surviving men from the Three

Tusk clan rode with Totila and Trasamund. The rest of the Red Dire Wolves were driving their musk oxen and mammoths off to the south and west to give them something to fall back on if they had to. Part of Hamnet Thyssen said that that was wrong, that the Bizogots should act as if they were sure of winning.

He soon decided that part was being stupid. Wasn't it the part that had clung to Gudrid, the part that had refused to see anything wrong? Wasn't it the blind part, the brainless part? He thought it was. The Red Dire Wolves were only being sensible.

But even as he nodded to himself, he worried. If you planned for the worst thing that could happen, weren't you more likely to bring it about? Wouldn't your warriors be more cautious, thinking, *Well, even if we lose here, it isn't the end of the world?* If you went into battle, shouldn't you go into it thinking you had to win no matter what?

Wasn't that, in fact, what made Bizogots fiercer than Raumsdalians most of the time? Raumsdalians, with all the resources of the Empire behind them, could more easily afford to lose than the mammoth-herders could. The Empire's soldiers could come back and win another day. The Bizogots lived, and fought, in the moment.

And the Rulers? What of them? As far as Hamnet could see, they couldn't afford to lose here. They had to go forward. Back, back towards the Gap and even beyond it, would be nothing but disaster for them.

Someone pointed. Shouts rang out. "There they are!" the Bizogots yelled. "Now we'll get them!" Totila's men were brave enough, no doubt of that.

"Revenge!" Trasamund bellowed. All his clansmen took up that cry. Liv's voice rang clear and high among the deeper ones. She was his woman, but she was a Three Tusk Bizogot, too, and always would be.

Mammoths in the center, riding deer on the outthrust wings. If Hamnet had commanded the Rulers, he would have deployed his forces the same way. Where were their wizards? That was another worry. Hamnet glanced to Liv, to Audun Gilli, to Odovacar farther away. They'd held off the spirit hawks, whatever those were. They'd barely done it, but they had. Could they withstand the invaders once more?

They'd better, Hamnet Thyssen thought. *We all go down if they fail.* He looked over at Liv again. If she failed, she wouldn't just be in danger of losing a battle. She risked dying a dreadful death by sorcery. His mind shied from that thought like a horse shying from a snake.

While the mammoths were off in the distance, they seemed like . . . animals. As they neared, the Bizogots and Raumsdalians got a better notion of their size. They seemed to swell and swell. If they charged, when they charged . . . Hamnet didn't know how the horsemen riding to either side of him could stand up to that.

"They look funny," a Bizogot said.

"They look *wrong*," another one agreed.

"Why, those sneaky sons of whores!" Ulric Skakki exclaimed in Raumsdalian. "They put leather armor on their God-cursed beasts."

He was right. That armor wouldn't stop everything, but it would turn some arrows and keep some of the woolly mammoths from running wild when they were wounded. It also proved that the Rulers paid attention to what their foes did. Trasamund's Bizogots had harried the mammoths with arrows in their raid up into their own grazing lands. They wouldn't have such an easy time of it now.

"Forward the Three Tusk clan!" Trasamund shouted. "There are the murderers, in front of us in a fair fight! Now we pay them back!"

Liv rode with the rest of Trasamund's clansmen. That meant Hamnet Thyssen also rode with the Three Tusk Bizogots. Nothing would happen to her if he could possibly help it. And if he couldn't help it, he wanted whatever happened to her to happen to him, too.

Shaking his head, Ulric Skakki stuck close to Count Hamnet. The adventurer would never have charged into battle on his own—Hamnet was sure of that. Striking from ambush was much more Ulric's style. But he spoke not a word of complaint. He just strung his bow, nocked an arrow, and peered ahead for a likely target.

Audun Gilli stayed with Hamnet and Ulric. Count Hamnet was sure no strategy went into the wizard's thoughts. He just didn't want to be separated from the only other two Raumsdalians for many, many miles. But his choice also pulled the Red Dire Wolves forward faster than they might have gone otherwise. With Liv and Audun speeding into the fight, Totila didn't want his clansmen warded by Odovacar alone. Hamnet Thyssen had a hard time blaming him for that. If the Red Dire Wolves stayed near the other two who knew magic, they might stay under their protection.

If they have any protection to give, Hamnet thought. *Well, we'll find out.*

Totila's Bizogots shouted their jarl's name. Trasamund's followers kept roaring, "Revenge!" And now Hamnet Thyssen could hear the Rulers' battle cries, too. They were deep and harsh, and in his ears might as well have been the calls of some fierce animals. No one on this side of the Glacier understood a word of the Rulers' language. *One more thing we should have started pulling from our prisoners,* Hamnet thought. *We've got to take care of that after the fight—if we have the chance.*

A warrior of the Rulers on mammothback bent his horn-strengthened bow and let fly. His arrow fell short and kicked up a little puff of snow. Ulric Skakki grinned. "See?" he said. "They get buck fever, too."

"So they do," Count Hamnet said. In every battle in which he'd fought, archers opened up before they had any chance of hitting their foes. It was only human—if you could see the enemy, you thought you could kill him.

Some of the Bizogots also started shooting too soon. Their hate burned hot and clean and pure. And then, well before Hamnet Thyssen would have loosed a shot, a deer with one of the Rulers aboard crumpled and crashed to the ground, pinning the fighting man under its thrashing body. That was a prodigious shot, one Hamnet would have had trouble believing if he hadn't seen it himself.

Trasamund thumped his chest. "Mine!" he bellowed, and held his bow over his head in triumph. "First blood to the Bizogots! First blood to the Three Tusk clan! Revenge!"

"Revenge!" his clansmen cried. Count Hamnet yelled, too, to make the war cry sound louder and fiercer. Whether that would do any good he had no idea. He was pretty sure it couldn't hurt.

Then the Rulers' arrows also started to bite. Bizogots and horses tumbled. Wounded horses screamed, high and shrill. So did wounded men. The horses sounded as if they suffered worse, and they probably did. The Bizogots at least knew why they were wounded. To the horses, it was all a dreadful, incomprehensible surprise.

Suddenly the mammoths loomed up right ahead, seeming as tall and vertical as the Glacier. Archers shot down from them with wicked effect. A lancer speared a Bizogot out of the saddle. The man shrieked as if demons had seized his soul.

The mammoth raised its trunk to trumpet. Could war mammoths feel triumph? Maybe they could. If this one did, its celebration proved premature. Ulric Skakki shot it in the tender and seldom exposed underside of the trunk. The spit-filled bugle call of victory turned to a squeal of pain.

One of the warriors of the Rulers on the mammoth's back whacked it with an iron-tipped goad when it started to rear. However well the Rulers trained their beasts, they didn't train them well enough to stay reliable when

wounded. Hamnet Thyssen had seen that in an earlier skirmish. It didn't
surprise him. Horses were liable to run wild if they got hurt. So were the
camels the Manches and other southwestern raiders rode. He would have
been surprised if the same *didn't* hold true for mammoths.

Of course, a mammoth wild with pain could do more than a horse or
even a camel. This one decided it didn't feel like being walloped. It reached
up with its bleeding trunk, plucked the driver off its back, and threw him to
the ground. He screamed, just as any man born on this side of the Glacier
might have done. Then the mammoth stepped on him. Count Hamnet
heard his ribs crunch as his chest caved in. The scream abruptly cut off.

Still trumpeting in pain, the mammoth lumbered off, careless of the
other men on its back. "There's one of the big cows out of the fight," Ulric
said cheerfully.

"So there is," Hamnet answered. But how many mammoths were still in
it? Too many, too cursed many.

An arrow hissed past his head like an angry serpent. Did the Rulers
know about snakes, or were they as ignorant of them as the Bizogots? Liv
hadn't wanted to believe there were such creatures. No snake could survive
winters like these. The Rulers might get some horrible surprises as they
moved farther south—*if* they moved farther south. Hamnet hoped they
didn't get the chance.

He shot at a heavily bearded man on a deer. His arrow missed the enemy
warrior but struck the deer in the haunch. It bounded away with the warrior
still trying to fight it under control. He didn't have much luck.

At its rider's command, another deer lowered its head and charged Hamnet's horse. The rider brandished a heavy curved sword. Even though the
tines of those antlers weren't pointed, Hamnet knew they could hurt or
frighten his horse. He guided the animal to one side and slashed at the enemy fighting man with his own blade.

Yammering something Hamnet couldn't understand, the warrior turned
the stroke. He cut at Hamnet, too. The Raumsdalian noble beat aside the
curved blade. He was taller in the saddle than the man from beyond the
Glacier, as his horse stood several hands higher than the deer. He chopped
down and laid open the deer's shoulder. The enemy warrior couldn't give all
his attention to his swordplay after that, and combat was too serious for
anything less. Hamnet Thyssen hacked him out of the saddle.

Mounted on horses, the Bizogots also had the advantage of height on
the deer-riding Rulers. Wherever horses confronted deer, the Bizogots

surged forward. But the enemy's mammoths were another story. They dominated their part of the field. The Bizogots could not stand against them.

"Hold fast! Hold fast!" Trasamund and Totila shouted, both separately and together. Hamnet admired the Bizogots for not giving way to panic. It was as if they were fighting a swarm of fortresses that moved as fast as any horse.

Hamnet looked around for Liv. He did that as often as he could. Getting into the battle meant he couldn't stay as close to her as he would have liked. But when he saw her with her arms upraised and a furious look on her face as she cried out to the heavens, he spurred towards her as fast as he could.

"No!" she shouted. "By God, no!"

She looked as if she had the weight of the world on her shoulders, as if she were trying to bear up under more than anyone was supposed to carry. Hamnet Thyssen slashed the air with his sword, hoping to help as he had when her spirit flew north to see what the Rulers were doing. If that did any good, he couldn't see it or sense it.

Where was Audun Gilli? Could he come to Liv's aid? Count Hamnet heard his angry cry—he too sounded like a man in over his head. What were the Rulers' wizards doing? Whatever it was, they were putting a lot of strength into it.

Hamnet looked around for Odovacar. If that wasn't a measure of his desperation, he couldn't imagine what would be. He didn't see the Red Dire Wolves' shaman. A moment later, he did hear a howl that sounded as desolate as the shouts that came from Liv's throat and from Audun's. No ordinary dire wolf would come so close to a battlefield till it could feed on corpses, so that had to be Odovacar.

And then, despite everything the Bizogot shamans and the Raumsdalian wizard could do, the sorcerous storm broke on the army Trasamund and Totila led. Hamnet Thyssen thought his eyes were playing tricks on him, making him see enemies where there were none, where there could be none.

But then a warrior of the Rulers almost killed him. Not all the foes he thought he saw came from his imagination alone. He watched Bizogots fall because they could not tell false foes from true. And he suspected, though he could not prove, that some of the false foes turned true because the Bizogots thought them true.

Liv cried out again. Her hands twisted in furious passes. For a moment, Hamnet's vision cleared—but only for a moment. And the effects of Liv's spell didn't reach very far. Bizogots more than a bowshot from her seemed as bedeviled as they ever had.

"No!" Trasamund's deep roar reached across the battlefield. "These lying mammoth turds can't get away with that!"

But the Rulers could. They did. And, with their enemies reeling in confusion, their wizards threw another spell at them. From what seemed every direction at once, icicles flew at the Bizogots like arrows. Shields turned some; thick leather clothes stopped others. But some struck home, wounding men and horses alike. The spell probably would have been more dangerous, more deadly, in the heart of winter than at the tag end of the season, but it was bad enough as things were.

"Stop them!" a Bizogot screamed at Liv, blood running down his face. "Don't let them do that!"

"I'm trying!" she screamed back. None of the darting, plunging icicles had struck or even struck at her. She seemed able to protect herself. Hamnet had shattered one with his sword, but only one. She could ward him, too, to some degree. She lacked the strength to extend her reach to the whole Bizogot host.

So did Audun Gilli and Odovacar. If they could have, they would have—Hamnet Thyssen was sure of that. Coping with wizardry and war mammoths both all but unstoppable . . . How long could the Bizogot army hold together?

Ulric Skakki shot a fellow who was plainly a leading officer among the Rulers off his mammoth. The man had been yelling orders and pointing this way and that, directing his men as a band leader might direct his musicians. Hamnet Thyssen hoped his fall—and he *did* fall, bleeding, into the snow—would throw the enemy into disarray and buy the Bizogots time to regroup.

Losing their commander did discomfit the Rulers . . . for a minute or two. Then another of their officers, noting or learning that the commander was down, took over for him. *He* shouted orders. *He* pointed this way and that. And the enemy army pulled itself together and went back to the business of crushing its opponents.

"They're good, God curse them," Ulric Skakki said.

"They're better than good. They're smoother than *we* are, let alone the Bizogots," Count Hamnet said. "We couldn't lose a captain and shrug it off like that." He didn't even talk about what would happen if Trasamund or Totila were badly wounded here. He knew, and so did Ulric—the Bizogots would fall to pieces.

Even without losing their chieftains, they fell to pieces anyhow. It didn't happen all at once, the way it might have if a jarl fell. No one could deny the Bizogots' courage. But when courage without much direction ran up against courage with discipline, and against war mammoths and superior sorcery, it came up short.

At first by ones and twos, then in small groups, then in clusters, the Red Dire Wolves—those who could—broke free of the press and rode off to the southwest. They knew where their herds roamed. If they were to survive as a clan, they had to protect the beasts. Men from the Three Tusk clan rode with them. Fierce and desperate as Trasamund's Bizogots were, they were made of flesh and blood; they had limits. The Rulers inflicted enough punishment on them to push them to those limits and beyond.

"Cowards!" Trasamund roared, watching his own clansmen retreat with the Red Dire Wolves. "Where are your ballocks?"

"Your Ferocity, what more can we do here but get killed to no purpose?" Hamnet Thyssen asked. "Can we beat the Rulers in this fight?"

Trasamund sent him a look full of hate. "Not you, too? Well, run away if you want to. I came here to fight, by God!" He'd done plenty of that; his great two-handed sword was smeared and splashed with blood all along the blade.

"Did you come here to throw yourself away?" That wasn't Count Hamnet—it was Liv. "We've lost this battle. We're beaten. If we try again, *when* we try again, it will have to be somewhere else. We still must have our revenge. But can't you see we won't win it here?"

Plainly, Trasamund didn't want to heed her. Just as plainly, she was right. Totila called, "We've got to get away, save what we can!"

Seeing his fellow jarl flee the field seemed to bring Trasamund to his senses. "Away, then," he said bitterly. "Away! Will we spend the rest of our lives running away from the accursed Rulers?"

It's possible, Count Hamnet thought. If the invaders could bring in enough men and mammoths through the Gap, they would be very dangerous indeed. Hamnet had feared they would fight well. They turned out to fight even better than he'd expected.

How hard would they pursue? If they pressed the chase with everything they had in them, they might shatter the Red Dire Wolves forever. But they didn't seem willing—or, more likely, able—to do that. They'd won, yes, but not easily. And so the Bizogots escaped them and broke off the fight. Hamnet Thyssen wondered how much difference it would make.

NOT MANY THINGS in the world were grimmer than the camp of an army that had just lost a battle. The wounded were sullen, feeling they suffered pointlessly. The men who'd got away safe were angry and embarrassed, having done their best to no purpose. And everyone was apprehensive, fearing the enemy would fall on them while their spirits were at a low ebb.

The warm weather around the camp made the snow melt, and the drips reminded Hamnet Thyssen of tears shed for the cause. That was more fanciful than he usually got, but he couldn't help it.

Several Bizogots screamed at Trasamund and Totila when their chieftains tried to get them to go on sentry duty. Trasamund had to knock one of the nomads down and kick him before he would. "Are we still warriors?" the jarl roared furiously. "Or are we made into voles and lemmings, sport for any weasel that would bite our throats?"

"Do you feel squeaky?" Ulric Skakki asked Count Hamnet. Somehow, the adventurer made his whiskers seem remarkably like a vole's.

Hamnet knew he should have smiled. He couldn't make himself do it, try as he would. "They beat us," he said gloomily.

"So they did," Ulric agreed. "Did you really look for anything different? The Bizogots haven't figured out this is no game yet."

"What will it take before they do?" Hamnet asked. "War mammoths trampling the lot of them?"

"Maybe." Ulric Skakki didn't sound as worried or as wearied as most of the men around him. "That would bring the Rulers down to the Empire's northern border—and Sigvat II hasn't realized this is no game, either."

"Marvelous," Hamnet Thyssen said. "By your logic, almost everyone ought to be almost ready to fight just when it's too late to do any good."

"Yes, that sounds about right," Ulric agreed. "Or don't you think so?"

The trouble was, Hamnet did think so, even if he didn't want to. "We have to find some way to beat them. If we don't, we're ruined."

"No one *has* to do anything. Haven't you noticed that yet?" Ulric Skakki said. "It would be nice if we did, but there's no guarantee." He gestured at the misery all around. "You can see for yourself there isn't."

Hamnet Thyssen winced. "You know what I mean."

"So what?" Ulric said. "Where's the connection between what you mean and what is? If you can't find one, what does what you mean have to do with the price of peas? We're in trouble. Wishing we weren't won't get us anywhere. Am I right or wrong?"

"Oh, you're right, sure enough," Hamnet said. "Do you suppose wishing you'd shut up anyway would get me anywhere?" Ulric Skakki laughed, for all the world as if he were joking. Any sort of cheery sound made most of the people who heard it stare at him, plainly wondering if he'd lost his wits.

Totila came up to Count Hamnet and Ulric. "Is it true that you Raumsdalians know more about curing wounds than we do?"

To Hamnet's way of thinking, it was hard to know less about curing wounds than the Bizoguts did. All the same, his nod and Ulric's were both cautious. Battlefield surgery was a risky business for anybody. "What do you want us to try to do?" Hamnet asked.

"Come see the wound. Judge for yourself," the Red Dire Wolves' jarl answered.

A Bizogot warrior writhed and groaned. He had an arrow embedded in his calf. When Hamnet made as if to touch it, the big, burly man said, "Don't. The point is barbed. You can't pull it out."

"Push it through?" Hamnet wondered aloud. The Bizogot groaned again. Count Hamnet understood why. That would add fresh torment and make the wound worse. But they couldn't leave the arrow where it was, either.

"You see?" the jarl said.

"I see," Hamnet said glumly. "I see, but I don't know what I can do. How about you, Ulric?"

Ulric Skakki took from a belt pouch a bronze contraption with a long, flat handle and a curved tip with a small hole in the center. "What's that?" Totila asked.

"Arrow-drawing spoon," the adventurer answered. "I slide it down the shaft, get hold of the point with the hole, and pull up. It lets me bring out the point, but keeps the barbs from doing too much more tearing when they leave the wound."

"Try it," the injured Bizogot said. "That God-cursed thing has to come out."

Hamnet Thyssen and Totila held his leg to make sure he couldn't twist away. "Have you ever used this thing before?" Hamnet asked in Raumsdalian.

"I've seen it done," Ulric answered in the imperial tongue. That wasn't the same thing. He switched back to the Bizogot language to speak to the wounded man: "I'm going to start. Do your best to hold still."

"I'll try." The mammoth-herder braced himself.

Despite that, he gasped and tried to jerk free when Ulric Skakki pushed the arrow-drawing spoon into the wound. The injured warrior groaned and

cursed, none of which did him any good. He gasped again when Ulric tried
to slide the very tip of the arrowhead into the hole in the spoon. "I'm sorry,"
Ulric said. "Remember, I'm doing this by feel. I'm not hurting you on purpose."

"I know," the Bizogot got out. "But that doesn't mean you're not hurting me."

"I'm close, curse it. It should be right about—" Ulric moved the spoon a
little. The Bizogot groaned on a different note. "There!" Ulric exclaimed.
"I've got it. I can feel it."

"So can I, by God!" the wounded man said.

"I'm going to bring it out now," Ulric told him. "I'll go slow, as slow as I
can. Try to hold still. It will help. Are you ready?"

"No," the Bizogot said honestly. "But go ahead. Waiting won't make it
any better."

"Hold him tight," Ulric warned Hamnet and Totila. "He won't like this,
but I've got to do it. Here we go."

The wounded Bizogot bit down hard to keep from screaming. He spat
red into the slushy snow, so he was chewing on his lips or tongue. His
bunched fists pounded the snow again and again. Hamnet had taken battle
wounds. He knew what the younger man was going through. The less he
thought about that, the better.

"It's out!" Ulric said. Not much flesh clung to the barbs on the point; the
drawing spoon really had shielded the wound from most of the damage it
would have taken otherwise.

"Thank you," the wounded Bizogot said. "Easier to bear now that that
cursed thing isn't sticking into me any more."

"That's what *she* said," Ulric answered, which made the wounded man
laugh.

"Let me see that spoon," Totila said. "Could we make it from bone or
horn?"

"I don't see why not. Here, keep this one if you want to." Ulric cleaned it
in snow and slush before handing it to the Bizogot. Totila studied it and
nodded thoughtfully.

Count Hamnet, meanwhile, bandaged the wounded man's leg. Down in
the Empire, bandages would have been made of linen. Here, the Bizogots
used musk-ox wool and dried moss to close wounds and soak up blood. If
anything, those worked better than their Raumsdalian equivalents.

"I thank you," the wounded man said. "Do you think it will heal clean?"

"That's in God's hands, not mine," Hamnet answered. "But I don't see any reason why it shouldn't."

"Those strangers really do fight from mammothback," the Bizogot said in wondering tones. "Who would have believed it?"

"We've been telling you about it all winter," Hamnet Thyssen pointed out with more than a touch of asperity.

"And so?" The wounded nomad seemed glad to have something to talk about besides the darkening bandage on his leg. "I can tell you about a sky-blue mammoth with pink horns that honks like a goose, but will you expect to see one if I do?"

"It depends," Count Hamnet said judiciously. "If I know you're a reliable man, I might. Why would we lie to you? By God, why would what's left of the Three Tusk clan lie to you? They fought the Rulers. They saw them using war mammoths."

To his surprise, the man from the Red Dire Wolves had an answer for him: "We all thought you were making them out to be worse than they really are so we'd join you and do what you wanted. We thought it was nothing but a trick to scare us, to make us fall in line behind you. We're Bizogots. We're free men. We didn't aim to do that."

"And so you had to get crushed before you decided we might know what we were talking about after all?" That sounded like something a Bizogot would do. Hamnet Thyssen counted himself to be lucky in a country where the closest walls—those of the stone houses the Leaping Lynx clan's summer homes by Sudertorp Lake—were many miles away. Otherwise, he would have been sorely tempted to pound his head against one.

The wounded man nodded. "Sure. Except we didn't expect to get crushed. We thought we'd do the crushing."

After rubbing snow on his hands to get the blood off them, Hamnet Thyssen walked away. He put on his mittens to warm himself up again. Ulric Skakki came after him. "This is what we came north for?" Ulric said.

"This is what we came north for," Hamnet answered stolidly. "The Bizogots are fools, but at least they're fighting fools. Down in Nidaros, Sigvat II is a blind fool. If you ask me, that's worse."

"Well, maybe," Ulric Skakki said. "But where are we going to find some people who aren't fools? That's what we really need."

"We really need to beat the Rulers. Fighting fools can do that—may be able to do that, anyhow," Hamnet said. "Blind fools won't."

They were both using Raumsdalian again; it let them speak their minds without worrying that the Bizogots would overhear and get angry. Ulric Skakki rolled his eyes. "All the Bizogots in the world couldn't stop the army that beat us today. God knows the Bizogots are brave. But God knows they're stupid, too. And the more I see of the Rulers, the more I see that they aren't. They're cruel bastards, but they aren't dumb bastards."

"And that sorcery . . ." Count Hamnet let the words hang in the air.

"That was pretty bad," Ulric agreed. "Some of those flying icicles almost skewered me. And some of them did skewer Bizogots—or else distracted them so the Rulers had an easy time killing them."

"Do you suppose our best wizards could have stopped the spell?" Hamnet asked.

"I don't know," the adventurer said. "One day before too long, chances are we'll find out."

"God help the Empire if its wizards don't have better luck than the Bizogot shamans up here," Hamnet said.

"God help the Empire. That'll do," Ulric Skakki said. "Somebody'd better, and it's not as if Sigvat's up to the job."

"God should help the Bizogots, too—and if he doesn't, we should lend a hand," Count Hamnet said. "Do you know whether Totila and Trasamund aim to send messengers to the other clans and tell them what's happened to the Red Dire Wolves?"

"I know they haven't done it yet. I know I haven't heard them talk about doing it," Ulric answered. "Whether the thought has trickled through their beady little minds . . . that I can't tell you."

"Beady little minds," Hamnet echoed sourly. The phrase fit much too well. "All right, then. We'd better make sure they do think of it. And we'd better make sure they don't just think of it, too. We'd better make sure they do it."

"You don't have much faith in them, do you?" Ulric said.

Hamnet Thyssen shook his head. "Now that you mention it, no."

IV

SPRING. DOWN IN the Empire, it was a time of renewal, return, re-
birth. In the Bizogot country, it was all of that and more, jammed into a
few frantic weeks. When the snow up on the northern plains melted, everything turned to mud and marshes and ponds. Getting from here to there
became a challenge. Getting from here to there in a hurry became a joke.

Bare mud and shallow water didn't last long. (There was no deep water
on the frozen steppe, which stayed frozen a few feet down regardless of the
season.) Plants came to mad life, coating the ground with green and burst-
ing into bloom. And in the marshes and puddles, the eggs mosquitoes and
flies and midges had laid the year before thawed out and hatched and gave
birth to a new generation of buzzing biters.

Hamnet Thyssen squelched and slapped and swore. The air was thick
not only with bugs but also with the birds that battened on them. The birds
grew fat and nested and laid eggs so their succeeding generation could feast
off bugs yet unborn. But far too many bugs remained uneaten.

"Can't you do anything about it?" Hamnet asked Liv, not for the first
time.

"Bear grease on your face and hands helps some," she answered. She was
bitten, too. So were all the Bizogots. So were their dogs and musk oxen and
mammoths, all of which shed their winter coats just in time to give the
mosquitoes tempting targets.

"You should have a magic to keep the bugs away," he said.

She looked at him. "You Raumsdalians like to think you're stronger than
the world around you. Up here, shamans know better. God lets us live on

the plains . . . as long as we don't push our luck too hard. How could one shaman hold off all the bugs that spawn every spring?"

Put that way, it was a different kind of question. Count Hamnet said, "Can't you hold off *some* of the bugs?"

That only made Liv smile. "What if we did? Don't you think the rest would be plenty to drive men and beasts wild?"

"Umm . . . Probably." Hamnet Thyssen managed a smile of his own, a crooked one. "You're telling me to give up and leave this alone, aren't you?"

"As a matter of fact, yes—except for the bear grease," Liv said. "That helps—as much as anything, anyhow." With a sigh, Hamnet smeared some on. Maybe it helped a little. On the other hand, maybe it didn't.

The Rulers didn't try to drive the Red Dire Wolves to destruction—not right away, anyhow. They could have pursued much harder than they did. Maybe the spring thaw slowed them down. Maybe they awaited reinforcements from beyond the Glacier. Maybe they just didn't care what the beaten Bizogots did. Hamnet had no way of knowing. He welcomed the respite, whatever the reason for it.

It also gave the Red Dire Wolves' messengers the chance to warn other clans. It gave them the chance, yes. How seriously the rest of the Bizogots took those messengers . . . One of the horsemen came back to the Red Dire Wolves' camp that evening. Days got long faster in springtime up here in the north than they did in the Empire; already the sun's setting point had swung far to the northwest, and twilight lingered late.

The slowly gathering gloom descending on the camp didn't come close to matching the gloom on the messenger's face. He bit into a leg from a roasted partridge and swigged from a skin of smetyn, but neither the food nor the fermented mammoth's milk did much to lighten his mood.

"They wouldn't believe me," he told Totila and anyone else who would listen. "By God, Your Ferocity, they wouldn't! They laughed at me. They asked me if I was chewing mystic mushrooms."

"They have their nerve!" Odovacar said indignantly—somehow, the deaf old shaman heard that fine. "Mystic mushrooms are shamans' food. The visions they send drive ordinary men mad."

Liv smiled behind her hand. "That doesn't stop ordinary men from eating them now and then," she whispered to Count Hamnet.

"I'm not surprised," he answered. "If smetyn were against the law, people would still drink it." She nodded.

Totila scowled at the messenger. "Did you manage to persuade 'em you had all your wits about you?"

"I showed 'em this." The messenger pulled up his sleeve and showed off a long cut on his arm, which was still held closed by several musk-ox-sinew stitches. "Even then, they had the nerve to ask me if I did it to myself when the mushrooms made me crazy. I told 'em I'd fight the next fool who asked me a question like that. They heard me out after that, anyhow. But even when they listened, they wouldn't believe."

"Why not?" Totila's face was a study in helpless rage.

"Almost makes you wonder if the Rulers have a spell in the air to turn Bizogots' wits to horse manure," Ulric Skakki said. His usual view was that Bizogots' wits weren't far removed from horse manure anyhow, but nothing in his tone or attitude suggested that now.

"Could it be so?" Trasamund asked.

"Not likely, Your Ferocity," Ulric said. "People can be plenty stupid all by themselves. They mostly don't need magic to help 'em along."

"I wasn't asking you," the Three Tusk jarl said. "I was asking the shamans here." He looked from Liv to Odovacar to Audun Gilli.

"I don't think it's likely, either, Your Ferocity," Liv said. Audun nodded; he'd finally picked up enough of the Bizogot language to get by in it, though he still butchered the grammar and threw in Raumsdalian words when he spoke it himself. As for Odovacar, he didn't seem to have heard Trasamund this time.

Trasamund looked dissatisfied. He'd seldom looked any other way since learning of the disaster that had overwhelmed his clan, but he seemed even less happy than usual now. "I don't want to know what you think," he rumbled. "I want to know what your magic tells you."

"Don't take me seriously here, for heaven's sake," Ulric Skakki said. "I was only joking."

"You Raumsdalians have a saying, don't you, about true words spoken in jest?" Trasamund said. "I think you did that here. You are a clever Raumsdalian. Sometimes you are too clever for your own good. I know you think Bizogots are nothing but a pack of fools."

"I never said that," Ulric protested.

"I don't care what you said. I wasn't talking about what you said. I know what you think here," Trasamund said. Ulric Skakki looked innocent. It wasn't easy, not when he was bound to be guilty as charged, but he brought it off. Hamnet Thyssen thought the Bizogots could be fools, too, and he knew his opinion of them was higher than Ulric's. Trasamund went on, "You think we are fools, yes. But without magic, could we be fools enough to ignore an enemy already beating our clans and stealing our grazing grounds?"

By the look on Ulric's face, he saw nothing too improbable in that, even if he didn't come right out and say so. But the way Trasamund put the question made Hamnet Thyssen wonder. Yes, the Bizogots could be fools, especially from a Raumsdalian point of view. Were they likely to be idiots?

"Maybe we ought to find out, if we can," he said.

Audun Gilli blinked. Liv said, "Not you, too!" Even Odovacar looked at Count Hamnet in surprise, and Hamnet was convinced the Red Dire Wolves' shaman had no idea what was going on.

"It's possible Ulric's right without meaning to be," Hamnet said stubbornly. "If the Bizogots farther south would rather believe in mystic mushrooms than in the Rulers, don't you think that says something's wrong with them?"

Liv looked exasperated. Odovacar went on looking blank. But Audun Gilli looked thoughtful. "It could be so," he said. "I don't say it is, but it could be." He turned to Liv. "Do you know a spell for seeing if someone is using magic?"

"Oh, yes," she answered. "We need a charm like that, for we often have claims that someone is bewitching someone else. We need to find out where the truth lies."

"If the truth lies, how do you find it?" Ulric Skakki inquired.

Audun Gilli didn't get the pun. Liv did, and winced. Trasamund muttered something under his breath. "We use that kind of spell in Nidaros, too," Audun said, taking no notice of what he couldn't follow. "Maybe we ought to try it here."

Liv sighed. "I think it's a waste of time, but if it makes you happy. . . ."

"Happy?" Trasamund spoke before Hamnet, Ulric, or Audun could. "Wise lady, nothing that has passed here since we traveled south into the Empire makes me happy. But if we find here a tool to use against our foes, or a way to keep them from using a tool against us, then I say we have done something worthwhile. Is this so, or is it not so?"

"If we find something, Your Ferocity, it is so," Liv answered. "Otherwise, we do nothing but waste time and strength. This last strikes me as more likely."

"Sometimes finding out the enemy isn't doing something counts for as much as finding out he is would," Hamnet Thyssen said. "If he isn't spreading confusion—"

"Then our neighbors truly are as idiotic as you Raumsdalians make them out to be," Trasamund broke in.

"You said it. I didn't," Hamnet said. "But if the Rulers *are* fuddling the rest of the Bizogots, we need to know that. And if they are, we need to stop them if we can."

"I said I would make the spell. I will," Liv said. "But I wouldn't bother if Trasamund hadn't decided Ulric Skakki meant what he said when he was only making one of his jokes." She sent the adventurer a severe stare.

Ulric looked embarrassed, a startling and unnatural expression on his face, whose normal bland expression could conceal anything. "I *said* I was joking," he protested. "No one wanted to believe me."

"See what happens when you tell so many lies?" Trasamund said. "Nobody wants to hear the truth from you."

"I'll find the truth, whatever it is." Liv nodded to Audun Gilli. "Tell me about your magic-sniffing spells." When he did, in a mixture of her tongue and Raumsdalian, she frowned for a moment, considering. Then she nodded to herself. "Those are not bad, but I think I'll use one I already know. It's simpler, and I won't have to worry about slipping with something new and unfamiliar."

"That makes sense," Audun agreed.

"She'll do it anyhow," Ulric Skakki said, as if to prove he didn't intend all his words to be taken seriously.

Then Liv explained to Odovacar what she intended to do. That took so much shouting, she might almost have told the Rulers what she had in mind, too. At last, the Red Dire Wolves' shaman said, "Anybody would think you figured the Rulers were using magic to make us stupid."

Liv sighed. "Yes. Anyone would think that."

She took from a pouch on her belt an agate, dark brown banded with white. Audun Gilli suddenly grinned when he saw the stone. "Oh, very nice!" he said. "Agate overcomes perils, strengthens the heart, and helps against adversities."

"We have them, sure enough," Trasamund said.

Her face a mask of concentration, Liv took no notice of either of them. She drew forth the dried foot of a snowshoe hare, bound it to the agate with a length of sinew, and tied them both to her left upper arm. "This to help me go where I will, in our world or that of the spirit, and to return without peril," she said.

"May it be so," Hamnet Thyssen murmured. He worried whenever she worked magic, for he knew the danger it put her in. That it was needful only made him worry more, since that meant he couldn't stop her.

She began to chant. Some of the strange little tune was in the Bizogot language. The rest might have been in the speech mammoths used among themselves—if mammoths used any speech among themselves.

As magic had a way of doing, the spell seemed to reach Odovacar. He pricked up his ears and followed her charm with all the attention he had in him. That his ears pricked was literally true; even in human shape, they were unusually large, unusually pointed, and unusually mobile. A bit later, he began to chant. His tune was much like the one Liv used, though not identical. Some of what he sang was in the Bizogot tongue. The rest might have been the speech dire wolves used among themselves—if dire wolves used any speech among themselves.

"The truth!" Liv and Odovacar sang the same thing at the same time, perhaps by chance, perhaps . . . not. "We must have the truth!" Then their songs went different ways again, into mammoth maunderings for Liv and dire-wolf woolgathering for Odovacar.

Both shamans began to dance, Liv plodding after the truth and Odovacar chasing with lolling tongue and hungry eyes. Hamnet Thyssen watched Audun Gilli watching them in fascination. The Raumsdalian wizard seemed altogether absorbed in the workings of a sorcery from a tradition different from the Empire's. If Liv was a mammoth and Odovacar a dire wolf, he might have been a bright-eyed mouse, taking everything in.

"We must have the truth!" Odovacar called again.

"Do lies and deceit stalk the Bizogots?" Liv sang, and then something muffled and mammothy that, Hamnet felt, somehow meant the same thing.

"Quite a show, isn't it?" Ulric Skakki whispered to Hamnet. "I never thought a bad joke could go so far."

"That should teach you to think before you let your tongue flap," Hamnet whispered back. "It probably won't, but it should." Ulric sent him an aggrieved look. He took no notice of it.

The two Raumsdalians might have quarreled then, even though the Bizogot shamans were still busy with their magic. But then Odovacar let out a sudden, startled yip. Liv gasped in surprise. Hamnet Thyssen and Ulric Skakki stared at them, their own disagreement forgotten. Audun Gilli's eyes got wider yet.

"They do!" Liv said. "By God, they do!" She sounded astonished. She also sounded outraged. "This must not be!"

"Banish the lies!" Odovacar bayed. "Banish the deception!"

"Begone!" Liv cried. "Begone! Let them be trampled!"

"Let them be eaten!" Odovacar bared his teeth. They were uncommonly long and sharp, as if he was beginning to take animal shape. The howl he let out argued that he was.

Hamnet felt something that had hovered over the Bizogot encampment—that had, for all he knew, hung over the whole of the frozen steppe—lift and pull back. He hadn't known it was there; it manifested itself more by its absence than it had by its presence. Was he smarter now that it started to withdraw? Maybe he was. Or maybe he was imagining that he was. How could he tell? He was no wizard, and never would be.

Audun Gilli gasped. "No!" he said in Raumsdalian, and began incanting frantically.

Two or three heartbeats later, Liv and Odovacar also gasped. The Red Dire Wolves' shaman staggered and pitched forward on his face. He lay unmoving, whether dead or smitten with something like an apoplexy Hamnet Thyssen could not have said.

Hamnet had more urgent things to worry about than the state of Odovacar's health. Liv, stronger—or perhaps just younger—than the other shaman, still stood, swaying as if in a breeze. But there was no breeze. The force of the Rulers' counterspell was what rocked her. Her lips skinned back from her teeth in a ghastly grimace as she gathered all her strength to resist the magic.

Audun Gilli clutched an amulet of sea-green beryl. Hamnet knew that was a stone sorcerers used to overcome their enemies and make them meek. Audun gabbled out a spell as fast as he could. Was he trying to save himself alone, or did he also include Liv and even Odovacar in his magic? Count Hamnet couldn't ask, not without distracting him and perhaps ruining everything he was trying to do.

Hamnet wondered what he could do by himself, but not for long. He drew his sword and began slashing the air around Liv, as he'd done a couple of times before. Once it had seemed to help, once not. He hoped it would do some good now.

Hoping, he called, "Do the same for Audun," to Ulric Skakki. "It can't hurt—I'm sure of that."

"Right." Ulric wasted no words, but drew his own blade. The adventurer loved to quibble when he found the chance, but he knew there was a time and a place for everything. This was the time for action.

Trasamund freed his great two-handed sword from its scabbard and passed it through the air above the fallen Odovacar. The Red Dire Wolves' shaman groaned and stirred—he wasn't dead, then. But only Trasamund's powerful wrists let him jerk the blade higher in the nick of time so he didn't slay the man he was trying to save. Odovacar howled like a wolf. Hamnet Thyssen wondered whether he had anything more than a wolf's wits in him.

Liv cried, "No!" again. This time rage filled her voice, not fear. "We broke their cursed snare! They won't set it again!" She clutched the hare's foot and agate with her right hand. "I throw back your curses!" she shouted. "May they come down on the head of the shamans who sent them forth, and may they fill their witless heads with coals of fire!"

"So may it be!" Audun Gilli said. Hamnet wouldn't have bet he could follow Liv's words, but he did. Maybe the magic she was working helped him understand.

And Odovacar also called, "So may it be!" His voice seemed scarcely human—it held as much of the dire wolf's howl as of words. But Hamnet Thyssen understood him even so, and Liv and Audun also seemed to.

"Coals of fire!" Liv cried again, gesturing with her left hand. Was it coincidence that Audun Gilli and Odovacar also made the same pass at the same time? Hamnet Thyssen didn't think so.

And he didn't think it was coincidence that the two Bizogots and Audun cried out again a moment later, this time in triumph. Now Audun shouted, "Coals of fire!" Hamnet didn't think he was conjuring with the phrase, but was using it to describe what was happening to the enemy wizards.

"Let them see how they like that, by God!" Liv said. "Let them see they've found foes who can strike back!" Odovacar howled like a hungry dire wolf.

"Is it over?" Hamnet asked.

"For now," Liv answered. "There will be other meetings. They are bound to come, and we will have to do our best in them. But this one has gone as we might have wished most." She looked over to Ulric Skakki. "You see what happens when you joke?"

"I'm afraid I do," he said. "I guess that ought to teach me to keep my mouth shut from here on out, the way Hamnet says I should—but it probably won't."

"No, it won't," Trasamund agreed. "Raumsdalians never know when to shut up."

"Which makes us different from Bizogots how?" Ulric asked politely. The jarl glared at him. Ulric smiled back. But two Bizogot shamans and a Raumsdalian wizard had found and beaten back the spell the Rulers laid over the frozen plains. Instead of quarreling, both men started to laugh. They too were liable to have other run-ins, but no trouble would spring from this one.

TOTILA AND TRASAMUND sent out messengers again. Now that the cloud of foolishness that had hung over the Bizogots was gone, the two jarls hoped their comrades would have second thoughts about what they'd heard before. "Maybe," Totila said hopefully, "we'll even have people riding into our camp to tell us they've decided to take us seriously after all."

But they didn't.

Hamnet Thyssen kept looking north—not, for once, towards the Glacier but towards the Rulers. They hadn't tried to restore the spell Liv and Audun and Odovacar had shattered. Hamnet wondered what that meant. Maybe their wizards had taken a serious defeat and lacked the strength to fight back. Or maybe they'd simply decided the spell was worthless now that the Bizogots knew it was there. Who could guess how the Rulers thought?

Even the captives the Bizogots held weren't sure. "Who knows how a shaman thinks?" one of them said when Hamnet asked him. "They know what they know, and it is not for the likes of us to learn. Maybe they tell the chieftains, but I am—I was—only an ordinary warrior. I rode, I fought . . . and I failed, for you hold me now."

"Do your folk have writing?" Hamnet Thyssen needed to use the Raumsdalian word, for the Bizogots didn't use letters. Naturally, the prisoner failed to follow him. He explained, as best he could, in the Bizogot language.

"This is another kind of magic you speak of," the captive said. His name was Rankarag. "I told you, I know nothing of what shamans do."

"No, not magic. Anyone can do it. I can do it, and I'll never be a shaman in a thousand years," Count Hamnet said. "Look." He took a sharp length of bone and wrote *Rankarag* in the mud. "There is your name."

Rankarag promptly reached out with his booted foot and smudged the characters beyond legibility. "No one will make magic with a picture of my name," he declared.

Hamnet Thyssen started to write his own name in the dirt to show the captive it was only a name, not magic at all. He started to, yes, but then he didn't. Who could say what a sorcerer might do with his name—and who could say whether Rankarag knew as little of wizardry as he claimed? Better, maybe, not to take chances.

Instead, Hamnet wrote *mammoth*. "These are the signs we use for the name of the great beast," he said.

"One of them is the same as one in my name," Rankarag said suspiciously. He had a quick eye.

"*Rankarag* and *mammoth* have the same sound in them," Hamnet answered. He said the name and the word again, stressing the first syllable each time. "The same character shows that sound."

Rankarag plucked at his thick, curly beard. "With enough—characters, you call them?—you could set down anything you can say, couldn't you?"

He was no fool. Nodding, Hamnet said, "We have a character for each sound in my language. We *can* set down anything we say."

"This is a strong magic," the warrior of the Rulers said. "This is a stronger magic than I looked for folk of the herd to have." By that he meant any human beings not of the Rulers. His folk looked at all other people as animals to be herded like mammoths and riding deer.

"It is not magic at all," Hamnet Thyssen insisted. "It is a craft, like making a bow or fletching an arrow. Anyone can learn it."

"So you say," Rankarag replied. "You are not part of the Bizogot herd. Do these Bizogots know this so-called craft?"

"No," Hamnet said.

"So your herd keeps it for itself, then," the warrior from the Rulers said. "One day, you will use it against the Bizogot herd. You will slaughter them all, except for the pretty women, and you will take their land." He had a very basic notion of what went into diplomacy. So did the rest of his folk.

Count Hamnet wanted to laugh in his face. Instead, he just shook his head. "We don't want the Bizogots' land. We have better land of our own."

"But you still keep these, these characters secret from the Bizogots," Rankarag said.

"No," Hamnet replied, as patiently as he could. "They can learn to write if they want to. A few of them have. Most see no use for it, though."

"Then this Bizogot herd is full of fools," Rankarag said—a view not too different from the one many Raumsdalians held. He pointed a finger at Hamnet Thyssen. "I can prove that you are lying. I can make you prove it, in fact. If it is only a craft"—he laughed at the very idea—"you will not mind showing me all of these characters."

After writing Rankarag's name again, Hamnet showed him the sound that each character in it made, finishing, "You see the r sound and the a sound are there together twice. These are the characters that make them, and they are also there twice. We have thirty-seven characters in all. Here they are." He wrote them out in order, saying the sound for each one as he did.

Rankarag stared at him, at the Raumsdalian characters, at him again. "You are not making this up," he said slowly.

"By God, no!" Hamnet said. "That would be more trouble than it's worth."

Like a lot of Bizogots, Rankarag proved to have an excellent memory for what he saw and heard. He took the bit of bone from Count Hamnet and wrote in the muddy ground, muttering to himself as he did. "So this would say *tent* in the tongue of the Bizogot herd, then?"

"Almost. Not quite. What you wrote is *tint*, which means a color. Here is the character for the *e* sound." Hamnet pointed it out, then wrote *tent* himself. In spite of himself, he was impressed that Rankarag had come so close after hearing the sound of each character only once.

"*Tent.*" Rankarag wrote it again, this time correctly.

"That's right," Hamnet said.

Rankarag eyed him. "I could put your name in the mud, the same as you put mine. I could work magic on it if I were a shaman."

Suddenly, Count Hamnet wondered whether showing him the way Raumsdalians wrote was such a good idea. Rankarag didn't see writing as a tool. He saw it as a weapon. The minds of the Rulers seemed to run in that direction. As casually as Hamnet could, he said, "You could try. Because we use characters all the time, of course we are warded against them." That sounded good. He wished it were true.

And it impressed the captive less than he hoped it would. "You folk of the herds, what are your wards worth?" Rankarag said. "Our shamans should have no trouble beating them down."

"Your magic is not always as strong as you think it is," Hamnet Thyssen replied, trying to fight down his unease. "Besides, what do you care what the Rulers do? You don't belong to them any more. You are a prisoner, a prisoner of the Bizogots."

Rankarag flinched as if Hamnet had threatened to hit him. The real threat probably wouldn't have scared him; he was a warrior to the core. "I wish you hadn't reminded me," he said in a low, sullen voice.

"You need to remember it. You failed. You were captured. The Rulers don't want you back. If you have any future at all, it's with us, not with them." Count Hamnet hoped he was right. If Rankarag escaped and brought writing and the idea of writing back to the Rulers' wizards, would that make him valuable enough to earn his way into the ranks of his folk once more? Hamnet couldn't be sure; he simply didn't know the enemy well enough to judge.

One thing he could do—and he did it. He warned the guards to keep an extra close watch on the prisoners. "We'll do it," one of them said.

Hamnet asked Trasamund and Totila to tell the guards to be careful, too. They would take an order from a jarl more seriously than a warning from a foreigner. He hoped they would, anyhow. He had the feeling he'd put a sword into the Rulers' hands. He hadn't intended to, but what did that have to do with the price of meat?

"NAME MAGIC, YOU say?" Ulric Skakki looked at Count Hamnet as if he'd found half of him in his apple. "Name magic with letters? Well, there's one more thing to have nightmares about. Thank you so much."

"I didn't mean to," Hamnet said sheepishly.

"Yes? And so?" Ulric said. "Probably the best thing we could do now would be to kill this Rankarag whoreson. Or do you suppose he's already passed on the news to the rest of the prisoners?"

"I hope not," Hamnet said. "But I wouldn't be surprised."

"No. Neither would I," Ulric said. "You and your big mouth—and you talk about me. If the Rulers were freezing, would you have told them to start a fire?"

"I didn't think they would think to use writing for sorcery," Hamnet said unhappily.

"Why the demon not?" Ulric Skakki rolled his eyes. "That's probably what we used it for first, too. After a while, some people figured out you could do other things with it, too. But they had to pry it out of the wizards' hands before they could—you can bet on that."

"How do you know? Were you there?" Hamnet asked.

"Of course," Ulric said easily. "This was in the days when mammoths weren't woolly and musk oxen were green, you understand."

"I wonder what Audun would say about that," Hamnet Thyssen remarked.

"Well, you can ask him if you want to." Ulric's voice was dismissive. "I didn't see him around then, though—I'll tell you that." He often took his whimsy more seriously than things any sensible person would have known were worth taking seriously.

As much to annoy the adventurer as for any other reason, Count Hamnet did hunt up Audun Gilli. "What do you know about how writing started?" he asked out of a clear blue sky—something the frozen steppe didn't see all that often, but something it enjoyed now.

The wizard blinked. "What on earth brought that on?" he asked.

Hamnet Thyssen explained his unfortunate introduction of the idea to Rankarag, and also his fruitless—at least from his point of view—discussion with Ulric Skakki. "So if you know anything about the days when the musk oxen were green, let's hear it," he finished.

"Green musk oxen," Audun Gilli murmured. "I wasn't there for that, I will say. But Ulric's right, I think—wizards likely did come up with writing first. We needed it more than other people would have."

"How much trouble can the Rulers cause if they start using it?" Hamnet asked.

"How should I know?" Audun answered—which was, Hamnet had to admit, a sensible response. The wizard went on, "My best guess is, they'll cause more trouble than we expect them to. They seem to be like that."

"They do, don't they?" Hamnet Thyssen said unhappily. "We've got to make sure none of our captives flees north, then. I've talked to the Bizogots about it, but sometimes talking to them is like talking to the Glacier. You can do it, but you wonder why you bother."

"They follow their own bent, don't they?" Audun said.

Hamnet laughed, not that he found it very funny. "That's the kindest way I ever heard to say they do whatever they cursed well please."

"They sure do," Audun said. "They ought to be able to see that this is important . . . except they don't write themselves, and so they don't understand why it would matter whether or not the Rulers do."

"If the Rulers start using name magic against them, they'll understand soon enough," Count Hamnet said. "Of course, that'll be too late." He spat into the mud between his feet. "Amazing how many things we understand too stinking late." He wasn't thinking of sorcery, at least not of the usual sort. He was thinking of Gudrid. As usual when he thought of his faithless former wife, he wished he didn't.

Luckily, Audun Gilli couldn't read his mind. "Even if we do have escapes," the wizard said, "it stays light so much longer now. They can't get a long start in the night. We have a much better chance of hunting them down."

"So we do," Hamnet said sourly. "It would still be better if they didn't get away at all. Can you do anything magical to make sure they stay here?"

"I doubt it. You need a willing subject for sorcery like that," Audun said.

"Oh, wonderful," Count Hamnet said, his tone more sour still. "If you've got willing subjects, you don't need to magic 'em to get 'em to stay where they're supposed to."

"Well, yes, there is that," the wizard admitted. As if he badly wanted to change the subject, he pointed up into the sky. "Look. The teratorns have come back from the south."

"So they have," Hamnet said. The great birds—scavengers big enough to dwarf vultures and even condors—stayed longer around Nidaros than up here in the Bizogot country. But when winter clamped down there, most of them flew south—corpses got too thin on the ground to let them stay.

As if thinking along with Count Hamnet, Audun Gilli said, "They're liable to have plenty to eat up here this summer."

"Yes, aren't they?" Hamnet said. "I hope they don't sick up the bodies of the Rulers they feed on. And I hope there are plenty of those."

"May it be so. May God hear your prayer," the wizard said. Hamnet hadn't been praying, or not exactly, but he wouldn't be sorry if God listened to him. God hadn't done much of that lately. But when he said as much, Audun Gilli cocked his head to one side and studied him like a bright-eyed bird. "No, eh? So you don't thank God for Liv, then?"

"I do," Hamnet said at once. "I do, and you're right. I was thinking of the world's affairs, not my own."

"Your own count for more most of the time," Audun observed.

"Most of the time, but not here," Hamnet Thyssen said. "If the world's affairs go to ruin, mine will, too. Down in the Empire, I could live in my castle and tell the world to go hang. I can't do that here—the world is more likely to hang me. Can we stop the Rulers? Can we even slow them down?"

"Would we be up here if we didn't think we could?" Audun Gilli answered.

"We thought we could when we came north," Hamnet said. "That was before we knew they'd crushed the Three Tusk clan. It was before they beat the Red Dire Wolves, too." He looked uneasily towards the north. How much of a fight could the Bizogots put up when the Rulers decided to strike again? Enough? Any at all?

The wizard's eyes went in the same direction. "They are strong," Audun murmured, as much to himself as to Hamnet Thyssen. "They are strong, yes, but we can stop them."

"How?" Hamnet asked bluntly.

"I don't know yet," Audun Gilli replied. "But I think we'll find out. The very strong have weaknesses in proportion to their strength."

"Is that so?" Hamnet Thyssen said. "Tell me of a lion's weaknesses, then."

"If a lion doesn't have lots of big animals to kill, it will starve," Audun said at once. "Foxes or weasels can live well and get fat on land that won't support a lion."

He was right. Hamnet couldn't deny it. Even so . . . "I don't see what that has to do with the Rulers."

"Neither do I," the sorcerer said. "You were the one who mentioned the lion, though."

"Well, so I was," Count Hamnet said gruffly. "What weaknesses do the Rulers have? We haven't seen many yet."

"No, we haven't," Audun Gilli agreed. "The way they discard captives may be one. If they didn't, we wouldn't have learned so much from our prisoners."

At the moment, Hamnet Thyssen worried more about what Rankarag and the other prisoners had learned from him. No one had tried to escape yet. Maybe the captives thought the Rulers wouldn't take them back no matter what. Maybe they were right if they did. That did seem to be a weakness to Hamnet.

But was it a weakness the Bizogots could use to beat the Rulers? If it was, he couldn't see how. Had the Bizogots found any weaknesses like that? If they had, he knew he had no idea what they were.

V

Fear made the scout's voice wobble when he rode into the camp. "They're moving!" he called. "The God-cursed Rulers are moving!"

And, like a spark setting kindling alight, the fear in the Bizogot rider's voice sent fear racing through the encampment where the Red Dire Wolves and the remnants of the Three Tusk clan dwelt. "They're moving!" became "They're coming!" became "They'll attack us!" became "They'll kill us all!" became "We have to flee before they *can* kill us all!"

Trasamund kept his wits about him, at least enough to hear what the scout truly said. "What do you mean, they're moving?" he shouted through the rising chaos. Hamnet Thyssen couldn't have found a better question if he tried for a week. Finding out what was really going on came ahead of everything else.

"Well, Your Ferocity, they're moving south," the Bizogot rider answered. He pointed east. "They're heading down into our country—into Red Dire Wolf country—over that way."

"They're not coming straight at the camp, then?" Trasamund demanded.

"No, Your Ferocity, or not when I saw 'em," the scout said. "But their war mammoths and riding deer are on the move, and the herds of mammoths and musk oxen they've stolen here." He had more diplomacy than most Bizogots; he didn't remind Trasamund that those stolen mammoths and musk oxen came from the Three Tusk clan.

Totila said, "This is bad enough. They move into the heart of our grazing grounds, may God afflict them with boils. We can't take *our* herds that way now, not without fighting."

"We're not ready for another fight yet," Ulric Skakki said in a low voice.

"Now tell me something I didn't know," Hamnet Thyssen answered. "Do you think the Bizogots ever will be?"

"Well, if the answer turns out to be no, we both rode a demon of a long way for nothing," Ulric said, which seemed like another obvious truth.

"What are we going to do?" Liv found one more important question. "Will we go over to the attack? Will we run from the Rulers? Or will we stay here and wait till they strike us?"

"Let's hit them!" Trasamund boomed.

He might have been a male grouse booming where no females could hear him. The Bizogots didn't take up the cry. They weren't eager to strike at the Rulers. One fight with the foe from beyond the Glacier had taught them how misplaced eagerness was. They might fight bravely against the invaders, but few of them would swarm forward to do it.

Trasamund didn't seem to see that. "Let's hit them!" he cried again.

Fear had kindled among the Red Dire Wolves. Ferocity wouldn't. Again, Trasamund's bellow fell into a deep, dark pool of silence. It raised no echoes. The jarl of the Three Tusk clan turned red with rage when he saw it wouldn't.

"Are *you* afraid?" Trasamund shouted, now in disbelief.

No one told him no. He clapped a hand to his forehead. Count Hamnet wondered if he would have a stroke, but he didn't.

"We know which direction the Rulers will come from now," Totila said. "We can work out how best to beat them back when they do."

"But—" Trasamund looked around. He sent Totila a withering glance, but realized standing fast was as much as he could hope to get from the other Bizogots. He had not a chance in the world of making them go forward. Shaking his head, he said, "We should be able to do more than this."

"Sometimes doing anything at all is as much as you can ask for," Hamnet Thyssen told him.

"Maybe." Trasamund didn't sound as if he believed it. "But if we're standing still and they're still coming forward . . . The chin stands still. The fist comes forward."

"And sometimes the fist breaks knuckles when it hits the chin," Hamnet said.

"Sometimes," the Bizogot jarl echoed gloomily. He'd broken knuckles on both hands. But he went on, "Most of the time, the fist strikes home and the fellow with the chin goes down." He looked at the clansmen all around. "By

God, Raumsdalian, what do we do if they smash us again? Where do we run? Where *can* we run?"

"The thing to do, Your Ferocity, is make sure they don't smash us." Count Hamnet hoped the Bizogots could do that. Trasamund wasn't wrong—another defeat would ruin the Red Dire Wolves. Another defeat might also persuade a lot of other clans to roll on their backs for the Rulers. Easier and safer to yield than to go up against an overwhelmingly strong foe in hopeless battle. So the nomads might believe, anyhow.

Or they might not. Hamnet Thyssen knew he was thinking like a civilized man, like a Raumsdalian, himself. The Bizogots were a proud and touchy folk. They might decide they would rather die than admit the invaders from beyond the Glacier were their superiors. He had no way to know ahead of time. He would have to see for himself.

When he said as much to Ulric Skakki, the adventurer said, "Here's hoping we *don't* have to find out, Your Grace." He turned Count Hamnet's title of nobility into one of faint reproach.

"How do you mean?" Hamnet asked.

"If we can beat the Rulers, we don't have to worry that they'll panic the rest of the clans into going belly-up."

"Oh. Yes. There is that." Hamnet sounded as dubious as Trasamund had a little while before.

"If you don't think we can, what are you doing here?" Ulric spoke in a low voice. He took Count Hamnet by the elbow and steered him away from Trasamund and the other Bizogots. The steppe squelched under their boots. The Bizogot country, which had been white for so long, was green now, the green of grass and rocks and tiny shrubs, all splashed with red and yellow and blue flowers. The brief beauty effectively disguised what a harsh land it was.

"What am I doing here?" Hamnet echoed. "The best I can."

"Don't make yourself out to be that big a hero," Ulric said. "You would have stayed down in the Empire if Liv stayed with you."

"Yes, I like her company," Hamnet said. "So what? I'm entitled to a little happiness if I can find it."

"Nobody is entitled to happiness. You'll lose it if you think you are." Ulric spoke with unusual conviction. "You may stumble over it now and again, but that's not because you're entitled to it."

He was likely to be right. No—as far as Hamnet could see, he was bound to be right. Recognizing as much, the noble changed the subject: "Even if I'd gone down to my castle instead of coming up here, I would have met the Rulers sooner or later. Or will you tell me I'm wrong about that?"

"I wish I could." Ulric Skakki sighed. "Well, you don't always get what you want. Sometimes you're stuck with things. We're stuck with the Bizogots now, and with the slim chances they have."

"See? You think so, too," Hamnet said.

"They're doing *something*, anyhow." Ulric sighed again, even more mournfully than before. "I wish they were doing more. I wish they knew how to do more. I wish they had some tiny notion of how to work together. And I wish Sigvat would have taken his head out of his . . ." He sighed one more time. "I said it myself a minute ago—you don't always get what you want."

"How about what you don't want?" Count Hamnet asked. Ulric Skakki made a questioning noise. Hamnet explained: "I don't want to get beaten again."

"Oh. That," Ulric said airily. "We'll find out."

FIGHTING AMONG HIS own countrymen, Hamnet Thyssen wouldn't have ridden out as a scout to keep an eye on what the enemy was up to. The Raumsdalians had soldiers who specialized in such things, as they had specialists who had dealt with catapults, sharpshooting archers, and others who could do one thing very well and the others not so well.

Up in the Bizogot country, shamans were the only specialists. Everyone else had to be able to do all the things people needed to do to live on the frozen steppe; there wasn't enough surplus to let the nomads be able to specialize. In bad years, there was no surplus at all—there wasn't enough. Starvation was an uncommon misfortune down in the Empire, but a fact of life here.

Motion drew Hamnet's eye. It wasn't a riding deer or a war mammoth in the distance, but a vole or lemming scurrying from one tussock to another almost under his horse's hooves. A moment later, a weasel streaked after the other little animal. Most of the weasel's coat had gone brown, with only a few small white patches left. The beasts needed no calendar to know spring was here.

Birds of all sizes from larkspurs to teratorns crowded the Bizogot country. Most of them fed on the bounty of bugs the springtime ponds brought. Others ate the birds that ate the bugs—hawks and owls lived here, too.

More waterfowl bred on the edges of Sudertorp Lake, south of the Red

Dire Wolves' grazing grounds, than anywhere else. But others found smaller ponds and puddles good enough. A goose rose from a pond and flew away as Hamnet came near. The bird couldn't know he wasn't hunting it. If he were hungry, he might have been.

He kept staring east. He was getting close to where the Bizogot had spotted the Rulers. The invaders' scouts would probably be prowling out this way. They would want to know how alert the Bizogots were.

Ulric Skakki rode somewhere not too far away, though Hamnet couldn't see him right now. The frozen steppe looked perfectly flat—and well it might, since the Glacier had lain on it so long and left so recently. But it wasn't, or not quite; it had its gentle swells and dips. Some of those hid the adventurer from sight.

What do I do if four or five enemies come at me? But Hamnet Thyssen knew the answer to that. If he was outnumbered, he would run away. He wasn't out to be a hero, or even a fierce warrior. All he wanted to do was make sure the Rulers weren't heading for the Red Dire Wolves' encampment along this line.

Something out there on the horizon . . . Hamnet's eyes narrowed. He shaded them with his left hand, trying to see better. "Animals," he muttered aloud. He urged his horse forward. Were those some of the Rulers' herds, or perhaps beasts they'd stolen from the Bizogots? Or was that their army on the move? He had to find out.

As he rode forward, he wondered how the Rulers treated enemies they captured. Not very well, was his best guess. He hadn't been a captured enemy the last time he stayed at one of their encampments. He'd been—what? A curiosity, perhaps, along with the other Raumsdalians and Bizogots who traveled beyond the Glacier.

But what he'd seen and heard made it clear the Rulers didn't think men and women of other folk were really human beings. They were hard enough on their own kind, casting them out if taken prisoner and expecting them to kill themselves if defeated. On others? Hamnet Thyssen didn't want to find out the hard way.

He hadn't gone very far before a couple of small shapes separated themselves from the larger mass there on the horizon and came his way. He nodded to himself. The Rulers were alert. He might despise them—he did despise them—but they made monstrously good warriors.

He kept going a while longer, long enough to satisfy himself that he was just seeing a herd, not the vanguard of the Rulers' army. That didn't let those riding deer—he could plainly make out that they were riding deer now—get within bowshot of his horse, but it did let them come closer than he'd intended. No, he didn't want to find out how the Rulers treated prisoners. He wheeled his horse and rode back more or less in the direction from which he'd come.

Hoarse shouts rang out behind him, faint in the distance. Had the enemy warriors thought he would oblige them by riding straight into their hands? Too bad for them if they had.

When he looked over his shoulder, they were coming after him as fast as their riding deer would go. He booted his horse up from a trot to a gallop. He kept zigzagging a bit, not wanting to show the Rulers exactly in which direction the Red Dire Wolves' camp lay.

They kept after him. If they ran their antlered mounts into the ground in the pursuit, they didn't seem to care. He had more trouble pulling away from them than he'd thought he would.

He began looking around for Ulric Skakki. He didn't want to be rescued, or not exactly, but he wouldn't have minded knowing where the adventurer was.

Then he found out. He chanced to be looking back again when one of the Rulers threw up his hands and slid off over his riding deer's tail. A moment later, an arrow struck the other one's mount. The deer crashed to the ground, pinning the warrior beneath it. Ulric Skakki galloped up, sprang down from his horse, and finished the man with a swordthrust.

By the time Hamnet rode back to him, he was already mounted again. "That was . . . nicely done," Hamnet said, reflecting that Ulric made a monstrously good warrior, too, even if he wasn't showy about it the way the Rulers were.

"Thanks," Ulric answered now. "You made it easy. They didn't pay any attention to me till much too late."

"The foxes chased the hare and didn't notice the dire wolf?" Hamnet wasn't sure he liked the idea of being nothing more than someone who distracted the foe from a real danger. He wanted the Rulers to think he was dangerous himself.

Ulric winked at him, disconcertingly sharp. "You've got the cutest whiskers."

"I'm so glad you think so." Hamnet Thyssen batting his eyes made Ulric laugh out loud. Count Hamnet couldn't keep his mood light for long. He asked, "Did you get a good look at the herd up ahead?" He pointed east. "How many of the Rulers were there with it?"

"At least these two." The adventurer pointed to one of the corpses. "I didn't see that many more. Did you?"

"I didn't think so," Hamnet answered. "I'd say we've proved the main thrust against the Red Dire Wolves won't come along this path."

"I'd say you're right." Ulric nodded. "And I'd also say we'd better get back to them anyhow. That thrust *is* coming, whether it's coming this way or not. I don't want to ride into camp and find out there's no camp left, if you know what I mean."

Hamnet Thyssen understood him much too well. He didn't want to think of getting back there and finding the Rulers had broken the Bizogots. If anything happened to Liv . . . He especially didn't want anything to happen to her if he wasn't there to do all he could to keep it from happening. That probably didn't make much sense, but he didn't care. "Let's ride," he said harshly.

Again he had the feeling Ulric Skakki knew exactly what he was thinking. He didn't care. As long as the adventurer kept his mouth shut about Liv, they would get along fine. If Ulric didn't . . .

If Ulric didn't, Hamnet would try to hurt him. He wasn't sure he could. The last time he tried, he flew through the air with the greatest of ease and ended up, suddenly and painfully, on his back on a hard stone floor. He was bigger than Ulric Skakki, and thought he was stronger. Ulric was faster and trickier. More often than not, that gave him the edge.

"We shouldn't quarrel among ourselves," Ulric said, not quite out of nowhere. "We should save it for the Rulers."

"Well, you're right." Hamnet Thyssen wasn't about to let Ulric know he'd been thinking about fighting him.

A short-eared fox trotted across their path. Like the weasel's, its pelt was going from white to brown. The hares up here were also short-eared and stocky next to the ones that bounded across the Raumsdalian prairie, while northern lynxes were more compact than bobcats. "What about the Bizogots?" Ulric Skakki asked when Count Hamnet remarked on that. "Why aren't they built like balls?"

"They wear clothes. They build fires," Hamnet answered. "And take a look at the Rulers. They *are* broader and thicker than most folk from this side of the Glacier."

Ulric grunted. "If I never had to look at the Rulers again, it wouldn't break my heart. You'd best believe that."

"Nor mine," Count Hamnet agreed.

"I wonder what their women are like, though," Ulric said, all at once thoughtful. "We haven't seen them."

"They're here now. Liv saw them in her spirit flight. She called them ugly bitches," Hamnet Thyssen said. "So the Rulers aren't just coming to raid. They're coming to settle."

"I want to see their women myself, in the flesh, not just in spirit," Ulric Skakki said. "They would mean we've beaten them so badly, we're coming up to their camps."

"Or it could mean they've captured us and put us to work there," Count Hamnet said. Ulric made a horrible face. "Besides," Hamnet went on, "you don't mean you want to see them. You mean you want to swive them."

"Well, yes," Ulric admitted, "but if you say that to a Bizogot girl named Arnora I won't be very happy with you."

Count Hamnet had noticed that Ulric had taken up with one Bizogot in particular instead of spreading himself through the mammoth-herders' women as opportunity, among other things, arose. Hamnet had a horror of infidelity. All the same, he said, "I won't blab. Sooner or later, though, you'll give yourself away."

"Let me worry about that." Ulric could have said a good many other things. He left them unspoken. Hamnet appreciated his tact, such as it was.

They spotted smoke an hour or so later. Hamnet feared at first it was the smoke of a sack, but soon realized there wasn't enough for that. It was only the normal smoke that rose above any Bizogot encampment. He breathed a loud, long sigh of relief.

Ulric Skakki sent him a crooked smile. "Now that you mention it, yes."

When they rode into the camp, the Bizogots cheered to learn they'd slain a couple of warriors from the Rulers. "Two more we won't have to worry about at the next big battle," Totila said, sounding a lot like Trasamund.

Arnora embraced Ulric after he got down from his horse. Her blue eyes shone. She was as tall as he was, and almost as wide through the shoulders. "Kill more of them," she said with Bizogot directness. "Kill many more. I'll make you glad you do." She led him off to a tent to attend to that on the spot.

"We only gave them a fleabite," Hamnet said, scratching as if reminded. "Before long, they'll try to do worse to us."

"Let them come!" Trasamund shouted. "Let them do their worst! Do they think we fear them? By God, we'll teach them a thing or two. Let them come!"

Hamnet Thyssen looked at Liv. She said what was in his mind, too: "Be careful what you ask for, Your Ferocity, or God may decide to give it to you."

THE RULERS CAME two days later, driving in the scouts patrolling to the east and sending them headlong back into the Red Dire Wolves' encampment in fear for their lives. "Arm yourselves!" the scouts shouted as they rode in. "We have to fight!"

"To me, Three Tusk clan!" Trasamund bellowed. "To me! Another chance for vengeance is here!"

Totila shouted for his warriors, too. Hamnet Thyssen wished other clans had ridden in. That would have given the Bizogots a better chance against their foes. *Or maybe,* he thought glumly, *it would have given the Rulers the chance to get rid of more Bizogots at once.* He knew too well that the Bizogots had had little luck against the invaders in battle.

"Can we stop them?" he asked Liv.

"Do you mean, can our fighters stop theirs? Man for man, we can match them," she said. "When it comes to shamanry, though . . . Well, Audun and Odovacar and I will do our best. I have to hope it will be good enough."

He gave her a quick kiss. He had to hope whatever magic the shamans and Audun Gilli could muster would be good enough, too. "If you can spook their war mammoths . . ."

"That would be good, wouldn't it?" Liv said. "We'll try. We'll try everything we can think of."

"This is our land!" Totila was shouting. "These are our herds! Are we going to let these flyblown mammoth turds steal them from us?"

"No!" the Bizogots yelled back. Their spirits still seemed high. Hamnet Thyssen admired them for that, at the same time wondering where they'd left their memories. The Rulers already held the heart of the Red Dire Wolves' grazing lands. The invaders had already beaten the clan once. Why did Totila think his countrymen could beat the Rulers now?

Maybe he didn't. Maybe he just thought they had to make the fight. If they didn't, if they fled, they would be invaders themselves, trying to take land from other Bizogots. And they would have a brand new war on their hands if they did. Sometimes you needed to fight even when the odds were bad.

"Well, well." Ulric Skakki looked up from the methodical examination he was giving the arrows in his quiver. "Doesn't this sound like fun?" His bright, cheery voice matched the wide smile on his foxy features.

Count Hamnet just shook his head. "No."

"What do you suppose the Bizogots will do if things go wrong again?" Ulric spoke Raumsdalian, so most of the mammoth-herders wouldn't understand. "What do you suppose *we'll* do if things go wrong?"

"Try to stay alive," Hamnet said, also in Raumsdalian. "What else can we do? What can anybody do when things go wrong?"

"A point. Yes, a distinct point." The adventurer tapped one of the points sticking up from the quiver. "Not too sharp a point, I hope."

The Bizogots and the Raumsdalians who'd come north rode out behind the scouts a little later. Women and old men stayed behind to tend the herds, though some women carried bows to battle. Arnora rode beside Ulric Skakki, and seemed as ready to fight as any of the men howling out battle songs.

If the Rulers broke the Red Dire Wolves again, would the herd guards be able to keep the Bizogots' animals out of the invaders' hands? Nobody could know something like that ahead of time, but Hamnet had his doubts.

"There!" The shout rose from up ahead. "There they are, the God-cursed rogues!"

"Are you ready?" Hamnet asked Liv.

"I'd better be, but how much difference would it make if I weren't?" she said.

He had no good answer for that. "*Can* you do anything about their mammoths?" he asked.

She smiled at him the way a mother might smile at a fussy child. "We can do things," she replied. "I don't know whether they'll work the way we hope, but we can do them."

He had to be content, or not so content, with that. He worried as he rode forward with the Bizogots. If Liv and Audun and Odovacar couldn't stop or slow down the mammoths, this battle was lost before it began. They had to see that, didn't they?

Liv did. Audun probably did. Odovacar? Hamnet Thyssen wasn't sure how much Odovacar saw, or how much it mattered.

Closer now. The mammoths loomed up ahead like perambulating mountains. The riding deer out to the flanks weren't nearly so formidable. Where were the Rulers' wizards? What new deviltry were they planning?

The Bizogots shouted Totila's name, and Trasamund's. They shouted for vengeance. They roared out their hatred of the Rulers. They shook their fists. They yelled curses that probably wouldn't bite. And the Rulers yelled back. Hamnet Thyssen still knew next to nothing of their harsh, guttural speech. All the same, he doubted that the invaders were praising the Bizogots or passing the time of day.

Arrows started to fly. "Do you see?" Ulric Skakki said. "They've put more armor on their mammoths."

Hamnet hadn't noticed, but Ulric was right. The thick leather sheets did cover more of the enormous beasts. "I don't care how much they put on," Hamnet said. "Leather won't turn a square hit." As if to try to prove the point, he nocked an arrow and let fly.

Ulric Skakki also began shooting. "I don't think they *can* armor their deer, or not very much," he said. "Those have all they can do to carry men. They don't have any weight left over for armor, too."

Down in the Empire, heavy cavalry horses would carry a trooper, his coat of mail, and iron armor of their own. Charges of such knights were irresistible . . . except, perhaps, by mammoths. But the Bizogots had neither such big horses nor such armor. Their warriors wore cuirasses of leather boiled in oil—when they wore armor at all. Their horses had no more protection than the Rulers' riding deer.

Deer and horses, then, made larger, easier targets than warriors. Wounded animals shrilled out cries of pain that reminded Hamnet Thyssen of women in torment. Listening, he wanted to stuff his fingers in his ears to block out the horrid sounds. But his hands had other things to do.

He methodically drew and shot, drew and shot. His bowstring didn't break, as it had in the last fight against the Rulers. Liv had set a spell on it, and on many others, to ward against the enemy's sorcerous mischief. Audun and Odovacar had also seen to the Bizogots' bows. So far, their charms seemed to be working.

Bizogot horsemen were at least a match for the warriors of the Rulers on riding deer. But horsemen could not withstand the Rulers' war mammoths. Fight as the Bizogots would, the mammoths drove a great wedge into the center of their line, threatening to split their force in two.

"If you can do anything at all about those God-cursed beasts, this would be a mighty good time!" Hamnet shouted to Liv.

"I'll try," she answered, and said something to Audun Gilli, who rode close by. The Raumsdalian wizard nodded. He began what Hamnet recognized as a protective spell, to keep Liv from having to guard herself while she made a different kind of magic.

Count Hamnet wouldn't have wanted to cast a spell while riding a bucketing horse and hoping no enemy arrow struck home. That was what Liv had to do, though, and she did it as if she had years of practice. Her voice never wavered, and her passes were, or at least seemed, quick and reliable. Hamnet admired her at least as much for her unflustered competence as for her courage.

And suddenly the ground in front of and under the Rulers' war mammoths began to boil with . . . with what? With voles, Hamnet realized, and with lemmings, and with all the other mousy little creatures that lived on the northern steppe. Some of them started running up the mammoths' legs. Others squeaked and died as great feet squashed them. Still others started up the mammoths' trunks instead of their legs.

The mammoths liked that no better than Hamnet would have enjoyed a sending of cockroaches. They did odd, ridiculous-looking dance steps, trying to shake free of the voles and lemmings. If they also shook free of some of the warriors on their backs, they didn't care at all. The Rulers might, but the mammoths didn't.

And those mammoths particularly didn't like the little animals on their trunks. They shook them again and again, sending lemmings flying. They didn't pay any attention to the battle they were supposed to be fighting.

Where the war mammoths had forced their way into the center of the Bizogots' line, now they suddenly halted, more worried about vermin than violence. The Bizogots whooped and cheered and fought back hard. Had the confusion in the enemy ranks lasted longer, and had they met with no confusion of their own . . .

Hamnet Thyssen often thought about that afterwards. Much too late to do anything about it then, of course.

In the battle, he shouted, "Ha! See how you like it!" He shot an enemy warrior who'd fallen from his mammoth, and then another one. They would have done the same to him. They'd tried to do the same to him. But he'd succeeded against them. And Liv and Audun and Odovacar had succeeded against their wizards.

No sooner had that thought crossed his mind than he discovered it did not do to count the Rulers' wizards out too soon. The air suddenly darkened around the Bizogots. Hamnet had thought he knew everything there was to know about bugs in the north when the steppe unfroze. He quickly found out how naive he'd been.

As Liv and her comrades called voles and lemmings to the Rulers' mammoths, so the enemy wizards called insects to the Bizogots and their horses. Some always buzzed about; all you could do was slap and swear. But now the mosquitoes and gnats and flies descended in a cloud as thick and choking as if woven from the long hairs of the woolly mammoth. Horses bucked and thrashed in torment, lashing their tails against the overwhelming onslaught.

Fighting was next to impossible with so many bugs assailing every unclothed inch of skin. Even breathing wasn't easy. Hamnet Thyssen coughed and choked. Something nasty that wiggled and tasted of blood crunched between his teeth. Gnats kept getting in his eyes. He rubbed frantically.

The bugs didn't seem to bother the Rulers or their animals, or no worse than usual. *Why am I not surprised?* Hamnet thought bitterly. The enemy's war mammoths were still distracted, but the warriors on riding deer seemed unaffected by either side's sorcery.

Not far from Hamnet, Liv was slapping and scratching and spitting as desperately as he was. "Make it stop!" he shouted to her. "By God, you have to!"

"If we do, we'll have to let go of the spell that calls the little animals to their mammoths," she answered.

He might have guessed that. "I think you'd better do it anyhow," he said. "They're hurting us worse than we're hurting them." Saying that tasted bad . . . but not so bad as the insects that filled his mouth and furred his teeth.

Liv said something that should have made every insect in the world burst into flames. It should have, but it didn't. She shouted to Odovacar, who didn't hear her, then to Audun Gilli, who did. Audun nodded—indistinctly, through the curtain of bugs.

A Bizogot right in front of Hamnet caught an arrow in the throat, gurgling when he tried to scream and drowning in his own blood. *That could have been me,* the Raumsdalian thought, and shuddered, and got another gnat, or another three, in his eye. He ducked to rub at himself, and an arrow hissed past just above his head. If he were sitting straight on his horse, it would have caught him in the forehead. Sometimes whether you lived or died was nothing but luck.

He could tell when Liv and Audun and possibly Odovacar began to fight the mad swarm of insects the Rulers' wizards had summoned. The bugs went from impossible to intolerable all the way down to extremely annoying. He could spit bugs out of his mouth faster than they flew in. He wasn't swallowing or inhaling so many. He could even see, sometimes for a minute or two at a time.

And what he could see was that everything had its price. As soon as the

Bizogot shamans and Audun Gilli abandoned their spell to fight the one the Rulers were using, the lemmings and voles they'd called to the battle-field did what anyone would expect little animals to do in the presence of big ones—they ran away. And the war mammoths, no longer bedeviled, surged forward once more.

"We can beat them!" Trasamund shouted again and again. He went on shouting it after he pulled an arrow out of his left hand. He went on shout-ing it after the Bizogots, having fought as hard as anybody could fight, had to retreat anyhow. He went on shouting it as retreat turned to rout. He went on shouting it—roaring it out at the top of his lungs—long after he must have stopped believing it.

Ulric Skakki was bleeding from a gashed ear—the kind of wound that splattered gore all over the place without meaning much. "How come we're going the wrong way if we can beat them?" he asked Hamnet Thyssen.

"Oh, shut up," Count Hamnet explained.

Ulric nodded gravely, as if the explanation meant something. "Makes as much sense as anything I could have come up with myself," he said.

Hamnet pointed south—actually, a little west of south. "Are those riding deer?" he asked.

"Well, they aren't glyptodonts—that's for sure," Ulric said.

"They're cutting us off from the other half of the army. They're cutting us off from the Red Dire Wolves' herds, too," Hamnet said.

"They're good at war. They're better than the Bizogots, because they come into fights with a plan," Ulric said. "They're going to be a lot of trou-ble."

"They're already a lot of trouble," Count Hamnet said. "And they're herd-ing us the way you'd herd musk oxen—or even sheep."

"Baaa," Ulric said—or was it *Bah!*? Hamnet couldn't tell. The adventurer went on, "What do you think we can do about it?"

"Right now? Not a cursed thing," Hamnet answered.

"Well, that's what I think we can do about it, too," Ulric Skakki said. "Nice to see we agree about something, isn't it? And it's nice to see the Rulers *can* run a pursuit when they feel like it, eh?"

"Fornicating wonderful," Hamnet said. Ulric laughed, for all the world as if that were funny . . . for all the world as if anything were funny.

"Where's Totila?" Ulric Skakki asked after looking around.

Count Hamnet also looked for the Red Dire Wolves' jarl. "Don't see him."

"He must be with the other bunch—if he's still anywhere," Ulric said. Glumly, Hamnet nodded. He didn't see Odovacar any more, either. Was the shaman still alive? Hamnet wondered if he would ever know.

Then he had more urgent things to worry about. A warrior of the Rulers, shouting something unintelligible, slashed at him with a sword. He parried and gave back an overhand cut. The enemy fighting man turned it with a little round leather buckler he wore on his left arm. His riding deer tried to prod Hamnet's horse with its antlers. The Raumsdalian cut again. He wounded the deer's snout. The animal let out a startled snort and started to buck, just the way a horse would have. The man on it had everything he could do to stay in the saddle. Hamnet Thyssen got a good slash home against the side of his neck. Blood spurted. The warrior let out a gobbling wail and crumpled.

A tiny victory—too tiny to mean anything in the bigger fight. The Rulers went right on driving this band of Bizogots north and west, away from the larger group farther south. Every so often, an arrow would bite, and a man or a horse would go down.

Spring days had stretched in a hurry. That let the Rulers push the pursuit longer and harder than they could have at a different season or, say, down in the Empire. After what seemed a very long time, night finally fell.

"We must be back up in the lands of the Three Tusk clan," Liv said when the Bizogots—and Hamnet, and Ulric, and Audun Gilli—finally stopped to rest. She sounded ready to fall over from exhaustion, or possibly from despair.

"What are they going to do—chase us till they smash us against the Glacier?" Maybe Ulric meant it for a sour joke. But it sounded much too likely to Hamnet Thyssen.

VI

THE SUN CAME up too early. Count Hamnet munched smoked mammoth meat. He scooped up water with his hands from one of the countless ponds, and hoped it wouldn't give him a flux of the bowels.

And then one of the rearguard shouted that the Rulers were coming. Swearing wearily, Hamnet climbed up onto his horse. The animal's sigh sounded all too human, all too martyred. It was weary, too. Hamnet didn't care. If he didn't ride, the Rulers would kill him. If he did, he might get away to fight again later on.

"What did we do to deserve this?" Trasamund groaned as they headed north and west again. "Why does God hate us?"

"It hasn't got anything to do with God," Ulric Skakki said. "The weather's warmer, so the Gap melted through. That's all there is to it."

"All, eh?" Trasamund said. "And who made the weather warmer? Was it you? I don't think so. Did God have a little something to do with it? Well, maybe."

Ulric grunted. The jarl's sarcasm pierced like an arrow. And the weather *was* warmer, without a doubt. This would have been a warm day down in Nidaros, let alone here on the frozen steppe. Count Hamnet wondered whether the steppe would stay frozen if weather like this persisted. What kind of country would this be if it ever thawed out all the way?

Up ahead, growing taller every hour, loomed the Glacier. Imagining it gone from the world seemed lunatic. Only a few years earlier, though, imagining it split in two would have seemed just as mad. Whether God had anything to do with it or not, the Glacier was in retreat.

"Does this land belong to the Three Tusk clan?" Hamnet asked. "Or have we come so far west, we're in the country of—what's the next clan over?"

"They are the White Foxes," Trasamund answered. "They are a pack of thieves and robbers, not to be trusted even for a minute."

To Raumsdalians, all Bizogots were thieves. The harsh land in which they lived made them eager to grab whatever they could, and not worry about silly foreign notions like ownership. If Trasamund thought the White Foxes were thieves even by Bizogot standards, that made them larcenous indeed . . . unless it just said the Three Tusk clan looked down its collective nose at its neighbors.

Ulric Skakki must have had that same thought, for he asked, "And what do the White Foxes say about the Three Tusk clan?"

"Who cares?" Trasamund missed the sly mockery in Ulric's voice. "With a pack of ne'er-do-wells like that, what difference does it make?"

"You still didn't say whose land this is," Hamnet pointed out.

"These are not Three Tusk grazing grounds. That much I know," Trasamund said. "Maybe they belong to the Red Dire Wolves, maybe to the White Foxes. But I have roamed every foot of our land, and this is none of it. Can you not see how much poorer it is than the lands we use?"

Hamnet Thyssen could see nothing of the sort. He doubted Trasamund could, either. The Three Tusk jarl reflexively boasted about the glories of his clan and its grazing grounds—or rather, the grazing grounds the clan had once held, the grazing grounds now under the Rulers' sway.

His horse thudded and squelched its way to the northwest. It was tired and blowing. He didn't know what he'd do if it foundered. He shook his head. That wasn't so. He knew all too well: he would die.

He was worn himself, worn and nodding. But he jerked upright when a deep rumble, as of distant thunder, came from the direction in which he was riding. He thought at first it *was* thunder, but thunder from a clear blue sky with the warm sun shining down would have meant God was taking a more direct interest in worldly affairs than he seemed to be in the habit of doing.

"What the—?" he asked Liv.

"I think it was an avalanche," she answered. She looked even wearier than he felt, which he would have thought impossible if he weren't seeing it with his own eyes. But she hadn't merely fought in yesterday's battle; she'd worked magic all through it, which would drain anyone. After a yawn, she continued, "Sometimes chunks of the Glacier will crash down when the weather is like this. It will melt near the top and sometimes set everything farther down in motion."

"Lucky it didn't do that at the Gap," Hamnet exclaimed.

"Farther north there—it's usually cooler." Liv pointed ahead. "Look at all the dust rising from the plain. It was an avalanche, and a big one, too."

Sure enough, a cloud of dust like the ones that sometimes rolled across the plains of the Empire was climbing into the sky, obscuring what lay behind it. Hamnet looked back over his shoulder. Riding deer and a few war mammoths still pursued, though the Rulers didn't seem to want to close.

And then, as if to grind the fugitives between two stones, Bizogots rode at them from straight ahead. They were men from the White Fox clan, which answered the question of whose grazing grounds these were. "What are you doing here, you saucy robbers?" one of them shouted angrily. "Get off our land, or we'll fill you full of holes!"

"Why don't you ride on by us?" Trasamund yelled back. "Then you can tell the Rulers the same thing. Do you think they'll listen to you?"

"What are you talking about?" the White Fox Bizogot said. Then he recognized Trasamund. "By God! You're the Three Tusk clan's jarl!"

"And much good that's done me," Trasamund answered bleakly. "I've lost my clan. The Rulers have taken our grazing lands, and the Red Dire Wolves', too. They'll come after you next. They're on the way." He pointed back over his shoulder.

The White Foxes reined in. They put their heads together. The warrior who'd been shouting was plainly a man of some importance in their clan. Hamnet Thyssen watched him bringing the rest of the White Fox Bizogots around to whatever it was that he thought.

He rode out ahead of them. "Pass on!" he said. "If you come to our herds, you may kill enough to feed yourselves, but no more. If anyone challenges you, tell him I, Sunniulf, have given you leave." He struck a pose, there on horseback, so they might see what a powerful fellow he was. Still holding himself straight and proud, he added, "As for the Rulers, we'll deal with them."

He waved the rest of the White Foxes forward. They trotted past the men fleeing the latest battle lost. "Shall we go with them and do what we can to help?" Count Hamnet asked.

"I wouldn't help that arrogant son of a rotten mammoth chitterling up on his feet if all the Glacier fell on him," Trasamund growled. "Did the

White Foxes do anything to help us? Let them find out for themselves and see how they like it. The ones who live may have more sense after that."

Hamnet didn't like it, but he wasn't in charge. Trasamund was if anyone was. After the disaster of the day before, Hamnet wasn't sure anybody could give orders with confidence these Bizogots would follow them. But then, Bizogots generally obeyed orders only when they felt like it.

"We ride!" Trasamund shouted. They rode.

Ulric Skakki looked back a couple of times. "Trying to watch the White Foxes get what they probably will?" Hamnet asked.

"Well, yes." Ulric sounded faintly embarrassed. "People always stare when a really nasty accident happens. You can't help yourself."

"Oh, spare me. You aren't even trying," Hamnet Thyssen said.

"Well, what if I'm not?" Ulric retorted. "I didn't like that Sunniulf item any better than Trasamund did. What about you?"

"He could have done worse. He could have pitched into us instead of the Rulers."

"As far as his clan is concerned, pitching into the Rulers will be worse. We likely won't be able to take his name in vain much longer—he'll be too dead to come back and defend his honor, such as it is."

Count Hamnet wished he could tell the adventurer he was wrong. But he thought Ulric was right. "Sunniulf's doing us a favor, though," he said. "He's keeping the pursuit off our backs."

"Huzzah," Ulric said sourly. "For one thing, he doesn't know he's doing us any favors. For another, he won't keep doing them for very long. He's not going to run into the Rulers. They're going to run over him."

Again, that marched too well with what Hamnet was thinking. He sighed. His breath didn't burst forth in a puff of steam: proof indeed that spring had come to the frozen steppe. He wondered if he would hear the sounds of battle behind the ragged band of fleeing Bizogots, but the White Foxes and the Rulers clashed too far off to let him.

With another sigh, he said, "Well, we'd better get as far away as we can while the Rulers are busy, and we ought to cover our tracks, too."

"Now you're talking," Ulric Skakki told him.

CONCEALING A TRAIL in the north country was at the same time simple and next to impossible. Splashing through shallow rills and puddles and pools—and there were no deep ones, thanks to the permanently frozen ground—gave long stretches where travelers showed no hoofprints. On the other hand, the mud all around that standing water showed tracks only too well.

If there were more high ground on the northern plains, concealment would have been hopeless. Anyone on a hill, even a modest hill, could have seen for many miles. But the swells and dips in the landscape were smaller than that. They were just enough to keep the ground from being perfectly flat, enough so that, when riders were in dips, swells helped hide them from those who came after them.

But when riders came up onto swells . . . Looking south and east a few hours after Sunniulf's White Foxes rode past to battle the Rulers, Hamnet Thyssen spotted war mammoths and riding deer silhouetted against the sky. Even though he swore, his heart wasn't in it.

Trasamund's was. "How the glory of the Bizogots is fallen!" he groaned. "These bandits thrash us as if we were naughty boys. How will we ever get away from them?"

Even he could no longer imagine beating the Rulers. Escaping suddenly seemed too much to hope for. Liv, by contrast, stuck to what was still possible. She pointed ahead. "There's a herd of musk oxen. Let's kill one and butcher it. We need the meat."

Three or four White Fox Bizogots and their dogs accompanied the herd. They shouted angrily when they saw strangers on their grazing grounds, and even more angrily when they discovered one of the strangers was the jarl of the Three Tusk clan. But Trasamund, still downcast, used Sunniulf's name without his own usual display of chest-thumping pride. And it worked . . . well enough, anyhow.

"Where is Sunniulf now?" one of the White Foxes asked. "Why isn't he with you?"

"He led his men off to fight the Rulers," Hamnet Thyssen answered when Trasamund hesitated.

"Ah." The White Fox Bizogot nodded. "That will have taken care of those rogues, then."

"Well . . . no," Hamnet said. "Not long ago, we noticed the Rulers were still coming after us."

That made all the White Foxes exclaim. "They couldn't have beaten Sunniulf," one of them said. "Nobody beats Sunniulf!" The others nodded.

Ulric Skakki jerked a thumb towards the southeast. "Maybe you should go tell that to the Rulers," he said. "I don't think they've got the news."

"What do you mean?" The White Fox Bizogot lifted his fur cap and scratched his head. "What are you talking about?"

"If you wait around here much longer, you'll find out," Ulric said. "Can we have our musk ox?"

"You can have it. Sunniulf said so." The Bizogot eyed him. "You're a foreigner. Don't see many foreigners around here."

"You will." Hamnet Thyssen, Ulric Skakki, and Trasamund all said the same thing at the same time. The White Fox scratched his head again.

They killed the musk ox downwind from the herd, then butchered it as fast as they could. The speed of the job meant they left some meat behind that they might have taken otherwise. Clucking, the herders started stripping that flesh from the dead beast's bones. The Three Tusk Bizogots and Red Dire Wolves and Raumsdalians left them to it. The refugees rode off. The Rulers wouldn't be far behind.

Liv pointed ahead, towards the Glacier, which loomed higher on the horizon than it had a couple of days before. "You can really see what the avalanche did," she said.

"You can, by God," Hamnet Thyssen agreed. It looked as if the collapse had started near the top of the ice sheet and extended all the way down. The jumble of freshly exposed ice boulders was whiter and brighter than the older ice to either side. The Glacier didn't rise straight up from the edge of the Bizogot steppe there, either; the slope was gentler, more gradual. "We might really be able to climb that if we had to."

"We might, yes. But why would anyone want to?" Liv said.

Instead of looking ahead, Ulric Skakki looked behind them. Count Hamnet imitated him. Yes, the Rulers' riding deer and war mammoths had come up over the horizon again. "If our lovely friends keep herding us in this direction, they may give us some reasons to think about it," Ulric said.

Liv bared her teeth, not at him but at the idea. "Is escape to the top of the Glacier—if we could get there—escape at all?"

"We've talked about that before," Hamnet said. "It depends on whether anything—and anyone—lives up there."

"If anybody does, getting up to the top may not be escape," Ulric Skakki said.

That made Hamnet bare *his* teeth, because it held too much truth and because he hadn't thought of it. "God grant we don't have to worry about that," he said.

Liv nodded. Even cynical Ulric Skakki didn't say no. Trasamund was the one who grunted and scowled. "God has turned his back on the Bizogots," he said gloomily. "He pays us no mind, not any more."

"Well, if you feel that way, why not ride back to the Rulers and throw yourself at them?" Ulric asked. "You might get two or three before they kill you."

"That is not revenge enough," the jarl answered. "Two or three? Pah! I want to kill them all. And if God won't help me, I'll cursed well take care of it on my own."

To Count Hamnet, that was on the edge of blasphemy. He didn't say so; he understood what drove Trasamund to feel the way he did. And Ulric Skakki slapped Trasamund on the back, saying, "There's the first sensible thing you've come out with since I don't know when. Why don't you do it more often?"

Trasamund said something about Ulric's female ancestors concerning which he could have had no personal knowledge. At another time, it might have started a fight to the death. Now Ulric only laughed and slapped him on the back again. Trasamund said something even more incendiary. Ulric laughed harder.

"If the weather stays so warm, will we see more avalanches like this?" Hamnet asked.

"I wouldn't be surprised," Liv answered. "We'll probably start getting a meltwater lake up here, too, like Sudertorp Lake down in the Leaping Lynx country."

"Yes, that makes sense," Audun Gilli said. The wizard looked towards the sun, which was going down in the northwest—not far above the avalanche, in fact. "It stays light a long time in these parts, doesn't it?"

Now Count Hamnet laughed at him. "You were up here last summer, too. You just noticed that?"

Audun smiled ruefully. "It does seem to matter more when the extra daylight means you're likelier to get killed."

Hamnet Thyssen grunted. A glance back over his shoulder said the Rulers were still there. A glance ahead said the sun wasn't going down fast enough to suit him, either. "We'll need to set plenty of sentries tonight, in case the Rulers try to hit us in the dark."

"Sounds like something they'd do," Trasamund growled.

"I would, too, if I thought it would work," Ulric Skakki said. "Wouldn't you?"

Trasamund didn't answer, from which Count Hamnet concluded that he would but didn't want to admit it to Ulric. The Bizogots and Raumsdalians rode on. Eventually, the sun did set and twilight did fade. On the other side of the Glacier, it was getting towards the season of the year where twilight lingered from sundown to sunup.

Setting fires seemed too great a risk. Raw musk-ox meat wasn't Hamnet's idea of a feast, but it was ever so much better than empty. He wolfed down a good-sized gobbet. So did Ulric. Audun Gilli looked revolted, but he ate, too. The Bizogots took raw meat in stride. They ate anything and everything.

The Three Tusk jarl sent Hamnet out to watch as soon as he was done eating. The gleam in Trasamund's eye, even in the dark, had to mean he was waiting for the Raumsdalian noble to kick up a fuss. Hamnet went without a word. Did Trasamund sigh behind him? He didn't turn around to look.

He did hope Liv would come out and keep him company while he stood sentry, but she didn't. He didn't get angry at that—she had to be wearier than he was—but it disappointed him.

Stars wheeled through the sky in circles set at a different angle from the one he knew down in the Empire. More of them stayed above the horizon all night long than was true in Nidaros. Somewhere off in the distance, a fox yipped at the half-goldpiece moon. Hamnet wondered if the yip was a signal, but it came from due west, a direction from which the Rulers were unlikely to attack. Sometimes a fox was only a fox.

When dire wolves off in the south started howling, Hamnet worried more. But nothing came of that, either. *Jumpy tonight, aren't you?* he asked himself with a wry chuckle. *Haven't I earned the right?* His answer formed as fast as the question.

He'd begun to wonder whether Trasamund intended him to watch till dawn when a Bizogot came out to take his place. "Anything?" the big, burly blond asked.

"Foxes. Dire wolves," Hamnet Thyssen answered. "I didn't see any Rulers or hear any signs of them. I didn't see any owls, either."

"Owls?" The Bizogot sounded puzzled.

"Their shamans spy on wings," Hamnet said. His replacement grunted. Count Hamnet stumbled back towards the encampment, splashing through little pools and rills he didn't see till too late. He might not have found the resting Bizogots if not for the whickering of their horses and then a small, sudden flare of witchlight.

That led him over to Liv and Audun Gilli, who were sitting close together on the ground and talking in low voices. Liv's Raumsdalian, by now, was fairly fluent. Audun had learned some of the Bizogots' tongue, and eked it out when he ran short, as he did now and again. They both looked up when Hamnet drew near.

"Oh, it's you," Audun said. "Anything out there?"

"Stars. Half a moon." Hamnet pointed up to the sky, then waved. "A fox. Dire wolves howling. No Rulers, God be praised—the dire wolves were only wolves. No wizards in the shape of owls, or none that flew close enough for me to see." Audun had asked the question in Raumsdalian, and Hamnet answered in the same language. His birthspeech felt strange in his mouth; even with Ulric, he'd been using the Bizogot tongue more often than not.

"I didn't sense any spies," Liv said, and Audun Gilli nodded. Liv went on, "I don't know why they'd need them; we're hardly worth worrying about anyway."

That held more truth than Hamnet wished it did. "What was the little flash I saw when I was coming into camp?"

"I was showing Liv a spell for piercing illusions," Audun Gilli answered. "The flash is sorcerous energy dissipating—think of it as steam rising when you boil soup."

"Steam won't betray us to the Rulers." But Hamnet Thyssen relented before either Audun or Liv could complain. "I don't suppose that little flash would, either, not unless they were already right on top of us." He yawned. "With any luck at all, I'm going to sleep for a week between now and sunrise."

With any luck at all, Liv would lie down beside him when he rolled himself in his blanket. With any luck at all, the two of them would lie under the same blanket. He was tired, yes, but not too tired for that. But all she said was, "Sleep well. I do want to learn this charm. It's better than the one we use."

Hamnet couldn't very well say he wasn't so sleepy as all that. With a martyred sigh—not that he hadn't done it to himself—he did go off and lie down. Liv and Audun Gilli went on talking quietly. She laughed once, just before Hamnet would have dropped off. The sweet, familiar sound brought him back to wakefulness.

He wondered if he ought to be jealous. *Of Audun?* he thought, and laughed, too—at himself. Yes, the wizard and Liv had sorcery in common, but if he wasn't a weed of a man, such a man had never sprouted. Liv, Hamnet Thyssen was comfortably certain, had better taste than *that.* He twisted and turned and did fall asleep.

Trasamund had to shake him awake. "Are you dead, or what?" the jarl rumbled. "Thought I'd need to kick you."

"One of us would have been dead after that," Hamnet Thyssen said. "I don't think it would be me."

"After we've beaten the Rulers, I'll fight you if you want," Trasamund said. "Till then, we've got other things to worry about."

"Why, what ever could you mean?" Count Hamnet asked. The Bizogot's answering laugh was sour as vinegar. Hamnet rolled up his blanket and ate another chunk of raw musk-ox meat. Then he climbed onto his horse. He hoped the poor animal wouldn't give out.

Somewhere not nearly far enough away, the Rulers would be climbing onto their riding deer. Before long, they'd be trotting out after the Bizogots. They seemed as stubborn in the hunt as a pack of dire wolves. They kept pressing the quarry till it had nowhere to go. Hamnet Thyssen looked ahead towards the Glacier and the remains of the avalanche. Before long, that would hold true for him and his comrades, too.

With a sad snort, the horse began to walk. It tried to turn its head and look back at him when he urged it up into a trot. It might have been saying, *You can't really mean that, can you?* But he could. He did. The horse might fall over dead if it had to work too hard. It *would* die, and so would he, if the Rulers caught up to them.

By the nature of things, the horse couldn't understand that. Count Hamnet couldn't explain it to the animal. All he could do was command. The poor horse, not understanding, had to obey.

Hamnet Thyssen waited for the shout from the rearguard, the shout that said the Rulers were in sight. The skin, even the muscles, between his shoulder blades tensed, as if anticipating an arrow. *As if?* he wondered. What else was he waiting for from those implacable pursuers?

He looked around, trying to gauge what kind of fight the Bizogots could make if—when—the Rulers attacked in earnest. He didn't like what he saw. A few men, Trasamund chief among them in spirit as well as rank, still had fight in them. Most of the Bizogots, though, were all too plainly beaten. They'd lost too many battles. They'd fled too much and too long. If—when—the Rulers hit them, they would break . . . or die.

"We're a jolly crew, aren't we?" As happened too often for comfort, Ulric Skakki divined what he was thinking.

"Oh, of course," Count Hamnet said in a hollow voice. He pointed ahead, towards some of the ice boulders from the avalanche that had bounced and bounded farthest across the Bizogot steppe. "The dance is just past those big rocks, isn't it?"

Ulric laughed as merrily as if they really were riding towards viols and a drum and plenty of beer and smiling, pretty girls. "It would be a better dance than the one we've been making, wouldn't it?"

"Couldn't be much worse." Hamnet looked around again, this time for his pretty girl, even if she had nothing to smile about right now. Liv rode beside Audun Gilli, earnestly talking about something sorcerous. Audun's hands shaped a pass. Liv tried to imitate it. He corrected her, with a little extra emphasis on the motion she'd missed. She tried again. He nodded.

Had Ulric Skakki not been riding beside him, Hamnet would have done some muttering. He misliked the tenor of his thoughts. Defeat ruined everything, even things that should have had nothing to do with it. But the last thing he wanted was for Ulric to know he had any worries like that. The adventurer might not say anything; he had to know Hamnet would ignite if he did. He would think whatever he didn't say, though, and that would be bad enough.

Worse than bad enough.

"The Rulers!" There it was, the cry Count Hamnet had waited for. He hunched down in the saddle to make himself a smaller target. He didn't realize he'd done it till he saw Ulric doing the same thing.

"How many arrows have you got left?" he asked Ulric.

"Some," the adventurer answered, reaching over his shoulder to feel what was in his quiver. "How about you?"

"Some," Hamnet Thyssen agreed. "They don't grow on trees, you know."

Again, Ulric Skakki produced a cheery laugh from nowhere in particular. "Even if they did, much good it would do us. What could we harvest here? Toothpicks, by God!" That made Count Hamnet smile, too. The birches and willows and other would-be trees that grew on the frozen steppe never got bigger than calf-high bushes.

Setting a hand on his sword, Hamnet said, "This doesn't shrink."

"It had better not," Ulric said. "But can we get close enough to cut up the Rulers, or will they shoot us before we do?"

"We'll find out," Count Hamnet said, and not even his argumentative countryman could disagree with that.

More and more riding deer and war mammoths came up over the horizon.

Closer and closer they drew. Till now, they'd seemed content to chase the Bizogots. By the way they came on, they had more than that in mind today.

"Can you summon the voles and lemmings?" Hamnet Thyssen called to Liv. "We'll have a better chance if they've got to fight without their mammoths."

"We can try," Liv answered—and then she turned to speak to Audun Gilli. Count Hamnet knew they were only planning their magic together. All the same, he frowned and looked away. That wasn't what he wanted to see right now.

It turned out not to matter. Liv and Audun had barely started their spell when whatever wizards the Rulers had with them struck first. It wasn't the spell they'd used before; bugs didn't choke the Bizogots and torment their animals. Instead, hawks and falcons and owls dove out of the sky, slashing at horses and riders alike. Wounded horses screamed in pain and surprise. A Bizogot not far from Hamnet Thyssen shrieked and clapped his hands to his face. Blood poured out between his fingers. Had cruel talons robbed him of an eye? Hamnet couldn't be sure, but feared the worst.

Were some of those wheeling, hurtling owls wizards in sorcerous disguise? He had no way to be sure, but he feared the worst there, too. Trasamund actually caught a hawk out of the air, wrung its neck, and flung the corpse to the ground. Hamnet marveled at the feat without imagining for a moment that he could imitate it.

Ulric Skakki slashed a falcon out of the sky. Hamnet thought he might do that, but had no time to dwell on the possibilities. The birds of prey flew off as abruptly as they'd appeared, leaving the Bizogots in disarray and confusion. Then, shouting their harsh war cries, the Rulers rode in for the kill.

Archers shooting from atop a war mammoth pincushioned the Bizogot with the bloodied face. An arrow hissed past Hamnet Thyssen's head, so close that he felt the fletching brush his beard. He shot at one of the men up there. The warrior of the Rulers jeered as the arrow went wide. Then one from Ulric Skakki caught him in the forehead. He crumpled, a look of absurd surprise the last expression he would ever wear.

Hamnet cut at another warrior on a riding deer. The fighter turned his first stroke, but the second one got home. When the Rulers were wounded, they cried out like any lesser breed. The warrior tried to fight on, but Count Hamnet cut him down.

He looked around again. Some of the Bizogots were still fighting fiercely. Others, though, streamed away from the Rulers as fast as they could. Riding deer trotted after horses. Seeing riding deer get past him sent a chill through Hamnet, a chill more frigid than any winter on the frozen steppe could bring. Surrounded, cut off . . .

"We've got to get out of this!" he called to Ulric.

"Well, yes," the adventurer said. His sword had blood on it. "But how? Do you want to cut and run?"

Yes! Count Hamnet thought. Then he saw Trasamund pull his horse's head around and ride off towards the northwest. "We can't stay any more," Hamnet said, and pointed after the jarl.

"By God!" Ulric Skakki exclaimed. "What is this world coming to?"

"An end, I think," Hamnet answered grimly. "When the Gap melted through, when the Rulers invaded . . . Everything we knew before is gone. It's all different now. Even if we win, even if we find the Golden Shrine, it will never be the same."

"I didn't expect a philosophy lesson—which doesn't mean you're wrong," Ulric said. "I'd better go look for Arnora, and you'll want to find Liv. We'll make for where the avalanche came down. I'll meet you there—or I hope I will."

"Luck," Count Hamnet said. Ulric Skakki nodded.

Do I need to look for Liv? Won't Audun take care of that? Hamnet swore at himself. Yes, he was letting defeat poison everything in his life. Before he could even think of finding the Three Tusk clan's shaman, he needed to fight off another warrior of the Rulers. He wanted to kill the curly-bearded fighting man, but had to content himself with driving him off with a bleeding forearm.

There was Audun Gilli. And, sure enough, not far away was Liv. She wasn't working wizardry against the Rulers now. She had a bow in her hands, and used it with as much skill if perhaps without quite the same strength as a man might have.

Neither she nor Audun saw the warrior riding up from behind them. Hamnet Thyssen shouted to distract him, then plucked out a dagger and threw it at the enemy. It wasn't a proper throwing knife; it didn't pierce him. But the thump against his side made him slow up and look around, which gave Hamnet time to engage him. Metal belled on metal as their swords clashed together.

"You are that one!" the warrior of the Rulers said in the Bizogot language. "They want you bad!"

"Well, they can't have me," Hamnet answered. His foe made as if to shout, but Hamnet's sword went home then. The warrior looked amazed. He slowly crumpled from his riding deer.

Hamnet forgot about him as soon as he stopped being a threat. He grabbed Liv by the arm. "We have to get away!" he yelled.

"We can't!" she said.

"The demon we can't. Trasamund's already gone," Hamnet answered.

Her eyes widened. Her head swung, as if on a swivel. When she didn't see the jarl, her features sagged in weariness and dismay. "Truly everything is lost," she said, her voice quiet and amazed and all but hopeless.

"Not while we're still breathing. Come on, before the Rulers close the sack around us," Hamnet said. A heartbeat slower than he might have, he added, "You, too, Audun."

"Yes," the wizard said. "Maybe we'll win another chance later. We can hope, anyhow." He didn't hesitate in talking to Hamnet Thyssen. Perhaps that meant he was a good dissembler. In another man, Hamnet would have thought it did. But he'd spent too much time at close quarters with the wizard to find it easy to believe. If Audun thought something, he usually said it. Ulric Skakki could smile and charm and say one thing and mean another. Not Audun.

Thinking of Ulric reminded Hamnet what the adventurer had said. "Let's ride for the avalanche," Hamnet said. "We can use the ice boulders for cover."

"For a while," Liv said. "We'll get hungry there. If the Rulers want to sit around and starve us out, they can. And where do we have to go?"

"Up to the top of the Glacier, by God," Count Hamnet answered. "They won't look for that, and we may get away. And it's something maybe no one's ever done in all the history of the world." The idea had intrigued him ever since it first crossed his mind.

It didn't seem to intrigue Liv. "No one's ever come back from doing it— that's sure enough." But she didn't say no, not straight out. And she did guide her horse towards the northwest. So did Audun. So did Hamnet Thyssen.

Some Bizogots were riding in that direction. Others tried to break out to the southwest. Hamnet supposed they wanted to join up with the White Foxes. If they could, they might stay safe . . . for a while. He feared climbing the Glacier gave a better long-term hope—and climbing the Glacier was pure desperation.

A few warriors on riding deer had already got between the Bizogots and the Glacier. Liv shot one of them out of the saddle. She had more arrows left than Hamnet. He relied on the sword, and slew a warrior himself. When one of the Rulers started to attack Audun Gilli, his deer seemed to go mad, bounding off across the steppe at random despite his curses and, soon, his fist

"Nicely done," Count Hamnet said, his tone as neutral as he could make it. "Would it work for more than one riding deer at a time?"

"I don't think so." Audun watched the animal's antics with solemn fascination. "I was surprised it worked once."

"So was he," Hamnet said. Then they were past the Rulers. Hamnet spied Trasamund a couple of bowshots ahead and to the left. He waved and shouted. After a moment, the jarl waved back and steered his horse over towards them. *Misery loves company,* Hamnet thought.

"What now? Up the Glacier?" Plainly, Trasamund didn't mean it.

He blinked when Hamnet Thyssen nodded. "Have you got a better idea?" Hamnet asked.

Trasamund spat. "I have no ideas left, and nothing else, either. If you say you want to take it out and piss your way through the Glacier, I'll try to follow. Everything I've tried, everything I've done, has turned to dung in my hands."

Count Hamnet shivered. It wasn't altogether in response to Trasamund's despair; here close by the Glacier, it was colder than it had been even a couple of miles farther south. This was where winter lived. The growing warmth might have weakened it, but it was a long way from dead.

They'd ridden past a house-sized chunk when Hamnet heard a shout from Ulric Skakki: "Over here!" Beside him, Arnora pressed a chunk of moss to a cut that split her cheek. She wouldn't be pretty any more, but that was a worry for later, if there was a later. Now, Ulric said, "Well, here we are, in this jolly place. Where do we go next?"

Hamnet told him.

VII

THIS IS MADNESS," Trasamund said, scrambling up over a tilted block of ice. "Madness, I tell you."

"Of course, Your Ferocity," Ulric Skakki said politely. He pointed down towards the edge of the frozen steppe, which now lay some distance below them. "Would you like to explain to the Rulers how mad it is?"

Hamnet Thyssen paused for a moment at the top of another jagged chunk of ice. He looked down towards the ground, too. The Rulers weren't coming after the dozen or so Bizogots and Raumsdalians who were trying to use the avalanche to climb to the top of the Glacier. In their boots, Count Hamnet wouldn't have, either. They were doing about what he would have done were their positions reversed: they were standing there pointing at the fugitives and laughing themselves silly.

"We got a chance to kill a couple of horses and hack off some of the meat," Liv said. "With the musk ox, that will keep us going . . . for a while, anyhow."

"Horseflesh tastes like glue," Ulric Skakki complained.

"How much glue have you eaten?" Hamnet asked.

"Well, I've eaten more crow, I must say," Ulric answered. "And it's plain enough I haven't eaten enough glue to know when to keep my mouth shut." He still sounded like a man on a lark, not someone fleeing for his life without much hope that even fleeing would stretch it very far.

"One thing," Audun Gilli said. "We can keep our meat fresh as long as we need to. We won't have any trouble putting it on ice." The wizard's laugh sounded slightly hysterical, or perhaps just slightly cracked.

That didn't mean he was wrong. Most of the ice in the world was either under their feet or ahead of them. Hamnet Thyssen was glad he had his winter mittens. Without them, his hands not only would have frozen but also would have been cut to ribbons: much of the ice over which he struggled was almost swordblade-sharp.

A couple of Bizogot men were without mittens. They'd wrapped cloth around their palms, which was better than nothing but probably not good enough. One of them, a big, blocky fellow named Vulfolaic, said, "Some of that horsemeat still has the hide on, yes? I can cut strips from that when we stop."

"It will spoil," Audun said, proving he really was learning the Bizogots' speech.

"Not if I piss on it a few times," Vulfolaic answered. "Not proper tanning, but it will have to do."

"Er—yes." The wizard's expression said he would rather do without gauntlets than wear that kind. Vulfolaic wasn't so fussy. Squeamish Bizogots wouldn't last long.

How long will we last anyhow? Hamnet wondered. Climbing to the top of the Glacier—if they could—might give them their best chance to escape the Rulers, but he knew that best was none too good. If they died here, and if scavengers didn't find them, they might stay perfectly preserved for a long time. What held true for horsemeat also held for human flesh.

"Come on," he said. "We ought to get as high as we can while the daylight lasts."

"What if we touch off another avalanche?" With the wound to her cheek, Arnora's voice was mushy and indistinct.

Hamnet Thyssen only shrugged. "If we do, we won't need to worry any more."

That made Vulfolaic laugh. "Spoken like a Bizogot, by God! I wouldn't have thought you southerners had the manhood to say such things—and to mean them."

"If I had a copper for every time a Bizogot wondered how long my prong was, I'd be too rich to want to leave Nidaros," Ulric Skakki said.

"He wasn't questioning yours—he was questioning mine," Hamnet answered. "And as long as Arnora doesn't worry about yours, I don't see that it's anybody else's business."

"You're no fun," Ulric told him. "Life would be so much duller if people didn't get all hot and bothered over stupid little things."

"You mean like being invaded? Like being beaten?" Count Hamnet said. "I'm bothered. I can't very well say I'm not. But I defy anyone to stay hot climbing the Glacier."

"Well, you've got something there." Ulric reached up to him. "Give me a hand, will you? You made it to the top of that block, but I don't think I can, not by myself. You're taller than I am."

"I wish I had hobnails in the bottom of my boots," Hamnet said, grabbing Ulric's wrist and yanking him upwards. With a grunt, the adventurer scrambled onto the top of the ice boulder beside him. "They'd make climbing a lot easier."

"Hobnails? No!" Trasamund shook his head. "You wear hobnails on ice or in snow, they bleed heat right out of your feet. Maybe they're all right in Raumsdalia, where it's warm, but not up here."

"Hadn't thought of that," Count Hamnet admitted. "You may be right. If we had boots with a couple of layers of hide between our soles and the nails, though . . ."

"If we had wings, we could fly up to the top of the Glacier," Trasamund said. "And we could piss on the miserable Rulers down below, too."

Hamnet shut up.

When he looked down to the Bizogot steppe now, he could hardly make out the invaders down there. They might have been ants or fleas or other small annoyances. They might have been, but they weren't. He looked behind, and then he looked ahead. How far had they come? Maybe a third of the way, he guessed. The going got no easier as they moved on. If anything, the slope grew steeper. Without the titanic avalanche, they wouldn't have had a prayer of reaching the top of the Glacier. Even with it, the climb wouldn't be easy. Anything but.

And something else was wrong, or at least different. He seemed to need an extra breath or two whenever he struggled up onto a new chunk of ice. Hauling Ulric after him had made his heart pound.

Then a light dawned. "We're climbing a mountain!" he exclaimed. "The air's getting thinner!"

"It would do that, wouldn't it?" Liv said. "No wonder I'm breathing so hard."

"Do you have a magic that would let us breathe the way we do down on the plain?" Hamnet asked her.

"*I* don't," she answered. "We never needed anything like that. What about you, Audun?"

Audun Gilli shook his head. "Maybe someone in the Empire does—someone in the west, most likely, who has to worry about mountains more than people around Nidaros do. But I've never needed a spell like that, either. Too bad."

"I hope there will be enough air to keep us going when we get to the top," Count Hamnet said.

"Don't you think you should have worried about that *before* we started climbing?" Ulric Skakki asked.

"Maybe we'll die up there," Hamnet said. "But maybe we won't. If we'd stayed down on the Bizogot plain, we'd all be dead by now." That wasn't quite true; the Rulers might have let Liv and Arnora live for a while, but the women wouldn't have been glad if they did. Most of the time, people didn't know what they were talking about when they spoke of a fate worse than death. Serving the enemy's lusts till he decided to knock you over the head, though . . . That came much too close to the real thing.

He started climbing again so he wouldn't have to think about it. Liv went up the broken blocks of ice beside him. Her face was particularly grim. Maybe she was trying not to think about what the Rulers would have done to her, too.

After a while, Ulric pointed to the plain far below and said, "Look. You can watch sunset spreading over the land."

Was it sunset or the shadow of the Glacier? After a moment, Hamnet Thyssen decided the two were one and the same. The sun wouldn't come up again till morning. And he could see the shadow or the sunset line or whatever it was stretching farther and farther till everything down there—the whole world he'd known up till now—was swallowed in deepening blue shadow. The sun kept on shining on his comrades and him for some little while. He watched the shadow creep up the avalanche from below them. At last, the sun set halfway up the Glacier, too, or however far they were.

"Well," Trasamund said as it got darker and chillier, and then again, "Well." He didn't go on; it was as if he couldn't go on.

When nothing came after those two false starts, Ulric Skakki nodded sagely and said, "I couldn't agree with you more."

The Bizogot jarl glowered at him. "Your whole world has just turned to a steaming pile of mammoth turds. Go ahead. Tell me how you feel about it."

"Well . . ." Ulric let it hang, too. Was he mocking Trasamund or sympathizing with him? Count Hamnet couldn't tell. By the way Trasamund muttered to himself, neither could he. Hamnet wondered whether even Ulric Skakki knew.

Raw meat made an uninspiring supper. Hamnet Thyssen had gone without often enough, though, to know how much better it was than no supper at all. As a smith stoked a furnace, so he fueled himself.

He wished he could have found a furnace somewhere closer than hundreds of miles away. A cold wind wailed down off the top of the Glacier. Even wrapped in a mammoth hide, he was chilly. Like any traveler, he carried tinder and a way to start a fire. He used flint and steel; the Bizogots, who didn't work iron, made do with firebows instead. But how they would have got a fire going didn't matter now, for they had nothing to sustain it.

Liv sat up for a while, talking about wizardry with Audun Gilli. Count Hamnet was too weary to be jealous, or to wait for her to go to sleep, too. The rough ice on which he lay might have been a feather bed. Exhaustion clubbed him down.

SUMMER MORNING CAME soon in the north country. Hamnet Thyssen didn't want to wake up, but light sneaking in between his eyelids left him little choice. He yawned and stretched. Down below, on the steppe, night still reigned.

Methodically, Hamnet cut bite after bite from a chunk of cold raw horsemeat. He chewed and swallowed, chewed and swallowed. He'd had breakfasts he relished more, but he knew he would miss the meat when it was gone. He ate now, while he still had the chance.

Not far away, Vulfolaic was doing the same thing. After swallowing a bite, he said, "I sat up a while in the night and watched."

"Did you, by God? Well, more power to you. You're a stronger man than I am." Count Hamnet made as if to tip the hat he wasn't wearing. "You didn't see the Rulers sneaking up on us—that's plain enough."

"No." Vulfolaic shook his head. He sent Hamnet a quizzical look. No Bizogot would have admitted another man was stronger than he, yet the Raumsdalian had fought bravely in all the battles and skirmishes just past. He scratched his head, then crushed something between his thumbnails.

When he didn't say anything more on his own, Hamnet prompted him: "Well, what did you see? You must have seen something, or you wouldn't bother telling me you did sentry duty."

"True enough." Now Vulfolaic seemed impressed at how clever he was. Count Hamnet wanted to pound his head against the Glacier. After another pause, Vulfolaic went on, "I didn't see the Rulers, no, but a big snowy owl flew around us. It must have known men well, for it stayed out of bowshot."

He blinked when not only Hamnet but also Liv, Audun Gilli, and Ulric Skakki exclaimed. "That was the Rulers, looking us over," Liv said.

"They won't be back, either—that's a sure thing," Ulric said.

"Why not?" Audun didn't follow.

The adventurer clicked his tongue between his teeth, as if surprised such naïveté could exist. "Don't be silly," he said. "The owl will have taken one look, laughed till it almost fell out of the sky, and flown away. Why bother coming back? I'm surprised they bothered checking at all. A ragged bunch like us won't give the Rulers any trouble even if we don't end up frozen for our trouble."

"Oh," the wizard said in a small, unhappy voice. He didn't try to argue.

Hamnet Thyssen wouldn't have, either. He saw things the way Ulric did. He and his comrades were likely just putting off the inevitable—and, chances were, not for very long, either.

Trasamund sucked horse blood out of his mustache. "Let's get going," he said. "If we have to do this, we'll *do* it."

Hamnet admired his determination. Living up to it was something else again. Every muscle in his arms and legs and back groaned when he got moving. He'd done too much the day before, and he hadn't slept on a feather bed after all. "I feel my age," he said.

"If you weren't old when you started this climb, you would be by the time you finished," Ulric Skakki said, which also held a painful amount of truth.

Whether they could finish the climb grew less and less certain as the day wore along. The slope got steeper as they neared the top of the Glacier. They had to try several different ways to get around or over tilted blocks of ice. They'd taken harness trappings from the horses they killed. Those helped, but Hamnet wished the leather lines were longer.

"Careful!" he called when he saw a block shifting under Trasamund's bulk. "You don't want to start another avalanche."

Trasamund held very still, then backed down instead of climbing on. The chunk of ice—bigger than he was—didn't move any more. He nodded to Count Hamnet. "Thanks. I wouldn't have had the chance to start more than one—that's for sure."

"Mm, no," Hamnet said. "And what you started, the avalanche would finish." Trasamund nodded again.

As they climbed higher, though, the Bizogots and Raumsdalians had to take more and more chances. It was either take them or have no way to go forward. They used what precautions they could. No one climbed right behind anyone else except when the going was uncommonly good or when there was no other choice. That way, if they did start an avalanche, it wouldn't wipe out all of them. They hoped it wouldn't, anyhow.

The long northern day helped. Even down in Nidaros, the sun would have set before they got close to the top of the Glacier. A mist coming off the frozen surface veiled the plains far below. "You know what someone looking up towards us would see?" Ulric Skakki said, pausing to pant atop an ice boulder as clear and sparkling as a jewel.

"He wouldn't see anything. If we can't see him, he can't see us." Hamnet Thyssen was panting, too. The air felt as thin as a cheap tapman's beer after he'd watered it. He couldn't get enough into his lungs to let him move as freely as he wanted. He felt weary unto death, and had a pounding headache.

He knew his logic was good, and started to get angry when the adventurer shook his head. But Ulric had an answer of his own: "He'd see clouds. We're above those clouds, looking down on them. Isn't that something you thought only birds and God could ever do?" No matter how cynical he was, awe filled his voice.

"Well, you're right," Hamnet said. "I hope they're not the last thing we see."

"So do I. I'd sooner look down on the Rulers than on clouds," Ulric said. Maybe because of the thin air scrambling his brains, Count Hamnet needed longer than he should have for the pun to sink in. When it did, it made his headache worse—or he thought so, anyhow.

"Come on!" Trasamund pushed himself to his feet again. "We're almost there. Let's finish the job. Up on top of the Glacier, by God! No one from down below has ever done that, or we'd have tales to tell of it. They'll remember us forever!"

In a low voice, Ulric said, "No one from down below's ever done it and then made it back to start tales. Will we?"

"Well, the Bizogot's right about one thing: we won't if we don't get moving." Hamnet Thyssen heaved himself upright, too. "And we *are* almost there."

They had one last bad stretch: nearly vertical, with the ice alarmingly shaky under them. Then they clawed their way up out of the scarp the avalanche had bitten from the edge of the ice sheet. Hamnet's breath smoked as he stared across the top of the Glacier.

It might have been spring down below, but winter still reigned here. Or maybe not. In the midst of all that white and blue, enough dirt had blown into crevices in the ice to let plants sprout here and there. And not too far away in the distance was what seemed an oasis in this frozen desert: a mountaintop that climbed out of the Glacier and showed green streaked with snow.

"Well, we know where we're going," Hamnet said. No one disagreed with him.

"Never mind where we're going for now," Liv said. "We're here. We did it! Isn't that enough of a marvel?"

"Before I started up, I thought it would be. Now I'm not so sure," he answered. She made a questioning noise. He explained: "Looking at what it's like up here, seems to me getting down again will be the real marvel."

She thought about that, then nodded. "You're bound to be right."

He wished she had told him he was wrong. He wished she had convinced him he was wrong. The more likely he was to be wrong, the better their chances were.

He wanted to ask her to sleep with him, to make love with him, that evening. But he held back, not so much for fear she would say no as for fear she would say yes and find him unable to perform. After all the fighting and climbing he'd done the past few days, he was far from sure he could. And the thin air up here atop the Glacier only made things worse. He felt as if he were moving under water, with every step costing far more effort than it should have.

He and Liv did sleep in each other's arms once the sun went down. But sleep was all they did. Hamnet woke once in the middle of the night. When he looked up at the sky, he wondered if he was seeing things. It was blacker than he'd ever known it to be, and a whole host of stars blazed down—far more than he'd seen on a clear night down on the ground.

People who came from the mountains talked about how many stars they could see. He'd always nodded when he heard talk like that, nodded without taking it very seriously. Now he saw he'd been wrong. So many shone here, he had trouble picking out the brighter ones that marked the outlines of the constellations. The Milky Way was a glisten of mother-of-pearl.

And then, despite the beauty, despite the wonder, he fell asleep again. He could admire the night sky for as long as he stayed atop the Glacier. Sleep, though, sleep he needed now.

He didn't want to wake up come morning, even with the sun smacking

him in the face. He yawned and stretched and groaned. Then he saw Ulric
Skakki gutting a snowshoe hare. For a heartbeat, that meant nothing special to him, which only proved how tired he was. Then he blinked. "Where
did you get that?" he asked through another yawn.

"Oh, I looked in my pocket, and there it was," Ulric answered airily.
Hamnet Thyssen growled, down deep in his throat. Ulric laughed. Then,
before Hamnet attempted mayhem on his exasperating person, he went on,
"It just came hopping along, happy as you please. It stopped to nibble on
one of those little patches of plants they have up here, and I put an arrow
through it."

"I wouldn't eat raw rabbit down below," Trasamund said. "I've known
too many who got sick after they did. Up here . . . Up here I'll eat anything I
can kill, and worry about getting sick later on."

They still had horseflesh and musk-ox meat, too. Hamnet Thyssen wasn't
hungry any more when he started trudging towards the peak that stuck up
through the Glacier. Tired, stiff, sore, trying to suck in more air than he readily could . . . all of that, but not hungry.

He saw more rabbits hopping across the Glacier, and other little creatures he couldn't name so readily. "Do they go from one mountaintop to another, like boatmen in the Southeastern Sea sailing from one island to the
next?" he wondered.

"Seems so," Audun Gilli said. "Those mountains *are* islands here, islands of life."

"Islands of life," Count Hamnet echoed. It was a pretty phrase, and one
also likely to be true. The two didn't go together all that often. "What would
we do if one of them weren't close by?"

Ulric Skakki had a one-word answer for that: "Starve."

That wasn't very pretty, but it too was likely to be true. Hamnet trudged
along the top of the Glacier. They might starve anyway, once their food ran
out. How many hares and voles and whatever other little creatures that
lived up here could they catch? Enough to live on? He would have been surprised.

A fox trotted past, unfortunately well out of bowshot. Spit flooded Hamnet's mouth as he watched it go. Fox meat was bound to be rank, but it was
meat. He got the feeling that if he stayed up here long he wouldn't sneer at
anything even remotely edible. In this thin air, in this cold, a man needed to
eat like a sabertooth to keep going.

But for its eyes and nose, the fox was white. Down on the Bizogot steppe, the animals had turned brown. There wasn't enough dirt up here to make that worthwhile.

"We can drink ourselves through every tavern in Nidaros with this tale, and never once touch our own money," Ulric said.

"If we get back," Hamnet Thyssen said

"Well, yes, there is that," the adventurer allowed, "though you didn't hear me being rude enough to talk about it."

"I'd like to drink my way through a tavern or two," Audun Gilli said wistfully.

He'd spent a lot of time in Nidaros drinking—mourning his family, lost in a fire. He'd had his head stuck in the ale vat for three years, but he'd done well enough and stayed sober enough since Ulric Skakki hauled him from the gutter and made him dry out. One thing seemed plain: he wouldn't have a chance to do much drinking up here.

No matter how far Count Hamnet and the other refugees walked, the mountaintop seemed no closer. Hamnet had heard the air in the southwestern deserts was clear enough to make things seem closer than they really were. God knew what air there was up here was achingly transparent.

"We should have brought some horses up the avalanche," Trasamund said.

For a moment, Hamnet thought he meant it. That only proved he wasn't getting enough air to keep his own wits working. Vulfolaic needed longer to realize it was a joke than he did, which made him feel a little better. The other Bizogot did a splendid double take, then sent Trasamund a dirty look. "You could have strapped three or four of them on your back and carried them up that way," Vulfolaic said.

"Don't be foolish." Trasamund shook his head. "The wizards could have shrunk them, and we'd each have one in our belt pouches."

"Why not?" Hamnet asked Liv. "If the Rulers' wizards can turn themselves into owls, why couldn't you do something like that?"

"Easier to work magic on yourself than on something else," she answered. Audun Gilli nodded. She went on, "We were a little rushed before we started climbing, too, or more than a little."

"If you're going to complain about every little thing . . ." Trasamund said.

"I ought to clout you with something," Liv said, "but I haven't got anything handy and I'm too tired to do a proper job of it."

On they went. Suddenly, the mountaintop seemed to loom just ahead of them. Hamnet wasn't sure how it had got so close without his noticing—probably because he'd been trudging along with his head down. It looked less inviting now that he could examine it better . . . but then, what didn't? The green that had drawn them from afar wasn't the green of rich upland meadows, as he'd hoped it would be. It was thin and patchy, with gray rock showing through here and there, or perhaps more often than that.

But it was undoubtedly a more hopeful place than the vast solitude of the Glacier all around it. Some of the plants had flowers. Some even had berries already. And if mosquitoes buzzed . . . well, they were life, too.

Something that looked like a rabbit with short hind legs and short, round ears stared at the newcomers from little black eyes. "Funny-looking creature," Trasamund remarked.

"It probably thinks the same of you," Ulric Skakki answered. Trasamund rewarded him with a glare. Ignoring it, the adventurer went on, "I do believe that's what they call a pika. They live up in the mountains south of the Glacier, too."

"I wonder if it tastes like rabbit," Vulfolaic said.

Before he could do more than wonder, the pika, if that was what it was, disappeared into a hole in the ground. "*That's* interesting," Liv said.

"Why?" Count Hamnet asked. "The hole can't be very deep. Chances are we can get the beast out."

She shook her head. "Not what I meant. Why would it be afraid of us if it never saw people before?"

"Because we're large and noisy and we smell bad?" he suggested.

Liv's grin was crooked enough to suit even Ulric Skakki. "Well, God knows that's all true," she said.

A few buntings and longspurs fluttered about, as they might have on the Bizogot plains. Hamnet Thyssen wouldn't have thought they could find enough seeds to eat up here, but they didn't seem to care what he thought.

They were meat, too, if the Bizogots and Raumsdalians could figure out some way to catch them.

A spring bubbled up out of the rock. Hamnet had been chipping off bits of ice and putting them in his mouth when he got thirsty. The spring water wasn't much warmer, but it tasted far better. He sprawled down not far away. "God, I'm tired!" he groaned.

The others rested, too. The rock, again, wasn't much warmer than the Glacier surrounding it, but it seemed so. The sun shone down brightly. "We have a refuge—for a while," Arnora said.

"How's your face?" Ulric asked her.

Her hand went to the moss covering her wound. "Sore," she answered. "The scar will make me lose my looks." She shrugged. "I'm still alive. I may stay alive a while longer, anyhow."

"You still look fine to me, sweetheart," Ulric Skakki said.

"You say that because you want to screw me and you have no other women handy," Arnora said with a wry, one-sided smile. "Tell me I'm wrong. I know men. I know how they work."

"No man in his right mind would say he knew how women worked," Ulric said.

"Of course not. But men are simple," Arnora replied.

"I feel pretty simple right now," Ulric said. "I won't argue with you there. I need food, and I need sleep. The more of each, the better. After that . . . well, my dear, after that I'll still think you look good."

"You tell me so now," Arnora said. "When we get down again . . . If we get down again . . . Well, if we get down again, that will be a miracle. Maybe I can look for another miracle afterwards."

Liv was methodically gathering dead plants. She eyed them none too happily. "They'll burn fast—they won't give a good, long-lasting fire the way musk-ox dung would. But maybe we'll be able to cook a little, anyhow."

Even getting a fire going proved harder than it would have down on the Bizogot plain. The air was so thin, sparks didn't want to form and the fuel didn't want to catch. Finally, though, they could cook, or at least sear, chunks of meat.

Chewing—and chewing, and chewing—Ulric Skakki said, "No matter what you do to this stuff, I don't think we'll see it at fancy eateries in Nidaros any time soon."

"Odds are against it," Count Hamnet agreed. The odds were against their ever seeing anything in Nidaros again, but he didn't dwell on that. Dwelling on it wouldn't have done him any good, anyhow.

While the sun shone, the mountaintop stayed warm enough. But they'd come to the eastern side of the mountain, and its bulk made the sun set for them earlier than it would have otherwise. They could watch the mountain's shadow stretch west across the Glacier. They could—but they didn't spend much time doing it. They spread across the rocks and screen, all of them looking for anything that would burn.

"We might as well be sleeping on ice," Hamnet grumbled as a frigid wind began to blow.

"As long as we're sleeping someplace where our enemies can't get at us, I'll worry about everything else later," Liv said. "Cold is only cold. It gets much worse than this in winter down on the plain."

Since she was right, Hamnet left it there. He spread out his bedroll behind a boulder that shielded him from the worst of the breeze. Liv lay down beside him. He looked around for Audun Gilli, but didn't see the wizard anywhere close by. That suited him fine.

"I never imagined anyone could come up here," Liv said.

Now that they were here, the mountaintop gave new meaning to the phrase *cold comfort*. Hamnet Thyssen tried not to dwell on that, either. Twisting to escape a pebble that was digging into his ribs, he said, "If it weren't for the avalanche, we couldn't have done it. We never would have made the climb straight up the side of the Glacier."

"No." Liv shook her head. "We barely got here as it was."

"I'm sorry things didn't work out better," Hamnet said. "Maybe if you and Trasamund had stayed up in the north . . ."

She shook her head again. "It wouldn't have made much difference. The Rulers would have beaten the Three Tusk clan anyhow. They are stronger than we are." She grimaced. Though the sun was down, twilight lingered long, as it did in these parts; Hamnet could watch her lips twist. "Strange to say something like that. Strange to have to say it. But it is true. Do you think they are stronger than the Empire, too?"

"They may well be," Hamnet said slowly. "Their wizards seem able to do things we can't match."

"It's true." Liv's voice was sleepy and sad. "Audun's had no better luck against them than any Bizogot shaman."

"You've spent a lot of time talking with him lately," Hamnet remarked, not casually enough.

"Magic," Liv answered. "Too much magic going on these days. He knows things I don't. I know some things he doesn't, too." She sighed. "Doesn't seem either one of us knows enough. Doesn't seem anyone does. Would we be here if we did?"

Count Hamnet didn't know where they'd be. "*Just* magic?" He knew he shouldn't ask the question, knew he especially shouldn't ask it like that, and asked it anyway.

Liv leaned up on an elbow. She searched his face. "Not just magic, no," she said. "We talk about things any people would talk about. Why? Is something wrong with that?"

In the wintertime, the Bizogots had a devilish way to kill dire wolves. They would skewer a chunk of meat with several long bone needles, then leave it out on the snow. A dire wolf would swallow it whole—would have to, because it froze hard as stone. But when it thawed out inside the belly of the beast, the needles would skewer from the inside out. Liv's counterquestion seemed just as dangerous.

"Well, I don't know," Hamnet Thyssen said, cautious now—cautious too late, the way people usually are cautious. "Is there?"

"You're jealous," Liv said. "Aren't you?"

"No," he answered, the way anyone asked that question would answer. And that question, answered that way, was almost always a lie. He knew it was here. As if to prove as much, he added, "Of course not."

"Uh-*huh*," Liv said, which could have meant anything at all—anything that wasn't good for the two of them. She went on, "Don't you think we have more important things to worry about right now?"

"Yes," he said, which couldn't—and didn't—mean anything but no.

"Staying alive, for instance," Liv said, as if he hadn't spoken. "Seeing if we can find a way down from the Glacier—with or without magic—that doesn't get us killed."

"I said yes," Hamnet reminded her. He needed to remind himself, too.

"I know you did." Liv sighed again. "I'm going to sleep—or I'm going to try to go to sleep, anyhow. Good night."

"Good night." He set a hand on her shoulder. She didn't shake it off. She just acted as if it weren't there. That might have been worse. He took it away himself, marveling that it wasn't charred to the wrist.

Before long, she started breathing deeply and regularly. If she wasn't asleep, she had a promising future on the stage—if any of them had a promising future anywhere, which seemed unlikely.

Hamnet Thyssen wondered whether sleep would find him. No matter how weary he was, he was also upset—with himself, for charging out onto thin ice and falling through; and with Liv, for not giving him the reassurance he craved. But, no matter how upset he was, he was also weary. He went from wondering how he could have put things better to complete unconsciousness without even noticing.

When he woke in the middle of the night, he was startled to find how dark and cold it had got and how many stars crowded the sky—even more than had on the way up the Glacier. And he was even more startled to hear several foxes yowl and yip out on the ice, not far from the base of the mountain. He opened his eyes to see Trasamund feeding the fire. Then he closed them and stopped thinking altogether.

He woke up again a little before sunup. Twilight already brightened the eastern sky, and would for some little while before the sun actually rose. He looked over at Liv. Had she been awake, they could have taken up where they'd left off the night before. That would have been a mistake, which wouldn't have stopped Count Hamnet from doing it.

Luck, or something like it, was with him, though he didn't think so at the time: Liv went on snoring. The longer Hamnet listened to her, the slower and more regular his own breathing got. Pretty soon, he was asleep again. *Why not?* he thought as he dozed off. It wasn't as if the refugees were going anywhere very far today.

He woke with the sun shining in his face. But sunshine wasn't what woke him. A kick in the ribs was. He started to grab for his sword, then froze when he saw that the man who'd kicked him had an arrow aimed at his chest from a stride away and couldn't possibly miss if he let fly.

Very slowly, Hamnet raised his hands. His captor recognized the gesture and nodded. A glance told Hamnet the whole camp was overrun. The fugitives hadn't imagined they needed to set sentries here atop the Glacier. That only proved their imaginations weren't so good as they might have been.

These weren't the Rulers. These men plainly lived on the Glacier all the time. They were short and stocky, with great barrel chests to take in all the thin air they could. They wore clothes pieced together from hare and fox hides. Their arrowheads and knives were of stone, which was primitive but would serve. Fear pierced Hamnet like an arrow. Would they think strangers in their frigid domain were anything but meat?

VIII

DO YOU KNOW this speech?" Hamnet Thyssen asked in the Bizogot language. The strangers looked something like Bizogots, though they didn't come close to matching them for size. They were fair-skinned and pale-eyed, with hair and matted beards of yellow or red or light brown.

One of them said a few words in his own tongue. It sounded something like the Bizogot speech. Count Hamnet couldn't make anything of it, though. By their frowns, neither could Trasamund or Liv or any of the other mammoth-herders.

To his amazement, Ulric Skakki said something in what sounded like the same language, or one much like it. And if Hamnet was amazed, the barrel-chested men of the Glacier were astonished. They all pointed at Ulric and said something that had to mean, *How can you talk with us?*

He replied, haltingly. Count Hamnet could *almost* follow him, but meaning somehow flitted away. Then Ulric spoke in the ordinary Bizogot language: "There's this little clan bumped up against the western mountains—the Crag Goats, they call themselves. They speak a dialect God couldn't follow. It's as old as those hills, and twice as dusty. That's what I'm using."

"Even if God couldn't, you learned it," Vulfolaic said.

A man of the Glacier shouted angrily and raised his bow in plain warning: the captives weren't supposed to talk in a tongue he couldn't readily follow. Then the man spoke to Ulric Skakki again.

Ulric answered yes. That much Hamnet Thyssen could make out, but no more. What he answered yes to, Hamnet had no idea. Ulric Skakki and the men of the Glacier went back and forth. He spoke slowly, feeling for words.

They answered at their usual speed. They seemed to have trouble grasping the idea of someone who spoke only a little of their language.

After pointing to his comrades, Ulric got some grudging nods from their captors. "All right," he said in the usual Bizogot language, though slowly and with an antique turn of phrase. "They give me leave to speak somewhat to you. I think their ancestors came up here the same way we did, and then found they could not return."

"How long ago?" Trasamund and Audun Gilli asked at the same time. They looked at each other in surprise; two men less likely to think alike were hard to imagine.

It did them no good. Ulric shrugged and spread his hands. "I have no idea," he answered. "They don't know, either. Longer ago than any of them remember—that's all I can tell you."

"What will they do with us?" Liv asked. *What will they do to us?* had to be what she meant. She was wise to phrase the question the way she did. No telling how much of the normal Bizogot tongue they might be able to grasp.

"Well, I don't *think* we're breakfast right now," Ulric said. Hamnet Thyssen's stomach did a slow lurch. That had already crossed his mind.

"Should we give them the meat we have left?" Arnora asked.

"That's a good idea. You're as smart as you're beautiful," Ulric told her, and she blushed like a girl. He went on, "They'll find it anyway. Better we give it to them than that they take it from us."

He spoke again in the ancient dialect the men of the Glacier used. The Bizogots had lived north of the Raumsdalians for a couple of thousand years. When in that time did these people's forebears come up here? Were they fleeing some disaster, or were they just exploring? Hamnet Thyssen shrugged a tiny shrug. If they didn't know any more, he was unlikely ever to find out.

When they understood Ulric Skakki, they could hardly hide their excitement. The strangers had meat? The strangers would *give* them meat? One of them pointed to his ear, as if to say he couldn't believe what he was hearing. He answered Ulric quickly. Count Hamnet couldn't be sure what he said, but thought it likely to mean, *If you're really going to do this, you'd better do it.*

The adventurer confirmed that, saying, "They want to see it. Time for us to cough up, I'm afraid. Go to the packs and get it out. Don't hold any back. And *don't* go for your weapons. We're all dead if you do."

When the men of the Glacier saw the chunks of raw horseflesh and musk-ox meat, they sighed in something close to ecstasy. Those gobbets were too big to come from any of the animals Hamnet had seen up here. One of the men of the Glacier used a stone blade to cut a mouthful of meat. He chewed and swallowed.

His face lit up in surprise. "Not man meat!" he exclaimed—Hamnet made that out very clearly.

Some of the other men of the Glacier sampled the new food. They nodded agreement. Then they tried to get Ulric Skakki to tell them what beasts it came from. *Horse* and *musk ox* were only words to them. When he talked about what the live animals were like, when he stretched out his arms to show how big they were, the men plainly didn't believe him. They'd forgotten too much.

They ate the horsemeat and what was left of the musk ox in nothing flat. Hamnet Thyssen knew the Bizogots could eat more at a sitting than Raumsdalians. That was what happened when you didn't always eat regularly. But the men of the Glacier effortlessly outdid the Bizogots. Trasamund's eyes widened to watch them put away the meat.

When the men of the Glacier finished, they seemed amazed themselves at what they'd done. They patted their bellies and swaggered around. Count Hamnet got the idea they weren't used to feeling full.

They didn't let down their guard, though. Several of them kept the Bizogots and Raumsdalians covered with nocked arrows. Their bows were marvels of bone and sinew and lashings of leather and roots: they had no wood to give them proper bowstaves. That meant they also had no spears, which had to make hunting harder.

"If we get the chance, we can take them," Hamnet murmured to Ulric without moving his lips.

"I think so, too." Ulric had also mastered that small but useful skill. "But will they give it to us?"

Hamnet wished he could talk to Liv or Audun Gilli, but neither stood close enough to let him do it without drawing the notice of the men of the Glacier. If they could use magic to distract the barbarians, who could guess what might happen next?

The opportunity passed. The men of the Glacier used gestures to get their captives to hold their hands out for binding. Again, the cords were strange to Hamnet's eyes, but they did the job. He strained at them, trying not to show he was doing it. He had no luck breaking free.

A man of the Glacier plucked a dagger from a sheath on Ulric Skakki's belt. He stared at the iron blade, holding it up close to his face. Then he tried the edge with his thumb. He tried his own stone knife a moment later. His shrug said he found them about equally sharp. Hamnet Thyssen waited to see what the shaggy men made of swords—especially of Trasamund's great two-handed blade. But they didn't disarm all their captives, though another man did rob Ulric of his bow and quiver. The men of the Glacier admired the bow and, even more, the few arrows he had left.

They still remembered something of herding. They got the Bizogots and Raumsdalians moving off the mountain refuge and back down to the Glacier. As soon as they could see it, they pointed to another peak that stuck up farther west. And off they went, surrounding their captives and urging them along. Having no choice, Hamnet went where he was bidden.

As long as the prisoners tried to keep up, the men of the Glacier didn't harry them. They also didn't seem to mind any more if the Bizogots and Raumsdalians spoke among themselves. Now that their hands were bound, they didn't seem so dangerous. That was Hamnet's guess, anyhow.

"Do they have any shamans with them?" he asked Liv as they trudged along.

"I don't feel any men of power," she answered after a moment spent doing whatever a shaman did instead of listening. "Maybe there is one where we're going, though. I can't imagine living your whole life without magic."

"No up here—that's for sure," Hamnet said. "I thought you Bizogots led a hard life. Well, you do, but this is harder."

Liv nodded. "These people are of our kindred," she said. "Not close kin, not now, but they were Bizogots once. Their looks and their speech say the same thing."

"So does Ulric Skakki," Count Hamnet agreed.

Some snow buntings fluttered by, looking for plants growing in the pockets of dirt that clung to the top of the ice. The men of the Glacier sprang into action as if they'd practiced for years—and so, no doubt, they had. They carried nets made from sinews and twisted dried plants: the same kind of cords they used to bind their prisoners. Flinging them up, they caught several little birds, then quickly killed them.

They seemed pleased with themselves afterwards. The birds didn't offer much meat. Nothing up here offered much meat. Every little bit meant the men of the Glacier wouldn't starve for a while longer. Hamnet Thyssen would have pitied them more if they hadn't shown they knew what man's flesh tasted like.

"Things could be worse," Ulric Skakki said a bit later.

"Oh, of course they could," Count Hamnet agreed sardonically. "They could have killed us all right away and started feasting on us back at the other mountain. Wouldn't that have been jolly?"

"Not quite what I had in mind," Ulric said with what was probably commendable restraint. "I was thinking we could have grown up here ourselves. The world's biggest frozen trap . . . God must have been in a nasty mood when he left these poor buggers stuck here."

He wasn't wrong, not even a little bit. To try to stay alive on terrain that gave a man so little—it would have driven anyone to the edge of madness, or maybe beyond. Hamnet's shiver, for once, had nothing to do with the vast plain of ice across which he tramped.

Then one of his captors let out a startled grunt and pointed north. Hamnet Thyssen's head turned that way. He saw more human figures moving in the distance. And those distant people saw his comrades and captors, too. They loped towards them.

The men of the Glacier who'd captured the Bizogots and Raumsdalians looked to their weapons. "They're people, all right," Ulric said. "Put a few of them together, and they make factions and go to war."

Inspiration struck Hamnet. "Tell these bastards we'll fight on their side if they turn us loose," he said urgently. "They didn't eat us right away, after all. And if we can get our hands free with something in them . . ."

Ulric gave him a foxy grin. "I'll try. No guarantees, but I'll try. If it doesn't work, how are we worse off?"

How could we be worse off? went through Hamnet Thyssen's mind. But there were ways; he and Ulric had both come up with some. The adventurer spoke to the men of the Glacier. They weren't altogether naive—they could see that Ulric didn't have only their benefit in mind. But they could also see that the approaching band of barbarians outnumbered them. If they didn't do something, they were liable to end up on a spit or in a stewpot themselves.

They went back and forth with Ulric. At last, he spoke in the regular Bizogot tongue: "I've promised them we won't attack them right after this fight. That seems fair to me. But if we get our hands free, we'll be equals or more than equals. Is it a bargain? They'll understand *yes*, I think."

"Yes!" everyone shouted.

The men of the Glacier cut their bonds then. The stone knives did the job about as fast as iron could have. Hamnet opened and closed his hands again and again, working circulation back into them. He hoped he wasn't frostbitten.

He drew his sword. His comrades were taking hold of their weapons, too. "You know you've been in a bad place when the chance of getting killed is better than what you had before," Ulric Skakki remarked with what seemed to Count Hamnet excessive good cheer.

Trasamund drew his great two-handed blade and swung it in circles so it thrummed through the air. "Let them come!" he roared. "Let them come, by God, and I will make them go!" The men of the Glacier exclaimed and pointed. They'd never seen anything like the weapon—and maybe they'd never seen anything like the Bizogot jarl, either.

Shouting, the members of the other clan or tribe or whatever it was trotted forward. If the sight of strangers with strange weapons fazed them, they didn't let on. One of them drew his bow and let fly. His arrow fell short, splintering against the Glacier. Before long, though, the missiles would start to bite.

Trasamund shouted a command much used in Bizogot warfare: *"Chaaarge!"* He lumbered towards the attackers. So did the rest of the Bizogot men. And so did Hamnet Thyssen and Ulric Skakki.

Hamnet threw himself flat on the ice when an arrow hissed through the space where his head had been a couple of heartbeats earlier. As he scrambled to his feet again, he said, "If we can close with them, we'll slaughter them. They don't have shields or armor or swords."

No sooner had the words passed his lips than he suddenly felt as if he were running through porridge, not air. The band of barbarians that captured him and his comrades might not have had a shaman along. These newcomers did.

A Bizogot howled and fell when an arrow pierced his leg. The attackers might pincushion all of them if something didn't happen in a hurry.

"Liv!" Count Hamnet bawled. "Audun! Do something!" Even in that moment of desperation, he wished he weren't calling for the two of them together. But he couldn't do anything about that now except hope they had a counterspell handy.

They must have, for all at once he could move normally again. One of the attackers, a fellow with streaks of gray in his beard (and how many men of the Glacier lived long enough to go gray?), hung back a little from the rest. When the counterspell freed the Bizogots and Raumsdalians from the magic that had slowed them, he stamped his foot and swore. The gesture was so obvious, and so universal, it would have got a big laugh on the stage in Nidaros. Having stamped and sworn, he started incanting again.

Hamnet Thyssen resolved to kill him before he could finish his new spell.

Resolving to do it and doing it were two different things, as Hamnet knew too well. But he got one lucky break, for an arrow from a man of the Glacier on his side pierced an attacker's hand before that attacker could finish pointing *his* arrow at Hamnet's midsection. The wounded archer howled, broke the arrow, and pulled it from the wound, exactly as any other injured warrior might have done. Seeing Hamnet bearing down on him, he took a stone knife from a sheath on his belt and got ready to defend himself.

A stone knife made a good enough weapon . . . against another stone knife. Against a good iron sword, it was hardly any weapon at all. Hamnet Thyssen didn't let the man of the Glacier close with him and grapple. A slash sheared off two fingers when the fellow tried. He stood there astonished, staring at the spouting stumps, till Hamnet cut deep into his neck with another stroke.

Then Count Hamnet ran on, towards the attackers' shaman. The man's eyes blazed at him, blue as the depths of the Glacier. They radiated power and hatred.

With a shout, the shaman started to aim a spell at him. Before the man of the Glacier could finish it, Hamnet swung his sword. Nimble as a hare dodging a fox, the shaman ducked away. He shouted something Hamnet couldn't understand. Whatever it was, though, he doubted it was an endearment.

Hamnet Thyssen swung the sword again. Again, the grizzled man of the Glacier evaded the cut. Again, it disrupted his magic. And again, he cursed Count Hamnet—the Raumsdalian noble thought so, anyhow. One of the phrases the shaman used sounded something like the Bizogot words for *go away.*

That Count Hamnet didn't intend to do. This time, he thrust instead of slashing. The man of the Glacier didn't know what to do about that. Hamnet felt the sword grate on a rib as it went home.

Those blue, blue eyes opened enormously wide, in astonishment and dismay and pain. The shaman opened his mouth, too, to shriek, but more blood than noise came from it. Slowly, he crumpled to the Glacier. Hamnet's wrist twisted as he pulled the blade free: a veteran's trick to enlarge the wound and make sure it killed. He probably didn't need it here, but drill-masters had beaten it into him when he was young, and he used it when-ever he got the chance.

With the enemy's wizard dying at his feet, he looked around to see how the rest of the fight was going. At least half a dozen of the barbarians were down, their blood steaming on the ice. One Bizogot was dead; a stone knife had slashed his throat. The man wounded during the spell was swearing with that arrow through his leg. Several men of the Glacier were running off as fast as they could go.

Ulric Skakki wiped blood from his sword on a dead man's trousers. "Thrusting it into earth would clean it better," Ulric said, "but earth's a little hard to come by right here."

"Just a little," Hamnet Thyssen allowed. "They've forgotten what to do about swords."

"A good thing, too, or they would have been tougher," Ulric said. "They put up a better fight than I thought they could. When you scragged their shaman, that took a lot of heart out of them."

"Did it?" Hamnet had been too busy to notice.

"Oh, yes. They must have thought he was the finest thing since raw meat." Ulric Skakki eyed the shaman's corpse. "Now he *is* raw meat. I won-der if our charming friends will turn him into the main course. And I won-der if they'll expect us to share."

"You come up with the most delightful ideas," Hamnet said. Ulric made as if to bow. As Hamnet's stomach twisted, he went on, "Maybe I could turn cannibal to keep from starving. Maybe. Just to feed myself? No. I hope not, anyway."

"Up here, the difference between needing to feed yourself and starving isn't likely to be very big," Ulric said.

Hamnet Thyssen grunted. Before he could say anything, a man of the Glacier came up to him and pounded him on the back. The fellow poured out a torrent of gibberish. "What's he saying?" Hamnet asked Ulric Skakki.

"That you're a demon of a warrior," the adventurer answered. "That he didn't think anybody could kill old Leudigisel, but you made it look easy. Uh, that you're entitled to his heart and liver and ballocks if you want them."

Reflecting that his stomach had twisted too soon, Count Hamnet said, "Tell him I don't want to offend him, but that's not our custom. Tell him I wouldn't pollute myself by eating any part of old what's-his-name."

"I'm not sure I can say that, but I'll try." Ulric Skakki did. He must have made his point, for the man of the Glacier said something and pointed to Hamnet. "He likes what you said," Ulric translated. "He says it shows a manly attitude." The man of the Glacier spoke again. "He asks if you mind if his clan feeds on their dead foes' flesh."

"They can do whatever they want," Hamnet replied. "We didn't come up here to reform them. We didn't even know they were here when we did come up." He switched to Raumsdalian so the man of the Glacier couldn't possibly understand: "And I'd rather have them butcher the shaman than us, by God."

"Yes, that crossed my mind, too," Ulric Skakki said. He spoke haltingly in the tongue the men of the Glacier used, the tongue related to an obscure Bizogot dialect.

The man with whom he was talking shouted to his comrades. They started butchering their fallen enemies. Hamnet Thyssen couldn't watch for long. He'd butchered many animals and slain many men, but he'd never seen people deliberately cut up human corpses for meat.

No man of the Glacier ate any raw man's flesh. Through Ulric, Count Hamnet asked why not. The man who answered him explained that there was a curse on the practice. "I bet they come down sick when they eat their neighbors raw," Ulric guessed shrewdly. "You have to cook pork gray to keep that from happening, and it's bound to be worse with your own kind. Lots of curses have common sense behind them if you know where to look."

That wouldn't have occurred to Count Hamnet. Ulric Skakki had a knack for eyeing the world sideways and seeing things other people missed. Hamnet said, "I hope there are enough rabbits and mice and berries and whatnot on the next mountain to keep us going for a while. Otherwise . . ."

"Otherwise we have to keep quiet forever if we do somehow make it down from here," Ulric finished for him. "Yes. If we don't, no one will want to do anything with us but kill us on sight."

"That's what I was thinking, all right." Hamnet wished it weren't. He didn't want to become a cannibal, to put himself beyond the pale of decency for the rest of his life. But he didn't want to starve to death, either.

Ulric spoke to a man of the Glacier who was helping to cut up a corpse. Hamnet caught something that sounded like the Bizogot word for *friends.* The barrel-chested barbarian nodded. He said something that had Leudigisel's name in it. Hamnet guess the man meant that anyone who'd killed Leudigisel was a friend of his.

When Ulric asked another question, the man of the Glacier shrugged and spread his gory hands. He paused and wiped his fingers clean—well, cleaner. Then the man of the Glacier said something more.

"What's going on?" Hamnet asked.

"I asked him if he knew how we could get down from the Glacier, get back to the rest of the world," Ulric replied. "He said he didn't. He asked me why anyone would want to when things were so much better here."

"Oh." Hamnet Thyssen put no stress on the word. He didn't think it needed any. By Ulric Skakki's crooked smile, neither did he.

Did vultures and teratorns come up here to the top of the Glacier? Hamnet couldn't remember seeing any overhead. If he had, he would have thought they were waiting for him to keel over. Marching and fighting in this thin air left him crushingly weary.

"We went to war for this clan," he told Ulric. "They owe us help getting down, if they have any to give."

The adventurer translated his words for the man of the Glacier. The barbarian shrugged. He spoke. "He says to wait for another avalanche," Ulric Skakki said.

"No, thanks," Count Hamnet answered. Scavenger birds might or might not come up here. But small-eared foxes, no doubt drawn by the scent of blood, already stood waiting just out of bowshot to clean up the remains the men of the Glacier didn't want.

Pointing to them, Ulric Skakki said, "They show these people have been up here for a long time, poor devils."

"How do you mean?" Hamnet asked.

"They know how far a bow shoots, and they know not to come that close."

"That makes them smarter than a lot of warriors I've run into." Hamnet pointed to the puddles of blood now freezing on the ice.

"Heh," Ulric said. "That's one of those jokes that would be funny if only it were funny—know what I mean?"

"Who said I was joking?" Hamnet Thyssen answered.

THE MOUNTAINTOP REFUGE to which the men of the Glacier led the Raumsdalians and Bizogots was larger and more hospitable than the one they'd found on their own. It had a broad, low south-facing slope that caught as much sun as there was to catch. Flowers and berries and other greens grew as thickly as they could at that height and in that weather.

Stone pens housed hares and pikas and voles. The men of the Glacier did everything they could to make themselves at home here. And everything they could do still left their little world terrifyingly bleak to anyone who came to it anew.

Count Hamnet saw his first women and children of the Glacier there. The only difference between them and their menfolk he could find was that they grew no beards, so their faces were only filthy, not shaggy. They hid behind rocks when they saw oddly dressed strangers accompanying their kinsmen, but came out with glad cries when the men of the Glacier told of the battle they'd fought and showed off the meat they'd brought back.

They used dried dung for their fires, as the Bizogots did down on what Hamnet had thought of as the frozen plain till he came to the top of the Glacier. Some of the dung was rabbit pellets. The rest . . . Well, the men of the Glacier couldn't even afford to waste waste.

"We can't stay here long," Trasamund said in a low voice.

"I wouldn't want to, God knows," Hamnet answered. "But why do you say we can't?"

"Because we'll eat them empty if we do," the jarl said. "I'll bet some of them starve every winter the way things are. Pretty soon they'll see they can't keep us, if they haven't seen it by now. And then they'll kill us and cook us, or try."

As soon as Hamnet heard that, he knew it had to be true. "We'd best keep sentries up while the rest of us sleep, then," he said.

"Already thought of it," Trasamund replied.

"Good," Hamnet said. "We don't want to be pushy about it. If we are, we're liable to give them ideas they don't need. But we don't want to let them talk us out of it, either."

"That's about how I see things, too," the Bizogot said. "We can whip them if we have to, I think."

"Maybe," Hamnet said. "But even if we do, so what? Do you want to be lord of this mountain?" He didn't come out and ask, *Are you utterly mad?*— but he didn't miss by much, either.

The idea appalled Trasamund. "I want to come down off the Glacier. I want to fight the Rulers. I want to beat them, by God. I'm jarl of the Three Tusk clan, and that's what I aim to grow old being."

No matter how he aimed, Hamnet Thyssen feared he was unlikely to hit his target. His clan was shattered beyond repair. So was the Bizogots' whole way of life on much of the frozen steppe, if not on all of it. Hamnet could hardly blame the jarl if that hadn't sunk in yet. Sooner or later, though, it would have to.

He looked around to see what Liv was doing. He seemed to be doing that more and more lately, and wished he weren't. She and Audun Gilli were both trying to talk to a scrawny woman of the Glacier with long, stringy blond hair. The woman's fur tunic and trousers were decorated with fringes and bits of sparkling crystal tied on with rawhide or cord. He nodded to himself. If she wasn't this clan's shaman, he would have been very much surprised.

"Can you translate?" Audun Gilli called to Ulric Skakki. "You're the only one of us who knows their language."

"It's a little like what I speak, but only a little," Liv added. "When I guess, I guess wrong half the time. And you don't want to guess wrong when you're talking about shamanry. A mistake can kill you."

"A shame you don't want to put any pressure on me," Ulric said with one of his lopsided smiles. "I'll try, but I don't know how much I can help. I didn't have a lot to do with the Crag Goats' shaman."

He squatted down beside the stringy-haired woman and spoke to her in her language. Listening, Count Hamnet felt he ought to be able to understand it, but couldn't except for a word here and there. It was at least as far from the regular Bizogot tongue as the old-fashioned Raumsdalian priests used in their liturgies was from the everyday speech of Nidaros.

A moment later, he forgot about the fine points of dialect, for the smell of roasting pork brought spit flooding into his mouth. He'd marched and fought on very little food, and that savory smell reminded him of it.

But it wasn't pork. He realized that a moment too late, a moment after the smell dug down deep and made his belly growl. Nausea and hunger warred within him. He'd wanted man's flesh. He hadn't quite known what it was, but he'd wanted it. Part of him still did, and that was worst of all.

Trasamund went from smile to scowl in a way that suggested the cooking cannibal feast had smelled good to him, too. The men of the Glacier watched their enemies' flesh sizzle with eager anticipation. They didn't think they were doing anything wrong by eating it. Had the men of the other clan won the fight, these barbarians would have been butchered. *And so would I,* Count Hamnet thought.

"Ulric!" he called.

"What is it?" The adventurer looked up from his colloquy with the shaman.

"Ask if we can eat some hares or whatever else they have instead of . . . that." Hamnet pointed to the meat cooking above the fires.

"Oh. Right." Ulric Skakki went back to the language the men of the Glacier could follow. The shaman sounded surprised as she answered. Ulric said, "She wants to know why, when man's flesh is so much sweeter. She says there's nothing better than the flesh of foes you've killed yourself."

"Wonderful," Count Hamnet said tightly. "Well, tell her it's not our custom or whatever you have to say to get us out of it. God knows you aren't lying."

"I'll do my best." Again, Ulric returned to the other dialect. The shaman shrugged and tapped her forehead with a callused finger as she said something in reply. "She thinks foreigners are crazy," Ulric translated unnecessarily.

"Well, we love her, too," Hamnet said, which made Ulric bark laughter and earned the Raumsdalian noble a sharp glance from the shaman. Hamnet Thyssen looked back impassively, and the woman of the Glacier was the first to turn her eyes away.

Instead of hares, the men of the Glacier fed their guests pikas and voles. Hamnet guessed they were being given the glove, but he wasn't inclined to fuss about it. He would have eaten worms and earwigs instead of the meat that smelled so damnably tempting.

The men of the Glacier didn't worry about it. Hamnet could see why. Life here was impossibly hard. They probably didn't recognize the folk of other clans as human beings at all. But when he watched them cut flesh with their stone knives and greedily stuff it into their mouths, he almost lost his own appetite.

Almost, but not quite. He was so hungry, before long he *would* have eaten man's flesh and been glad to get it. That thought made him despise the locals less as he watched them feast.

"How much does their shaman know?" he asked Liv. If he could talk about anything else, it had to help.

"Hard to be sure, but more than I expected," she answered. "They have so little up here—they *can't* use much for shamanry. But what will can do, will and bone and stone, Marcovefa does. I suppose that's true for the other one, too, the one you killed."

"I've never seen anything like that tanglefoot spell before—I know that." Hamnet shivered. "I hope I never do again, either." He remembered the choice morsels he'd been offered from the dead shaman. With another shiver, he wondered if one day before too long he'd regret not eating them when he had the chance.

"It was different, sure enough." Liv looked at him from under lowered eyebrows. "Why do you think I'm cheating on you with Audun?"

Count Hamnet started to deny that he thought any such thing. He started to, yes, but found he couldn't. It wasn't so much that he minded lying as that he minded minded lying and getting found out. His voice dull with a mixture of anger and embarrassment, he answered, "I imagine because I saw it happen before with Gudrid."

"I'm not Gudrid, thank God. I hoped you might have noticed," Liv said tartly. "And I'm not sleeping with Audun Gilli, either. If you keep trying to watch me all day and all night, though, I'm liable to start, just to give you something to watch."

He got out two syllables of a laugh before he realized she wasn't joking. She thought spying was as big a betrayal as infidelity, and she *would* repay the one with the other. He hesitated. He knew the words he needed, but bringing them out came hard, hard. But he had no choice, not if he wanted to keep her. Hating himself, hating her a little, he mumbled, "I'm sorry."

"Are you?" Liv expected words to mean what they said. Bizogots weren't much for polite hypocrisy, but she'd seen that Raumsdalians could be. She eyed him narrowly, trying to scent dissembling. She must not have, for at last she nodded. "Yes, I think you are. All right, then—let it go."

He nodded, too. It wasn't done between them; he knew that. But it wouldn't crash down on them like a great ice avalanche, either—not right now, anyway. He changed the subject: "Can we sleep safely?"

"Sooner or later, we'll have to," Liv answered. "We may as well do it now. No quarrel between us and them for the time being."

"Except about what they eat." Hamnet Thyssen couldn't get the smell of roasting pork out of his nostrils or out of his mind.

"We can't do anything about that except not eat it ourselves." Liv tossed a pebble up into the air. It fell with a small click. "Not eating it may make them leery of us, but I don't think we can do anything about it."

"Nothing we'd want to do, anyhow," Hamnet said.

He curled up on the slope. Liv lay down beside him. He slid his arm around her and pulled her close to him. She moved willingly enough. It should have been comforting, reassuring. It seemed anything but, instead reminding him of how they'd quarreled and of what he feared. He couldn't keep his arm around her all the time. What would she do when it wasn't there?

She'll look around to see if you're watching her, that's what, he told himself. *And you'd better not be, or she'll make you sorry.* But how could he not watch? Gudrid had taught him that unwatched women cheated whenever they felt like it, and you wouldn't know they were cheating because you weren't watching them. Then, when you couldn't not know any more, you hurt all the worse because they'd been doing it for so long. You couldn't win.

He couldn't even stay awake. He'd done too much and slept too little. His eyes slid shut in the middle of a worry. He never knew he'd slid under. If anyone tried to rouse him to stand sentry, it didn't work. Except for breathing, he might have been dead.

When he woke, he was confused, not realizing he'd been asleep. Wasn't the sun over *there* a moment earlier? Or had he somehow shifted so that what he thought was east was really west? No and no, he finally decided. This was morning, and the sun truly did lie in the northeast. The men of the Glacier hadn't tried to murder him while he slept, either.

Liv still lay beside him, snoring softly. Sleep stole weariness and years from her face. Hamnet Thyssen could see the girl she had been, not the desperate shaman with the strange foreign lover she'd become.

When Liv woke a little later, she smiled at Hamnet. But the expression soon faded as she remembered where they were and, no doubt, what they'd been talking about before exhaustion claimed them. They had a lot of repair work to do . . . if they lived.

IX

W E'VE GOT TO get down from here," Hamnet Thyssen said. "If we don't—and if we don't do it soon—we'll have a war on our hands."

"Yes? And so?" Trasamund sent a hooded but scornful glance towards the men of the Glacier. "It wouldn't last long, and we'd cursed well win. We'd slaughter them, as a matter of fact, and we wouldn't have much trouble doing it, either."

"I know. That's what I'm afraid of," Count Hamnet answered. The Bizogot jarl sent him a quizzical look. He explained: "We slaughter the men. We take the women and sire our own children on them. We raise rabbits and voles on this crag, and we fight with the men of the Glacier who live on other crags. Then what? We turn into men of the Glacier ourselves, that's what, and the children we sire will think everything we say about what it was like down in the Bizogot country is a pack of lies. Is that what you've got in mind?"

Trasamund bared his teeth in a horrible grimace. "Good God, no!"

"Well, I don't, either," Hamnet said. "And so we'd better take as much food as they'll let us have and get out of here before the fighting starts."

"Where can we get down, though, except where we climbed up?" Trasamund said. "If we try that, the Rulers are liable to be waiting for us."

"I doubt it. We're only an afterthought to them—if that, by now," Hamnet said. "They've got bigger things to worry about farther south—not just the Bizogot clans down there, but the Empire. Odds are they've forgotten about us."

"Maybe." The Bizogot didn't sound as if he believed it. He was so self-important, he couldn't imagine that anyone else, even his enemies—perhaps especially his enemies—wouldn't think him important, too.

"At least we're here in the summer." Hamnet felt like stretching in the sun like a cat. It was almost as warm as it would have been down on the Bizogot plains. And, up so high, the sun was harder on the skin than it would have been down there. A swarthy man, Hamnet had got darker. Many of the fairer Bizogots were sunburned, some of them badly.

With a grunt, Trasamund nodded. "Winter up here wouldn't be much fun." From a Bizogot, especially a Bizogot who'd lived his life hard by the edge of the Glacier, that was no small admission.

"No, not much." Count Hamnet didn't want Trasamund outdoing him at understatement. "Maybe, though, it will melt enough of the Glacier to touch off a new avalanche at the edge. And maybe we can use that to get down."

"Even if it does, how would we know?" Trasamund replied. "And how long do you want to wait around and hope? You were the one who said we couldn't wait long, and I think you're right."

"If a big chunk does let go, we might hear it even though we're a long way from the edge of the Glacier," Count Hamnet said. "Not a lot of other noise between there and here." He growled, down deep in his chest. "As for the other . . . You're right, I did say that, and it's true, curse it. Not enough food up here to keep guests long."

"What are you talking about?" Trasamund retorted. "Up here, guests *are* food."

"Not for us. If we turn cannibal, there's no point going down again. Next to that, the Rulers are welcome to do as they please."

"Not to me they're not, by God," the Bizogot said. "I'd eat man's flesh if it was that or starve. Not before, but then. It happens in hard winters once in a while."

"Mm, I can see how it might." Hamnet tried to sound calm and judicious, not revolted. "But what do you think afterwards of the people who did it?"

"Depends. If they really had no other choice, then it's just one of those things. If it's not like that, or if the friends and kin of the ones who got eaten decide it's not like that . . . Well, the cannibals don't last long then."

Hamnet Thyssen found himself nodding. By the Bizogots' rough standards, that seemed fair enough. Even down in the Empire, there were stories of men who ate neighbors and relatives when the Breath of God blew strong and the harvest failed. People laughed at those stories more often than not, which didn't mean some of them weren't true. Sometimes you laughed because screaming was the only other choice.

Ulric was translating for Audun Gilli and the shaman from the men of the Glacier, whose name was Marcovefa. The adventurer suddenly straightened and stiffened like a dog that had taken a scent. "Ha!" he said, turning. "Thyssen!"

"I'm here," Hamnet answered. "What do you need?"

"Come over here, why don't you? That way, I won't have to yell," Ulric said. "Besides, you may understand pieces of this in the original, and it's better if you try. I might make a mistake."

Grunting, Hamnet got to his feet. Parts of him creaked and crunched as he moved. He had enough years to feel sleeping on hard ground after marching and fighting, enough years to make him feel half again as old as he really was. He creaked again when he squatted beside Ulric and Marcovefa and Audun. He had to make himself nod to the Raumsdalian wizard. Audun nodded back as if nothing was wrong.

"What's the story?" Hamnet asked.

"She may know another way down," Ulric answered.

That got Hamnet's interest, all right. "Tell me more," he said.

Ulric spread his hands in frustration. "I can't—or not much more, anyhow. The verbs are driving me crazy. Here. Wait. I'll have her tell you what she told me. Maybe you'll be able to make some sense out of it."

"I couldn't," Audun Gilli said. But Audun had needed a year to get something more than a smattering of the ordinary Bizogot language. Whatever his talents as a wizard, he made anything but a cunning linguist.

"Well, I'll try." Hamnet knew he sounded dubious. He thought he recognized words here and there in the language the men of the Glacier used. A couple of times, he'd made out a sentence, as long as it was short and simple.

Ulric spoke to Marcovefa. Hamnet thought he said something like, *Tell him what you just told me.* He wouldn't have bet anything he cared about losing, though.

Marcovefa answered. It was her birthspeech; she didn't stumble or hesitate the way Ulric did. That made her harder for Hamnet Thyssen to follow, not easier. He frowned, listening intently.

When she finished, he said, "Didn't she say she knows where a way down will be?"

"Ha! You heard it like that, too!" Ulric said. "Maybe the verbs are strange, but that sure sounds like a Bizogot future tense, doesn't it?"

"It did to me," Hamnet said. "Why don't you ask her?"

"I've tried. It didn't help." Ulric sighed and tried again.

"Past? Now? Later? All the same." That was what Hamnet thought Marcovefa said. He looked a question at Ulric.

The adventurer sighed. "I think she's saying there's no difference between one time and another. Crazy little bird, isn't she?"

He spoke in Raumsdalian, which the shaman couldn't possibly understand. Nothing in his face or his tone of voice gave him away. But Marcovefa let out an indignant sniff and slapped his arm the way a mother would slap a child who'd done something rude and silly. She might not have followed the words, but she knew—she *knew*—he hadn't treated her with the respect she deserved.

"Maybe there's more to it than you think," Count Hamnet said slowly.

"Maybe." Ulric didn't sound as if he believed it, but now he didn't sound as if he dared disbelieve it, either. That left him sounding . . . confused. He went on speaking Raumsdalian: "Maybe up here there's so little going on that *now* and *then* can blend like salt and garlic in a stew. Nothing up here would surprise me very much any more. I mean, what is time but a way to keep everything from happening at once?"

Hamnet Thyssen half—more than half—expected Marcovefa to slap him again for being flip. He wouldn't have been surprised if she was crazy, at least by the standards that prevailed at the bottom of the Glacier. This was too strange and too harsh and too different a world to expect standards to stay the same. But instead of being insulted, the shaman nodded vigorously. She let out what was, to Hamnet, mostly a stream of gibberish.

By the bemused look on Ulric's face, he understood a good deal more of it, but was none too happy that he did. "What was that all about?" Hamnet asked when Marcovefa finally fell silent.

"She says I get it after all," Ulric replied, shaking his head. "She says she thought I was as vacant as a vole—which is a demon of a phrase, even in her weird dialect—till I made my snide joke. But everything I said was true, she told me. She feels it in her heart."

Marcovefa laid a hand over her left breast. She might not understand Raumsdalian in any ordinary sense of the world, but she could sense truth and falsehood . . . or she thought she could, anyhow. By what Hamnet was seeing here, he would have had a hard time telling her she was wrong.

Then she said something else, something that sounded very self-assured. Ulric's jaw dropped. "What *now*?" Hamnet asked. "Do I really want to know?"

"Well, I'm damned if I want to be the only one who does," Ulric answered. "She says she's going with us, to the edge of the Glacier and over it."

"But what about her clan?" Hamnet said. "Won't they end up a feast for some of the others up here if she leaves them? How can she do it?"

The adventurer spoke to her. She pointed to a young man scraping flesh from the inside of a pika hide with a sharpened bit of flint. "That's Dragolen," Ulric said. "He's well on his way to turning into a shaman himself. By what she can tell, nothing too horrendous happens—not *will happen,* but *happens*—to the clan till he finishes learning the things he needs to know."

"Tell her we don't eat man's flesh down below," Hamnet said. "Maybe that will make her want to stay here."

But Marcovefa only shrugged at the news. Like a lot of shamans and wizards, she could be imperious when she chose. "I go," she said, and even Hamnet couldn't misunderstand her—however much he might have wanted to.

No matter what Marcovefa thought of Dragolen as an up-and-coming shaman, Hamnet Thyssen wondered whether the clan chief—he didn't have enough people under him to count as a jarl in the Raumsdalian's mind— would be eager to let her leave. But he said not a word against her. He was probably so glad to get rid of the dangerous strangers that losing his shaman seemed small by comparison.

Hamnet asked both Liv and Audun Gilli if they foretold trouble by bringing Marcovefa along. Liv simply shook her head. On matters that didn't touch their private lives, she and Hamnet still worked well together. On those that did . . . they didn't.

"We're already in so much trouble, what's a little more?" Audun said. Having no good answer for that, Hamnet walked away shaking his head.

Ulric dickered with the clan chief over how many hares and pikas and voles the Bizogots and Raumsdalians would take with them when they left. When he didn't like the deal the chief proposed, he sweetened it by offering to leave a couple of swords behind with the men of the Glacier. That made the chief cheer up.

"Swords won't help them catch rabbits," Audun said, a puzzled note in his voice.

Ulric eyed him with something approaching pity. "Rabbits aren't the only meat they hunt, and swords *will* help them with the other."

"The other . . . ? Oh!" Light—a revolted light—shone in the wizard's eyes.

Marcovefa led them off the mountainside and down onto the surface of the Glacier. Count Hamnet shook his head in wonder. He'd never dreamt he would need to descend to travel over the Glacier. He'd never dreamt of a lot of the things that happened to him till they did. A good many of them, he would have been happier to avoid. That was afterwards, though, and afterwards was always too late.

Here and there, puddles dotted the top of the Glacier. Marcovefa eyed them dubiously. She said something. When Hamnet looked a question at Ulric, the adventurer translated: "In her grandfather's grandfather's days, this didn't happen, she says."

"Is she sure she's not talking about her grandchildren's days?" Hamnet asked. "She's the one who can't keep time straight."

Before Ulric could render that into Marcovefa's dialect, she sent Hamnet a severe look, as if he were a child acting snippy around grownups. That shouldn't have been easy to bring off; he thought he was older than she was. But when she wanted to, she could assume as many years and as much dignity as she pleased. It was an unusual gift, and not a small one, either.

She led the Bizogots and Raumsdalians south and west with a fine display of confidence. Count Hamnet wondered what lay behind it. He wondered if anything did. Maybe she was willing to sacrifice herself to strand them on the Glacier and rid her clan of the threat they posed. But when that thought bubbled up from the dark places at the bottom of his mind, he shook his head. He could imagine it, but he couldn't believe it. She acted like someone who knew what she was doing and where she was going.

Of course, a madwoman would act that way, too. Hamnet was much less certain Marcovefa and the real world touched each other very much.

Why are you following her, then? he asked himself. But the answer to that was all too plain: even if she was leading them to disaster, what did they have to lose? Staying up here was only disaster of a different kind. The miserable cannibal life the men of the Glacier led showed that all too clearly.

He skirted another puddle atop the Glacier. "What do you suppose would happen if it all melted?" he asked.

"Never happen," Trasamund said. "Not while we still live."

Those two things weren't the same, though the jarl didn't seem to understand it. Even if he and Hamnet Thyssen lived to grow long white beards—which seemed most unlikely at the moment—they would die in an eyeblink of time as far as the world went. Not so far long ago, as far as the world went, the Glacier had pushed down to not far north of Nidaros. The country around the present capital was much like the Bizogot steppe in those days. If the Glacier disappeared, this northern land might turn out not to be so useless, too.

But Trasamund wouldn't be here to see it. To him, nothing else mattered. Well, that made a certain amount of sense, or maybe more than a certain amount. But Hamnet tried to take a longer view.

Marcovefa said something. Ulric answered. She said something else. Ulric translated: " 'The day is coming,' she says, or maybe, 'The day is here.' "

"Not here yet, by God," Hamnet said. "Or what are we walking on?"

Again, Ulric turned that into words Marcovefa could understand. She gave back one word. "Illusion," Ulric said.

"Well, as long as it fools my feet, I'm not going to worry about it," Hamnet said.

The Bizogots caught a few voles in patches of greenery. Marcovefa had a bird net and a chant that seemed to lure birds into it. But there weren't many to lure. They steadily went through the meat they'd got from the shaman's clan. Count Hamnet began to wonder if they would have enough to get back to the crag at need. Before long, he stopped wondering: they wouldn't. Marcovefa led them towards the edge of the Glacier—the rim of the world, she called it—with perfect and sublime certitude.

When they got there, they could look down at a sea of curdled white clouds that hid the Bizogot country from the eye. Count Hamnet and Ulric stared at each other, both appalled, but neither, somehow, enormously surprised. Liv glanced over towards Marcovefa as if wondering what her fellow shaman would do now. Audun Gilli, by contrast, only shrugged, as if to say, *Well, this is interesting, isn't it?*

But Trasamund exploded like a tightly shut pot forgotten atop a fire. He didn't just curse Marcovefa—he screamed at her. He pulled his two-handed sword from the sheath he wore on his back and brandished it, bellowing, "We ought to carve steaks off you, you worthless, mangy trull!"

Marcovefa answered more calmly than Hamnet Thyssen thought he could have managed under such circumstances. She said something that set Ulric giggling helplessly. "What was that?" Hamnet asked.

"Something like, 'Why didn't your mother spank you when you were little?' " the adventurer answered.

Trasamund didn't ask for a translation. He kept on raving. When Count Hamnet thought he really might swing that sword, his feet went out from under him and he sat down, hard, on the Glacier. He was lucky the sword didn't skewer or slice him. Marcovefa looked the slightest bit smug—enough to convince Hamnet that the Bizogot's pratfall was no accident.

Even Trasamund seemed convinced after trying four times to stand and failing again and again. "Give over!" he told Marcovefa, holding up a hand in token of surrender. "I'll put the blade away. By God, I will!"

The shaman didn't speak the ordinary Bizogot tongue. What Trasamund said couldn't have meant much to her. But she seemed to grasp the essentials behind or under language. She knew what the jarl meant even if she didn't know what he said. With a nod whose somber dignity the Raumsdalian Emperor might have envied, she signaled that he was free from her spell. When he tried to get to his feet once more, he succeeded.

He shuddered. "She knows somewhat of shamanry, all right," he said to Hamnet Thyssen. "But why the demon didn't she know the Glacier here is just like the Glacier everywhere else except at that one big avalanche?"

"If I could tell you, I'd be on my way towards making a pretty fair shaman myself," Count Hamnet answered.

Liv shook her head. "I am a fair shaman, or I like to think I am," she said. "I have no idea why we're here." Then she turned to Audun Gilli and asked, "Do you?" Hamnet wished she hadn't, even if he understood why she had.

Audun started to shake his head, too, but hesitated. "Nooo," he said slowly, "not unless . . ." He did shake his head then, firmly and decisively. His voice firmed as he repeated, "No," and continued, "The whole idea is too ridiculous."

"And what about this mess isn't?" Ulric asked. "Come on—out with it."

But Audun wouldn't talk. All he said was, "If we know, we'll know without any doubt. And if we don't, we'll be too busy starving to worry about it."

"You so relieve my mind," Ulric said. Not even his sly mockery could pry any more words out of the Raumsdalian wizard. Marcovefa looked on with what Hamnet would have called innocent amusement if he hadn't already figured out that she was much less innocent than she seemed, and in a way that had nothing to do with her taste for cannibal feasts.

Arnora came over and linked her arm with Ulric's. "We may as well camp here," she said. "We're not going anywhere—that's for sure."

Marcovefa asked a question. Hamnet Thyssen would have bet it was, *What did she say?* The shaman didn't understand everything that went on around her. Words spoken without strong emotion behind them remained opaque. Ulric translated for her. She said something else. Ulric asked her a different question. She repeated herself—Hamnet could hear that—more emphatically.

"What now?" he asked Ulric.

"She says we all die before our time if we camp here," the adventurer replied.

Arnora tossed her shining head. "What does she know?"

"More than you do, sweetheart, when it comes to things up here," Ulric said. Arnora pulled her arm free and glared at him.

"I think maybe the woman from the men of the Glacier is right. Maybe." Audun Gilli always spoke the Bizogots' language slowly and clumsily. Now something new was in his voice. Only the way he looked at Marcovefa helped Hamnet Thyssen give it a name. Awe. Without a doubt, it was awe.

"Where do we camp if we don't camp here?" Trasamund asked, eyeing the westering sun. "Wherever it is, we'd better take care of it before too long. I know twilight lingers, but not forever."

Marcovefa led them away from the edge of the Glacier, back in the direction of the mountain refuge from which they'd come. She still had an imperious certainty that made anyone else doubt her at his peril.

"Why didn't she just tell us to stop where she wanted us to stop?" Arnora grumbled. "Instead, she almost led us off the tallest cliff there is."

"I don't think she knew the cliff was still there," Ulric answered.

"You don't think she knew?" the Bizogot woman said shrilly. "And you followed her anyway?"

Ulric only shrugged. "Have you got a better idea?"

Arnora opened her mouth. Then she closed it again. Up here atop the Glacier, there were few good ideas to have. The best one, to Hamnet Thyssen's way of thinking, was not to get stuck here in the first place. But when the only other choice was staying where you were and getting slaughtered, trying to reach the top of the Glacier suddenly looked a lot better. It had to Hamnet not long before, and it must have to the ancestors of the men of the Glacier some time in the dim and vanished past.

Marcovefa stopped without warning in the middle of an icefield which looked no different from the rest of the Glacier that stretched as far as the eye could see. She spoke. As usual, Ulric translated: "This will do, she says."

"Do what?" Hamnet asked.

She looked at him even before Ulric turned the dour question into words she could understand. He thought she would be angry at him for presuming to talk back, but amusement glinted in her eyes. She said a few words. Ulric asked her something. She nodded. "Do to keep the Glacier under our feet," he reported. "That's what she says."

"Well, where else would it be?" Trasamund rumbled. "Up our—?" He didn't finish that, but went far enough to leave no doubt of his meaning.

Hamnet Thyssen waited for Marcovefa to get angry at him. Instead, the shaman started to laugh. When she spoke, so did Ulric. "She says you're welcome to put it there if that makes you happy." She added something else: "She'd like to watch if you try."

Trasamund turned red. "Never mind," he muttered. "I'll keep my mouth shut from now on." Hamnet didn't believe he would—or could. That he said he would was surprising enough.

They set stones on the Glacier and dried dung on the stones so they could make fires and cook their meat. Marcovefa carried cuts that did not come from a hare or vole. Now that Hamnet had got used to the smell of that flesh roasting, he decided it didn't quite smell like pork after all. It smelled better than pork, as if it were perfectly right for the nose, for the mouth, for the belly. He supposed it was—in a way. In every other way, though . . . He'd done a lot of things for which people could blacken his name. Better to walk off the edge of the Glacier than to earn the name of cannibal.

It didn't bother Marcovefa. Man's flesh was only food to her. Count Hamnet couldn't match her detachment, and didn't want to try.

Twilight lingered long even after the sun went down. Trasamund posted sentries. "Never can tell who saw the fires," he said. He looked to Marcovefa to see if she had anything to say about that. She didn't. She was getting ready to sleep. Lying on the Glacier was like lying on frozen rock. Hamnet Thyssen didn't care. When you were tired enough, frozen rock felt like a mattress stuffed with eiderdown.

Morning twilight was already turning the eastern sky gray when a Bizogot shook him awake for sentry duty. "Anything look funny?" he asked around a yawn.

"Everything up here looks funny," answered the Bizogot, whose name was Magnulf. "Nothing looks any worse than it did before, though."

"All right." Hamnet climbed to his feet. His back and shoulder and one knee creaked. Maybe frozen rock wasn't so wonderful to sleep on after all. The Bizogot pointed northeast to show Hamnet where he should go. Knee still aching, he trudged in that direction.

After taking his place out there, he looked back towards the camp. In happier times, in easier times, Liv would often come out to keep him company while he stood watch. Not now. She lay there sleeping. She might have done that anyway. Hamnet Thyssen knew as much. But he chose to resent it this morning.

In due course, fire struck the edge of the world in the northeast: the sun climbing over the horizon. For the moment, Hamnet could look at it without hurting his eyes. That wouldn't last long; the higher it climbed, the hotter it would seem. And the day would be warm, too. How long could the Glacier last if weather like this came every year?

It'll last longer than I do, by God, Hamnet Thyssen thought, and he turned away from the sun. His shadow stretched out before him across the glaciertop, many times taller than he was. It would shrink as the day advanced and then advance as the day shrank, and finally darkness would swallow it. *As the shadow goes, so the man.*

Come morning, his shadow would be reborn. Himself? He had much less hope about that.

Looking away from the sun meant looking in the direction from which he'd come. People there were starting to stir. Someone waved in his direction: Ulric. Even at a couple of bowshots' distance, the adventurer's sinuous grace made him stand out. Ulric gestured to him to come back in. With the sun in the sky, anyone could see trouble coming.

Ha! Count Hamnet thought. *If people could see trouble coming as easily as that, we'd all have less of it.*

Small plumes of smoke rose from dried dung on flat stones. The air above the fires shimmered with heat. The Bizogots and Raumsdalians cooked small animals. Marcovefa roasted the abominable meat she liked better.

"Now what?" Hamnet asked, carefully licking all the grease from his fingers.

Ulric's head swiveled as he surveyed the Glacier all around. "As far as I can tell, the plan is for us to sit here till we starve." He didn't sound like a man who was joking, but he did sound absurdly cheerful at the prospect.

"No." That wasn't Hamnet Thyssen; it was Audun Gilli. The wizard shook his head. "Oh, no."

"You know something." Count Hamnet sounded accusing, even to himself. "What is it?"

"*Something* is about what I know," Audun agreed. "*Something* is going to happen, and happen soon. What?" He spread his hands and shrugged. "Your guess is as good as mine, maybe better."

"Will it happen before we starve?" Hamnet asked. "That would be nice, because Ulric's right—we're going to."

"By God, we won't starve to death up here," the wizard said. "I don't know what will happen to us, but not that."

"You so relieve our minds," Ulric said.

"You notice Marcovefa isn't coming over here and slapping him silly— well, sillier," Hamnet said, which won him a wounded look from Audun Gilli. That worried him not at all. He went on, "Must mean she thinks he knows what he's talking about."

"Happy day," Ulric said. "Which of them is crazier, do you suppose?"

"Both of them," Count Hamnet answered. That confused the wizard, but Ulric nodded in perfect understanding. Marcovefa eyed Hamnet as if wondering whether to say anything. When she didn't, he was more relieved than he hoped he showed.

"What *are* we going to do today?" Trasamund demanded. "Sit around here freezing our arses off?"

"If you do much sitting around here, you *will* freeze your arse off," Count Hamnet said. "On the other hand, where do you propose to go?"

"Back to the edge of the Glacier?" But Trasamund didn't sound sure of himself—almost a first for the big, rambunctious Bizogot.

"Why?" Ulric asked. "What can you do there besides jump off? How long do you suppose you'd have to regret that before you went *splut*?"

He picked a particularly expressive noise to describe how Trasamund would sound when he hit. The jarl glared and muttered into his beard. Then he walked away shaking his head.

"Sometimes the worst thing you can do to somebody is tell him the truth," Count Hamnet remarked.

"No doubt," Ulric said. "And do you have any idea how many people get old and gray without ever once figuring that out?"

"Too many, or I miss my guess," Hamnet said.

Marcovefa seemed happy enough sitting around doing nothing. Once, halfway through the day, a raven flew up and landed on her shoulder. It sat there as if it belonged, preening and making soft croaking noises and peering around with disconcertingly clever beady black eyes. Marcovefa took its presence for granted. She scratched its head. Instead of pecking her with its formidable bill, it bent forward like a cat so her hand could better find its itches.

"A familiar?" Ulric wondered out loud.

"Not exactly, or I don't think so," Audun Gilli said. "Seems more like a friend."

The longer Count Hamnet watched, the more he thought Audun was right. Marcovefa croaked, too, as if she and the raven shared a language where she didn't share one with the Bizogots and Raumsdalians all around her. The big black bird seemed to understand what she was saying, and she also seemed to follow it. Hamnet told himself nothing the shaman could do surprised him much any more. He'd already told himself the same thing several times, and been wrong every one of them.

After a while, the raven flew off towards the edge of the Glacier. Ulric's eyes followed it. "Good bit of meat on a bird that size," he remarked. "Those cursed things have got fat off us on every battlefield since the beginning of time. We could start paying them back."

Even as he spoke, his gaze slid to Marcovefa. He might have known she would understand the essence of what he was saying. She came over to him and pulled his ear, exactly as if he were a naughty boy. Then she gave him a piece of her mind in her own language.

"She eats man's flesh, but she draws the line at raven." Audun Gilli shook his head.

"Maybe she does. She's sure making Ulric eat crow, though," Count Hamnet said, deadpan.

Audun started to nod. Then he caught himself and drew back from Count Hamnet as if the Raumsdalian noble had some rare, dangerous, and highly contagious disease. Chances were he did, too. At any rate, people often treated foolishness that way.

An hour or so later, the raven came back. No one tried to catch it or kill it. It perched on Marcovefa's shoulder again and croaked in her ear. One of the croaks sounded like *soon* to Hamnet Thyssen. He scratched his ear, wondering if he'd heard that or only imagined it. He knew ravens could be trained to speak, but he had trouble believing this one had been. He had even more trouble believing it had been trained to speak a language he understood.

Was he becoming like Marcovefa, then, and gaining the ability to grasp meaning even without knowing a language? He had an enormous amount of trouble believing that.

The shaman scratched the base of the raven's beak with a forefinger. That beak might have been able to bite the finger off. Instead, the raven nuzzled her like a lovesick pup. Getting it to do something like that—getting it to want to do something like that—probably wasn't magic in any ordinary sense of the word, but Hamnet had a hard time deciding what else to call it.

A warm breeze ruffled his beard and the raven's feathers. For the moment, maybe even for the season, the Breath of God, the cold, ravening wind from the Glacier, had failed. It would blow again when the year turned; Hamnet was sure of that. But for now, even here, the wind came up from the south.

Liv and Audun Gilli both stiffened at the same time, like two hunting dogs taking a scent. Liv stared at Marcovefa. Audun exclaimed, "She really did!"

Hamnet Thyssen felt the Glacier shudder under his feet. *Earthquake,* he thought. He was safer here than he would have been in Nidaros. In bad earthquakes, people died when heavy things fell on them. The only thing that could fall on him here was the sky.

Along with the shaking came a deep bass rumble from the south, a rumble and a crashing and a roar. When Hamnet looked that way, he didn't see anything. Maybe his wits were slow, because he didn't grasp what the noise might mean.

Clever as usual, Ulric did. His trouble was different: he tried hard not to believe it. "She couldn't have known an avalanche was coming . . . could she?" he said, his own doubt showing in the last two words.

Although the raven fluttered its wings when the shaking and rumbling started, it stayed on Marcovefa's shoulder. The shaman stroked the bird, calming it. Did she look pleased with herself? If she didn't, Hamnet lacked the words to describe the way she did look.

At last, the commotion subsided. Marcovefa said something in her language. Everyone else looked towards Ulric for a translation. Reluctantly, he gave one: "She says we can go down now."

"She knew. She *knew.*" Audun Gilli made it sound more like an accusation than praise. "Even back on the mountainside, she saw the avalanche coming."

"He's right," Liv said, not something Hamnet wanted to hear from her but not something he could disagree with, either. "She must have known."

"She's a shaman, not a sham, sure enough," Ulric said. "The only thing she didn't know was just when it would happen—and I don't think she cared."

Marcovefa said something else. Even Hamnet thought he understood it: when didn't matter. Maybe she was right, maybe she was wrong. Either way, she sounded very sure. She didn't wait to give Ulric a chance to translate. She just started walking south. Every line of her body made it plain that she didn't care whether the Bizogots and Raumsdalians went with her. No matter what they did, she would try to descend from the Glacier.

They did follow, of course. Something occurred to Count Hamnet as they tramped along over the Glacier. He caught up with Ulric, who was walking not far from Marcovefa, and said, "Ask her if she knows of the Golden Shrine."

"Well, I will, but what are the odds?" Ulric said.

Before he could ask the question in Marcovefa's dialect, she stopped dead and stared at Hamnet Thyssen. A flood of words burst from her. Ulric held up his hands, as if to dam the flow. He didn't have much luck. A moment later, he started to laugh. "What is it?" Hamnet asked.

"You impressed her—that's what," Ulric replied. "Up till now, she thought we were a bunch of godless savages. But if we know about the Golden Shrine, we can't be so bad after all."

"She understood me before you translated," Hamnet said slowly, and the adventurer nodded. Hamnet went on, "What does she know, then?"

Again, Marcovefa started talking without waiting to hear the question in her tongue. She pointed north, then south. Ulric said, "She knows it's somewhere not under the Glacier. It's a salve for the good and a snare for the wicked, she says. You get from it what you bring to it. It makes you even more what you are already. I'm not sure what that means. I'm not sure she's sure what she means, come to that."

Marcovefa let out an indignant sniff. "I think she is," Count Hamnet said. "Eyvind Torfinn talked about the place the same way, and he knows more about it than anybody." *Anybody except maybe a cannibal savage,* he thought. How strange was that? Stranger than anything else here atop the Glacier? Hamnet doubted it.

The avalanche they'd heard proved even bigger than the one they'd climbed to get here. Marcovefa and her raven both looked smug. The way down lay open—if the travelers could take it.

X

Hamnet Thyssen had thought climbing up tumbled and shattered blocks of ice was bad. And it was. How many times had he almost killed himself in the desperate scramble to escape the Rulers? Probably more than he realized, which said everything that needed saying all by itself. But descending made going up child's play by comparison.

If you slipped while you were climbing, someone below you had a chance to catch you and save you. If you slipped on the way down, you went down yourself, maybe all the way down, and you had a good chance of starting another avalanche when you did it.

"By God, I wish we had more rope," Trasamund said before they'd gone even a bowshot. "If we could tie all of ourselves together, a slip wouldn't be so bad."

"It might be worse," Count Hamnet said. "If one of us slipped, he might carry everybody he was roped to down with him."

The jarl grunted. He looked as if he wanted to tell Hamnet he was wrong. He didn't, though, because too plainly the Raumsdalian was right. Disaster waited under their feet at every step they took. They might have done better staying up on the Glacier . . . except that they would soon have begun to starve.

"That other avalanche had a chance to settle down before we tackled it." As usual, Ulric sounded most cheerful when the going was worst. "This one's still shifting and sorting itself out."

"You noticed that, too, did you?" Hamnet pointed down the steep slope.

Crashes and thuds farther down told of more shifting below. "This one's a long way from finished—but it can finish us any time it wants to."

"Don't give it ideas. It's bound to have enough of its own," Ulric said.

"I wish I could call you a liar," Hamnet said. The Bizogots and Raumsdalians had separated into little groups of three and four and five, each group staying as far from the others as it could. If one set of climbers did touch off another avalanche, with luck it wouldn't sweep them all to their doom. With luck.

Marcovefa descended without a care in the world. Sometimes the raven stayed on her shoulder. Sometimes it flew off and soared and spun and swooped through the air. Hamnet Thyssen had seldom had the chance to watch a bird flying from above it. He didn't have much of a chance now; he was too busy watching where he put his hands and feet. Killing himself for the sake of an unusual sight struck him as excessive devotion.

Maybe Marcovefa thought she could stop any trouble with a quick spell. Maybe she was right . . . and maybe she wasn't. Count Hamnet noticed that Liv and Audun Gilli both seemed much less carefree. Audun, probably the clumsiest person in the band, seemed scared out of his skin. Hamnet had a hard time blaming him—for that, anyway.

Not only were they above the raven—at least from time to time—they were also above a bank of clouds that bumped up against the side of the Glacier. And then they weren't above the clouds any more, but in them. Count Hamnet discovered what mountain dwellers already knew: clouds up close were nothing but fog. Not being able to see more than a few feet as he struggled down towards the ground only made the descent even more alarming than it would have been otherwise.

He was on the point of complaining about that when Trasamund beat him to it. Ulric loaded his voice with treacle as he answered, "You poor dear. Maybe we should go back up to the top and try again when the weather gets nicer."

The Bizogot's reply should have melted the Glacier all by itself. Somehow, it didn't. It didn't scorch Ulric, either; the adventurer only laughed, which infuriated Trasamund all over again. Hamnet Thyssen went right on scrambling down the steep slope of the avalanche, glad he hadn't offered himself as a target for Ulric's merciless wit.

Little by little, what had been a layer of clouds below and then a layer of fog all around became a layer of clouds above. That seemed normal to Hamnet, as it doubtless did to the other Raumsdalians and the Bizogots.

Marcovefa said something that sounded intrigued as she looked up. Ulric started to laugh again, this time, Hamnet judged, without sarcasm.

"Well?" Hamnet asked.

"She says, 'There's something you don't see every day,' " Ulric said. "She's more used to the tops of clouds than to their bottoms."

Marcovefa looked down then. That also seemed to interest her. There, at least, Hamnet Thyssen could understand why. She was closer to the ground than any men of the Glacier had come for who could say how many hundred years. She spoke again.

This time, Ulric translated without waiting for anyone to ask him: "She says even the air feels heavy and thick down here."

"Tell her we think there isn't enough of it up where she lives," Hamnet replied.

Ulric did. The comment only made the shaman laugh and shake her head. "Oh, no, she says," Ulric reported. "It's just right up there. . . . All what you're used to, I suppose."

"No doubt," Count Hamnet said. "Of course, she's also used to eating neighbors she doesn't get along with." He paused. "Considering a few of the people I know in Nidaros, that does have something to recommend it. But still . . ."

"I know some of the people in Nidaros you wouldn't mind seeing dead," Ulric said. "Anybody who ate 'em would sick 'em up again afterwards."

"It could be," Hamnet said. "I—"

He broke off. Someone in the group of climbers farthest to his right let out a wild scream of terror. "Watch out!" Two Bizogots and Audun Gilli shouted the same thing at the same time. It was much too late and altogether useless. That whole group—except for Arnora, who was trailing—plunged down the still-steep side of the ice mountain in an avalanche they'd touched off themselves. Hamnet Thyssen never knew what went wrong. A misplaced hand? A foot that came down where it shouldn't have? Odds were whichever Bizogot made the mistake didn't have long to regret it, either. How long could you last in a tumble of snow and icy boulders? If you were lucky, you would die fast, before you got buried alive.

Ulric slid half a step towards Arnora, then checked himself. Any move he made, or any she made, might start things sliding again. One of the Bizogots in the next group over did have some rope. He threw it to her. White-faced and panting with terror, she tied it around her waist. Then, moving as if walking on eggs, she sidled towards the man who'd thrown it. He hauled in the rope, and eventually hauled in Arnora with it.

She threw her arms around him and kissed him when she was safe—or as safe as she could be on the side of the Glacier. Count Hamnet glanced over to Ulric to see how he liked that. "I'd kiss him myself, but he's bound to like it better from Arnora," Ulric said. Hamnet only nodded. Either Ulric really worried less about such things than he did or hid his worries better. Whichever it was, the adventurer had the advantage there.

"We knew this was dangerous before we started down," Trasamund said. "Now we truly *know* it is. Let's remember till we—"

"Hit bottom?" Ulric suggested.

"Yes," Trasamund said, and then, "No, curse it. Will you be serious for once in your life?"

"Oh, I'm serious enough," the adventurer said. "Hard to stay jolly for long when you watch people die on a slope only maniacs would try."

"Even sane, sensible people will try anything if they see their other choices are worse," Count Hamnet said.

Ulric didn't try to argue, from which Hamnet concluded that he didn't think he could. They'd all decided taking the chance of dying was better than turning into men of the Glacier. Hamnet wondered whether the men the avalanche had buried would still agree. He wouldn't have the chance to ask them, not in this world he wouldn't.

The rest of the climbers gingerly went around the new avalanche as they kept descending. They couldn't go too far around, not unless they got away from the slope of the bigger avalanche they were using for their route down. The rest of the Glacier wasn't dangerously steep—it was impossibly steep.

Hamnet Thyssen looked up towards the top of the avalanche, back the way he'd come. The clouds that had been below him now hid most of the route. It might have been just as well; seeing what he'd done would only have convinced him he'd been out of his mind to try this.

Or had he? What other choice was there? If he and his comrades hadn't climbed the Glacier, the Rulers would have killed them. If they hadn't come down, they would have turned into cannibals. This was bad. Those, as he'd told Ulric, were worse.

"We've been beyond the Glacier and on top of it," he said. "Not many can claim that."

"You, me, Ulric, Audun, Liv," Trasamund said. "Not many fools in the world."

"You're welcome to speak for yourself, Your Ferocity, but I'll thank you to include me out," Ulric said.

"Yes, tell me you're not a fool. Tell me and make me believe it," the Bizogot jarl said. Ulric maintained a dignified silence. Trasamund made a noise somewhere between a grunt and a snort. "Didn't think you could."

Marcovefa pointed down towards the ground—specifically, towards a herd of musk oxen in the middle distance. She said something that made Ulric snort, too—a snort that came close to a giggle. "Well?" Hamnet asked.

"She says we're either closer to the ground than she thought or those are the biggest voles she's ever seen," the adventurer reported.

After a moment, Count Hamnet started to laugh, too. There he was, clinging like a fly to the side of the Glacier, unable to fly away if by some mischance he slipped, and he laughed hard enough to have trouble holding on. "What will she think when she sees mammoths?" he said when he could finally speak again.

"Probably that the pikas should have gone to the dentist before they grew up," Ulric answered. That set them both laughing again, and got Trasamund and Audun Gilli started.

"I think we're losing our minds." Audun didn't sound especially dismayed.

Trasamund shook his head. "We lost them a long time ago. We wouldn't have gone up there if we hadn't."

Marcovefa asked a question. Ulric answered. By the way he kept going back and forth, he was having a hard time getting her to believe him. She kept screwing up her face and making derisive gestures. At last, he said something that turned her thoughtful. "She doesn't want to believe the musk oxen are as big as I say," Ulric said. "I reminded her of the chunks of horseflesh we had when we got to her mountain. Beasts really do grow bigger down below the Glacier."

The raven croaked in Marcovefa's ear. She answered it as seriously as she'd replied to Ulric. It croaked again. She shrugged and nodded.

"She'd sooner believe the bird than you," Hamnet Thyssen said.

"Proves she knows them both," Trasamund put in.

"I laugh. Ha. Ha, ha. Ha, ha, ha," Ulric said.

Hamnet pointed to the ground in front of the musk oxen. "We really are getting close," he said.

"Pay attention to where you are, not to where you want to be," Trasamund said. "We're still plenty high enough for the Glacier to kill us if it sees a chance."

He spoke of it as if it were alive and malevolent. After two long climbs, one up, one down, and a little while atop its frozen immensity, Hamnet would have been hard pressed to tell him he was crazy. And he gave good advice. A careless mistake now could still be the last one somebody ever made.

They all talked one another down. Hamnet let out a sigh of commingled exhaustion and relief when his boots squelched in mud made soft and slimy by meltwater. Trasamund knelt down to kiss the dirt. That should have been laughable. Somehow, it wasn't.

"There is a world below the Glacier. Who would have believed it?" Marcovefa said, Ulric translating.

"In one way, it's no different from the world you just left," Count Hamnet said. After Ulric did the honors, Marcovefa made a questioning noise. Hamnet explained: "Plenty of enemies will want to kill you here, too."

As THE SUN SET, the Glacier's shadows stretched farther and farther and darker and darker across the Bizogot plain. The travelers had moved a couple of miles south from the Glacier, not least because they didn't want to risk another avalanche thundering down on their heads. Marcovefa marveled at everything she saw: the swarms of birds, the variety of voles and mice and lemmings in the undergrowth, and the sheer scope and exuberance of the undergrowth itself.

"This land is so rich," she said through Ulric. "So wide, so many plants, and even the air makes me think I've chewed magic mushrooms."

"So much more air to breathe down here, it's probably making her drunk," Hamnet Thyssen said, again remembering the thin stuff atop the Glacier. "I hope it doesn't make her sick."

"Nothing we can do about it if it does—short of sending her off to the mountains, I suppose," Ulric said.

Marcovefa almost stepped in a mammoth turd. When she realized what it was, she stared down at it in disbelief, then yammered in her own language. Whatever she said, it set Ulric laughing. "Well?" Trasamund said. "Tell all of us."

"She wants to know if a mountain shit here, or maybe the Glacier," Ulric told him. Marcovefa added something else. "She says no animal could be big enough to leave a turd like that."

"She may say it, but that doesn't make it so," the jarl said. "Now maybe she'll believe we weren't pulling her leg when we told her what the beasts down here were like. She'd better, or she'll have a thin time of it when she meets her first lion or dire wolf."

Ulric translated that for the shaman from the men of the Glacier. Count Hamnet found he could make out more words now than he'd been able to when he first met that folk. It was a dialect of the Bizogot tongue, sure enough, but a strange one, and a very old-fashioned one as well.

"You just told her a dire wolf was a fox that weighs as much as a man, didn't you?" he asked the adventurer.

"That's right," Ulric said. "Do you want to take over some of the interpreting? I wouldn't miss it, by God."

"I don't think I could," Hamnet said. "I can figure out what some of the words are when I hear other people say them, but I don't know how to say them myself."

"Does make it harder," Ulric allowed. "Marcovefa's got to learn the ordinary Bizogot language. Trouble is, till we made it up to the top of the Glacier she didn't imagine there were any other languages. I don't know if she'll have an easy time finding new words for things."

Marcovefa looked down at the mammoth turd again. She quickly lost Count Hamnet when she spoke again; he had an easier time following Ulric's efforts to speak her tongue. With a small sigh, Ulric did the honors: "She says we can have big fires whenever we want if we've got turds like that to burn."

"I wonder what she'd think if she saw rounds of hickory burning in a fireplace down in Nidaros," Hamnet said. "Anyone who imagines the Bizogot country is rich—"

"Has been living on a mountaintop above the Glacier her whole life long," Ulric finished for him.

That wasn't what Hamnet would have said, which made it no less true. "Maybe you ought to tell her about horses and riding deer and riding mammoths," he remarked. "We may have to travel fast now that we're down here again."

"Why? Just because we'll be one jump ahead of the Rulers again—one jump ahead if we're lucky?" Ulric had a knack for knowing where the worst troubles lay, all right. He went on, "Well, I'll try. She's not going to understand about riding, you know, not till she sees somebody doing it."

He spoke slowly to Marcovefa. He had to keep backing up and starting over. At last, he had Hamnet get down on hands and knees and straddled him to show what riding meant. Marcovefa went into gales of giggles; it might have been the funniest thing she'd ever seen. "Why didn't you let me do the riding?" Hamnet asked irritably.

"Because I didn't want to look like an idiot?" Ulric suggested, and Hamnet tried to buck him off. Marcovefa laughed harder than ever. Unfazed and unthrown, Ulric went on, "Besides, you're bigger than I am, even if you make a fractious horse. I wanted to show her people ride bigger brutes."

"Thank you so much," Hamnet ground out. "Now that you've shown her, get the demon off me."

Ulric did, which was lucky for him. Count Hamnet's next move would have been to stand. Ulric couldn't very well have ridden him then, any more than he could have sat in someone's lap after the former lapholder rose.

"Well?" Hamnet said, an ominous rumble in his voice. "Does she understand what riding's all about now?"

After more back-and-forth between Ulric and Marcovefa, the adventurer nodded. "She understands it, all right," he said. "She isn't sure she believes it. She isn't sure it's any good. But now she knows what the word means, and she didn't before."

Hamnet Thyssen had to think about that for a little while. He'd made cracks about how impoverished the men of the Glacier were. Now he saw he'd barely begun to understand that. Even their language was a poor, starveling thing. So many things they couldn't do . . . and if you couldn't do something, you didn't need words to talk about it. So the words had fallen out of their vocabulary, and taken the ideas with them.

He looked back towards the Glacier, and then up towards the top. Both the layer of clouds through which he'd descended and gathering darkness kept him from seeing all the way up. But he didn't really need to. He knew where he'd been and what he'd done. And if the rest of the world didn't want to believe him, that was the world's lookout, not his.

Then he looked south. "I suppose we ought to be glad the Rulers weren't waiting for us when we got to the ground again," he said.

"And I suppose you're right," Ulric said. "Don't lose any sleep over it, though. They aren't likely to leave us alone very long."

"No, I suppose not," Hamnet said.

Nothing could have made him lose sleep that night. Slightly muddy ground made a better mattress than ice or bare rock. But he suspected he could have lain down on a porcupine the size of a glyptodont and still started snoring two heartbeats after he closed his eyes.

The sun had to climb up over the Glacier before morning came to the land by its base. That won him more sleep than he would have had a little farther south. He woke grabbing his sword hilt when Trasamund shook him. "We need food," the Bizogot said. "We need to find out whose land this is, too, and turn them against the Rulers if they aren't already."

"Are we still on the White Foxes' grazing grounds?" Hamnet asked. "Or have we come farther west than that? Which clan lies west of theirs?"

"West of the White Foxes are the Snowshoe Hares," Trasamund answered. He knew, and had to know, the Bizogot plain the way a native of Nidaros knew the capital's streets. "They chase the Foxes more often than the Foxes chase them."

"For all we know, the Rulers are here ahead of us," Liv said. "Everything that's held true on the steppe for generations is scrambled now. Even if we beat the Rulers, sorting things out afterwards will take years."

"We'll spill a lot of blood doing it, too." Trasamund sounded matter-of-fact about that, not dismayed the way a Raumsdalian would have. "But at least that will come by our own choosing, not on account of these God-cursed invaders."

"Not that the people who get maimed and killed will care," Ulric said.

"Of course they'll care," Trasamund insisted. "In a fight, doesn't who wounds you matter?"

"I'd rather not let anybody wound me, if it's all the same to you," Ulric said.

Hamnet Thyssen's eyes slid towards Liv. He'd given her the power to wound him. He'd done the same with Gudrid all those years before, only to discover he'd made a mistake. That kept him from doing it again . . . till he did. He couldn't prove Liv would make him sorry, too. No, he couldn't prove it—but he worried about it.

She could have reassured him. She could have . . . and she hadn't. He feared she was as out of sorts with him as he was with her. That wouldn't do anybody any good. It was, in fact, a recipe for disaster. Sitting down and talking with her might help—if they ever found a moment to sit down together, and if he could figure out what to say if they did. They hadn't yet, and he hadn't yet, either, and the silence between them was starting to fester.

And Trasamund got to his feet, saying, "We have to find a herd, and we have to find the folk in charge of it. We need food, and we need mounts, and

we need to get back into the fight against the invaders. Come on. Let's get
going."

As Count Hamnet wearily rose, too, and started trudging across the Bizogot plain, he almost hated the jarl. The nobleman needed other things,
too, and Trasamund wasn't giving him a chance even to figure out how to
find them. The things he needed were much less important in the grand
scheme. He knew as much. Knowing was scant consolation, if any at all, because what he needed was no less important to him.

THEY WERE ON the Snowshoe Hares' grazing grounds. They found out
when two horsemen pulled away from a herd of musk oxen and rode up
to look them over. Marcovefa stared at them. Then she stared at Ulric and
Hamnet Thyssen. And then she started to laugh. She said something.

Hamnet thought he understood it. When Ulric translated, he proved
right: "So you weren't making it up after all." Ulric said something in reply,
something on the order of, *Did you really think we were?* And Marcovefa answered, "Well, you never know. Who would have thought beasts could
truly grow so big?" Again, Hamnet followed her well enough to get meaning from her words before Ulric turned them into the ordinary Bizogot
speech.

"Who are you ragamuffins?" one of the Snowshoe Hares shouted. "What
the demon are you doing on our land?"

"We escaped the Rulers," Trasamund answered. "We had to climb up
onto the Glacier and then come down again, so we did that."

The Snowshoe Hare laughed in his face. "By God, I've heard some liars
in my time, but never one who came close to you."

Marcovefa stepped forward to get a better look at him. She said something in her language. "She says you're a noisy fool even if you can ride a
horse," Ulric translated, helpfully adding, "She's never seen anybody ride
before, so that impresses her more than it does us."

"What do you mean, she's never seen anybody ride a horse before?" the
Snowshoe Hare demanded.

"I usually mean what I say. You should try it. It works wonders," Ulric
said. "And she's never seen anybody ride a horse because the biggest animals up on top of the Glacier—except for people—are foxes."

"More of those lies!" the Bizogot from the Snowshoe Hares jeered.

Marcovefa spoke again. Hamnet Thyssen was afraid he understood what
she said. Ulric's translation confirmed it: "She says she's eaten better men

than you, and she doesn't mean it any way you'd enjoy. Believe me, she doesn't."

The expressions on the faces of the other Raumsdalians and the Bizogots with them told both riders from the Snowshoe Hares exactly how Marcovefa did mean it. As soon as they understood, they looked revolted, too. "Why don't you kill her, then, if she does things like that?" asked the one who'd done the talking.

"Because she's a shaman, for one thing," Ulric answered. "Because two-legged meat is a good bit of what they've got to eat up there, for another. It's a hardscrabble life on top of the Glacier, believe you me it is."

"Maybe." The way the Snowshoe Hare said it made it sound like an enormous concession. In his mind, it probably was.

"Now will you answer what I asked you?" Trasamund demanded. "Are you still free of the Rulers? Have the White Foxes gone down before them yet?"

That made the two horsemen put their heads together. When they separated, neither one looked happy. "*Something's* happened to the White Foxes, anyway," admitted the one who liked to hear himself.

"We thought it was a feud inside the clan," the other one said, proving he wasn't mute after all.

"It's worse than that, by God." Trasamund gave his own name, continuing, "You may have heard of me. I am the jarl of the Three Tusk clan—and what's left of the free Three Tusk clan stands here in front of you. The Rulers are that bad."

"Well, they haven't troubled us," the talkier Snowshoe Hare said. The other one nodded.

"They're probably heading south instead," Hamnet Thyssen said.

"Toward the Empire," Audun Gilli added.

How much would that matter to the Snowshoe Hares? Not much, not unless Count Hamnet missed his guess. The Raumsdalian Empire seemed barely real to most Bizogots up here by the Glacier, just as their world was strange and alien to the folk who dwelt below the tree line, and especially to those who lived south of the great forests.

"Let us talk to your jarl," Trasamund said. "Feed us, if you will—we're not your foes. If you don't help us, you help the God-cursed Rulers."

Hamnet Thyssen hoped he didn't ask the other Bizogot for horses for all his comrades. The Snowshoe Hares were unlikely to have enough to give them to him. They were less likely to want to do it even if they did have horses to spare.

But Trasamund must have made the same mental calculation himself. Instead of barking out more demands, he stood there waiting with as much calm dignity as he could muster, doing his best to seem like a man who'd asked for no more than he was entitled to.

Calm and dignity were in short supply among the Bizogots, and so all the more impressive when they did get used. The two Snowshoe Hares put their heads together again. Then the mouthier one said, "Yes, come with us. We'll feed you, and we'll take you to Euric, and he'll decide what to do next. I'm Buccelin; this is my cousin, Gunthar."

One by one, the Bizogots and Raumsdalians with Trasamund named themselves. Marcovefa came last—or Count Hamnet thought she would, anyhow. But after she told Buccelin and Gunthar her name, the raven on her shoulder croaked out a few syllables, too. Was that a coincidence, or was it also naming itself? Hamnet Thyssen wasn't sure. By the way Buccelin and Gunthar muttered, they weren't, either.

Marcovefa? She smiled and scratched the big black bird's formidable beak. The raven couldn't very well smile back, but Hamnet got the feeling that was what it was doing.

The Snowshoe Hares led the travelers who'd come down from the Glacier off towards the southwest. They traveled at what was a slow walk for their horses, so the men and women on foot wouldn't fall behind. Marcovefa watched them intently. After a couple of miles, she spoke up.

"She says she'd like to try to ride for a little while—she's never done it before," Ulric said.

Plainly, the mounted Bizogots wanted to say no. Just as plainly, they didn't have the nerve. Their eyes kept going from her face to the raven and back again. Gunthar reluctantly reined in and dismounted. He showed Marcovefa how to set her left foot in the stirrup and swing up over and onto the horse's back.

She managed more smoothly than Hamnet would have expected. When she was in the saddle, she smiled again. "She says she feels so tall!" Ulric said. "She says she can see as far as the raven can."

Gunthar laughed. "Is she witstruck?"

"Not the way you mean," Hamnet answered. "Everything down here is new to her. They haven't got much, there up on top of the Glacier."

"You're still going on about that, are you?" the Snowshoe Hare said.

"It's the truth," Hamnet Thyssen said stonily. "If you don't believe it, try crossing Marcovefa and see what happens."

"No, thanks," Gunthar said. "I don't know where the demon she's from. For all I can say, she fell from the back side of the moon. But I know a shaman when I see one. We've had a witstruck shaman or two in our clan. It doesn't mean they can't use spells well enough."

Buccelin showed Marcovefa how to use the pressure of her legs to urge the horse forward, and how to guide it to the right and left with the reins. She proved an apt pupil. The first question she asked was, "How do you make these big beasts your slaves?"

"We train them, starting when they're small," Buccelin answered.

After Ulric translated, the shaman nodded. Then she asked, "And what do you do when they rebel?"

"She really doesn't know anything about this business, does she?" Buccelin remarked. With a shrug, he went on, "We train them some more. We punish them. If we still can't break them, we can always kill them and eat them."

"Ah," Marcovefa said. "You are men, sure enough."

"What's that supposed to mean?" the Bizogot demanded. The woman from atop the Glacier said not another word. After a few more minutes, she dismounted, and did so with more grace than she'd used getting up on the horse. Buccelin mounted. Marcovefa sketched a salute. He gave back a brusque nod, then made a point of not riding anywhere near her.

In midafternoon, they approached a herd of musk oxen. Marcovefa pointed towards them. "So many large animals! Do you get up on top of these, too?"

"Maybe we could, but we don't." By then, Buccelin seemed resigned to playing guide. "We use them for their meat and hides and milk and wool and bones and horn." He chuckled. "Everything but the grunt."

Marcovefa thought that was funny, which proved she came from the back of beyond. A couple of other Snowshoe Hares rode out from the herd. "Who are these ragamuffins?" one of them shouted. "Where did they come from? Down off the Glacier?" He threw back his head and laughed at his own wit.

"Yes, I think they really did," Buccelin answered, which made the other Bizogot's jaw drop. "We're taking them to Euric. They know what the mess to the east is all about. This one"—he aimed a thumb at Trasamund—"used to be jarl of the Three Tusk clan."

"And I still am, by God." Pride rang in Trasamund's voice . . . for a little while. But he seemed to deflate as he continued, "It's just that the clan . . . has run into a few problems lately."

"A few problems have run over the clan, he means," Ulric whispered to Hamnet Thyssen, who nodded.

"We need to feed them," Buccelin said. "They seem hungry like they just came down off the Glacier, that's for sure. Any beast in bad shape?"

"We've got a cow that's limping," the other Bizogot said. "It's not slowing up the herd or anything, but we can kill it."

They did, and butchered it, and got a big fire of dried grass and dung going to cook the meat. Meanwhile, Trasamund and his clansmates and the Raumsdalians told what they knew of the invasion of the Rulers. They also told how they'd climbed the Glacier and what they'd found on top of it. None of them, though, mentioned some of Marcovefa's dining habits. Maybe that was coincidence. Maybe it was shared revulsion. Maybe it was some subtle spell from the shaman. Hamnet Thyssen couldn't be sure.

He was sure he stuffed himself like a Bizogot, gobbling down meat and fat and breaking big bones to reach the marrow. His hands and face got all greasy. He didn't care. He'd been empty a lot lately. Not having the fist of hunger pounding his stomach felt wonderful.

So did not needing to worry about standing watch. The Snowshoe Hares insisted that was their job. None of the travelers tried to argue with them. "We're out of danger for a little while, anyhow," Hamnet said.

"Danger from the outside, anyhow," Liv said.

"What's that supposed to mean?" he asked.

"I'm like you and Ulric—I usually say what I mean," she answered. "We have trouble—you and I have trouble—because you can't get over being jealous."

"Can you blame me?" Hamnet said.

But Liv nodded. "Yes, by God, I can blame you, because I haven't done anything to make you jealous."

"The demon you haven't." Hamnet didn't like arguing in a near-whisper to keep the others from hearing what was going on. He wanted to shout and raise a fuss and pound on things. He wondered why he didn't. It wasn't as if they didn't know about his squabbles with Liv. But he went on quietly: "If you haven't been clinging to Audun Gilli—"

"I haven't!" Liv's voice was also soft, but fire filled it all the same.

"You sure haven't clung to me lately. God only knows the last time we made love—*I* have trouble remembering," Hamnet said.

"I could say I'm not your toy. I could say we've had a few other things going on lately. I could even say you've been spending a lot of time around Marcovefa."

"Her?" Hamnet Thyssen clapped a hand to his forehead. "You *are* out of your mind! She's a barbarian, a savage."

"You mean you don't think the same thing about me?" Liv retorted. "And why am I out of my mind for doubting you when you're not out of yours for doubting me?"

"Because nothing's going on between me and the cannibal," Count Hamnet answered. She couldn't accuse him of thinking *that* about her. "I'm just trying to learn a little of her language and teach her some of yours."

"Well, what do you think I'm doing with Audun?"

"I don't know what you're doing with Audun. That's what worries me."

"You pick stupid things to worry about, especially when we have so many real ones that are bigger." Liv turned her back on him and rolled herself in her hide blanket. "Finding enough sleep is a real one. I had trouble up on top of the Glacier. I never thought I was getting enough air."

Count Hamnet felt the same way, but he would sooner have jumped from the top of the Glacier than admit it. He got under a hide, too, and closed his eyes. He didn't think he would sleep at all—too much anger seethed inside him—but exhaustion sneaked up from behind and clubbed him over the head.

When he woke in the middle of the short northern summer night, Liv was leaning over him. He wondered if he ought to grab for one of the knives on his belt. But all she did was shake her head and say, "You fool."

"What? For loving you too much?"

"Yes. For loving me *too much.* It makes you stupid, and you aren't stupid often enough to know how to do it right." Shaking her head, Liv slid under the hide with him. "Well?" she said: a one-word challenge, as if he didn't deserve what she was giving him. She probably thought he didn't.

He did the best he could. It seemed to be good enough. But even if it was, he knew it didn't really settle anything.

XI

W E'VE STAYED UP in the north too long," Hamnet Thyssen said as
the Bizogots and Raumsdalians and Marcovefa approached the
Snowshoe Hares' encampment.

"Well, God knows I'm not about to argue with you, but why do you say
so?" Ulric Skakki asked.

Count Hamnet pointed to the gaggle of tents made from mammoth and
musk-ox hides. "Because that's starting to look like civilization to me."

"Oh, my dear fellow! Are you well?" Ulric grabbed his arm and made as
if to take his pulse. Swearing and laughing at the same time, Hamnet
jerked free. Not a bit abashed, Ulric went on, "Much as I hate to admit it, I
feel the same way. And if that's not a judgment on both of us, what would
you call it?"

"It can't really be civilization, though, and I'll tell you why not," Hamnet
said. Ulric Skakki made an inquiring noise. Hamnet explained: "Euric may
want to listen to us, and Sigvat sure didn't."

"There is that," the adventurer agreed. "Sigvat turned out to be one of the
best arguments in favor of barbarian invasion anyone ever saw, didn't he?"

"I hadn't thought of it like that, but . . . yes," Hamnet said.

Fierce Bizogot dogs—some of them, by their looks, at least half dire
wolf—ran out of the encampment towards the newcomers, barking and
snarling. Buccelin and Gunthar shouted at them, which slowed them down
but didn't stop them. When Hamnet and Ulric and several of Trasamund's
Bizogots drew their swords, the dogs *did* stop—they knew that meant danger. Audun Gilli looked disappointed. He had a spell that made him seem

like what God would have been if God were Dog instead, one that terrified even the fiercest beasts. Now he wouldn't get to use it.

Marcovefa eyed the big dogs and their big teeth. She said something in her language. "What's that?" Hamnet asked Ulric.

"She says they really are foxes the size of men," Ulric answered. "One more thing we told her that she didn't believe."

"Tell her these are tamed, like the horses. Tell her the real dire wolves are bigger and fiercer," Hamnet said. Ulric Skakki did. Marcovefa raised an eyebrow. She said something else. "Well?" Count Hamnet asked.

"She says these will do," Ulric reported.

"I think so, too," Hamnet said. He frowned a moment later. He had the feeling you can sometimes get when someone is staring at you from behind—not quite sorcery, but the next thing to it. He also had the feeling he knew who it would be, and he was right. When he turned, not quite so casually as he would have liked, he caught Liv's eye on him. *It was nothing!* He didn't say it, for it was too obviously true to need saying. She eyed him even so.

Had he eyed her and Audun the same way for as little reason? He didn't shake his head, since Liv was still watching him, but that was how he felt. He hadn't been thinking anything untoward about Marcovefa. He knew that, down deep inside. He didn't know what Liv thought about Audun Gilli.

He also didn't know how unfair that comparison was. But he didn't know that he didn't know, and so it did him no good.

The dogs reluctantly moved back and to the sides as the travelers advanced. Children stared at them, too: particularly at Hamnet and Ulric and Audun, who, in spite of their clothes, plainly weren't Bizogots. Marcovefa stared at everything: the dogs, the children, the tents, the fires burning in front of them, the pots—trade goods up from the south—bubbling on top of those fires. The shaman sighed and spoke.

When Count Hamnet raised a questioning eyebrow, Ulric translated: "She's going on again about how lucky the Bizogots are. They have big animals to get big hides for their tents. They have big bones to use. They have these big fires because of all the dung. They have those—things—to cook in. She wonders why the men of the Glacier never thought of those."

Hamnet Thyssen tried to imagine the men of the Glacier making pottery. They almost certainly didn't have the clay they would need. They would have trouble making fires big enough and hot enough to bake the clay even if they did have it. "I didn't even see any baskets up there, let alone pots," he said. "I was surprised they could make rope—and what they do make is the strangest stuff I ever saw."

"That it is," Ulric said. "It does the job, though." It had done the job on the descent from the top of the Glacier. No one could ask more from it than that.

Buccelin held open a tent flap. "Here is the jarl. You will show him the respect he deserves."

"We will," Trasamund agreed, "if he shows us the respect we deserve."

Buccelin looked dismayed at that, but did not contradict it. Along with Trasamund, Hamnet and Ulric and Audun went into Euric's tent. So did Liv and Marcovefa. Liv stayed as far from Marcovefa as she could. Inside the tent, especially with so many people in it, that wasn't very far.

Butter-burning lamps and the open tent flap gave what light there was inside. The smell of the lamps warred with that of indifferently cured hides and with the smell of Euric himself. He was a big, burly man a few years younger than Hamnet. Nodding to Trasamund, he said, "Hello, Your Ferocity. I've heard a lot about you."

"I've heard a lot about you, too, Your Ferocity." Seeing that Euric did treat him as an equal made Trasamund preen.

"Tell me who your comrades are," the jarl of the Snowshoe Hares said. Trasamund named them one by one. When he got to Marcovefa, Euric's eyebrows leaped upwards. "Men from the south are one thing," the other Bizogot observed. "A woman from the north—a woman from the north and from on high—is a different story."

"We were there," Hamnet Thyssen said. "We had to go up there, or the Rulers would have killed us. They are another story, too, and one you need to worry about. You won't find the men of the Glacier coming down to eat your musk oxen."

"Or your clansmen," Ulric Skakki added, too quietly for Euric to hear.

"We've heard there is trouble with the Three Tusk clan, and lately with the White Foxes, too," Euric said.

"Worse than trouble," Trasamund said. "The only free folk left from the Three Tusk clan are with me here. The White Foxes have also been broken."

"So have the Red Dire Wolves, south of the Three Tusk clan's grazing grounds," Count Hamnet said. "The Rulers make bad enemies."

"Do they make good friends?" Euric asked, proving himself as practical and cynical a diplomat as any Raumsdalian ever born.

Hamnet Thyssen, Ulric Skakki, and Trasamund all looked at one another.

They'd come looking for an ally, not an opportunist. Ulric had the quickest tongue among them, and he gave an answer upon which Hamnet couldn't have hoped to improve: "Good luck, Your Ferocity."

Euric grunted. He was neither foolish nor innocent enough to imagine that Ulric meant the words literally. "How do you know?" he asked. "Did you try?"

"We spent a good bit of time talking with them when we went through the Gap last summer," Hamnet said. "As far as they're concerned, anyone who isn't of their folk is less than human. They call other people herds. It's hard to make friends with somebody who thinks he can drive you or shear you or slaughter you whenever he wants."

The Snowshoe Hares' jarl grunted again. "Well, you may be right," he said—hardly a ringing endorsement. "But then, you don't seem to have had much luck fighting them, either."

"They're not easy, by God!" Trasamund burst out. "They ride mammoths, and—"

"I'd heard that," Euric broke in. "I didn't know whether to believe it."

"It's true." All the Bizogots and Raumsdalians who'd met the Rulers spoke together in a mournful chorus.

Euric didn't seem to know whether to be appalled or amused. He finally just nodded. "All right. I believe it now."

"And their magic is stronger than anything we use," Liv added. "They can do things we can't, and they hurt us when they do. They've won battles because of it."

Marcovefa said something. Euric stared at her in surprise. Her speech sounded as if it might belong to the Bizogot language, but when you tried to understand it you couldn't. "What's that?" the jarl asked.

As usual, Ulric Skakki translated: "She says the Rulers' wizards aren't so strong as Liv makes them out to be. I should point out that she's never seen them, let alone tried to match her power against theirs."

"Fat lot she knows about it, then," Euric said scornfully.

Scorning Marcovefa was not a good idea. Had Euric asked him, Hamnet Thyssen would have said as much. The shaman from the mountain refuge atop the Glacier murmured more incomprehensibilities to herself.

Euric started to say something else. Instead, looking much more surprised than he had a moment earlier, he developed a sudden and apparently uncontrollable impulse to stand on his head. Then he whistled like a longspur. Then he yipped like a fox. Then he croaked like a raven. Marcovefa didn't know much about horses or musk oxen or mammoths, or the jarl probably would have impersonated them, too.

"Tell her that's enough," Hamnet whispered to Ulric. "We want him to respect us, not hate us."

"Right. I hope she listens to me." Ulric spoke to Marcovefa. She shook her head. He spoke again, this time with a definite pleading note in his voice. She sniffed, but at last she nodded and murmured to herself once more.

Euric collapsed in a heap. He needed a moment to sit up straight, and another moment to regain his aplomb. When he did, he proceeded to prove himself no fool, for he inclined his head to Marcovefa and said, "I cry pardon, wise woman."

She acknowledged him with another sniff, this one quite regal. Hamnet understood what she said next. Since Euric probably wouldn't, Ulric Skakki translated: "And well you might."

"What do you people want from the Snowshoe Hares?" Euric asked, this time with the air of someone who might think about giving it. Getting turned upside down—literally—might do that to a man.

Trasamund took advantage of the edge they'd gained: "Food to keep us going, and horses to let us move as fast as the Rulers."

"I can give you meat and suet and berries. We've had a good year with such things," Euric said. "But horses for so many?" He shook his head, even though he sent Marcovefa an apprehensive look while he did it. "I cry your pardon, too, Your Ferocity, but we haven't got so many beasts to spare." He might have—would have—said no before, but he said it much more politely now.

"How many can you give us?" Hamnet Thyssen asked. "If we can get some from you, maybe the next clan farther south will give us more."

"The Rock Ptarmigans?" Euric didn't quite laugh in his face, but he came close. "Well, maybe they will, since your shamans are so strong. But most of the time you can't pry a dried musk-ox turd out of them, let alone anything worth having."

In Raumsdalian, Ulric said, "I wonder what the Rock Ptarmigans have to say about the Snowshoe Hares."

"Nothing good, I'm sure," Euric said in the same language, "but they're only the Rock Ptarmigans, so what do they know?"

Hamnet Thyssen had rarely seen Ulric abashed, but he did now. "You caught me by surprise there, Your Ferocity," the adventurer admitted.

"That will teach you to talk behind somebody's back in front of his face," Euric said. Then he swung back towards Count Hamnet. "How many horses can we spare? A dozen, at the most." He looked horrified as soon as the words were out of his mouth. Plainly, he'd wanted to name some smaller number. Just as plainly, he hadn't been able to.

Marcovefa looked pleased and innocent at the same time. Did some small spell of hers make the Snowshoe Hares' jarl tell the truth regardless of what he wanted? Hamnet wouldn't have been surprised.

By Euric's sour expression, neither would he. On his own, he probably would have said four and haggled up to eight or so. "Well, I will not make myself out to be a liar," he said now. "You may take them. But when times come right again, you will pay the clan for the use you got of them."

"Agreed," Count Hamnet and Trasamund said in the same breath. And Marcovefa nodded. She might not speak the usual Bizogot language, but sometimes she understood it even so.

When Euric clasped hands with the Raumsdalian noble and his fellow jarl to seal the bargain, he also held out his big, square hand to the shaman from atop the Glacier. That struck Hamnet as only fair; without her, they wouldn't have had a bargain. They certainly wouldn't have had the one they had. More than a little relief in his voice, Euric said, "And now—we feast."

Bizogots could usually outeat Raumsdalians, not least because the mammoth-herders went hungry more often. When Marcovefa got a chance to show what she could do, her appetite amazed even the Bizogots. "I've seen a man twice her size who couldn't put away that much," Euric said admiringly.

"You may have hard times here, Your Ferocity, but I promise you that it's worse up on top of the Glacier," Count Hamnet said. "No horses or musk oxen or mammoths, just hares and voles and little animals halfway between called pikas. When Marcovefa's folk get hungry, they get *hungry*."

"I suppose so," the Snowshoe Hares' jarl said. He no longer seemed to doubt that the shaman did come from the top of the Glacier. Thoughtfully, he added, "I'm surprised they don't start eating each other when times get tough."

Hamnet Thyssen decided it might be just as well to pretend he didn't hear that. He counted himself lucky that Euric left it there.

Someone passed him a skin of smetyn. Next to wine or even beer, fermented milk was no great delight, but he was glad to drink something besides water. And, even if the Bizogots' brew was thin and sour, pouring down enough of it would let him forget his troubles for a while.

Trasamund started drinking as if he intended to forget about his troubles for a month. When Marcovefa tasted the smetyn, she looked puzzled. She asked a question of Ulric Skakki. "What does she say? Does she like it?" Euric asked.

"She asks, what is it you drink besides water?" Ulric said.

That set Trasamund laughing. He'd already downed enough to let almost anything set him laughing. "What do we drink besides water?" he echoed. "Anything we can, by God! Anything we can."

"Why?" Marcovefa asked. Hamnet Thyssen understood her on his own; the question was almost identical to the Bizogot phrase, *Because of what?*

"Tell her she'll find out after she drinks for a while." Trasamund laughed some more, this time in anticipation.

Ulric Skakki put that into Marcovefa's tongue. She nodded as if accepting a challenge and began to drink as seriously as she'd eaten. Before long, her eyes grew bright, her smile went slack, and she swayed even though she was sitting down.

"They don't have smetyn on top of the Glacier?" Euric asked, his voice dry.

"We didn't see any or hear of any," Hamnet answered. "Would you want to try to milk a rabbit or a vole?"

"Well, no," the jarl said with a wry smile.

Marcovefa said something else. "She wants to know why her head is spinning," Ulric said. "She says she hasn't eaten any shaman's mushrooms, but she's all dizzy anyway."

Liv looked interested when she heard that. "They have magic mushrooms up on that rock, do they?" she said. "I can't say I'm very surprised. Mushrooms grow almost everywhere."

"She's talked abut them before," Count Hamnet said.

"I didn't notice." Liv's voice was chilly.

"Tell her people down here use smetyn and things like it instead of mushrooms most of the time," Audun Gilli said.

Ulric Skakki did. Marcovefa spoke in return. "She says this isn't as good. She doesn't see all the colors she would with mushrooms, and she doesn't feel as if the sky were about to break." Hamnet didn't know what that meant; by Liv's nod, she evidently did. Marcovefa added something else. "She says this isn't *bad,* mind you—just not as good."

"In the morning, she'll feel like her head's about to break," Audun Gilli said. "And so will Trasamund."

"Yes, but Trasamund will know why," Hamnet Thyssen said. "For Marcovefa, it'll be a big surprise, and not one she likes very much."

"Everything that happens to Marcovefa down here is a surprise," Ulric Skakki said. "Some of the surprises, she'll like. Others? Her first hangover? Well, maybe not."

Some of the Snowshoe Hares began pairing off. That was another thing that happened at Bizogot feasts. Euric found women for Trasamund and the Bizogots who accompanied him, and one for Audun Gilli as well. They weren't all beauties, but Hamnet didn't think any of the Bizogots would have to close his eyes to lie down with one of them.

Then Euric surprised him. The jarl inclined his head to Marcovefa and said, "If you feel like it . . ."

Yes, the shaman from atop the Glacier sometimes understood what people meant without understanding what they said. She also surprised Count Hamnet—she smiled and nodded and, none too steadily, got to her feet and went back into Euric's tent with him.

"Well, well," Ulric said, a slightly bemused grin crossing his foxy face. "That ought to be interesting."

Arnora set a hand on his shoulder and shook him. "What about us?" she said with drunken intensity. "Don't you want to be intereshting—interesting—too?"

"My reputation would never be the same if I said no," the adventurer replied. "I aim to please, and God forbid I should fail in my aim." He rose, too, more smoothly than Marcovefa had done, and went off into the deepening twilight with his scar-faced lady friend.

That didn't quite leave Hamnet and Liv all alone, but not many people were close by, and none of them paid any attention to the Raumsdalian noble and the Bizogot shaman. "Well?" Liv said, an odd note of challenge in her voice. "Shall we?"

"I'm with Ulric," Hamnet replied. "I aim to please, too."

They went into one of the tents and slid under a mammoth-hide blanket. Bizogots lived in one another's pockets, especially during the long, hard northern winters, and needed less in the way of privacy than Raumsdalians did. They were better at looking the other way and pretending not to hear, too. By now, Hamnet had spent enough time among them to worry less about who might be watching and listening than he would have down in Nidaros.

All the same, he wasn't sure how well he would respond after everything he'd eaten and drunk. Making love with a full belly took more effort nowadays than it had when he was younger. And his quarrels with Liv didn't help, either.

But he succeeded. By the way she responded, he was better than good enough tonight. "You do still care," she murmured as they lay in each other's arms afterwards, their hearts slowing towards calm.

"I've always cared," he answered.

"Too much, maybe." Liv had said that before.

Hamnet Thyssen frowned. "How can a man care too much about a woman?"

"Easy enough," Liv said. "If you care so much, if you worry so much, that you drive her away instead of pulling her towards you, isn't that too much?"

"Are you saying I do that?" he asked.

"Sometimes," she replied, which was just polite enough to hold off a row. "But sometimes not, too." She caressed him. "*Not* is better."

"Better for you, maybe," he muttered.

He was lucky: she didn't hear him. She sprawled across him, warm and soft and, for the moment, happy. He found himself yawning. He didn't usually fall asleep right after making love, but he didn't usually eat and drink as much as he had beforehand, either. His eyes slid shut. He and Liv both started to snore about the same time.

LIV WOKE HAMNET the next morning by poking him in the ribs. His automatic response was to grab for his sword. Then he discovered he wasn't wearing it—or anything else. "What's going on?" he asked.

"I don't know," she answered. "But it's noisy out there, and it doesn't sound like good noise. We'd better find out."

Hamnet listened and found himself nodding. No, the racket out there didn't sound happy. If that wordless keening wasn't a woman in mourning, then it was a woman desperately ill. The groaning man also sounded none too healthy.

Despite the noise, some of the Bizogots in the tent stayed asleep. Others, like him and Liv, were waking up. Down in the Empire, Hamnet wouldn't have wanted to get out from under the blanket and dress with so little privacy. He especially wouldn't have wanted Liv to put herself on display like that. Bizogot customs were different, though. He didn't worry about it . . . much.

The bright sunlight hurt his eyes and made his head ache. Yes, he'd poured down too much smetyn the night before. But he wasn't nearly so bad off as Trasamund and Marcovefa. Their moans and groans had fooled Liv and him into thinking some real disaster had befallen the Snowshoe Hares.

Trasamund found a skin of water and poured it over his head. He came out blowing and snorting like a grampus. Then he found a skin of smetyn. That he applied internally. "I'll be better in a while," he said. "The hair of the dire wolf that bit me."

Marcovefa said something that sounded pitiful. Hamnet Thyssen looked around for Ulric Skakki and didn't see him. Maybe the adventurer figured out what the commotion was about. Or maybe he was just an uncommonly sound sleeper. Without Ulric around, Hamnet had to work out for himself what Marcovefa meant. He pointed to a skin of water and mimed pouring it over her. She looked at him through bloodshot eyes, then nodded.

She spluttered and coughed, then gasped out something Hamnet only half followed. He thought it meant, *This is supposed to make me feel better?*

"Here." Trasamund thrust a skin of smetyn at her and showed her she was supposed to drink from it.

She recoiled in horror, water dripping from her hair and her chin and the end of her nose. The way she held out her hands as she spoke told Hamnet what she had to mean—that she didn't want to get near smetyn ever again.

"Curse it, Thyssen, tell her it'll make her feel better, not worse," Trasamund said.

"I'll try," Count Hamnet told him. And he did, with the regular Bizogot speech and the few words of Marcovefa's dialect he thought he knew and a lot of gestures. She didn't want to believe him, for which he could hardly blame her. If it had poisoned her once, why wouldn't it poison her again?

He tried to show her that a little would help but a lot would make things worse. At last, warily, she drank. It wouldn't be a miracle cure; Hamnet knew that from somber experience. But chances were it would do her some good.

Euric looked more sympathetic than Count Hamnet had thought he would. He even kissed Marcovefa on the cheek. She must have pleased him when they went back into his tent together. What *would* she be like under a blanket? That was probably not the kind of question Liv wanted him asking himself.

Even if Marcovefa had pleased the jarl of the Snowshoe Hares, Euric did his best to wiggle out of the bargain he'd made with her the day before. He didn't refuse to turn over a dozen horses. He did do his best to give the refugees the dozen worst the clan owned. A couple of them were visibly on their last legs. None of the ones he wanted to turn over looked capable of anything more than a lazy canter.

A few swigs of smetyn had made Marcovefa more nearly reconciled to staying alive. Ulric took her aside and murmured in her ear. When she pointed at Euric, he blanched. She spoke. Ulric translated: "She says not to be niggardly. If you can't give with both hands, at least give with one."

"But—" Euric began. Then he swallowed whatever else he might have been about to say. Hamnet Thyssen had no trouble figuring out why. After what he and Marcovefa had done the night before, she was able to work the most intimate kind of magic against him. He didn't know she would, but he didn't know she wouldn't, either. Hamnet wouldn't have wanted to take that chance himself.

Then he glanced over to Liv—glanced more nervously than he wished he would have. Whatever Marcovefa could do to Euric, Liv could do to him . . . if she decided she wanted to. When you fell in love with, or even made love with, a shaman, you took chances you didn't with an ordinary woman.

Euric did give with one hand. He still passed on some of his clan's horrible screws, but he also gave away some horses that didn't look as if a strong breeze would blow them over. He sighed and moaned and mourned about every one of them, so much so that Hamnet wondered if he was laying it on too thick. But Hamnet knew more than a little about horses himself, and the replacements weren't bad animals. Euric was just unhappy he had to give them up.

With half the Bizogots and Raumsdalians mounted but the rest still on foot, the band of refugees moved no faster than it had before. If the clan south of the Snowshoe Hares had enough horses to let everybody here ride, things would pick up. In the meantime, the nags didn't slow the travelers down.

Liv and Arnora and Marcovefa rode most of the time. The men took turns on the other horses. Hamnet didn't mind walking. He'd got used to it. He did begrudge their sorry pace, though. "Who knows what the Rulers are doing farther east?" he said.

"Come on—you know and I know and the rest of us know," Ulric Skakki said. "They're chewing up every Bizogot clan that gets in their way."

Hamnet Thyssen winced, not because he didn't find that likely but because he did. He wished Ulric hadn't been so blunt. "You don't think we'll be able to pull the Bizogots together to fight them, do you?" he said.

"Well, it gets harder when they're going south faster than we are," Ulric replied—another painful truth.

"We may have to ride south and warn the Empire," Hamnet said. "When we get the horses to do it, I mean—and if it's not too late by then."

"Yes. If." Ulric was nothing if not discouraging. But then, with the way things were, there was too much to be discouraged about.

THEY GOT NO help from the Rock Ptarmigans. Well before they found the clan's encampment, Hamnet Thyssen began to fear that might be so. His first moment of worry came when the travelers approached a herd of mammoths.

The beasts awed Marcovefa. "The Rulers ride these, you say?" she asked, and Hamnet had no trouble following her.

"That's right," Ulric Skakki answered.

"Well, I can see why," Marcovefa said. Then she added something Hamnet couldn't follow. Ulric translated: "She wants to know if there are any beasts bigger than these."

"Some of the forest mastodons get a little bigger, I think, but not much," Hamnet said. Ulric nodded. As he relayed that, Count Hamnet went on, "But whales are supposed to be a lot bigger than any mammoths or mastodons, aren't they?"

Getting the idea of whales across to Marcovefa wasn't easy. Getting the idea of the sea across to her was even harder. She understood what streams and ponds were. But a pond full of salt water, bigger than the Glacier and deeper than a mountain was tall, strained her credulity.

Again, she spoke too fast for Count Hamnet to keep up with her. "She says we're joking with her. She says that just because the mammoths and the musk oxen turned out to be true, now we think she'll believe anything," Ulric reported.

Hamnet Thyssen raised his right hand as if taking an oath. "By God, it's the truth," he said. Marcovefa didn't care much for God, either, and remained unconvinced.

"Nobody's riding out to see who the demon we are," Trasamund said. "That's not how things ought to work."

He was right. Bizogots were as territorial as bad-tempered dogs. They should have spotted the strangers and come forth to challenge them, maybe to try to order them off the clan's land. Her voice troubled, Liv said, "I don't think there are any men with those mammoths."

As Count Hamnet drew closer to the herd, he decided Liv was right. And that was out of the ordinary, out of the ordinary in a bad way. Hamnet had trouble imagining any innocuous reason why the Bizogots would let a herd of mammoths wander on its own. Those animals meant food and wool and hides to the clan. Knowing where they were at a given moment was no light matter.

Audun Gilli nodded. "No dogs, either."

"More likely to see dogs around musk oxen than around mammoths," Trasamund said. "Musk oxen pay attention to them, because dogs remind them of dire wolves. But dire wolves don't trouble mammoths, except maybe to nip in and kill a calf once in a while, so mammoths don't care so much about them. Still . . ."

"It's not a good sign," Ulric Skakki said, and the jarl of the Three Tusk clan nodded.

The mammoths didn't seem to care much about strangers on horseback, either. The Rulers really tamed their mammoths. The Bizogots followed them, sometimes guided them, and used them, but the mammoths here below the Glacier remained their own masters in a way dogs and horses and even musk oxen didn't.

When Trasamund's Bizogots and the Raumsdalians with them came upon a herd of musk oxen with no riders or dogs nearby, Hamnet Thyssen began to worry in earnest. The Rock Ptarmigans would have had to have someone along to keep an eye on animals even more vital than mammoths . . . wouldn't they?

A cow musk ox was trailing the herd. Trasamund and some of the Bizogots from his clan cut the beast away from its fellows and killed it. After the feast Count Hamnet had had with the Snowshoe Hares, he'd been groaningly certain he would never want to eat again. A couple of days of travel showed him how foolish that was. He stuffed himself full of tough, stringy, half-charred musk-ox meat, and he was glad to get it.

When morning came, Ulric Skakki pointed to the southwest. Count Hamnet didn't need long to spot the carrion birds sliding down from the sky. "There are a lot of them," he said. "More than there would be for a dead musk ox."

"More than there would be for a dead mammoth, too," Ulric said. "What do you want to bet?—that's where the Rock Ptarmigans had their camp."

"Keep that bet or find a fool," Hamnet answered. "I won't touch it."

"If we weren't fools, what would we be doing up here?" Ulric asked: much too good a question.

The Bizogots and Raumsdalians rode and walked towards the spot where the birds were landing. More and more birds kept coming: crows and ravens, vultures and teratorns, even owls and hawks hungry for meat that hadn't got too high. Before the travelers saw corpses, they saw mammoth-hide tents in the distance and nodded to one another. Yes, this was where the Rock Ptarmigans had lived.

And this was where the Rock Ptarmigans had died. Owls and hawks notwithstanding, the stench of death filled the air. Corpses of Bizogots and their dogs sprawled in unlovely death among the tents. The scavengers rose in skrawking, screeching clouds as the travelers neared. Teratorns, some of them with wingspans more than twice the height of a man, had to run along the ground before they could get airborne.

"Do you see any wounds on those bodies?" Trasamund asked heavily.

"After the birds, would we?" Hamnet Thyssen returned.

"Some," Trasamund said. "Yes, some, by God. Do you see any arrows? Do you see any broken spearshafts? Do you see any signs of battle?"

Looking around, Hamnet didn't. Cold chills walked up his back. "What killed them, then?" he asked.

Before Trasamund could answer, Marcovefa and Liv began to keen at the same time. They looked at each other in surprise, but both kept on. Audun Gilli didn't keen. He was on horseback, and leaned over and noisily lost the meat he'd eaten for breakfast. Spitting and coughing, he gasped out one word: "Magic."

"Strong magic. Foul magic," Liv added. Marcovefa said something in her own language. Ulric Skakki didn't translate it, but Count Hamnet had no trouble guessing what it meant.

"If the Rulers can do this . . ." Trasamund didn't go on.

Ulric did: "If they can do this, the Empire is in even more trouble than we thought it was. We need to get down there as fast as we can."

"Bugger the Empire! What about the rest of the Bizogots?" Trasamund roared.

"What about them?" Ulric looked him in the eye. "Odds are we write them off, because they're already lost anyhow."

Trasamund gaped. He must not have looked for the adventurer to be so frank. Count Hamnet could have told him that was a mistake. If anyone didn't like such forthrightness, Ulric Skakki lost no sleep about it.

"If the Empire can beat the Rulers, we'll redeem the Bizogots," Hamnet said. "If the Empire loses, we're all ruined together."

Audun Gilli pointed past the encampment that death had struck. "Aren't those the Rock Ptarmigans' horses?" he said.

The death that had struck men and dogs spared the horses, as it had spared mammoths and musk oxen. Count Hamnet supposed the Rulers expected to use the herd animals for themselves. They wouldn't have got to use the horses unless they showed up soon, though, not when the beasts were tied in a line. If dire wolves didn't find them, they would soon perish for want of water and food.

"I didn't want to get mounts for the rest of us like this," Trasamund muttered as he cut the animals loose one after another.

"Better us than . . . them." Hamnet Thyssen looked east. "I wonder if they're on the way now."

"We can't fight them." Trasamund sounded as if he wanted Hamnet to tell him he was wrong.

But the Raumsdalian nodded. "I know we can't. The best thing we can do is disappear before they get here. Chances are they'll just think we're a band of brigands who happened on the camp before they did."

"Well, what else are we?" Ulric Skakki sounded proud, not ashamed.

Trasamund didn't gape this time—he glared. However much he must have wanted to, though, he did no more than glare. Count Hamnet took that to mean he feared Ulric was right. Hamnet cut another horse free and watched it start to graze. He feared Ulric was, too.

XII

HAMNET GREW HARDENED to the saddle. With the horses from the Rock Ptarmigans' camp, the travelers could switch mounts as beasts tired, which let them travel till they got too weary to go on themselves. The long days and twilight-filled nights of the Bizogot steppe in summer also kept them going longer than they would have at any other season of the year.

Riding straight south, or rather a little east of south, would have taken them to Nidaros by the shortest route. Hamnet would have liked to go that way. But trying it was also more likely to make them bump into the Rulers. And so they went south and west, away from the newcomers who had irrupted into the land of the Bizogots.

Trasamund and his clansmates didn't know much about the clans who dwelt on that part of the plain. Ulric Skakki, by contrast, had been there before, and was on good terms with several of the jarls they met.

"This is embarrassing," Trasamund whispered to Hamnet Thyssen after the jarl of the Green Geese greeted Ulric like a long-lost brother. "What business does a Raumsdalian have knowing Bizogots better than a Bizogot does?"

"Why ask me?" Hamnet said. "Why not ask Ulric, or even Grippo here?" Grippo was jarl of the Green Geese. Hamnet went on, "Ulric would tell you. You know that."

"And he'd gloat while he was doing it," Trasamund said. "He gloats even when he doesn't know he's gloating."

Ulric did enjoy trotting out what he knew and showing it off. "Well, ask Grippo, then," Hamnet said.

"I can't. I don't know him. And Ulric Skakki does, curse it."

Grippo raised a skin of smetyn to Ulric in salute. "Warmer than the last time you were here, isn't it?" the jarl of the Green Geese said.

"Oh, just a little," Ulric answered. "Couldn't very well be colder, by God."

"When were you here before?" Trasamund inquired.

"A couple of winters ago," Ulric Skakki answered lightly. He glanced over towards Trasamund. "That was the winter I slipped up through the Gap."

Trasamund looked as if he didn't know whether to laugh or curse. He ended up doing some of each. "Why, you lying sack of horse turds!" he burst out. "You expect me to believe that? You would have had to go right on past the Three Tusk clan without ever letting us know you were around."

"Yes? And so? What's so hard about that?" Ulric said. "You stuck by your tents and by your herds. No one had any idea I was there."

"You can't make me believe that," Trasamund said. "By God, *I* was the first one through the Gap, the first one to see what was on the other side of the Glacier. Why would I have come down to the Empire if I wasn't?"

"Because you're not as smart as you think you are?" Ulric Skakki suggested. His voice stayed mild, but he had no give in him.

Trasamund sent a glance of appeal to Hamnet Thyssen. "Tell him to ease off, Your Grace," he said, as if Ulric weren't standing there a few feet away. "Tell him I don't want to thump him, but I will if he doesn't quit spewing nonsense like this."

"Your Ferocity, I don't think it is nonsense," Count Hamnet answered. "In fact, I'm pretty sure I believe him. He told me about this when we were going up through the Gap last summer. He sounded like somebody who knew what he was talking about, too, and when we got beyond the Glacier some of the things he said turned out to be true."

He might have stabbed Trasamund in the back. "You want me to think a Raumsdalian is as good up here as any Bizogot?" the jarl said. "You want me to think a Raumsdalian is better up here than most Bizogots? I won't do it!"

"Do you know what you sound like?" Ulric said. "You sound like one of those tiresome Raumsdalians who go on and on about how Bizogots are too barbarous to do this, that, or the other thing. They're stupid bores, if you ask me." He didn't say what Trasamund was if you asked him, but you didn't need to be a scholar of logic to figure it out.

Trasamund certainly had no trouble. "If any of your drivel is true, why didn't you come out with it a long time ago?" he demanded.

"Well, I did tell Count Hamnet here—and I told him to keep it quiet," Ulric Skakki replied. "I didn't tell you before because I thought you'd get tiresome yourself if you knew—and I was bloody well right, wasn't I?"

"I ought to thump you from here to Nidaros and back again," Trasamund snarled.

"You're welcome to try," Ulric said politely. Trasamund was much the bigger man. Ulric was quicker and, as Hamnet Thyssen had painfully discovered, knew more fighting tricks than anyone had any business knowing. If the Bizogot and the adventurer fought, Count Hamnet knew which way he'd bet.

Trasamund was no coward—anything but. He'd hurled himself at the Rulers without the slightest worry about what might happen next. But something in Ulric's matter-of-fact invitation seemed to give him pause. He grabbed a skin of smetyn and took a long pull. With the air of a man being more magnanimous than he might, he said, "I am going to let you live, and I'll tell you why."

"I hang on your every word, Your Ferocity." Ulric Skakki's tone suggested that the jarl was welcome to hang himself.

Ignoring it, Trasamund said, "I am going to let you live because the Rulers are the enemies we have to fight. Once they're beaten, we can worry about each other again."

"Congratulations," Ulric said. "You see? You *can* make sense if you put your mind to it. I wasn't sure, but you can after all."

"Enough," Hamnet Thyssen said quickly. Ulric was working on making Trasamund lose his temper. Volcanic as the Bizogot was, that wouldn't be hard. It might be good for the sake of Ulric's amusement. But it also might end in blood—and Trasamund was right when he said fighting the Rulers was more important.

"You're no fun," the adventurer said petulantly.

"Yes, I know. That seems to be how things work for me," Count Hamnet said. "But Trasamund's trying hard to do the right thing. He deserves credit for it. He doesn't deserve you pushing him into a brawl he's doing his best to walk away from."

Ulric Skakki pushed out his lower lip. "You're really very ugly when you're right, too—just in case you didn't know."

"Thank you," Hamnet said. If Ulric was trying to bait *him* now, he wouldn't have any luck. By his sour stare, Ulric was trying to do exactly that.

"You are a band of brothers," Grippo observed. Before Count Hamnet could figure out a polite way to call the jarl of the Green Geese an idiot, Grippo continued, "My brothers and I, we would fight like dire wolves in mating season. You seem the same way—you know one another too well, and you've been too close together too long."

Instead of calling Grippo a fool, Hamnet Thyssen bowed. "You have good sense, Your Ferocity."

"Maybe. And even if I do, how much will it help me if these invaders decide to serve us the way they served the Rock Ptarmigans?"

That was a good question. In a way, it was too good a question, because Hamnet had no answer for it. "We're all doing what we can," he said, which was true but liable to be less than helpful.

"Will it be enough?" Grippo inquired—another pointed query. "And if it isn't, then what?"

"I don't know, Your Ferocity," Count Hamnet answered. "But if the Rulers win, I don't expect to be alive to see it."

"If the Rulers win, not many of us will be," Grippo said, "not unless we bend the knee to them, anyhow."

"And maybe not even then," Hamnet Thyssen said. "Anyone who is not of their folk is part of the herd, as far as they're concerned. Why would they treat a herd of people any better than a herd of mammoths?"

The Bizogot grunted. He lived in a mammoth-hide tent. He slept under a mammoth-hide blanket. He ate mammoth meat, used mammoth fat and butter in his lamps, wore mammoth-leather clothes, and used mammoth ivory for everything from ornaments to arrow points. The mammoths had no say in any of that. Under the Rulers, neither would he.

"By God, any Bizogot who bends the knee to the Rulers deserves whatever happens to him," Trasamund declared. "Any Bizogot who bends the knee to anyone deserves whatever happens to him. Are we not the free folk? Is it not better to die on our feet than to live on our knees?"

"People say so," Grippo answered. "The ones who do say so are all alive, though. I haven't heard what the dead ones say."

There was a piece of cynicism worthy of any diplomat from Nidaros, worthy even of Sigvat II himself. Hamnet Thyssen bowed his head in admiration of a sort. Euric had shown him that the Bizogots could aspire to civilized deceit. Listening to Grippo, he found that they'd truly mastered the art.

"We ought to bring him with us," Ulric Skakki murmured in Raumsdalian. "He'd swindle the Emperor right out of his shoes."

"For which I thank you, though you do me too much honor," Grippo said in the same language, his accent elegant and educated.

First Euric, then Grippo—again . . . Count Hamnet had rarely seen Ulric nonplussed, but he did now. "You never let on that you could speak Raumsdalian!" the adventurer yelped.

"Life is full of surprises, isn't it?" replied the jarl of the Green Geese.

"If you deal with the Rulers, you'll get your share," Hamnet Thyssen told him. "You may not like them once you have them, though."

"You've made yourself very plain," Grippo said. "I will do . . . what I do. Whatever it is, I won't harm you by it. I could, you know. If I seized you, if I gave you to the Rulers, I'd win favor from them. Will you tell me I'm wrong?"

"You wouldn't enjoy it long." That was as much as Count Hamnet could say. If he tried to tell Grippo the Rulers wouldn't reward him for turning over such persistent nuisances, the jarl would know he was lying.

"So I judge," Grippo replied calmly.

Marcovefa said something—a long, angry burst in her own language. How much of the talk had she understood? She was learning the usual Bizogot tongue, and she had that gift for understanding whether she knew the words or not. She glanced expectantly towards Ulric Skakki. *Well—go on*, her attitude said.

And he did: "She says you have her curse, Grippo, if you go against what is best for your folk for the sake of what you think best for you." Marcovefa nodded, as if satisfied with the feel of the translation.

"How much should this worry me?" By the way Grippo asked the question, he thought the answer was *not much*.

Marcovefa muttered to herself. Grippo started to say something else, something that probably would have been sardonic or cruel or crude. What came out instead was a deep, gabbling honk—the honk a goose the size of a man might have made. Grippo looked astonished. Then he started pecking for seeds on the ground. His face wasn't built for that the way a goose's was, but he didn't seem to care. And then he started preening. Unlike a goose, a man had no business being able to stick his head into his armpit. Grippo's neck seemed to stretch to accommodate. He honked some more, now seeming seriously alarmed.

"Tell her she's made her point," Hamnet Thyssen whispered to Ulric. "Too much is too much, same as it would have been with Euric. She should let him be a man again." Ulric nodded and spoke in Marcovefa's language.

Grippo raised his head. He went on honking for a few heartbeats, but then found ordinary words: "What the demon did you do to me?"

Ulric translated his question and then her reply: "She says she showed you what a silly goose you would be if you kissed the Rulers' backside."

"By God! I guess she did!" the jarl of the Green Geese said. "It was the oddest thing. Some of the seeds I found there were really *good*. Now I know they had to be disgusting, but I sure liked them when I pecked them up. And I knew what my honks meant, even if you didn't."

"Shamans sometimes take beast shape themselves, you know," Liv said.

"Oh, yes." Grippo nodded. "I've seen that. But I never thought I'd do it. I'm a man, and that's flat. But now I'm a man with a different look at things."

"I hope it's a look that says dealing with the Rulers wouldn't be such a good idea," Hamnet Thyssen said.

"Oh, yes. *Oh*, yes." Grippo nodded again and shivered at the same time. "Next time, if there were a next time, your shaman might turn me into a bird louse instead of a bird."

Marcovefa gave him a grin full of teeth. No one had said anything about her eating habits atop the Glacier. That grin suggested them despite the silence. Grippo flinched from it, and from the idea that she'd followed him without knowing his language.

WHEN THE TRAVELERS rode south the next morning, the Green Geese gave them more horses and everything they asked for in the way of supplies. Count Hamnet had the feeling Grippo would have done anything at all to get them away from his clan. Unlike Euric, he didn't invite Marcovefa to sleep with him. Hamnet thought he would sooner have slept with a serpent—and Grippo had never seen a serpent in his life.

"She does make an impression on people, doesn't she?" Hamnet said as the tents of the Green Geese shrank behind them.

"Who? Our cannibal princess? Oh, just a little," Ulric Skakki replied. "Yes, just a little. And if he gave her half a chance, she *would* make an impression on him." He mimed biting down hard. Hamnet Thyssen winced. That wasn't what he'd meant, which didn't mean it wasn't so.

The sun seemed to stay in the sky forever. It was high summer on the northern plains. For a few weeks, you could forget all about the Glacier—unless the Breath of God decided to blow down from the north even at that time of year. If it did, all kinds of strange things could happen, from snowstorms that blighted a growing season to twisters that picked up anything from a mammoth to a whole Bizogot encampment and flung it across the landscape.

But now the Breath of God might have been a million miles away. It got as hot as it ever did down in Nidaros—maybe hotter. The hunting was good . . . and Grippo sent one of his men with the travelers down to the edge of his grazing lands. The man from the Green Geese ordered musk-ox herders to kill a beast for the Bizogots and Raumsdalians passing through.

"What? Are you sure?" one of the herders said. "Grippo never tells us to do things like that."

"He did this time." The other Bizogot sent Marcovefa a sidelong glance. He didn't explain his jarl's embarrassment, not in public, but he sounded very sure of himself. The herder stopped grumbling.

Audun Gilli shaved bits from the musk ox's horns after it fell. "Why are you doing that?" Liv asked him.

"I don't know, not exactly." The wizard sounded a little sheepish. "But here we are, and here I am, and here's the musk ox, and the horns are strong, and they may be good for some kind of magic one of these days."

That sounded like a stretch to Hamnet Thyssen, but Liv only nodded. "I do the same sort of thing sometimes," she said. "My tent used to be full of this and that and the other thing—back when the clan was strong, I mean. And maybe I would have used some of what I gathered and maybe I wouldn't, but I had it just in case."

"When I had a house down in Nidaros, it was the same way," Audun said.

Wonderful, Count Hamnet thought. *They've found something else they have in common—they're both packrats.* Liv kept telling him he was worrying over nothing. Every time he looked, though, the nothing seemed bigger.

"What about you?" Liv asked Marcovefa. "Do you save things even when you don't know if you can use them?"

"Yes," Marcovefa answered in the regular Bizogot tongue. She was learning what she needed to know—or maybe her capacity for understanding helped whether she knew the words or not.

"You're going to be out of a job when she can speak for herself all the time," Count Hamnet remarked to Ulric Skakki.

"Well, it won't break my heart," Ulric answered. "Arnora already says I spend too bloody much time talking with her and talking for her." He rolled his eyes. "Women won't leave you alone when they think you might be fooling around."

"Right." Hamnet showed less enthusiastic agreement than he might have. Would Liv have said something like, *Men won't leave you alone when they think you're fooling around?* Would she have pointed at him when she said it? Would she have had reason for pointing at him that way?

Then Marcovefa pointed off into the middle distance and said something in her own dialect. *What are those?*—that was what it had to mean.

Those were lions: a couple of males, three or four females, and several cubs. Maybe the smell of blood from the butchered musk ox drew them. They were wise in the ways of men, though, for they stayed well out of bowshot. Whatever was left of the carcass, they would take after the Bizogots moved on.

A wry, self-mocking smile on his face, Ulric explained about lions. Marcovefa seemed intrigued—maybe even impressed. She said something more. Ulric translated: "She asks if we'll spare one if she calls it close enough to get a good look at it."

"Can her shamanry make sure it spares us?" Trasamund asked.

Instead of answering in words, Marcovefa walked over and patted him on the cheek, as if she were reassuring a nervous little boy. The jarl of the Three Tusk clan muttered something that probably wasn't a compliment. Marcovefa ignored him. She began a crooning chant, one that made Liv prick up her ears. "*We* use that tune for summoning spells," she said.

"The men of the Glacier spring from Bizogots," Hamnet Thyssen said. "Should you be surprised they still share some things with you?"

"When you put it that way, I guess not. I—" Liv broke off. The larger male lion trotted towards Marcovefa.

Hamnet Thyssen started to string his bow, then cut off the move before it was well begun. An arrow seemed more likely to enrage the big cat than to kill it outright. And Marcovefa had a way of knowing what she was doing. Of course, if she turned out not to this time, it would be the wrong moment for a mistake. . . .

Down in the Empire, lions had manes not much more than stubble. This one boasted a full, luxuriant growth. Its coat was thinning with summer, but still far heavier than any the beasts in the south grew. It needed all the help it could get against the ferocious winter weather in these parts.

When the lion drew near to the shaman from atop the Glacier, it flopped down on the ground and rolled with its paws in the air, for all the world like a pampered house cat. But these paws could rip the guts out of a man—or, for that matter, a horse. Marcovefa scratched the lion under its chin. A deep, rasping purr rewarded her. The beast yawned, exposing fangs that wouldn't match a sabertooth's but that were more than savage enough for all ordinary use. She rubbed its belly, and the purr got louder.

"By God, I wouldn't want to do that," Ulric Skakki muttered.

"I'd want to," Trasamund said, "but I wouldn't dare." From the fierce Bizogot, that was no small admission.

When Marcovefa had seen as much of the lion as she cared to, she chanted a new song. The great murderous beast stopped acting like a happy kitten. It got to its feet and trotted away from her. Only when it got back to the rest of the pride did the spell suddenly seem to wear off. The lion began washing and washing, going over its hide with its large, rough tongue.

"Cleaning the stink of us off it," Ulric said, amusement in his voice. "It doesn't think we're fit to associate with."

"It must have met people before, then," Count Hamnet said, and the bitterness in his voice made everyone who heard him either stare or else look away from him in embarrassment.

What kind of embarrassment? he wondered. *That I made a fool of myself? Or that I told a truth that hurts but that they can't deny?* He shrugged. What difference did it make? Anyone who still took a sunny view of human nature after what the Rulers visited upon the Rock Ptarmigans was too big a fool to deserve to wander the Bizogot plains alone, anyhow.

Marcovefa pointed out towards the lion and spoke. "She says we're lucky to live in a land that has such beasts," Ulric said. "She says they give us something to measure ourselves against."

"Measuring myself against a lion is easy," Audun Gilli said. "I am less than a lion, and I hope I have sense enough to know it."

When Ulric Skakki translated, Marcovefa shook her head. "Could the lion have called you away from other men and made you come to it?" she asked through the adventurer.

"I hope not, by God!" Audun blurted, which struck Count Hamnet as the truth wrapped in a joke. The wizard went on, "I wouldn't have called it here, either. Maybe I could have—maybe—but I wouldn't."

"Why not?" Marcovefa asked.

"For fear something would go wrong with my magic, that's why," Audun said.

"Never fear," the shaman from atop the Glacier said seriously. "Never. When you fear, it makes your magic small."

"Well, yours isn't. We've noticed that," Audun Gilli said.

"You see?" Even with Ulric Skakki translating for her, Marcovefa sounded sure of herself.

"I think she is of our blood," Trasamund said. "Bizogots know better than to fear."

"Not fearing isn't always good, either," Hamnet Thyssen pointed out. "Sometimes you can run straight into something you would have stayed away from if only you'd had the sense to fear it."

"I don't believe that," Trasamund said.

What about your clan? Hamnet thought. If they'd kept proper watch at the Gap, they might have kept the Rulers from getting through for a long time. But they hadn't known enough to fear the mammoth-riders. They'd found out soon enough: too soon, in fact.

He knew Trasamund would quarrel with him if he pointed that out. Life was too short. They bickered often enough as things were, sometimes over things that might actually get fixed. They were stuck with the past, though, however little either one of them liked it.

Instead of chaffing the jarl, Hamnet asked, "What will we do if we run into the enemy on our road south?"

"What will we do *when* we run into the enemy? That's what you mean." Ulric Skakki was rarely shy about throwing oil on the fire.

But Count Hamnet shook his head. "I said *if.* I meant *if.* We're trying to stay out of the paths the Rulers are likely to take."

"The answer is the same any which way," Trasamund said. "If we find them—if they find us—we fight them." He reached back over his shoulder to touch the hilt of his great two-handed sword. "They can die. We can kill them. We have killed a good many of them—not enough, but a good many." He scowled. "Unless we kill them all, it is not enough. I don't know how to do that. I wish I did."

"We can kill them, yes. But they can kill us, too, and they're rather better at that than we are at the other." Ulric enjoyed irritating Trasamund, where Hamnet Thyssen didn't. "Wouldn't we do better staying away from them than fighting where we can't win?"

"If you are afraid—" Trasamund began: a Bizogot's automatic retort. But then he shook his big head. "I know you too well. You are not afraid. You are only annoying me, like any other gnat. Well, I don't feel like letting you bite today. If we run into the Rulers, do whatever you please. You will anyhow."

Hamnet looked down at the ground so Ulric wouldn't see him smile. When he had his features under control, he raised his head once more. Ulric Skakki was using the edge of a blade of grass to rout out something stuck between his teeth. If Trasamund's thrust bothered him, he didn't show it. But, to those who knew him, his very nonchalance said he knew he'd lost the exchange.

"How does it feel to be a gnat?" Hamnet asked.

"Natural enough," Ulric replied easily. Hamnet started to nod. Then he grimaced and found something else to do. If Ulric had lost the exchange to the Bizogot jarl, he'd just lost it to Ulric, and the adventurer needed only two words to make him do it.

He wasn't sorry to take sentry duty when the sun finally went down. A few stars came out, but only a few. Twilight lingered long in the north, and the moon filled the southern sky with pale light. Everything was grayish, colors muted and distances confused. Even motion seemed indistinct. It was like watching half in dreamland.

Sounds, though, were somehow magnified. A dire wolf that howled far off to the south might almost have been sniffing at Hamnet's boots. An owl's hoot made his hand drop to his swordhilt. The Rulers' wizards flew through the night—and sometimes through the day—as owls. He needed another hoot or two to realize how distant this bird was. Real or sorcerous, it would not come across the travelers' encampment.

And a footfall that sounded as if it came from right behind him was much farther away than that. For a moment, there in the uncertain light, he wasn't sure who was coming out to him. But Liv was impossible not to recognize. The way she moved spoke to him in his blood, at a level below words.

"Is it all right?" she asked as she came up.

"It seems to be," Hamnet answered. "Why aren't you sleeping?"

She shrugged. "With the sun in the sky so long, I don't seem to need as much." Hamnet found himself nodding. He'd noticed the same thing. When he had to, he could go longer without sleep here than he could have down in the Empire. The long, deep winter darkness in the north made him want to curl up and hibernate like a bear, though.

"I heard an owl not long ago," he said.

"Yes, I heard it, too," Liv said. "I think it was only an owl. I hope it was only an owl." She looked around. The twilight *was* deepening, but almost imperceptibly. "This stretch of days makes up for the rest of the year. It tries to, anyway."

"Half light and half dark anywhere you go," Hamnet Thyssen said. "Only the way they're blended is different."

"Yes." Liv stared up at the moon. It washed the shadows and lines from her face; she might have been a marble bust, not a woman of flesh and blood. Seeing her lips move as she spoke again, seeing that her lips *could* move, seemed startling. "I suppose people are the same way. Only the— what did you call it?—the blend is different."

"It could be," Hamnet said. "I don't know that it is, but it could be. Even the wickedest man won't tell you he's wicked. He won't think he is. What-ever he was doing, he was doing for the best of reasons—or he thinks he was, anyway."

"Even the Rulers are heroes in their own eyes." Liv's mouth twisted. "But not in mine. Oh, no—not in mine."

Her clan was shattered. She hadn't been there when the Rulers struck, hadn't pitted her wizardry against theirs. That the Rulers would have rolled over the Three Tusk clan anyhow seemed as certain to Hamnet Thyssen as tomorrow's sunrise. Telling Liv as much was pointless. He knew, because he'd tried.

What could he have done to keep Gudrid from betraying him all those years ago? Nothing, very likely; faithlessness was in her blood. That didn't keep him from lacerating himself even now, or from wishing things might have been different.

It also didn't keep him from lacerating himself about Liv whether he needed to or not: indeed, it drove him to do just that. But it blinded him to why he did it, too, and blinded him to his being blind. That, of course, he could not see.

"What are we going to do?" Liv cried. Hamnet thought she meant the two of them, but she went on, "What are the poor sorrowful Bizogots going to do?"

"Fight the enemy," Hamnet answered. "What else can you do?"

"But every time we try, we lose!"

He shook his head. "You've beaten them—we've beaten them—in raids."

She brushed that aside, as being of no account: "We can nip them when we catch them without a shaman. But when they have one, we lose."

"The Empire's wizards aren't to be despised," Hamnet said.

"Don't you think the Rulers will smash them?" she returned. "Their magic is of much the same kind as ours. Maybe they know a bit more, or maybe they can do a bit more, but it is of the same kind. And how much good has that kind of magic done against the Rulers?"

"Not enough," Count Hamnet admitted.

"Hardly anything!" Liv cried in a passion of fury most unlike her. "Whatever we try, even against their mammoths, they do something better—or rather, something worse—to us. Do you really think the Empire's wizards can stop them, or even slow them down very much?"

"If they can't," Hamnet said slowly, "then this whole land is in even more trouble than we thought it was."

"It is!" Liv said. "It is!"

"The only other choice is rolling on our bellies, the way the jarl of the Green Geese was thinking of doing," Hamnet said. "I can't do that. Can you?"

"No. I can't do anything at all, and I hate it," Liv said. "One of the best things about being a shaman is that you're able to change things, able to make them better. Against the Rulers, I can't, and it drives me wild. We're running away from them, and that seems to be the most we can do."

He put an arm around her. She clung for a moment, then broke away. He bit down on the inside of his lower lip. He couldn't even manage to comfort her.

"Why did you come to me?" he asked, his voice wooden.

"Because—" She broke off. "Oh, never mind."

"Because why?" he asked. He could come up with answers on his own. The likeliest one was, *Because Audun Gilli's asleep.* Even imagining that one did wonders for the way he felt about himself.

Liv didn't say that, though. "Because if I kept quiet any longer, I thought my head would explode," she told him. "There. Is that enough? Or do you want to stick any more thorns in me?"

Somehow, she'd twisted things so he was in the wrong. "I never wanted to do that," he said.

"No, eh? Or did you just want to stick something else in me instead?"

"You know I do," he answered, as steadily as he could. "I thought it went both ways. Maybe I was wrong."

"No, but . . . Do you have any idea how impossible you are?"

"I do my best," he said with a certain somber pride.

In spite of everything, that made her laugh. This time, she put her arms around him. He squeezed her, which made him do exactly what she'd said. For a moment, she squeezed him back. Then she twisted away again.

"Not now," she said. "It wouldn't be right."

"Why not?" With the blood pounding in his veins, he couldn't see any reason.

"Because that's something you should do when you're happy," Liv answered. "I'm not happy now, not when I miss the clan so much."

"I walked away from the Empire," Hamnet Thyssen said. *I walked away, and I want to make love with you anyhow.*

"Yes, but you walked away from somewhere you didn't fit any more," Liv said. "I belonged in the Three Tusk clan. I'll never find any other place where I belong half so well."

She was right about him. He'd stayed on the fringes of imperial life as much as he could for years before deciding to give it up and come north. She'd had a place where she belonged till the Rulers robbed her of it. He'd thought he fit with Gudrid. After he found out how wrong he was there, he'd been on his own, an uncomfortably independent island in an ocean full of people sure of their places and comfortable in them.

"Let it go, then," he said gloomily—not that he wanted to let it, or her, go, but that he had not the energy to quarrel over it. He wondered what he would have had the energy to quarrel about just then. A sudden irruption of the Rulers, perhaps. Getting excited about anything smaller seemed more trouble than it was worth.

Maybe Liv caught some of that in his voice. "I don't mean never," she said. "I only mean not right now."

"I know." Hamnet Thyssen couldn't make himself get very excited even about being turned down. And if that wasn't a sign of something badly wrong deep inside his spirit, then it wasn't, that was all.

"Well," Liv said. The word seemed to hang in the air. Hamnet knew he ought to say something, anything, but nothing came to him. He couldn't even care about not caring. Liv sighed. "I'll go back to the rest of them, then, and leave you here to stand your watch." She walked away, looking back over her shoulder once. Was she hoping he would call out to her? He nearly did, but again kept silence.

After what seemed a very long time—but, by the slow wheeling of the moon and stars, was no longer than it should have been—a Bizogot came out to relieve him. "Anything funny going on?" the man asked. "Anything strange?"

"No," Hamnet Thyssen said. "It's been pretty quiet."

He walked back to the encampment, lay down, and got a little sleep before the early-rising sun stuck slivers of light under his eyelids and forced them apart. Someone had built up the fire. Hamnet carved off a gobbet of musk-ox meat and began toasting his breakfast. "You look cheerful," Ulric Skakki said.

"I doubt it," Hamnet answered.

Mechanical as if moved by clockwork, he climbed aboard his horse and rode off with the rest of the travelers. If he nodded in the saddle, he wasn't the only one. And then Trasamund pointed south and let out a bellow of mingled fear and fury.

Riders ahead . . . Riders not on horses but on deer . . . The Rulers! Apathy fell from Count Hamnet like a discarded cloak. He strung his bow and made sure his sword was loose in its sheath. If they wanted to go on, they would have to fight. Yes, he was ready for that.

XIII

Fighting held a welcome simplicity. No time to brood. No time to think. Only to do, and to do fast. Your body knew far ahead of your mind. Hamnet's mind had spun in too many circles. Better to snuff it out and let his body show what it knew.

He would rather have done that lying with Liv. Since he couldn't pleasure her, killing someone else would do almost as well.

The Rulers, though, took a deal of killing. Even if their deer didn't measure up to horses, their bows made them formidable enemies. And they had no fear. The Bizogots and Raumsdalians might outnumber them, but they rode to the attack without the slightest hesitation.

By the way they came on, they thought the men who followed Trasamund would scatter like chaff before them. They were used to victory, and expected nothing else. Hamnet Thyssen nocked an arrow. No matter what they expected, he vowed that they would get a beating instead.

They started shooting before he would have. With those powerful compound bows, they could afford to. But their deer were a little slower than horses, so they couldn't stay out of range of the Raumsdalians and Bizogots they faced. They didn't seem interested in staying out of range, anyhow.

An arrow hissed past Hamnet's head. At such a range, that was fearsomely good shooting, or perhaps fearsomely lucky. Had the arrow hit him, which wouldn't have mattered.

He let fly himself. The enemy he aimed at didn't fall. Shooting from a bucketing horse at a foeman on a galloping deer wasn't easy. He swore anyhow, and reached over his shoulder to pull another arrow from the quiver. He drew the bow, aimed, and released all in one smooth motion, guiding the horse with his knees while he did. The bowstring thrummed against his wrist.

A moment later, the riding deer that carried the man he'd shot at crashed to the ground. That wasn't quite what he'd had in mind, but it would do.

Out in front of him, Trasamund bellowed, "A hit! A hit for the Three Tusk clan!" The jarl let out an alarming—and alarmingly authentic—mammoth squeal. He shook his fist at the Rulers and bawled obscenities their way. He hadn't seen who shot the deer, and wasn't likely to give a Raumsdalian credit in place of one of his own. To be fair, many more Bizogots followed him, so the odds were on his side even if he happened to be wrong.

One of his Bizogots tumbled from the saddle with an arrow through the chest. The remnant of the Three Tusk clan had just got smaller. Hamnet shot a couple of more arrows at the Rulers. He didn't see any of them or their mounts go down after either one of those shots, but all he could do was keep trying.

Then he set his bow aside and drew his sword. It was going to come down to handstrokes, the way fights always did. That gave him and his companions the edge, for their mounts were bigger than the ones the Rulers used. They could strike down at their foes from horseback. And the enemy didn't seem to have a wizard along. If they had, odds were the Raumsdalians and Bizogots would already have come to grief.

That thought had hardly crossed Count Hamnet's mind before the Rulers' riding deer seemed to go mad. They started leaping and bounding like oversized rabbits, and refused to answer their riders' commands. The Rulers' shouts mingled fury and dismay.

Hamnet glanced over towards Liv. She looked as surprised as he was. He looked at Audun Gilli. The Raumsdalian wizard was having trouble staying on his own horse—not the kind of trouble the Rulers were having, but the kind of trouble any bad rider might have in battle. Whoever was driving the Rulers' mounts crazy, it wasn't either of them.

Which left . . . As soon as Hamnet Thyssen saw Marcovefa, he knew he'd wasted his time with his first two glances. The shaman from atop the Glacier was almost hugging herself with glee. Hamnet had no idea how she'd done it, but he had no doubt that she'd done it.

He also had no doubt that his side needed to take advantage of it. "Come on!" he yelled. "Let's hit them while they're having trouble!"

The Bizogots from the Three Tusk clan and the others who'd joined them needed little encouragement. Slaying their foes while the warriors of the Rulers were fighting to control their riding deer wasn't sporting, but it was

very effective. The enemy would have done the same to them—had done the
same whenever their sorcerers let them. Revenge was sweet.

They took no captives. The Rulers tried to flee when they saw things going so far against them, but had no luck—their riding deer couldn't outrun
horses. Three Bizogots died in the fight. Several more were hurt. Ulric
Skakki looked at Count Hamnet. "You're bleeding," he remarked.

"Am I?" Hamnet said in surprise. Then he looked down and saw the cut on
the back of his hand. As soon as he noticed it, it started to hurt. "So are you."

"I know. I know." Ulric had a scratch on his left ear. He shrugged. "My tunic is stained. So what? It'll make me look fierce and warlike, won't it?"

He looked anything but. That didn't mean he wasn't, but he didn't look
as if he were. Like the northern beasts that changed color with the seasons,
he concealed his talents as best he could.

"Tell Marcovefa she did a good job spooking their deer," Hamnet
Thyssen said.

"She did, didn't she?" Ulric looked around for her, then called out in the
strange, old-fashioned dialect she used.

She replied at some length. "What does she say?" Hamnet asked.

Ulric looked bemused. "She says we've been going on and on about how
strong their magic is, but it wasn't anything much."

"How does she know?" Hamnet said. "They had no wizard with them."

"Good point." Ulric Skakki put the question into Marcovefa's tongue.
Knowing what he was going to say helped Count Hamnet follow some of it.

Marcovefa answered volubly. When she spoke, Hamnet could find a
word here and there, but not enough to piece together into meaning. "She
says you can always tell," Ulric Skakki reported. "She says you can taste it
on the wind, smell it in their sweat."

The adventurer shrugged. "I don't know whether to take that literally or
not. Considering her eating habits up on top of the Glacier, I hope I'm not
supposed to."

Marcovefa scowled at him. She had to understand what he meant. She
could follow the regular Bizogot language, but not Raumsdalian, which he'd
used—not usually, anyhow. But when she decided to, she understood whatever she wanted. Now she chose to be affronted, or at least to act affronted.
It wasn't the same thing. Were she really angry, she would have made Ulric
as sorry as Grippo.

Trasamund bowed in the saddle to Marcovefa. "For your aid I give
thanks, wise woman," he said. "Any blow against the Rulers is a good one."

"They are not so much," Marcovefa said clearly in the Bizogot tongue. Then she added something Hamnet couldn't follow.

Neither could Trasamund. "What was that?" he asked.

She repeated it. This time, Ulric translated: "They deserve drowning, like little beasts a mother cannot raise. They will get what they deserve."

"By God, may it be so," the jarl boomed. He pointed to the corpses dotting the steppe. "If you're hungry, you're welcome to them."

Again, Marcovefa spouted gibberish. Again, Ulric translated: "She says she would not touch ill-omened flesh."

"That suits me. Let the crows have them, then," Trasamund said. "We ride on." And they did.

THEY'D SWUNG EVEN farther west than Hamnet Thyssen thought. He expected they would have to travel along the northern edge of Sudertorp Lake, and looked forward to showing Marcovefa the wide expanse of water. (She'd lived her life above a much wider expanse of water, but that didn't occur to him till later. The Glacier yielded meltwater, yes, but it didn't really cross his mind when he thought of the lake. It was, or felt like, something altogether different.) But they were west of its westernmost tip, and had to find a way to cross the little Sudertorp River, which flowed out of it. He was stuck with talking about the lake instead of having it there in front of him.

Through Ulric Skakki, Marcovefa asked, "Why does the water stay in the lake? Why doesn't it all run out through the river?"

Count Hamnet frowned at him. "You know the answer to that as well as I do."

"Well, yes, but so what?" Ulric said. "You were playing tour guide, and I wasn't. You do the explaining."

"Fine." Hamnet pointed east, back towards the outlet to the lake. "Tell her about all the dirt and rocks and ice that dam up the end and hold the water in the lakebed. Tell her they're leftovers from the days when the Glacier came this far south."

Ulric did. Hamnet could follow bits and pieces of what he said to Marcovefa, and of what she said to him. That meant he was braced when Ulric translated another question from her: "What would happen if the dam gave way?"

The idea was plenty to make him shudder. "The biggest flood anybody ever saw. You know about the badlands west of Nidaros, where Hevring Lake flooded and tore everything to pieces. Tell her about those, and tell her we'd have more just like them up here if Sudertorp Lake broke the dam."

Ulric did, with gestures. Marcovefa seemed suitably impressed, but Hamnet wondered how much she really understood. How much *could* she understand, when she'd had so little to do with running water before descending from the Glacier?

"Where's the closest ford?" he asked Ulric.

The adventurer pointed west. "About an hour's ride that way, I think. There's a closer one we could use if the water were lower, but I don't think we could get away with it now." He knew the steppe like a Bizogot—knew it better than a lot of Bizogots, in fact, for he'd ranged it widely while they stayed on their clan's grazing grounds most of the time.

Dire wolves drank by the river. Their heads rose when they saw or heard or smelled the riders coming. They peered towards the approaching Bizogots and Raumsdalians, as if wondering whether to stand their ground and fight. One of them let out a querulous whine. That must have been the signal for all of them to leave. They trotted away, tails held high as if to say they weren't really afraid.

"Big foxes," Marcovefa remarked. "Friendly foxes. They go in bunches, like the musk oxen." Yes, she was learning the regular Bizogot tongue.

"Packs. We call them packs," Trasamund said. "And you wouldn't think they were so friendly if you ran into them by yourself."

Count Hamnet wondered about that. If anyone could stay safe in the company of hungry dire wolves, the shaman from atop the Glacier seemed a likely candidate. But she hadn't meant they were friendly to people; she was talking about how they behaved with one another.

Rocks sticking up out of the water showed where the first possible ford lay. Seeing the white water churning around them, Hamnet shook his head. "I don't think we want to try to get across there," he said. "Looks like a good way to drown."

"I told you it wouldn't be good with this much water in the river," Ulric Skakki said.

"You tell me all kinds of things," Hamnet replied. "Some of them are true. Some . . ."

"I'm so insulted." Ulric laughed out loud.

They reached the real ford a little later. The water there didn't get up past the horses' bellies. It was cold, but that was no great surprise. Marcovefa watched with eyes as wide as a child's as the horse carried her across to the southern bank. Up above the Glacier, were any streams big enough to make such a thing possible, even if they'd had horses up there? Hamnet didn't think so.

"Is this still Leaping Lynx country?" he asked after splashing up onto the far bank.

"I think so. Or maybe their lands end farther east," Ulric Skakki answered. "Either way, they'll be in trouble when the Rulers get this far south."

Hamnet Thyssen nodded. The Leaping Lynx clan were rarities: semi-sedentary Bizogots. In winter they roamed like any other mammoth-herders. But in the warm season they lived in stone houses near the eastern edge of Sudertorp Lake. The swarms of waterfowl that bred in the reeds and marshes there gave them so much food, they didn't have to roam. They wouldn't even be a moving target when the invaders swept down on them.

"Hard to feel real sorry for the Leaping Lynxes," Trasamund said. "They aren't really proper Bizogots at all."

"Set against the Rulers, everybody from this side of the Glacier is proper," Hamnet Thyssen said. "If we lose sight of that, we lose, and there's the end of it."

The Bizogot jarl grunted. He didn't want to lose his particularism—it suited him too well. Anything bigger than a clan had to feel artificial to him. "People across the steppe are saying, 'Well, the Three Tusk clan can't be proper Bizogots, because they lost a battle and lost their grazing lands,'" Ulric Skakki said. "Are they right?"

"No, by God!" Trasamund shouted.

But he couldn't or wouldn't see that that had anything to do with the way he looked at the Leaping Lynxes. Ulric sighed but didn't seem surprised. Hamnet Thyssen wasn't surprised, either—saddened, yes, but not surprised. Trasamund always had trouble seeing that he'd made a mistake, or even that he could.

There wasn't really time to worry about it or time to quarrel about it. Audun Gilli asked, "Are the Rulers over this river yet?" That was the burning question.

"If they are, we may find out about it soon," Hamnet said. "Sudertorp Lake will have pushed them either this way or off to the east. If it is to the east, God help the Leaping Lynxes." *And if it's not, God help us,* he thought.

"This land is so rich," Marcovefa said. "It can hold so many. Such a shame to need to fight over it."

Hamnet and Ulric looked at each other. She saw the land was richer than the mountaintop sticking up through the Glacier. But she didn't see how very poor that was. Rich by comparison didn't mean truly rich—not even close.

Trasamund pointed. "There are mammoths," he said.

In the days before the Gap melted through, the Bizogots and Raums-dalians would have welcomed that news. It would have meant more mammoth-herders were close by. Now it might mean mammoth-riders were near. The difference sounded small, but was even bigger than the one between Marcovefa's homeland and the Bizogot steppe. It was the difference between safety and disaster.

They approached the mammoths with as much caution as they could muster. If the great beasts belonged to the Rulers, what could Trasamund and those with him do but flee? And what kind of chance would they have if they did? *Not good,* Hamnet Thyssen thought. *No, anything but good.*

But they breathed easier when the man who rode out to see who they were and what they were up to rode a horse, not a deer. The hair under his fur hat was Bizogot yellow, not the shiny black of the Rulers. Even his brand of bluster sounded familiar: "Who the demon are you, and what the demon do you think you're doing here?"

"You're Marcomer, aren't you?" Hamnet Thyssen shouted back, pleased he remembered the fellow's name. "We met when I guested with the Leaping Lynxes last year."

"Thyssen?" Marcomer called, and Hamnet nodded. The Bizogot barely waited for that before he went on, "What in blazes is going on farther north? We've had more people coming down through our grazing grounds than anybody in his right mind would believe. . . . And that's Trasamund with you again, isn't it?"

"It's me, all right." Trasamund was never shy about speaking for himself. He and Count Hamnet took turns talking about the arrival of the Rulers. The jarl of the Three Tusk clan finished, "It's even worse than we thought it would be when we came through going north last winter."

"We've heard some of this from others," Marcomer said. "We didn't know how much to believe. Men riding mammoths . . . Mad sorceries . . . But I've got to believe you when you tell me you went to the top of the Glacier. Nobody would be daft enough to make that up and expect the folk who heard him to listen."

Marcovefa stirred but held her tongue. She must have realized the Bizogot with the name that sounded like hers wasn't trying to offend.

"Will you let us pass on?" Ulric Skakki, as usual, went straight to the point.

"You ought to go back to the stone houses and talk to the jarl," Marcomer answered.

"If we go back to the stone houses, we're liable to run into folk we don't want to meet," Hamnet said. "I hope not, but we don't care to take the chance."

"Folk you don't want to meet? What are you talking about?" Marcomer might have heard what the travelers told him, but he hadn't really listened.

"I don't know whether the Rulers have come this far south, but I wouldn't be surprised," Hamnet said. "I do know they haven't come west of Sudertorp Lake, because we would have met them instead of you if they had. But if they have come this far and they've gone east of Sudertorp Lake, where are they likely to be?"

"At the stone houses!" Marcomer went pale. Now he understood what Count Hamnet and Trasamund were talking about. "We'd better send someone over there to warn the jarl." Without any kind of farewell, he rode back towards the mammoths, shouting at his fellow herders as he went.

"Well, we livened up his morning, didn't we?" Ulric Skakki sounded more proud of himself than anything else.

Before long, Marcomer and another horseman trotted east. Hamnet Thyssen silently wished them luck. Maybe they could warn the rest of the Leaping Lynxes. He feared they were more likely to run headlong into disaster. But that was also part of life—an all too common part.

"Let's ride," Trasamund said. "They won't kill a mammoth calf for us—I'm sure of that. We need to go on till we find a herd of musk oxen."

"Before too very long, we'll be able to see the tree line," Hamnet said. "We're more than halfway across the Bizogot steppe. When we started, I never would have believed we could get this far."

"Something to that." One corner of Ulric Skakki's mouth quirked up. "I wonder what the Rulers will think of trees. I wonder what their mammoths will think of them."

That hadn't occurred to Count Hamnet. No denying Ulric had something, though, or at least might have something. The land beyond the Glacier was also far beyond the tree line. The unfamiliar terrain might slow down the invaders. Or, on the other hand, it might not. *Brilliant*, Hamnet thought sardonically. *You covered all the choices, and you didn't settle a cursed thing.*

After that, riding on came as something of a relief.

THE WORST, OR something close to it, had befallen the Leaping Lynxes. Two days after the meeting by the mammoth herd, Marcomer and several other Bizogots from the lakeside caught up with the travelers from the north from behind. Along with his companions, Hamnet Thyssen had feared they might be warriors of the Rulers.

"I never got to the stone houses. These—Rulers—attacked before I could," Marcomer said. "They struck the clan, and they scattered us. Riccimir is dead. He had his quirks, but he was a good jarl."

"He was," Hamnet agreed. The Leaping Lynxes had the richest hunting grounds in the Bizogot country. Riccimir defended them well against other clans, some bigger and stronger than his, that wanted to take them for themselves.

"Some of our houses fell down," said one of the Bizogots—a woman—with Marcomer. "The mammoth-riders made a magic, and the houses fell down. The jarl died in the wreck of his, when a rock smashed his head. Then the strangers swept down on us. We tried to fight, but how could we? God only knows what happened to the ones who couldn't get away."

"They're part of the Rulers' herd now," Hamnet Thyssen said. That did nothing to cheer the Leaping Lynxes. He hadn't thought it would.

"What can we do?" Marcomer asked. "I want to go back and kill as many of those demons as I can before they get me."

That might have done well enough if he were likely to kill any of the Rulers at all before they killed him. As things were, Hamnet answered, "You have a better chance for revenge if you come with us. We think the Empire can fight back against the invaders." *Well, we hope the Empire can, anyhow. That's not the same thing, even if I don't want Marcomer thinking about the difference.*

Marcovefa said something incomprehensible. Hamnet looked a question towards Ulric Skakki. The adventurer didn't sound happy as he translated: "She doesn't understand why we're getting so upset about the Rulers. She says they're nothing much."

She'd said that before. She'd proved it, too . . . against a raiding party that had no wizard of its own along. "When she beats their shamans, she may talk any way she pleases," Trasamund said. "Till then, seeing as we've been running from the Rulers ever since we came down from the Glacier—before that, too!—I wish she'd keep her mouth shut."

Count Hamnet waited for Marcovefa to resent that, and to show it by making Trasamund do something embarrassing or absurd. But she didn't—she just smiled and blew him a kiss. The jarl muttered under his breath. He also seemed willing to leave it there, though.

Audun Gilli tried to look on the bright side: "We're a stronger party now. If we have to fight the Rulers, we stand a better chance."

"Something you really need to learn is the difference between *better* and *good*," Ulric Skakki said. Audun Gilli looked wounded. Hamnet Thyssen would have sympathized with him more if he hadn't been thinking the same thing. Ulric put it better than he would have and spoke first—that was all.

WHEN THEY CAME down to the tree line the year before, they'd been racing winter—and winter moved south faster than they did. This time, summer was sliding towards fall, but hadn't got there yet. Although days were getting shorter, nights hadn't yet outdistanced them. The firs and spruces remained dark, no snow stippling their needles.

"I've heard about trees," Marcomer said. "I never thought they'd be so big, though." Up on the Bizogot plain, which began where the forest could no longer grow, wood was an imported luxury, scarce and expensive.

"I thought they would be bushes," Marcovefa said. "I thought they would be bushes taller than me. But they aren't really like that, are they? And he is right. I never thought they would be this big."

Hamnet Thyssen, Ulric Skakki, and Audun Gilli all smiled, then tried to pretend they hadn't. So did Trasamund and Liv, who'd come south before. They knew about trees. For the rest of the Bizogots, as for Marcomer and Marcovefa, these scraggly samples just below the line where the ground froze were far and away the biggest living things they'd ever seen.

As Hamnet peered first east and then west, Ulric sent him a quizzical stare. "What are you looking for?" the adventurer demanded.

"A border station," Count Hamnet answered.

Ulric arched an eyebrow. "Why? Those snoops are nothing but nuisances. And, if you remember the way we left, they're liable to have orders to arrest us on sight."

"Let them try," Hamnet said. "We've got thirty warriors and three wizards with us. If that isn't enough to make border guards leave us alone, we're in real trouble. And when we find a station, we'll find a road leading south from it."

"Mm, there is that," Ulric admitted. He looked along the edge of the forest, too. "It would be easy in the wintertime."

"So it would," Hamnet Thyssen said. During the winter, the border guards kept big fires blazing to stay warm. A column of smoke pointed the way to each post. At this season of the year, though, the men didn't need to worry about freezing. Hamnet shrugged. "I don't see one, but our wizards can tell us which way to go to find one close by. They'd better be able to, anyhow."

Audun Gilli had a bit of lodestone on a string that he used for finding directions. The spell wasn't so accurate up in the far north as it was in the Empire, but the wizard thought it would work here. Count Hamnet judged him likely to be right, but they didn't need enormous precision now. Knowing whether to ride east or west would do.

"West," Audun said after chanting and making passes and watching the way the lodestone swung.

They went west. Marcovefa tried to question Audun about his charm. Ulric Skakki translated with a martyred expression on his face. Hamnet understood that; for a non-wizard, nothing was more boring than trying to render sorcery's technical terms from one tongue to another. He'd done it himself before Audun learned the Bizogot tongue. Now he wasn't sorry to see Audun talking with Marcovefa and not with Liv.

Jealous? Me? he thought, and then, *Well, yes.*

They reached the border post in a couple of hours; the stations were scattered thinly across the frontier between civilization and barbarism. This one looked like all the others Hamnet Thyssen had seen: a wooden hut held by a handful of Raumsdalian soldiers who didn't have the clout to get posted anywhere else. The Raumsdalians seemed horrified to see such a large party approaching them.

"What you do?" one of them shouted, using the Bizogot language badly but understandably. "No war here!"

"No, no war here yet," Hamnet answered in Raumsdalian. "But how long will it be? Have you heard of the coming of the Rulers?"

"What we hear and what we see are two different things," the soldier answered. "When we see these Rulers or whoever they are, maybe we'll worry about them. If they deserve it, I guess we will. Meantime, though, who the demon are you?"

"I am Count Hamnet Thyssen." Hamnet waited to see what would happen next.

One of the border guards started violently. "He's that one!" he exclaimed.

"That's right. I'm that one. What are you going to do about it?" Hamnet asked with a certain somber pride.

Before answering, the guards put their heads together. Then one of them said, "What'll you do after we let you into the Empire?"

"Try to persuade people there really is a danger to the north. You'll see for yourself soon enough. So will everybody, and it won't be much longer."

The border guards put their heads together again. When they drew apart, they all wore almost identical unpleasant smiles. "Pass on," one of them said. "You'll do worse to yourselves than anything we can do to you."

"Thank you so much." Count Hamnet wasn't about to show that he thought they were much too likely to be right. He translated the permission to advance for the Bizogots who spoke no Raumsdalian. Ulric rendered it into Marcovefa's dialect. She said something in return: something he *didn't* translate. "What's the closest town down this road?" Hamnet asked the guards.

"Malmo," answered the man who'd spoken before. "It's about half a day's ride from here." He sighed wistfully. "I sure wish it were closer." Hamnet believed that. A stretch at a border station could seem too much like one in jail.

As they rode past the border station, Marcovefa murmured to herself. Her hands twisted in quick passes. The guards got down on all fours and started cropping grass. When a noise from the travelers startled them, they bunched together in a ring, heads facing out. They weren't musk oxen, but they didn't seem to know they weren't.

"How long will the spell last?" Count Hamnet asked.

"A day. Maybe two." Marcovefa seemed pleased with herself.

Hamnet looked over his shoulder. The border guards were grazing again. He hadn't cared for their arrogance. Maybe they wouldn't act quite so high and mighty when they regained full humanity. Or maybe they wouldn't notice any difference. Either way, they weren't his worry.

"On to Malmo," he said, and Marcovefa nodded.

THE SHAMAN FROM atop the Glacier wasn't so happy by the time she reached the forest town. Several Bizogots from the frozen steppe were also in a bad way. "These trees!" one of them said with a shudder. "They're pressing in on me!"

"Where is the sky?" another one added. "Where is the . . . the space?" He threw his arms wide, as if to push back the branches that hung out over the road—which was hardly more than a track—and the dark trees from which they grew.

Out on the plains to the north, Count Hamnet often felt he was too small and the landscape much too large. Here where things closed in, Bizogots had the opposite trouble. He'd seen that before when traveling towards Nidaros with Trasamund and Liv. Liv didn't seem too happy now, but she'd been through this then and knew what to expect now. The mammoth-herders who hadn't got an unpleasant surprise. So did Marcovefa, who'd also lived her life in a land of wide horizons.

She sighed in relief when they rode out into the clearing that surrounded Malmo. "The sun!" she said. "Not shadows in my face all the time." Then she dropped into her own tongue.

"What's she saying?" Hamnet asked Ulric Skakki. "Something about wood, but I can't make out what."

"She's excited about all the ways you can use it," Ulric said. "The palisade, the houses . . . She called them wooden tents."

That was amusing and clever at the same time. "Wait till she sees the fires at the serai," Hamnet said. Malmo wasn't a very big town, but it was bound to have a place where travelers could stay . . . wasn't it?

As things turned out, it was. The serai was nothing special, even by the standards of provincial towns. But it had a bathhouse and cooked food and rooms with beds. Hamnet Thyssen wasn't inclined to be fussy. After so long among the Bizogots—to say nothing of the sojourn on top of the Glacier— even the rough edges of civilization seemed wonderful.

Marcovefa marveled at everything. She'd never known real buildings before. Bathing in hot water with soap must have seemed indescribably luxurious to her. She didn't want to come out and let some of the other travelers wash.

At supper, she ate roast pork. When she first tried it, she looked surprised. "Is this—?" she started.

Count Hamnet knew what she was driving at. "No, by God, it isn't," he told her. "When it cooks, it smells like that, but it's not."

"It tastes like that, too," she said. "Maybe not just like that, but close." She added something else in her own dialect.

Ulric translated: "She didn't think we ate each other, but she would have believed you if you told her that was what it was."

"We don't. It isn't." Hamnet Thyssen drained a mug of ale, glad to be spared at least one sin. After smetyn, ale seemed very good to him. He didn't ask for wine. The tapman might have had some, but this far north it was bound to be painfully expensive. Ale would do.

Through Ulric, Marcovefa asked, "If I drink a lot of this, will my head want to fall off tomorrow morning?"

"Yes." Hamnet and Ulric and Trasamund and Audun Gilli all said the same thing at the same time.

Then she asked, "How much is a lot?"

That was harder to answer. Hamnet said, "It's different from one person to the next. It depends on how big you are and how much you usually drink and on who knows what."

"Have to find out, then." Marcovefa finished her mug and waved to the tapman for another. She was starting to figure out how things worked here. But when Ulric gave the fellow a coin for the fresh mug, she got puzzled all over again. To her, copper and silver and gold made good ornaments, but that was all. Trying to explain why money was money wasn't easy. "What good is it?" she asked, over and over.

The way she asked it made Hamnet Thyssen wonder himself. "We make lots of different kinds of things—you've seen that," Ulric said after several false starts. He got a cautious nod from Marcovefa. Thus encouraged, he went on, "We find it easier to give coins for things than to trade things all the time. It makes dealing simpler."

"How did you decide to do that?" she asked.

Now he shrugged. "I don't know. I do know we've been doing it for a long time. Everybody down here does it. That makes it work."

"You have strange customs," Marcovefa said seriously. A Raumsdalian talking about the ways of the folk who lived up on the Glacier would have used the exact same tone of voice.

Up on the Glacier, it was impossible to be rich. There wasn't enough for anyone to get a surplus. Having enough wasn't easy. Trading with one another and with the Empire, Bizogots *could* get rich—Trasamund had been, before his clan fell on hard times—but it wasn't easy. For that matter, it wasn't easy in the Empire, but it was easier, because there were more goods to move around—and because there was money to make the moving easier.

Was that good or bad? Hamnet had never wondered before. It was what Raumsdalia and every other civilized land had, and what the Bizogots and other barbarians aspired to. If the clans atop the Glacier had lost it, that was only because they'd lost so many other things as well.

"Everyone has strange customs—to people who don't have the same ones," he said, and waited to see if the shaman would need Ulric to translate for her. Her nod said she followed on her own.

Audun Gilli emptied his mug of ale, yawned, and went upstairs. Several

Bizogots had already drunk themselves sleepy. Ulric Skakki grinned. "They haven't got the head for real drinking," he said.

"Seems that way," Hamnet agreed, glad he was drinking ale instead of smetyn.

"Who says?" Trasamund demanded, and shouted for a fresh mug. Ulric also waved for a refill. So did Hamnet.

"Drink yourselves foolish if you please, but I'm going upstairs." Liv set down her mug and did just that.

After Hamnet Thyssen had more ale in front of him, he found he didn't feel like getting getting blind drunk just to make a point. He knew what he could hold, and so did Ulric and Trasamund, the people he would have been most interested in impressing. He drained the mug in a hurry—no point in letting it go to waste, after all—then pushed back his stool and stood up. "I'm going upstairs, too," he said.

His friends jeered at him. He'd known they would, so he had no trouble ignoring them. The room spun a little as he walked to the stairs. Yes, he'd already had plenty.

He climbed the steps with exaggerated care and quiet. At the top of the stairs, he stopped dead. There stood Liv and Audun Gilli, kissing in the hallway.

XIV

SOMETIMES WHEN YOU were wounded, you didn't feel the pain for the first few heartbeats. Sometimes it pierced you right away. When Hamnet Thyssen heard a noise like a dire wolf's growl, he needed that handful of heartbeats to realize it came from his own throat.

The other two also needed a moment to hear it through their more enjoyable distraction. It reached Audun before Liv. He sprang away from her with a gasp of horror. "I can explain," he gabbled. "You have to understand—"

"Understand what?" Hamnet said, still growling. "Understand how many pieces I'm going to cut you into?" His hand already lay on the hilt of his sword, though he didn't remember telling it to go there.

"Don't be foolish, Hamnet," Liv said. "It's over. You know it is. It's been over for a while now. You know that, too."

He did know it, even if he hadn't wanted to look at it. That made things worse, not better. "It can't be!" he said. He'd lost Gudrid. How could he stand losing another woman? "I loved you! You loved me!" He wished that hadn't come out in the past tense. Maybe his mouth was wiser than his brain.

Liv nodded. "I did, for a while. But when you started herding me the way dogs herd musk oxen, when you started wondering whether I was faithful every time I breathed . . . You caused what you wanted to cure. Killing Audun won't get me back, even if you can. It's too late for that."

"I ought to kill you, too," he ground out. He should have done that with Gudrid. Then she wouldn't have been able to torment him all these years after they broke apart. Would Liv do the same? Would she revel in it the way Gudrid had?

"You can try," she said. "But what good would it do? It won't bring me back to you. Nothing can do that now. What we had was good while it lasted. Why not remember it that way?"

Hamnet started to say that killing her and Audun would make him feel better. But he wasn't even sure that was true. It might make him feel better for a little while, but he knew he would be sorry afterwards if he did it. He couldn't tell them he hoped they would be happy together; he didn't. He didn't see much point in telling them he hoped they would be unhappy together—they could figure that out for themselves.

And so he pushed past them without a word. Audun Gilli shrank from him. Liv didn't. She had as much courage as any Bizogot. She looked as if she wanted to say something, but she didn't do that, either. After their first spell of intoxication with each other, neither of them had been able to find enough to say to each other. That was part of the trouble, though Hamnet didn't realize it.

When he walked into the mean little room he'd thought he would share with Liv, he found she'd already taken her meager belongings out. He said something that should have made the roof cave in and the walls collapse. Everything stayed up, though, and the bed didn't collapse when he threw himself down on it, even if the frame did groan.

After losing Gudrid, he'd wept for days—weeks, in fact. He wept now, too, but even he knew the tears were more drunken self-pity than anything else. Gudrid had had a hold on him that Liv couldn't match. Knowing he would probably be all right before too long made him all the more mournful.

One good thing: Audun Gilli's chamber lay halfway down the hall. If he'd had to listen to the mattress in the next room creaking rhythmically, he really might have drawn his sword and done his best to slaughter the wizard and the shaman.

Instead, he fell asleep with his boots still on, sprawled out across the bed. After that, he didn't hear a thing.

WHEN HE CAME downstairs the next morning, some of the Bizogots were already eating breakfast. So was Ulric Skakki. He sat next to Trasamund. Both of them cautiously spooned up porridge of rye and oats and sipped from mugs of beer. By their sallow skins and red-tracked eyes, they hoped the beer would soothe aching heads. By the way the corners of their mouths turned down, it hadn't done the job yet.

Trasamund stared at Count Hamnet. "By God, man, what ails you?" the jarl burst out. "You went to bed long before we did, but you look worse than either one of us."

Ulric, by contrast, had a way of cutting to the chase. He did it now with two words: "He knows."

Hamnet scowled at him. How long had they known? How long had everybody known? How long had people been laughing at him behind his back? Hadn't he had enough of that with Gudrid? Evidently not.

"What'll it be, friend?" The tapman sounded cheerful. Why not? He hadn't just lost his woman.

"Beer," Hamnet said. "Porridge." Even if part of him wished he were dead, his belly craved ballast.

"Sorry, Thyssen," Ulric said when Hamnet sat down across from him. "It happens, that's all. It'll probably happen with me and Arnora before long."

"Yes, but—" Hamnet began, and then stopped.

"But what?" Ulric asked, his voice deceptively mild.

"But you and Arnora aren't in love."

"No. We just screw each other silly, which isn't bad, either. But you and Liv aren't in love any more, either, if you ever were," Ulric said.

"I still love her!" Hamnet cried.

"Which has nothing to do with what I said." Ulric was most dangerous when he was most accurate. "You may love Liv, but it's pretty plain she doesn't love you right now. And if she doesn't, you two aren't in love, no matter how much you may wish you were. Or will you tell me I'm wrong?"

Count Hamnet wanted to. He knew too well he couldn't. "No," he mumbled. A serving girl who might have been the tapman's daughter brought him his breakfast.

"Dig in," Ulric said cheerfully. "You may as well."

And Hamnet did. The porridge had onions and bits of smoked sausage in it. No matter how the rest of him felt, his belly was happy. Arnora came down a few minutes later. Instead of sitting by Ulric, she made a point of plopping herself down at a far table and scowling at him. He grinned back, which only seemed to annoy her more.

Then Liv and Audun Gilli came down together. They were holding hands. Liv looked pleased with herself. The wizard looked happy and frightened at the same time. Hamnet's glower said he wished they would both catch fire. Liv shook her head and Audun flinched, but they stayed unscorched.

They did have the courtesy to sit where Hamnet couldn't see them without twisting to do it. That helped a little, but only a little. Every time he heard Liv's voice, he felt vitriol dripping down his back.

Ulric Skakki waved to the serving girl and pointed at Hamnet. "Bring this man another mug of beer."

"Are you sure that's a good idea?" Trasamund asked.

"I'm not *sure* of anything," Ulric answered, "but I think one more will numb him. Three or four more . . . Well, three or four more wouldn't be a good idea right now."

The girl set the mug in front of Count Hamnet. He drained it. Ulric was a nice judge of such things, no doubt from experience. The beer built a wall—a low wall, but a wall—between him and what he was feeling. A few more, though, and he wouldn't have cared what he did.

Marcovefa was one of the last travelers to come down to the taproom. When she did, she noticed right away how people were sitting. The clans atop the Glacier must have had their quarrels and squabbles and scandals, too. People were people, no matter where and how they lived. They would fall in love with one another.

They would fall out of love with one another, too.

Marcovefa sat down by Hamnet. "I am sorry," she said in the ordinary Bizogot tongue. "It happens."

He looked at her—through her, really. "Go away," he said.

She looked back. "No."

"Then keep quiet and leave me alone."

She said something to Ulric Skakki in her own dialect. Hamnet could follow just enough of it to know it wasn't complimentary to him. He ignored it. He made a point of ignoring it. He made such a point of ignoring it, in fact, that Marcovefa thought it was funny. The only response he could find was to keep on ignoring her. She thought that was even funnier.

WHEN THEY RODE out of Malmo, Count Hamnet got fresh salt rubbed in his wounds. After Gudrid finally left him, she went off to Nidaros, and he hardly saw her till she came with Eyvind Torfinn on the journey up beyond the Glacier. He brooded that she was gone—brooded and brooded and brooded—but at least he didn't have to watch her with whatever lovers she'd had before latching on to the scholarly earl.

But he couldn't get away from Liv. There she was, not far away, talking animatedly with Audun Gilli, her face glowing the way it had not long before when she talked with him. Even when he rode too far away to make out what she was saying, he could hear the lilt in her voice. She talked to Audun the way a woman talked to a lover who pleased her. Hamnet knew the tone too well to mistake it. Now that she used it with someone else . . .

He ground his teeth till his jaw hurt. He wished a short-faced bear or a lion would spring out of the woods and devour Audun Gilli. *Slowly,* he thought, *so I can savor his screams.* Once the wizard was gone, he reasoned, Liv would come back to him. That she might have other choices didn't occur to him, which showed his reasoning wasn't all it might have been.

They rode on through the Empire's northern forests. The deeper they got, the more Marcovefa and the Bizogots who'd never before come down off the steppe marveled. That marveling wasn't always of a happy sort; they seemed to feel the trees pressing in on them more than ever. To Hamnet, it was only a forest: not the same kind as grew by his castle farther south, but close enough. The jays here had dark heads and blue bellies, not blue heads and white bellies. But their screeches weren't much different from those of any other jays.

Sedranc, the next town farther south, was larger and more prosperous than Malmo. As Marcovefa had before, she ate barley bread and oatcakes. In Sedranc, though, she really seemed to notice what she was eating and how unlike anything she'd known atop the Glacier it was. "What is this?" she asked. "How do they make it?" She sounded almost as wary as a Raumsdalian at one of her folk's cannibal feasts.

Some of the Bizogots also seemed curious. No crops grew on their plains, either. They gathered berries and roots and leaves, but they knew nothing of grain. Explaining how Raumsdalian farmers raised their crops and harvested them, how the seeds were ground into flour and the flour baked, took quite a while.

"A lot of work." Marcovefa delivered her verdict. "Too much work, maybe."

"Lots of food," Count Hamnet said. "More than we could get from hunting and picking berries. That food lets us have towns." *Lets us be civilized,* he thought. The two amounted to the same thing.

"What good is a town?" asked the shaman from atop the Glacier. "Why have this place? Why not wander?"

She wasn't being sardonic, or Hamnet didn't think so. "To let us have beds. To let us have bathtubs. To let us build houses the Breath of God has trouble blowing away," he replied.

"To let us buy and sell and trade," Ulric Skakki added.

"Money." Marcovefa used the Raumsdalian word as if it were a curse.

"Money." It sounded different in Ulric's mouth.

"To stay safe behind the wall," Audun Gilli said. He was right, too. Hamnet Thyssen glared at him anyway.

"Wall is not so much, either," Marcovefa said.

"What would you do different? How would you do better?" If Hamnet argued with her—if he argued with anyone but Audun—he wouldn't have to dwell on his own misery.

For the first time, a question seemed to give her pause. "I don't know," she said at last. "Something not like this, though."

"These are just country towns, and back-country towns at that," Ulric Skakki said in the ordinary Bizogot tongue. Then he had to go back and forth with Marcovefa, no doubt explaining what a back-country town was and why it wasn't so much of a much. When he dropped back into speech Hamnet could understand, he added, "Plenty of places farther south much finer than this."

"It's true," Liv said. "When I first came down to Raumsdalia, I thought each place was the finest one I'd ever seen. Then the next one down the road would be grander still."

Hamnet remembered that, remembered it with heartbreaking clarity. She'd shared her amazement and delight with him only the autumn before. Now, if she still had them, she'd share them with Audun Gilli. Hearing her voice stabbed Hamnet in the memory, and what wounds hurt worse than that?

He'd felt the same way about Gudrid last year. She'd gone out of her way to bait him, too, which Liv didn't seem to be doing—a small mercy, but a mercy even so. And yet, when a short-faced bear burst out of the forest, killed Gudrid's horse, and menaced her, he'd ridden to her rescue without a thought in his head except driving the bear away or killing it. Even at the time, he'd wondered why. Did he hope she'd be grateful? If he did, she disappointed him yet again.

What would he do if a short-faced bear came after Liv now? He was lucky—if it was luck—he didn't have to find out.

The forest's northern edge was clear-cut: there was a line past which trees simply could not grow. Its southern border was more ambiguous. Men could farm on south-facing slopes even in the midst of the trees. In good years, in warm years, in years when the Breath of God didn't blow too hard, they'd bring in a crop. Chances were they could bring in enough to last out one bad year. Two long, hard winters in a row, though, and they would start to starve.

More farmers seemed to be trying to carve out steadings up here than had been true before Count Hamnet's beard started going gray. More seemed to be making a go of it, too. In his grandfather's day, the forest's lower edge lay miles to the south.

Go back enough generations and it hadn't been forest here at all, but frozen steppe. Go back further than that, and the Glacier had ground forward and back, and who could say what it ground into oblivion? Only a few legends and—maybe—the Golden Shrine survived from those days.

If I found the Golden Shrine, could I make Liv love me again? Hamnet wondered. *God, could I make Gudrid love me again? Could I make myself not care if I couldn't make either one of them love me again?* Without love, poppy juice for the soul seemed plenty good.

He looked around, as if he would find the Golden Shrine in the middle of this frontier district. That would have been funny if it weren't so sad. He hadn't found the Golden Shrine even beyond the Glacier. What chance of stumbling over it in these mundane surroundings did he have? None, and he knew it.

What chance do I have? he wondered bitterly. The question was hard enough to answer all by itself.

He looked back over his shoulder, back past the forest, back towards the Bizogot steppe. He wondered why he cared so much about beating the Rulers. What did he care if they smashed the Bizogots and hurled Raumsdalia down in ruins?

Part of the answer to that seemed plain enough. If the Rulers smashed the Empire, he was all too likely to get caught and killed in the collapse. Even if he didn't, he would have to bend the knee to the invaders from beyond the Glacier. Every fiber in his being rebelled against that. Better to fight them for . . .

For what? For the love of a woman? Gudrid lay in Eyvind Torfinn's arms—and in any other arms she happened to fancy. And now Liv had thrown Hamnet over, too—and for whom? For a wizard lost in the real world. Why care whether he lived or died himself, let alone the Bizogots or the Raumsdalian Empire?

Another question easier to ask than answer.

Big, sharp-nosed, rough-coated dogs that looked to be at least half dire wolf ran snarling at the travelers from a farm cabin near the woods. Almost without thinking, Hamnet strung his bow and let fly. The arrow caught a wolf-dog in the flank. Its snarls turned to yelps of pain. It ran off faster than it had come forward. The other beasts, hearing their friend wounded, seemed to think twice.

"What did you go and do that for?" The farmer shook his fist at Count Hamnet. "He's a good dog!"

"Good dogs don't act like they want to tear my throat out," Hamnet answered. He nocked another shaft. If he had to shoot again, it might not be at a dog.

But the farmer, no matter what he thought, had better sense than to pick a fight with a band of thirty or so Bizogots and Raumsdalians. He went back to weeding. Each stroke of the hoe against some poor, defenseless plant said what he would have done to Hamnet Thyssen if only he were a hero.

Hamnet glanced up at the sky. It was blue—a watery blue, but blue. A few puffy clouds sailed across from west to east. No sign of dark clouds, threatening clouds, riding the Breath of God down from the north. But if the wind changed, when the wind changed . . . It could happen any day, any time. Hamnet Thyssen knew that well. The farmer had to know it, too. To Hamnet, it was a fact of life. To the farmer, it was a matter of life and death.

Which brought Hamnet back to the question he'd asked himself before. Why did he want to hold on to the one and hold off the other? He looked over at Liv, who was chatting happily with Audun Gilli. Yes, why indeed?

ONCE THEY CAME out of the forest and down into country where crops would grow most years, Marcovefa started marveling all over again at the richness of the landscape. Boats with sails astonished and delighted her, as the mere idea of them had delighted Liv a year before. Hamnet Thyssen wished he hadn't had the earlier memory; it meant he took no pleasure from the shaman's discovery.

"What happens in winter?" Marcovefa asked.

"About what you'd think. The rivers and lakes freeze. They haul the boats out of the water." Hamnet illustrated with gestures. Marcovefa followed well enough.

They were well to the west of Nidaros, and had to work their way south-east. Hamnet didn't think local officials in this part of the Empire were warned against them. He didn't see any couriers hotfooting it off to the capital to say he'd presumed to come back.

When he remarked on that to Ulric Skakki, the adventurer shrugged and said, "Well, no. But if these people have any idea what they're doing, you wouldn't see it. They'd make sure of that."

"If they knew what they were doing, they wouldn't be here," Count Hamnet said. "They'd be in the capital or somewhere else that mattered."

"Most of the time, you'd be right." Now Ulric was the one looking north. "If the Rulers come down—no, when the Rulers come down—it won't be like an ordinary Bizogot raid, though. The Bizogots likely wouldn't get this far any-way. I don't know if the Rulers can, either. I don't know . . . but they might."

"Yes. They might." Hamnet Thyssen's scowl covered the invaders and the Empire impartially. "I don't even know if I care."

"You need to spend some silver," Ulric Skakki said seriously.

The quick change of subject confused Hamnet. "What are you talking about?"

"You need to spend some silver," Ulric repeated. "Go to a whorehouse or pick a pretty serving girl who's easy—God knows there are enough of them. Once you lay her or she sucks your prong or whatever you happen to want, you won't hate the whole cursed world."

Hamnet shook his head. "It wouldn't mean anything."

"A pretty girl's got you in her mouth, it doesn't have to mean anything," Ulric said. "It feels good. Nothing wrong with that."

"Nothing wrong with it while it's going on," Count Hamnet said gloomily. "But afterwards you know she only wanted money, and she'd spit in your eye if you didn't pay her. If she doesn't care about you to begin with, why bother?"

"*Because* it feels good?" Ulric suggested with exaggerated patience.

"Not reason enough," Hamnet said. Ulric threw his hands in the air.

They came to the town of Burtrask just as the sun was setting. Burtrask had outgrown its wall; suburbs flourished outside the gray stone works. The gate guards hardly bothered to question the newcomers. Burtrask was used to prosperity, and seemed to have not a care in the world.

Touts just inside the gate bawled out the virtues of competing serais. Others bawled out the vices of competing bawdy houses. Count Hamnet felt Ulric's ironic eye on him. He didn't give the adventurer the satisfaction of looking back. Ulric's chuckle said he knew exactly what Hamnet wasn't doing, and why. Hamnet went right on ignoring him.

The seraikeeper they chose seemed surprised to have so many people descend on him at once, but he didn't let it faze him. "We'll have to set out pallets in the taproom for some of you, I'm afraid," he said. "We'll keep the fire going all night—no need to worry about that. I don't believe in freezing my guests. Neither do the girls down the street." The brothel stood a few doors away. That was also true of the other serais in Burtrask. They knew what travelers wanted. Most travelers, anyhow.

Thunk! Thunk! A hatchet came down on the necks of chickens and ducks out back. No doubt supper would be fresh. A couple of servants rolled barrels of beer into the taproom. Everybody in the Empire's northern provinces knew how Bizogots could drink.

Food and drink did make Count Hamnet feel better, but not enough. He bedded down on the taproom floor himself. Ulric Skakki and Arnora stayed together, and Trasamund had found a friendly serving girl without needing any suggestion from Ulric.

Strangers coming in for breakfast woke Hamnet not long after sunup. The seraikeeper, with work to do, didn't bother keeping quiet. He rattled pots and pans and thumped mugs down on the counter. Anyone who didn't like it, his attitude declared, was a lazy slugabed who should have paid for a room far from the racket. That his serai didn't have rooms enough for all his guests bothered him not a bit.

As Hamnet sat up and yawned, one of the men who'd come in for breakfast walked over to him: a nondescript fellow, not too tall or too short, not too fat or too thin, not too young or too old, with features altogether unmemorable except for gray eyes of uncommon alertness. "You are Count Hamnet Thyssen," he said. It was not a question.

Count Hamnet got to his feet. *Here we go,* he thought as he belted on his sword, which had lain beside him. "That's right," he said aloud. "I'm afraid you have the advantage of me, sir." That sounded politer than *Who the demon are you?* even if it meant the same thing.

"I'm Kormak Bersi," the man replied—a name as ordinary as his looks. "I have the honor to serve His Majesty."

That was a polite phrase, too. It meant *I'm an agent,* though it sounded nicer. "Well, what Raumsdalian doesn't?" Hamnet said. He pointed to the oatcakes and mug of beer Kormak was carrying. "Do you mind if I get myself some breakfast, too? Then we can talk, if talk is what you've got in mind."

"By all means, Your Grace, feed yourself," Kormak said. "And talk is the only thing I have in mind, believe me. I'm a peaceable man."

"That's nice," Hamnet said. "But whenever somebody says, 'Believe me,' I usually take it as a sign I shouldn't. I hope that doesn't offend you . . . too much."

Kormak Bersi's smile didn't reach his eyes. "Not . . . too much, Your Grace." He had a blade on his hip, and looked to be in good shape. Count Hamnet thought he could take him if he had to, but didn't want it to come to blood. He stepped over a couple of Bizogots who kept snoring away despite the noise and got a breakfast like the one the Emperor's man had bought. Kormak sat down at a small table. "Will this do?"

"As well as anywhere." Hamnet perched on a stool across from him. "Well? What's on your mind?" He tore off a chunk of oatcake, put it in his mouth, and deliberately began to chew.

Kormak also ate and drank a little before answering. Then, steepling his fingers in front of him, he said, "A bit of a surprise, discovering you back in Raumsdalia."

"Life is full of surprises," Hamnet said stolidly. He had to fight a scowl as he raised his mug to his lips. The surprises he'd got lately weren't pleasant ones.

"What do you suppose Sigvat II will think of your return?" Kormak Bersi asked, as if it mattered no more than the price of a jug of wine.

"I hope he'll think I wouldn't come back unless it was important," Hamnet replied. "You know about the Rulers?"

"I'm familiar with what you said last year," Kormak answered, which was no surprise at all. "And some, ah, wild rumors have also come down from the Bizogot country more recently."

"I'll bet they have. Most of what you've heard is less than what's really going on."

"Oh? How do you know what I've heard?"

"Have you heard that the Rulers have already conquered most of the steppe?" Hamnet demanded. "Have you heard they've smashed the Leaping Lynxes? They're that far south, and getting closer."

"I don't believe it!" Kormak Bersi exclaimed. "You're making that up so you can watch me jump and shout like a man a wasp just stung."

"By God, servant of His Majesty"—Hamnet laced what should have been a proud title with scorn—"I am not. Some of these Bizogots lying here in the taproom are Leaping Lynxes. They're what's left of the Leaping

Lynxes now, or what's left that's still free." He switched to the Bizogot tongue: "Marcomer! Are you awake there?"

"Afraid I am," Marcomer answered glumly. "Why? What do you want? Who's that sour-looking fellow with you? I don't know enough Raumsdalian to follow the two of you going back and forth, jabber, jabber, jabber."

"His name's Kormak Bersi, or that's what he says, anyway," Hamnet replied, drawing a glare from Kormak and proving the imperial agent understood the Bizogots' language. Hamnet went on, "He serves Sigvat II. He doesn't believe you're from the Leaping Lynxes. He doesn't believe what happened to them, either."

"Well, he's a bloody fool if he doesn't," Marcomer said, ambling over to join them.

"Watch your mouth, you." Kormak not only understood the Bizogot tongue, he spoke it well—and arrogantly.

"Oh, go bugger a weasel," Marcomer said. "What the demon do you think you can do to me that the God-cursed Rulers haven't already done?"

"What *did* they do?" Kormak Bersi demanded. "So far, I've heard nothing but noise. What really happened?"

"Most of the noise is your own jaws flapping, seems like. Raumsdalians like to hear themselves talk, don't they?" the Bizogot said. If he was trying to annoy Kormak even more, he succeeded. In fact, he succeeded even if he wasn't trying. But while the imperial agent steamed, Marcomer told him of riding back to the stone huts at the eastern edge of Sudertorp Lake and discovering that the Rulers had got there ahead of him. He told of rescuing a tiny fragment of his clan and then riding after the band Trasamund led. And he finished, "Here we are in the Empire. If you think the Rulers are very far behind us, you're even stupider than I give you credit for."

Kormak Bersi didn't seem any angrier, which proved he'd got caught up in Marcomer's tale. "His Majesty must hear of this, and quickly," the imperial agent said. "Our officers up in the forest need to know of it, too."

"If they don't know already, it isn't because we haven't spread the word," Hamnet Thyssen said. "Of course, they may not want to listen. We can't do anything about that."

"When do Raumsdalians ever listen to Bizogots?" Marcomer sounded more resigned than bitter.

"I'm no Bizogot," Count Hamnet reminded him. "Neither is Ulric Skakki . . . and neither is Audun Gilli." The last name tasted like bad fish in his mouth; he spat it out as fast as he could, and wiped his lips with the back of his sleeve afterwards.

"If what I hear is true . . ." Kormak Bersi began, and then stopped in alarm, for Marcomer's growl sound much like an angry dire wolf's. The Raumsdalian agent had nerve, for after gathering himself he repeated, "If this is true, it changes the nature of the orders I have."

"What kind of orders are those?" Hamnet asked. "Lock me up, lose the key, and God forbid you should pay attention to anything that comes out of my mouth?"

"Something like that." Kormak could sound almost as dry as Ulric Skakki. "But I may have to think twice."

"That would be nice. Most people have trouble enough thinking once," Count Hamnet said.

"Your precious Emperor must, if he doesn't believe the things he's heard about the Rulers," Marcomer said.

Kormak looked at him—looked through him, really. "You will find it a good policy not to speak ill of His Majesty," he said, his voice as chilly as if blown on the Breath of God.

"Why? If somebody's an idiot, how's he going to find out he's an idiot unless somebody else tells him so?" Bizogots didn't waste a lot of respect on their clan chiefs. To Marcomer, Sigvat II was nothing but a jarl writ large.

To Kormak Bersi, the idea that the Emperor might be an idiot wasn't far from blasphemous. "His Majesty is not an idiot," he said stiffly. "His Majesty cannot be an idiot."

"Why not?" Now Marcomer sounded honestly puzzled. "Isn't that like saying he can't shit? Everybody's an idiot now and again, on one thing or another. Over women, usually, or over men if you're a woman, but other stuff, too."

"His Majesty is not an idiot," Kormak repeated in tones more gelid than ever. "Anyone who says otherwise will be very, very sorry."

By Marcomer's expression, he thought the threat was idiotic, too. Hamnet Thyssen kicked him under the table to keep him from saying so. Hamnet also thought the threat was idiotic, or at least juvenile, but he knew the agent could enforce it. Marcomer glowered but, for a wonder, took the hint.

Ulric Skakki came down then, looking indecently—and that was probably just the right word—pleased with himself. He stopped and grinned. "Well, well! Kormak Bersi, as I live and breathe!"

"Hullo, Skakki," Kormak answered. "Have you really been daft enough to hook up with these fools and renegades? I heard it, but I didn't want to believe it."

"You may as well, because it's true." Ulric's grin got wider and more engaging—and, if you knew him the way Hamnet did, less reliable. "Life would be dull if you did the same old things over and over. Besides, there's real trouble loose up there, no matter what His Majesty thinks—or even if he thinks."

"Don't you start!" Kormak exclaimed.

Ulric looked more innocent than ever. "Who, me? What did I do?"

"You imagined that the Emperor might not be perfect," Hamnet said. "Now Bersi here has to decide whether to roast you over a slow fire or just cut off your head."

"Well, if he does cut it off, I can't very well tell him the Rulers are on the way down to cut off His Majesty's," Ulric said. "You'd think that was something people would want to know, but maybe not." His shrug was a small masterpiece of its kind.

"So you people plan on going to Nidaros and telling the Emperor he's been wrong all along?" Kormak said.

"You'd think he could see it for himself, but somebody's got to tell him if he can't," Ulric replied. "Since nobody else seems to want to, we'll do it."

"I'd better come with you," the imperial agent said.

"Why not? The more, the merrier." Ulric nodded to Count Hamnet. "Isn't that right, Your Grace?"

"How could I be any merrier?" Hamnet replied. "It's only my face that doesn't know it."

Kormak Bersi gave him a tired and dutiful smile. Marcovefa came downstairs just then, and Kormak forgot about everything but her. His focus was so quick and so intent, Hamnet wondered if he was something of a wizard himself—enough to sense that she was one, at any rate. "Where are you from?" he asked her in the Bizogot language.

"On top of the Glacier," she answered. "What about you?"

"Me? From Nidaros." Kormak looked surprised that he'd told her. "Are you really from atop the Glacier? Does that mean the stories these rogues were telling are true?"

"I don't know their stories," Marcovefa said. "But why would they lie?"

"Plenty of reasons." Kormak Bersi sounded sure of that. "How did you live, up there on top of everything?"

Marcovefa shrugged. "As best I could. We did not know we had little. No one else up there has more. Only when I come down here do I see there is more to have."

"What don't you have?" Kormak asked. "Up there, I mean."

"Bread. Meat from beast larger than fox. Hide from beast larger than fox." Marcovefa didn't mention meat from men, which was bound to be just as well. She went on, "Smetyn. Beer. These are great wonders."

By the way the agent smiled, he didn't think so. He took them all for granted, as Hamnet had before he saw how the clans atop the Glacier lived. "What do you think of the sorcery you've seen down here?"

Marcovefa snapped her fingers. "About that much. You are puny shamans. You have so many things, you do not trouble with wizardry the way you should."

That rocked Kormak Bersi back on his heels. He must have expected her to praise it to the skies. "What will you do now that you're down here among civilized people?" he asked.

"Don't know. Knock some sense into you, maybe," Marcovefa replied.

Kormak cast about for another question. He seemed to have trouble finding one that wouldn't land him in trouble. At last, he said, "Would you like to see Nidaros? Would you like to meet the Emperor?"

"Nidaros, yes. Big buildings . . . We have no big buildings. You must be clever, to make them so they don't fall down," Marcovefa said. Then she shrugged. "Your clan chief? Who cares? I have met plenty of clan chiefs. Man like other men, yes?"

"His Majesty Sigvat II, Emperor of Raumsdalia, is no clan chief," Kormak Bersi said haughtily.

"That's true. Most clan chiefs have better sense," Ulric Skakki said.

"Not you, too!" Kormak's scowl said he might have expected such things from Hamnet Thyssen, but not from Ulric.

"Yes, me, too," Ulric said. "What am I supposed to think when the Emperor's flat-out wrong and doesn't want to set things right?"

"Anything you say will be remembered," Kormak warned.

"That would be nice," Hamnet said. The agent stared at him. He explained: "Up till now, everyone's forgotten what we've said. Otherwise, somebody would have paid a little attention to it. I can hope so, anyhow."

"You aren't helping yourself," Kormak Bersi said.

"Take us to Nidaros. Tell the Emperor how naughty we've been," Count Hamnet said. "My guess is, he already knows."

XV

KORMAK BERSI RODE out of Burtrask with the travelers. "Are you our nursemaid, our shepherd, or our jailer?" Count Hamnet asked him.

"Not your jailer," the agent answered. "Plenty of others to tend to that. If you're lucky, I may keep you out of their clutches."

"And if we aren't?" Hamnet persisted.

"If you aren't, I may not."

There didn't seem to be much to say to that, so Hamnet Thyssen didn't try. Short of murder, they weren't going to shake Kormak. And murder seemed pointless when he went at least halfway towards believing them. Plenty of others in the Empire, from Sigvat II on down, didn't. Was riding on towards Nidaros pointless, then? Hamnet could only hope it wasn't, and wouldn't be.

As if to remind him of why he was taking the chance of returning, Raumsdalia spread itself out to best advantage before him. The weather stayed fine and mild. Fields of barley and rye ripened under that watery but steady sunshine. Horses and cattle and sheep grazed on the meadows. When the Raumsdalians and Bizogots rode through woods, red and gray squirrels frisked through the trees above, chattering and scolding as the horses clopped past.

With their soft fur, large eyes, and clever, handlike paws, squirrels charmed the Bizogots. Ulric Skakki, who knew them better, liked them less. "Nothing but rats with fluffy tails," he sneered.

"And people are nothing but dire wolves who comb their hair," Hamnet said.

"Oh, I don't know," Ulric said. "We'd go to war less often if we could lick our own privates."

They eyed each other. Hamnet wondered which of them was more cynical. By the look on Ulric's face, the adventurer was wondering the same thing. Better that, better admiring the scenery, than brooding about what would happen when he came to Nidaros. The Emperor's displeasure awaited him there. So did Gudrid's.

Thinking of her made him think of Liv. He'd hoped he would never think of the two of them together. But, like Gudrid, Liv was proving herself happier with someone else than with him. How Gudrid would laugh when she found out about that! She'd bedded Audun Gilli, too, before setting out from Nidaros. Hamnet wondered why. Probably so as not to leave anyone out.

Thinking about Sigvat or Gudrid or Liv hurt. Yes, better to watch squirrels in the pines and beeches and maples, better to watch wind rippling through growing grain, better to watch beasts fattening on long, green grass than to think of his own personal and political follies.

He'd just ridden out of a stretch of woods when he spotted vultures and teratorns and ravens spiraling down out of the sky ahead. "Well, well," he said. "Is that a sabertooth's work, or dire wolves', or bandits'?"

"All we have to do is ride on, and we'll find out . . . one way or another," Ulric Skakki said.

"Let it be bandits," Trasamund rumbled. "My sword has rested too long in its sheath. It grows thirsty." He reached back over his shoulder to stroke the hilt of the great two-handed blade.

"Fighting is too important to make a sport of it," Ulric said.

Count Hamnet was inclined to agree. Trasamund shook his head. "What better sport than scattering your enemies before you?" he said.

"What happens when they scatter you instead?" Ulric returned. "Where's the rest of your clan, jarl of the Three Tusk Bizogots?" Trasamund gave him a horrible look, one that proved looks couldn't kill, for Ulric stayed upright and smiling his usual mocking smile in return. Trasamund started to reach for the sword again, but arrested the gesture before his hand reached it. Ulric Skakki hadn't told him anything but the truth. Of course, the truth often hurt worse than any lies. Hamnet Thyssen knew that too well—and if he hadn't, one look at Liv riding alongside of Audun Gilli would have flayed the lesson into him forever.

Instead of looking at her, he grimly stared straight ahead. After he rode to the top of a low rise, he could see what the carrion birds were waiting for. A sabertooth had pulled down a cow in a meadow, and was tearing great chunks of flesh from the carcass. The big cat's short, stumpy tail quivered in delight as it ate.

The rest of the cattle in the herd had run off. They were starting to graze again, a couple of bowshots away. Every so often, their heads would rise—they knew where the sabertooth was, all right. But they also knew the killer wasn't likely to go after them now that it had other meat.

And what it didn't eat, the birds would. They waited in an expectant ring around the cat and the carcass. A raven hopped up and grabbed a gobbet of meat. Two more ravens tried to steal the dainty. The first one flew off, croaking angrily. One of the others chased it; the second seemed to decide its chances were better by the dead cow.

The sabertooth had ignored the thieving raven. Maybe it wasn't big enough to seem a competitor. Teratorns were another story. A bird with a body bigger than a turkey's and a wingspan as wide as three or four tall men—more to the point, a bird that size with a hooked beak in proportion—was enough to draw even a sabertooth's notice. This one lashed out with a mitten-sized front paw, warning the teratorn back. The oversized vulture squawked irately and retreated. Teratorns had a name for being stupid, but this one wasn't dumb enough to take on a sabertooth.

And the sabertooth wasn't dumb enough to take on three dozen people on horseback. Its short tail quivered again, this time in fury, as they approached. It roared, baring its formidable teeth. When it saw it couldn't scare them off, it slunk away. Its short hind legs gave it a peculiar gait, different from any other big cat's.

As soon as the sabertooth scuttled off towards the woods, the teratorns and lesser vultures and ravens—and a couple of opportunistic foxes—swarmed over the dead cow. There was plenty of meat for all of them, but they snapped and screeched at one another just the same.

Eyeing them with wry distaste, Ulric Skakki asked, "Remind you of anything you've seen before?"

"What? You mean Nidaros?" Count Hamnet replied, and Ulric nodded. Hamnet went on, "I think they have better manners here."

Kormak Bersi looked from one of them to the other. Hamnet had the feeling he was remembering everything they said, and he would use it against them when they got to the capital. *How can I land in worse trouble, though?*

he wondered, and smiled a little. Being in bad odor at the court had advantages he hadn't suspected.

AS THE TRAVELERS made their long, crablike progress towards Nidaros, Hamnet Thyssen wondered what news was coming straight to the imperial city from the Bizogot plains. Were couriers pounding down from some border post farther east with news that the Rulers had shattered the Leaping Lynxes? Did they have word that the Rulers were closer to the tree line than that? Were the Rulers already over the border themselves?

If Sigvat II got news like that, what would he think? Would he decide he'd been hasty when he looked down his nose at Hamnet and his warnings? Would he set Raumsdalia in motion to fight the danger pressing down from the north?

Would he care at all? Or would he be so busy with his pleasures in the capital that it wouldn't matter a bit to him? *One way or the other,* Hamnet thought, *I'll find out pretty soon.*

One thing didn't happen: they didn't pass couriers galloping out from Nidaros with orders for the imperial armies to assemble. Maybe that was a good sign—maybe it meant the Rulers weren't close to the border. Or maybe it meant that Sigvat wasn't going to worry about them even if they were. Again, Count Hamnet had the feeling he'd know the answer before long.

The scarred badlands that stretched out west from what had been Hevring Lake slowed the journey to the capital. Shrubs and clumps of grass sprouted here and there; birds and rabbits and other small game prowled the pocked landscape. The road had to make its way around and through all the scabby ravines and canyons, often doubling back on itself like a snake with a twisted spine. No farmers worked that land; it was far too rough to be broken to the plow. Some of the handful of people who did live there were hunters. Others were men and women who hoped everyone outside the badlands had forgotten they were alive.

Ulric Skakki raised a sardonic eyebrow in Hamnet Thyssen's direction. "Always good to get a look at your future home, isn't it?"

"I won't end up here, by God," Hamnet said.

"On the gibbet, maybe, but not here," Ulric said.

Hamnet only shrugged. "The gibbet would be better."

"What makes land like this?" Marcovefa asked. "We didn't see any other land—how do you say it?—torn up like this before."

As best he could, Hamnet Thyssen explained about how the flood that burst from Hevring Lake when its dam of dirt and ice finally failed scarred the land over which it poured. "Sudertorp Lake, farther north, has the same kind of cork in the jug—you saw that," he added. "One day it will open up, too, and pour across the Bizogot country. When everything is done up there, more badlands will stretch out to the west."

She thought about that, then nodded. "Could happen," she agreed. "Yes, could happen. Did magic make this, uh, dam go down?"

"No." Hamnet pointed north. "Once, a couple of thousand years ago, this was the edge of the Glacier. Yes, all the way down here. But it moved back, the weather got warmer, and the ice in the dam melted through. Sometimes big things happen all by themselves."

"Maybe." Marcovefa sounded more as if she were humoring him than as if she believed it.

They saw Nidaros' smoke rising into the sky days before they came to the capital. "People. Lots of people," Marcovefa said, pointing towards the dark smudge, and she was right. Any town let travelers know it was there well before they came to its walls because of the smoke that poured from hearths and cookfires and torches and lamps and all the other useful flames men and women kindled. An experienced traveler could gauge the size of a town from the smoke plume it sent up. The shaman from atop the Glacier was anything but an experienced traveler, but she saw that this smoke rose up from anything but an ordinary town.

"Are you glad to be coming home?" Kormak Bersi asked Count Hamnet.

The Raumsdalian noble didn't laugh in the agent's face, which to his mind only proved his restraint. "This is not my home. I wouldn't be glad to come here even if I weren't in hot water with the Emperor," he answered. "My home, such as it is, is a castle in the southeast, not far from where the woods begin. I wouldn't mind going there and forgetting about everything else, but I don't think everything else will forget about me. Sooner or later—likely sooner—the Rulers would end up besieging the place, and I doubt I could fight off the whoresons with my own retainers."

Kormak stared at him. "You think those barbarous savages can beat our glorious soldiers? For shame!"

"For one thing, our glorious soldiers have never fought lancers on mammothback," Hamnet Thyssen said. "For another, I'm not really worried about our glorious soldiers. I'm worried about the Rulers' wizards. Ask . . ." He ran down with a growl deep in his throat. He'd started to say, *Ask Audun*

Gilli. Ask Liv. Now he didn't even want to think about talking to them, though he knew he would have to. Growling still, he went on, "Bizogot shamans couldn't beat them—couldn't come close. And neither could our wizard." He pointed towards Audun. He wasn't aiming an arrow at the man who'd stolen Liv from him. It only felt that way.

"I don't think much of the kind of magic Bizogots can muster." Kormak sounded smug and patronizing. Raumsdalians often looked down their noses at their northern neighbors. They often had good reason to look down their noses at them, too. Here . . .

"Their shamans are good enough. And they work magic the same way we do. I've heard that from the shamans and from our sorcerers," Hamnet said. "The Rulers don't. They have their own way. Not surprising, not when they've been separate from us since the last time the Glacier came down, whenever that was."

Kormak Bersi surprised him by saying, "Since the days when we could go to the Golden Shrine."

"Yes, that's right. Since those days, or maybe even longer—who knows where their ancestors were back then?" Hamnet said. "But that doesn't matter. What matters is, their sorcerers are stronger than ours."

Kormak looked anything but convinced. He had no reason to believe Hamnet—he'd never faced the invaders' wizardry. Before he could say anything, Marcovefa asked, "What are you going on about?" She was getting ever more fluent in the ordinary Bizogot tongue, but Raumsdalian remained a closed codex to her—except when her sense of understanding spilled out like Hevring Lake after the dam broke down. That didn't seem to be happening now.

"About the Rulers' shamans," Hamnet Thyssen answered in the Bizogot language.

Many a Raumsdalian noblewoman would have envied Marcovefa's sniff. "Oh. *Them.* They're not so much," she said.

"Maybe not to you," Hamnet said. "They're better than anything we have. They've proved that, even if we wish they hadn't."

"Too many things," Marcovefa said impatiently. "You, these Bizogots . . . Too many *things.*" She freighted the word with scorn. "You have so many *things,* you don't pay enough attention to your shamanry."

"The Rulers have as many things as the Bizogots," Hamnet pointed out.

Marcovefa only sniffed again. "They don't pay enough attention to their shamanry, either. Maybe a little more than these Bizogots, a little more than you Raumsdalians. But not enough. Not close to enough. Up where I come from, they would be nothing. Nothing!" She snapped her fingers to show how much of a nothing they would be.

No one in his right mind wanted to go up where she came from. The clans atop the Glacier had no easy time climbing down, either. Did their poverty in all material things really make them such formidable wizards? Hamnet hadn't seen that when he was up there himself, but he hadn't looked for it, either. Down here, Marcovefa did seem uncommonly accomplished. Did that mean she was a powerful shaman, or that she came from a powerful school of sorcery? Hamnet didn't know, and he wasn't convinced she did, either.

"Maybe you'll just have to beat them all singlehanded," he said.

She looked at him, then back up towards the north. "Maybe I will."

THE BADLANDS ENDED as abruptly as they'd begun. All at once, the winding road ran straight and true towards Nidaros' western gate. What had been the muddy bottom of Hevring Lake was now some of the richest cropland in the Raumsdalian Empire. The travelers rode past orchards and fields and meadows finer than any they'd seen to the north and west. The farmers reacted to the sight of so many Bizogots on the road by hiding their livestock and shutting up their houses. They were brave and stupid at the same time: if these Bizogots really were invaders, only fleeing might have saved the locals.

"It would be funny if it weren't so sad," Trasamund said. "They haven't seen raiders in a long time, and they don't know what to do any more. God help them when they have to find out."

"First time I've heard you sound like you care about Raumsdalians," Ulric Skakki drawled.

The Bizogot jarl screwed up his face, then let his anger go in a long, loud sigh. "I care about anybody the Rulers hurt," he said. "Will you tell me I haven't earned the right?"

Not even Ulric had the crust to claim he hadn't.

All the Bizogots and Marcovefa exclaimed at the quality of the serai where they stayed that night. The roast pork *was* better than most, but the serai itself was nothing out of the ordinary to anyone who'd seen Nidaros itself and what the hostels there boasted. Hamnet found his bed wide and soft and inviting—far too much for someone sleeping in it by himself. He tossed and turned all night.

Ulric and Arnora had the room next door. The walls weren't thick enough to mute their screaming row—or the way they made up afterwards. Hamnet Thyssen plopped his pillow over his head. It didn't block out the sounds of lovemaking, which did nothing to help him drop off.

He came downstairs the next morning pouchy-eyed and grumpy. Beer and bacon made a good breakfast, but couldn't get him moving very fast. That Liv and Audun Gilli came down right after him only made things worse. They sat at a table halfway across the taproom—they weren't trying to torment him, as Gudrid would have—but his eyes kept sliding towards them.

Audun faced him. The wizard was smiling and happy and voluble. Hamnet knew the feeling; he'd enjoyed it himself not long before. He could see only the back of Liv's head. The way she held it made him sure she was happy, too. Maybe he was imagining things, but he didn't think so.

Ulric Skakki walked in and sat across from Hamnet. That kept him from seeing Liv unless he peered around the adventurer, which was probably part of what Ulric had in mind. It didn't help much, though. He didn't need to see Liv with his body's eyes to see her inside his mind.

To try to blot out that bright, shining image, he glowered at Ulric and said, "You're bloody noisy—you know that?"

"Not all my fault," Ulric said. "Arnora gets her share of the blame. More than her share, to tell you the truth—she enjoys quarreling over nothing, and I don't."

"Cursed walls are thin," Count Hamnet said, sipping from his mug. "By now, I know just about everything she enjoys—and you, too."

"I told you you needed to get laid," Ulric said with what sounded like exaggerated patience. "All that stuff is turning sour inside of you. It can't be healthy. You'll end up like one of those bull mastodons in"—he snapped his fingers, looking for a word—"what the demon do they call it?"

"Musth," Hamnet answered.

"That's it!" Ulric agreed. A serving girl came over to the table. He ordered breakfast, then turned back to Hamnet Thyssen. "They'd be a lot happier if they found a friendly female, and so, by God, would you."

"There's no such thing as a friendly female," Hamnet said stonily. "Not if you're looking for something that lasts."

"Not always true. A lot of the time, maybe, but not always," Ulric Skakki said. "Besides, if all you're trying to do is steer clear of musth, you don't care whether it lasts or not. You musth believe me, my deer fellow." He lisped with malice aforethought.

Count Hamnet grimaced at the pun and at the sentiment. "It wouldn't mean anything," he insisted.

"It would mean you could sleep at night. Is that so bad?"

"It would take more than that," Hamnet said.

"That would be a good start." Ulric looked back towards the stairs to make sure Arnora wasn't coming. He lowered his voice: "If you want to take my not quite beloved off my hands, I won't say a word. I'll be glad I don't have to worry about her, to tell you the truth. And since you say you know what she enjoys . . ."

"No, thanks." Hamnet's ears heated. "I know what I'd enjoy, too, and she isn't it."

"Too bad." The adventurer eyed him, one corner of his mouth canted up in rueful amusement. "I always remembered you were a hard case, but I didn't think you'd be quite so hard as this."

"Well, I am," Hamnet said, not without a certain somber pride.

"All right. Fine." Ulric made flapping motions with his arms, as if he were trying to get a duck to go where he wanted it to. "Some people are stupid enough to enjoy being miserable. I didn't think you were one of those, but if you are, you are."

The girl brought him breakfast then. He settled in and began to eat. He ignored Hamnet Thyssen altogether, or seemed to. Hamnet grumbled to himself; he didn't think he enjoyed being miserable. He hated it. He would much rather not have been miserable—but who'd given him a choice? Not Gudrid. Not Liv, either. That was how it looked to him, anyway.

Kormak Bersi came down just then. He sat down next to Ulric and nodded across the table to Count Hamnet. "You look cheerful this morning," he remarked.

"Oh, drop dead," Hamnet snarled.

Some men would have drawn sword on him. Kormak only turned to Ulric and said, "He sounds as happy as he looks, too."

"Somewhere down inside, I think he is," Ulric answered. "Only he hasn't told his face about it yet."

"You should go up on stage and tell jokes," Hamnet Thyssen said. "You could set a bowl at the edge, and everybody who laughed would throw money into it. You'd get rich in nothing flat. Then you wouldn't need to go adventuring."

"Matter of fact, I've done that," Ulric said. "If you think this is a hard way to make a living, you ought to try it. And mostly they don't throw money. What they do throw . . ." He held his nose.

Hamnet had helped jeer bad comics and jugglers off the stage. He'd never thought about what they were feeling when the audience booed them and flung old vegetables or rotten eggs. They were doing the best they could, even if it wasn't good enough. All at once, he understood that much too well.

WHEN THE TRAVELERS came to the western gate, they had to wait behind carts filled with produce and donkeys carrying baskets of fruit. The old lake bottom was Nidaros' larder these days. A peasant woman with a young porker under each arm sassed the gate guards. By the way they gave back her cheek, they'd been harassing one another a couple of times a week for years.

A mounted party made up mostly of fierce-looking Bizogots was something else again. Aside from likely being dangerous in their own right, the travelers broke routine. That was plenty to make the gate guards suspicious all by itself.

"Give me your names," ordered the fat, sloppy-looking sergeant in charge of the guards. One by one, the newcomers did. When Hamnet Thyssen announced himself, the sergeant jerked as if a wasp had stung him. "You can't be here! I'm supposed to arrest you if you show your face around here!"

"Good luck," Hamnet said. Not only did his companions outnumber the guards about four to one, each of them was probably worth at least two of these soft timeservers in a fight.

"He's in my custody. No arrest needed," Kormak Bersi said.

The sergeant sent him a fishy stare. "And who the demon are *you*?"

Kormak Bersi told him who, and what, he was. The agent displayed a bronze badge that proved he wasn't lying. "Any more questions?" he asked, his voice ominously mild.

"No, sir." The sergeant seemed to shrink into himself, and to shrink away from Kormak. He waved. The travelers rode into Nidaros.

Even Trasamund and Liv, who had been to the imperial capital before, stared in wonder. For the other Bizogots, Nidaros raised more than wonder—it raised slack-jawed astonishment. And for Marcovefa . . . What went beyond astonishment. Hamnet Thyssen had no word for it, but he knew it when he saw it.

"So *many* people," she whispered. She used her own dialect, but he managed to understand it.

Nidaros' streets ran from southeast to northwest, from northeast to southwest. A few ran from east to west. None went from north to south. If they had, they would have given the Breath of God a running start. Houses stood close together, so as not to let too much of the wind squeeze between them. They all had high-pitched roofs that would shed snow. All but the poorest had two walls on their north-facing side, the space between filled with air that helped blunt the cold. Doorways, without exception, faced south.

People from all over the Raumsdalian Empire, and from beyond, crowded the streets. Some of them looked to be tourists, gawking at the tall buildings and at the shoals of mankind of which they made up a part. Others hawked everything from mammoth ivory to fine swords to sabertooth fangs to tobacco from the far south.

Ulric Skakki bought some tobacco first chance he got. He charged his pipe, lit it with a twig he ignited at a sausage-seller's brazier, and puffed out happy clouds of smoke. Marcovefa said, "I have seen you do that before. What good is it?"

"I like it," Ulric answered. "I don't need any more reason than that."

She wrinkled her nose. "It stinks."

"I don't think so," Ulric said. "But even if it does, so what, by God? Plenty of other stinks in a city the size of this one."

Marcovefa couldn't very well argue with that. The odors of all sorts of smokes rode the air. So did the stenches of sewage and garbage. Horse and horse manure were two more strong notes, unwashed humanity yet another. Hot, greasy food had a place in there, too. Whether that was a stench or an appetizing smell depended on your point of view—and, perhaps, on the quality of the cooking.

"If we stay here long and the Emperor just ignores us, we'll run low on money," Hamnet Thyssen said. "Everything here costs more than in the provinces."

"Whatever Sigvat does, he won't ignore us," Ulric predicted. "He may listen to us. He may take our heads for being rude enough to show he was wrong. But he won't ignore us."

Count Hamnet thought that over. After a few heartbeats, he nodded. By riding north when Sigvat II wanted him to forget about the Rulers and the Bizogot steppe, he'd forced himself on the Emperor's attention. Sigvat wouldn't have forgotten about something like that.

"There." Kormak Bersi spoke in the Bizogot language. Pointing straight
ahead, he went on, "You can see the palace over the closer buildings."

Someone in that high spire who looked out over Nidaros could see the
approaching travelers, too. Could that someone make out that most of
them were Bizogots? Would he know they were refugees fleeing the invaders from beyond the Glacier? *If he doesn't know it, it's not because nobody
told him,* Hamnet thought.

"Try our hostel! Best in town!" a tout yelled.

Trasamund and Ulric Skakki and Count Hamnet and Kormak Bersi
looked at one another. They all nodded at the same time. "Take us there,"
Hamnet called. The best hostel in Nidaros would cost more than an ordinary one, but he would have bet the tout didn't really work for one of the
fancy places the capital boasted.

The man looked astonished and delighted and dismayed, all at the same
time. "What? The lot of you?" he said.

"Yes, the lot of us, by God," Hamnet answered. "You're not the best hostel in town if you can't make us fit."

"Well, we'll try," the tout said. "Come with me, and I'll show you what
we've got."

Merchants had to stop their wagons and pack trains as the travelers
turned off the main thoroughfare and onto a little side street. The traders
sent some hard looks their way, but no one seemed inclined to quarrel
with a small army of mounted and armed Bizogots—and the handful of
Raumsdalians with the northern barbarians looked like dangerous cus-
tomers, too.

The hostel turned out to be better than Hamnet Thyssen had expected,
but it was still a long way from the best. No southern wines graced the taproom, only beer and ale and mead. The rooms were cleaner than most, but
small and plain, not as opulent as chambers in the palace, the way they
would have been at a first-class establishment. And the proprietor proved
willing to haggle, which he wouldn't have in a fancy place. In one of those,
you went somewhere else if you couldn't afford what the landlord asked.

Hamnet made sure he didn't get a room next to Ulric and Arnora. The Bizogots between whom he tried to sleep didn't rut their way through the
night. Instead, the big blond man on one side invited in friends, and they all
started to sing. The racket was appalling, but Count Hamnet wasn't appalled.
It wasn't the kind of noise he had to pay attention to, the way lovemaking
would have been. Even though drunken discords woke him a couple of

times, they didn't infuriate him or leave him quivering with unslaked lust. He had no trouble dropping off again.

After breakfast the next morning, he nodded to Kormak Bersi. "Well, you've captured me, or near enough," he said. "Take me to the palace. Let's get this over with."

"Are you sure you know what you're doing?" the imperial agent asked.

"No, but then neither does Sigvat, and it doesn't stop him. It doesn't even slow him down," Hamnet answered. "We'll see what he says when he finds out I've come back in spite of everything."

"Yes, we will, won't we?" On that encouraging note, Kormak rose from the table. Hamnet Thyssen followed him.

THEY WALKED TO the palace. Count Hamnet would have ridden, but Kormak Bersi didn't seem to think it was a good idea. Hamnet thought about arguing, but let it go. Approaching any way at all was arrogant enough. Sigvat II was bound to see it like that, anyhow.

A Raumsdalian in Bizogot furs and leather walking through the streets of the capital got his share of curious looks and more. Hamnet Thyssen stolidly ignored them. He hadn't trimmed his hair and beard, either.

When he and Kormak came to the palace, the gate guards gaped at him, too. Kormak displayed his emblem for them. That got him respect, at least. "Who's the wild man with you, sir?" a guard asked.

"I am Count Hamnet Thyssen," Hamnet growled, sounding like the proudest of nobles. "And who the demon are you?"

The guard's jaw dropped. His eyes all but bugged out of his head. "By God, you *are* him," he choked out. "What are you doing here?"

Kormak Bersi had asked him the same question in different words. Couldn't anybody in Nidaros see out past the city walls? It didn't look that way. "Reporting to His Majesty," Hamnet answered. "I know more about what's going on in the Bizogot country than anybody he's talked to lately. I hope he'll listen to me, for the Empire's sake."

"But he's angry at you. Didn't you know that?" the guard said.

Count Hamnet shrugged. "I'll take the chance. I have to. If I can come back for the Empire's sake, he can listen to me."

"Go report that Count Hamnet has returned to the palace," Kormak Bersi said.

The guard didn't do it himself. Instead, he told off a couple of his men and sent them hotfooting it down the corridor. Hamnet Thyssen knew what that meant: this fellow didn't want to be associated with bad news. Had Hamnet been in good odor here, the squad leader would have done the job himself.

A couple of disbelieving courtiers came back with the guards. They stared at Count Hamnet as if at some fierce animal unaccountably running loose instead of being caged in a zoological garden. "Good day, gentlemen," he said, as if to show them he could be civilized after all.

They flinched from the sound of his voice. "What the demon did you come back here for, Thyssen?" one of them said. "Don't you know the Emperor would just as soon kill you as look at you?"

"Well, he can do that," Hamnet said. "The Empire won't be better off if he does, but he can."

"You don't care whether you live or die, do you?" the courtier croaked.

After examining what lay inside himself, Count Hamnet shook his head. "Now that you mention it, no."

That made the courtiers back away in a hurry. He didn't suppose he could blame them. Self-preservation did matter to most people, and especially to people who had anything to do with princes and potentates. It would have mattered to him, too, if Liv weren't giving herself to a no-account wizard.

But she was. Next to that, anything Sigvat or his torturers could do hardly seemed worth getting excited about.

Another courtier came out, this one with a fat gold chain around his neck to show what an important fellow he was. "So you want to see the Emperor, do you?" he said in a voice that sounded barely alive.

"That's right," Hamnet answered. "Can you take me to him?"

"I can. I doubt I would be doing you a favor, but I can."

"Let me worry about that," Count Hamnet said.

"I intend to. And you have more to worry about than you can imagine," the courtier replied. "But, if you must, come with me."

Hamnet Thyssen did. The palace seemed badly overdecorated; he was too used to serais and to Bizogot tents. It also seemed too warm. How much wood did Sigvat and his servitors go through every day? *Is that why I came back? To preserve such waste?* Hamnet wondered.

The courtier with the gold chain led him to the throne room. There he and Kormak Bersi had to stand and wait for a while. Sigvat II was busy talking to an elderly merchant whose fur robe celebrated his wealth. At last, the fellow bowed and tottered away. The courtier stepped forward. In ringing tones, he announced Count Hamnet.

"Your Majesty." Hamnet went to one knee before the Emperor. Beside him, Kormak, who was not a noble, dropped to both knees.

"So. You came back to mock me, did you?" Sigvat's voice was too thin and light to give him a proper growl. He was at least ten years younger than Hamnet Thyssen, and perhaps had more than his share of a young man's worry about whether his elders respected him as much as he thought they ought to.

"No, Your Majesty." Count Hamnet shook his head. "I came back to warn you. The Rulers turn out to be even more dangerous than I thought they were last year."

"So you say," Sigvat jeered. "*I* say one set of barbarians up beyond the woods is the same as another. *And* I say you disobeyed me when you went north last fall. You weren't supposed to do that. How do you propose to defend yourself, eh?"

"By telling you it was necessary," Hamnet Thyssen answered. "I understood the frozen plains better than you did, since I've been there and you haven't."

"Your Majesty, what's happening on the plains now shows that Count Hamnet has a point," Kormak Bersi said. "He—"

"He is a traitor," the Emperor broke in. "If you back him—and I see you do—then you're another." He raised his voice to a shout: "Guards! Take this wretch—take both these wretches—to the dungeons!"

XVI

Hamnet Thyssen had always known the imperial palace had dungeons. He hadn't expected to make their personal acquaintance. Wasn't a big part of real life the difference between what you expected and what you got?

Fighting a dozen guards would have been suicidally stupid. Hamnet took a certain dour satisfaction in noting how astonished Kormak Bersi seemed when the guards laid hold of him. His only crime had been to tell the truth as he saw it. To Sigvat, that was perfidious enough all by itself.

The guards hustled Count Hamnet and Kormak out of the throne room. The last thing the Raumsdalian noble saw there was the courtier's smirking face. "What's going on here?" someone asked as the guards frog-marched the new prisoners through the corridors down which Hamnet had come on his own not long before.

"They made the Emperor angry," one of the guards answered. He didn't seem to think he needed to say anything more. By all appearances, he was right.

How many times had Hamnet walked past a stairway without wondering where it went? Now he found out with this one, and wished he hadn't. Dungeons were supposed to be dark and gloomy, weren't they? This one, built below ground level, lived up to—or down to—that specification. Mold clung to the massive stones of the wall. Only a few torches gave fitful light. The air was cold and damp, and smelled of sour smoke and stale straw.

"In you go," the guards told Kormak Bersi. One of them opened a massive wooden door with a small iron grate at eye level. Kormak's captors shoved him in, closed the door (the hinges didn't squeal—they were rustproof bronze), and made sure it stayed closed with a heavy wooden bar.

"Now it's your turn," a guard said to Hamnet. He went into a cell some distance from Kormak's. He supposed the guards didn't want him plotting with the agent. That was a compliment of sorts, but only of sorts. No matter how much plotting he and Kormak did, he couldn't see how it would help them get away.

His cell had stone walls, a stone floor and ceiling, a musty pallet and wool blanket that were bound to be verminous, and a stinking slop bucket. Maybe a wizard could have put that together and used it to escape, but Hamnet knew he couldn't. The only light came through the grate.

After a bit, the door to the cell opened again. Three guards pointed bows at Hamnet while a fourth set a jug and a loaf on the floor and then hastily withdrew. When Count Hamnet sniffed the jug, he sighed. It held water. If he drank from it, it would probably give him a flux of the bowels. Of course, if he didn't . . . The loaf wasn't very big, and seemed almost as full of husks and chaff as his mattress. He ate about a quarter of it, and found it tasted as bad as it looked. Saving the rest for later—he had no idea how often they would feed him, but feared the worst—was no hardship. Eating more when he got hungry probably would be. Again, though, not eating was bound to be worse.

He paced off the cell. Six strides from the door to the back wall. Seven from one side to the other. With nothing else to do, he walked back and forth and around and around for a bit. That soon palled, as he'd known it would. He sat down on the miserable pallet. The blanket that went with it would be warm enough now. When the Breath of God started to blow? How many prisoners died of chest fever every winter?

As his eyes got used to the near-darkness all around, he saw more sharply than he had when the guards first shoved him in here. That might have been useful if there were anything much to see in the cell. Or so he thought at first.

After a while, he got up and went back to the far wall. No, his eyes hadn't tricked him. Prisoners who'd been here before had used—well, who could say what?—to scratch their names and other things onto the stones there. Some proclaimed their innocence. Some named the women they'd loved. One had carefully shown a woman loving him. The man wasn't a bad artist, and he must have had plenty of time to complete his work. Hamnet wondered how many other luckless souls in this cell had wandered over to the obscene drawing to remind themselves of what they were missing.

His mouth tightened. If he thought of Gudrid or Liv, he wouldn't necessarily think of them doing that with him. He might be more likely to see them in his mind's eye loving someone else.

And some of the prisoners cursed the people who'd caused them to end up here. Emperors' names figured prominently there. Some of them went back hundreds of years. Viglund had been a great conqueror in the days when the Raumsdalian Empire was much younger than it was now. Someone he'd conquered hadn't appreciated it.

Much good it did the poor bastard, Hamnet Thyssen thought. *Much good anything does anybody.*

With nothing better to do, he went back to the pallet and sat down again. He started reciting poetry, and wished he knew more of it. A bard might be able to entertain himself for a long time.

Or he might not. A guard's head blocked the grate, killing almost all the light in the cell. "Shut up in there!" the man snarled. "No noise allowed!"

Hamnet Thyssen laughed in his face. "What will you do to me if I make noise? Throw me in the dungeon?"

When the guard laughed, too, it was not a pleasant sound—anything but. "You want to find out, smart boy? Keep mouthing off and you will, by God! There's never been a bad place that couldn't get worse."

He spoke with great assurance. After a couple of heartbeats, Count Hamnet decided he was bound to be right. The guards could do whatever they wanted to a prisoner who annoyed them. "I was only trying to make time pass by," Hamnet said.

"It'll pass whether you do anything or not," the guard said. "So shut up. That's the rules." He stomped off.

A kidney stone would pass, too . . . eventually. And it would hurt all the time while it was passing. As for the rules, well, the people who enforced them always liked them better than those at whose expense they got enforced.

Swearing to himself, Hamnet—quietly—lay back on the miserable, lumpy pallet. When he and Kormak Bersi didn't come back to the hostel, Trasamund and Ulric Skakki would realize something had gone wrong. No doubt they would have a good idea what, too. But what could they do about it? When the Emperor was angry, could they do anything at all?

They would probably come straight to the palace to try to find out what was going on. And what would happen then? Count Hamnet's best guess was that they would end up here in the dungeons themselves in short order.

If Audun Gilli and Liv came along . . . Hamnet Thyssen ground his teeth. He didn't suppose they would end up here, or Marcovefa, either. But the Emperor was bound to have some place where he could put wizards who caused him trouble—a place warded by other, stronger wizards, no doubt.

Did the Raumsdalian Empire have any wizards stronger than Marcovefa? Count Hamnet wasn't so sure about that. She was liable to give Sigvat's arrogant sorcerers a surprise of the sort they hadn't had in many years, if ever. But was she stronger than all of them put together? Hamnet had trouble believing she was.

While he wondered about such things, time seemed to move at its normal rate. When his river of thought ran dry, though, it was as if everything stopped. He might have been in the cell for centuries, with another eternity or two to look forward to. He wasn't too hungry. He didn't need to ease himself. In the unending dim, damp twilight in there, those were his only clues that he hadn't already spent a very long time indeed down below all the parts of the palace he'd ever visited before.

If I do stay here long enough, my nails will grow out into claws and my beard will reach down to my waist. He might measure months and years that way. Days and weeks? The gauge wasn't fine enough. Sunrise? Sunset? He was even more cut off from them than he would have been in winter up beyond the Glacier. The sun might stay below the horizon for weeks up there, but you knew it would come back sooner or later. Down here, he had no guarantee of ever seeing another sunrise again.

He must have slept, for he jerked in surprise when the cell door opened and a guard threw in another miserable loaf. He still had some left from the last one. They weren't trying to starve him, anyway. Was that any favor to him? Again, he wasn't so sure.

HE LISTENED FOR Ulric Skakki's sly tones and Trasamund's bellow outside the door. It wasn't that he wanted them mewed up in here with him. But he did expect them to come after him. When they didn't, he wondered what had happened to them—what had gone wrong with them, in other words.

He'd been there for seventeen loaves—another way to count the time—when a guard looked in through the grate and said, "C'mere, Thyssen. You've got a visitor."

"A visitor?" Hamnet's voice sounded rusty even to himself. He hadn't used it much lately. He also sounded astonished—and he was. He had trouble imagining any of the travelers talking their way down here without ending up prisoners themselves.

"That's right," the guard said. "You want to talk or not?"

"I'm coming." Count Hamnet hurried to the door. Somebody thought enough of him to come down here. That had to be good news, didn't it? He eagerly peered out.

Gudrid looked back through the grate at him.

She wore attar of roses, the same scent she'd brought with her when she traveled beyond the Glacier the year before. The flowery sweetness seemed even more incongruous against the stenches in the dungeon than it had up on the frozen steppe.

"Hello, Hamnet," his former wife said. Her red-painted mouth stretched into a broad, happy smile. "So good to see you where you belong at last."

"I don't know what I did to deserve you," he answered. "Whatever it is, by God, I'm paying for it now."

"I thought the very same thing when we were together," Gudrid said.

He'd thought she loved him. He'd always known he loved her. Part of him still did, and always would. That only made her betrayal more bitter. He tried to show she couldn't wound him—a lying, and a losing, battle. "Are you enjoying yourself? Stare all you please," he said.

"I should throw peanuts, the way I would at monkeys in cages," she said, smiling wider yet. "What would you do for a peanut, Hamnet?"

He told her where she could put a peanut. He told her where she could put a year's worth of peanuts, and how well they would fit there, and why. She only laughed. Why not? She was on the outside looking in. He was on the inside looking out. It made all the difference in the world.

"Did Eyvind Torfinn tell you I was here?" he asked.

That only made Gudrid laugh again. "Don't be sillier than you can help, darling. Dear Eyvind knows, yes, because I told him. But Sigvat told me."

She sounded smug as a cat in a creamery. She no doubt had the right to sound that way, too. Hamnet Thyssen used a shrug for a shield. "He can say what he wants. He can do what he wants. He's the Emperor, after all."

"Oh, you do know that!" Gudrid exclaimed in mock surprise. "He didn't seem to think you did."

"Well, there is one thing," Hamnet said. "If the Rulers overrun Raumsdalia, he won't stay Emperor for long."

Gudrid sneered. "How likely do you think that is?"

"You were up there. You saw the Rulers last year. You saw more of some of them than I did, by God." Count Hamnet wasn't quite sure Gudrid had slept with their chief; he hadn't watched them in the act, for which he was duly grateful. But he was sure enough, and that was the kind of thing Gudrid did. For good measure, he added, "They've spent the time since last winter smashing up the Bizogots."

His former wife didn't bother denying anything. She did ask, "Is Trasamund all right?"

"He's not hurt, but his clan's wrecked. He's down here in Nidaros, too." Hamnet Thyssen didn't think he was giving anything away with that news.

All Gudrid said was, "Ah." Then she asked, "And your new barbarous beloved?"

"Liv is here, too."

Count Hamnet didn't think he revealed anything by how he said that. He must have been wrong, though, for Gudrid pounced—or rather, burst out laughing. "So she's gone and left you, has she? Well, that didn't take long."

How did she know? How could she tell? Whatever the answer was, her instincts were unfailing. "Yes, she's left me," Hamnet said. "She doesn't torment me for the fun of it, anyhow."

"Don't worry about it, sweetheart. Sooner or later, she will." With that casual reassurance, Gudrid blew him a kiss and swept out of the dungeon. A guard followed her. Hamnet watched them as far as the grate allowed, which wasn't very. Then, shaking his head, he went back to the pallet and lay down again.

The guard spoke to him: "You were married to that gal?"

"Afraid so," Hamnet said.

"I was married to her, I'd be afraid, too," the guard said. "She's nothing but trouble."

"I found that out. A little late, but I did," Hamnet Thyssen said.

"She why you're shut up here?"

"No." Hamnet shook his head. "I found out about the Emperor a little late, too."

"Here, now. You can't talk like that," the guard said. "You do, and—"

"I know. I know. It'll be even worse than it is already," Hamnet said wearily. "But you asked. I tried to tell you the truth."

"That's what they all say." The guard didn't want to listen. And he didn't have to listen, either. He walked away instead.

What will they do to me now? Hamnet wondered. He knew how it could get worse, all right. They could stop feeding him. They could stop giving him water. Or they could just grab him and haul him off to the torturer. If enough of them came in, he hadn't a prayer of fighting them off.

They didn't do any of those things. The loaves and the water kept coming. He stayed in the cell . . . and stayed, and stayed. That might not have been worse, but it was bad enough and then some.

"YOU! THYSSEN!" A guard with a raspy voice barked at him through the grate.

"What now?" Count Hamnet asked. Any change in routine worried him. Silence, being ignored, was routine. Getting noticed? He didn't expect good news.

"Somebody here wants to talk to you," the guard said.

Do I want to talk to Gudrid again? Hamnet wondered. After what had to be days of doing nothing, even a quarrel with his former wife might seem entertaining. If that wasn't madness, he didn't know what would be. All the same, it was so. He got to his feet and walked up to the door.

Seeing him approach, the guard nodded. "Here's the bum," the man said, and stepped to one side.

Hamnet braced himself to start snarling at Gudrid again. But those were not her aging but still attractive—still beautiful—features on the other side of the grate. Instead, Hamnet Thyssen found himself face-to-face with Earl Eyvind Torfinn.

Gudrid's husband. Gudrid's husband who hadn't, or acted as if he hadn't, the slightest idea how many times she'd put horns on him.

"I grieve to see you like this, Your Grace," the scholarly noble said.

"I'm not too happy about it myself, Your Splendor," Count Hamnet answered. "Did Gudrid finally tell you I was here?"

Earl Eyvind didn't notice that *finally*. He shook his head. His jowls wobbled. He'd regained the comfortable plumpness he'd enjoyed before his journey to the north the year before. Scratching at the edge of his whiskers, he said, "No. I don't think she knows you're here."

That only proved the right hand didn't know what the left was doing— nothing new where Gudrid was concerned. "Well, how the demon *did* you find out I was stuck here, then?" Hamnet demanded.

"Ulric Skakki is a resourceful chap," Eyvind replied: a truth so obvious, even he could see it. "He got word to me that you were having, ah, difficulties. I was shocked. I truly didn't believe His Majesty would be so, ah, unaccommodating."

"Oh, you can't say that." Hamnet Thyssen wagged a finger at him. "No, you can't, by God. After all, here I am—accommodated."

"Er, yes." Eyvind Torfinn laughed uneasily. "So you are. But whether you should be . . . That, perhaps, is a different question."

"Sigvat's got the answer. He says I should." Count Hamnet sounded more nearly resigned than outraged, which only proved he made a better actor than he'd ever dreamt he could.

"So I discovered," Eyvind said. "I urged your release—urged it in strong terms, too—but His Majesty was not amenable to reason."

He sounded surprised that reason couldn't sway the Raumsdalian Emperor. Reason would have swayed him, and so he believed it should sway everyone. That might have been logical—but it wasn't reasonable. Gudrid would have known better. Even Count Hamnet knew better.

"Thank you for trying," he said, and meant it. He couldn't dislike Eyvind Torfinn, even if the man was—occasionally, no doubt—sleeping with Gudrid. Eyvind's fondness for her aside, he was a decent man.

"It was my pleasure, my privilege," he said now. "And Skakki hinted at some remarkable adventures. Ascending to the top of the Glacier. Meeting people who dwelt up there . . . Extraordinary! I wish I could have been with you."

You had your chance last winter, and you stayed here, Hamnet Thyssen thought. Then he didn't just think it—he said it out loud. If Eyvind Torfinn didn't like it, so what? What could he do that Sigvat wasn't already doing?

The scholarly earl winced. "I am not a young man, Your Grace," he said stiffly. "I thought myself unequal to another journey up into the wilds so soon after the first, and Gudrid would have been adamantly opposed to setting out again, you know. The travels were a considerable hardship to her."

Poor thing. She only had Bizogots and warriors from the Rulers to seduce. Hamnet didn't say that. No one had told him when Gudrid was sleeping with other Raumsdalians, either. He'd had to find out for himself. Earl Eyvind would, too. Or maybe he already knew, and chose to look the other way. Hamnet had wondered about that before. He knew himself to be incapable of it.

Eyvind Torfinn wasn't lying to him here. He was sure of that. The other noble's white hair and paunch declared his years. And he seemed to listen to, and to obey, Gudrid as if her fidelity were perfect and unquestioned.

"If you talked to Ulric, you'll know the Rulers have come south of Sudertorp Lake," Hamnet said. "You'll know they've smashed the Leaping Lynxes."

"Yes, he did tell me that." Eyvind's voice was troubled. Maybe he'd done his best not to believe it. "It isn't good news."

"Too bloody right, it isn't," Hamnet Thyssen agreed. "If those bastards aren't over the border, they will be soon. You saw some of what their sorcery can do. Will we be able to stop them? Will we even be able to slow them down?"

"I have to hope we will, Your Grace," Eyvind said.

"I've had all kinds of hopes," Hamnet said harshly. "Gudrid's married to you. Liv is sleeping with Audun Gilli. I'm spending my time in this stinking dungeon. So what the demon is hope worth?"

Eyvind Torfinn lurched back two steps, his face as shocked as if Count Hamnet had slapped him. "I'm—I'm sorry," he got out after a couple of heartbeats. "Ulric . . . said nothing of your misfortunes with Liv."

"No, eh? I wonder how often people have accused him of discretion," Hamnet said. "But he didn't need to keep his mouth shut. It's true. Everybody who came down from the Bizogot country with me knows it. It'd be all over the city if people all over the city gave a curse about me."

"My condolences. Losing one woman is hard. Losing another is much more than twice as hard." Earl Eyvind's thoughts marched uncomfortably well with Hamnet's. The old man sounded as if he spoke from experience. He might well have. He was old enough to have loved and lost any number of times before wedding Gudrid. Did he love her, or was she only an ornament to him? If she was, she was an expensive ornament with a sharp pin.

"Not much I can do about it from here. Not much I can do about anything from here," Hamnet Thyssen said. "If you have the pull to get me out, Your Splendor, I'm in your debt the rest of my days. And what I owe, I pay. If you know me, you know that's so."

"I do know you, and I know that," Eyvind said. "I don't want your service, Thyssen. I want you free, to do what you can for the Empire. I am already doing everything I know how to do to get you out. This does not sit well with my wife, but I am doing it nonetheless." He set his chins and looked as heroic as a peaceable, mild-mannered scholar was ever likely to look.

He would try in spite of what Gudrid thought? How much luck was he likely to have, when Gudrid's thoughts and those of Sigvat II were so much alike? Hamnet had no idea of the answer, though he doubted the omens were good. He took a step back and bowed to Eyvind. "I thank you, Your Splendor."

"It's the least I can do, or try to do," Eyvind Torfinn answered. "I make no promises, however much I wish I could. God keep you." He sketched a salute and stepped away from the grate.

The guard who'd told Hamnet he'd come led him away. Hamnet listened to his footfalls even after he was out of sight. Someone out there hadn't forgotten. God didn't dole out many miracles. For Hamnet Thyssen, Eyvind's remembering came closer than most of the things he'd seen.

So Hamnet thought right after Eyvind Torfinn visited him, anyhow. But loaf followed nasty loaf. One jar of stale water replaced another. Guards came into the cell to empty the slop bucket, then left again. The air in the dungeon grew chillier. Hamnet didn't think it was his imagination; was the Breath of God starting to blow outside?

When the guards lifted the bar and opened the cell door when it wasn't feeding time, he quivered with fear, though he tried not to show it. Another break in routine. It couldn't be good news.

"Thyssen!" the lead guard barked.

"Yes, that's me," Hamnet agreed.

"Come along," the guard said.

"Or?" Hamnet asked.

"Or rot in there. No skin off my nose one way or the other."

Hamnet came. The guards paused in front of Kormak Bersi's cell, opened it, and got him out, too. "What's this all about?" the imperial agent asked as he emerged.

"You'll find out," the guard snapped. "Now shut your fool mouth and follow me." His mouth twisted in disgust. "You stink. And so do you, Thyssen."

"Do I?" Hamnet couldn't smell himself any more. He hardly noticed the stenches of the dungeon. When he first came here, they'd seemed horrible. You could get used to almost anything.

Hope came to life within him when they left the dungeon by the stairs that had brought him down into it. He hadn't gone very far before he realized the guards could be taking him and Kormak out to the chopping block. What price hope then?

"Winter's here," Kormak remarked even before they came up to ground level. The chill in the air was more obvious now that they drew closer to doors and windows that gave on the outside world.

Instead of the block, the guards brought them to a bathroom that held two copper tubs full of steaming water. "Wash yourselves," the lead guard growled. "Like I told you, you stink."

Without a word of argument, Hamnet stripped off the clothes he'd been wearing ever since they threw him into the cell and got into the closer tub. Kormak Bersi was only a heartbeat or two behind him. The soap sitting on a tray on the edge of Hamnet's tub wasn't perfumed, but it got the filth off him and didn't sear his skin. Soap alone wouldn't kill nits, though. He wondered if the guards knew, or cared.

Another guard gave him some nasty-smelling lotion and said, "Rub this into your hair—all your hair." Maybe the stuff was intended to deal with his lice. Standing up, he smeared it over his scalp and in his crotch and under his arms. In the other tub, Kormak was doing the same thing.

When Hamnet rinsed the lotion out of his hair, he got a little in his eyes. Then he quickly splashed more water into them. "Be careful," he warned Kormak Bersi, spluttering. "Burns like fire."

"Now you tell me," Kormak said, which doubtless meant he'd found out the same thing for himself.

Hamnet's old clothes had disappeared while he was bathing. So had the imperial agent's. The tunic and trousers Hamnet put on when he got out of the tub fit him tolerably well, but no better than that. The boots they gave him were loose, but that was all right. He asked for a second pair of thick wool socks, and the guards brought them to him. If the season really had turned, as seemed likely, the extra layer would help keep his feet warm when he had to go outside.

Kormak Bersi put on a similarly bland outfit. As soon as they were both dressed, the guards hustled them out of the bathroom. "Will you tell me where you're taking me?" Count Hamnet asked.

"Shut up," one of the guards explained.

"You'll find out," another one added. Hamnet Thyssen asked no more questions. The men seemed jumpy—and they were armed, while he and Kormak weren't. If they wanted to dispose of a couple of prisoners, they could. Hamnet consoled himself by thinking they wouldn't have bothered cleaning him and Kormak off if they were just going to take their heads. He hoped not, anyhow.

"In here," growled the guard who'd told him to shut up. Hamnet got shoved through a door into what looked like a small meeting room. So did Kormak Bersi. Hamnet wasn't astonished to discover Sigvat II sitting behind a small table there. Nor was he particularly surprised that the Emperor looked as if he hated him. Sigvat had looked at him that way often enough to get him used to it.

No matter how sour Sigvat looked, he remained lord of the Raumsdalian Empire. The forms had to be observed. Dropping to one knee, Count Hamnet murmured, "Your Majesty." Beside him, Kormak went to both knees.

"Get up, you two," Sigvat snapped. As Hamnet and the imperial agent rose, the Emperor went on, "I hope you're happy, now that you've gone and shown how smart you are."

"Your Majesty?" This time, Hamnet Thyssen used the phrase as a question. He couldn't very well know what had happened while he was in the dungeon. The Emperor couldn't expect him to . . . could he? Sigvat couldn't reasonably expect him to, no, but how reasonable was His Majesty? One more question Hamnet wished he hadn't thought of.

Sigvat didn't look reasonable now—he looked angry enough to bite horseshoe nails in half. "You've gone and shown how cursed smart you are," he repeated, vitriol in his voice. "These—these *Rulers,* that's what." He spat out the name of the tribe from beyond the Glacier.

"What have they done, Your Majesty?" Kormak Bersi asked . . . reasonably.

"They wrecked an army of ours near Vesteralen," the Emperor answered. "Wrecked it, I tell you. We had wizards attached to the army—whether you people think so or not, I did listen to you, by God. I don't think any of the wizards got out. For all I know, the Rulers ate them."

He wasn't joking, or not very much. Hamnet Thyssen tried to remember just where Vesteralen lay. Somewhere up in the northern woods—he knew that much. He couldn't come closer than that; as far as he knew, he'd never gone through the town.

"What do you want us to do about the Rulers, Your Majesty?" he asked.

Sigvat looked at him as at any idiot. "Stop them!" he exclaimed.

"How?" Hamnet asked. "What do you think a couple of men fresh from the dungeons can do that an army and a squad of wizards can't?"

"You have friends. I have trouble imagining how or why, but you do." The Emperor might have been accusing him of some nasty vice, like accosting little girls. Scowling and spiteful, Sigvat continued, "Some of those friends have been whining that I should have let you out a long time ago, or even that I never should have jugged you in the first place."

I really do *have friends,* Count Hamnet thought with some surprise. Maybe Eyvind Torfinn had done what he'd said he would do. Maybe Ulric Skakki had greased a few palms. Maybe—no, almost certainly—Trasamund had made a nuisance of himself. *For me.* Hamnet had trouble believing it.

But, as if to confirm it, Sigvat said, "Your friends, taken all in all, are a sneaky slither of snakes. Put all of you together and you should be able to give the Rulers trouble if anyone can."

"Yes. If," Kormak Bersi said, which perfectly echoed what was going through Hamnet's mind.

"I will do what I can, Your Majesty, on one condition," Hamnet said.

"You dare bargain with me?" Thumbscrews and racks and endless gallons of water roughened Sigvat's voice.

Hamnet Thyssen nodded anyway. "I do, sir. Whatever you do to me here, it won't be worse than letting Gudrid come north with me. She is no friend of mine. If you send me against the Rulers, don't send her. If you send her . . . well, I'd rather go back to the dungeon."

"If I take you up on that, you won't come out again," Sigvat warned. Count Hamnet only shrugged. The Emperor filled his lungs to call for guards to take Hamnet away.

"Wait, Your Majesty. Think," Kormak Bersi urged. "You need Thyssen more than you need me. He knows more about this business than I do, and he's a better man of his hands than I am, too."

Sigvat looked as astonished as if one of his chairs had spoken to him. He rounded on Count Hamnet. "Gudrid is no fonder of you than you are of her."

"Then why would she want to come north again?" the Raumsdalian noble asked.

But that question almost answered itself. Hamnet wanted nothing more than to stay away from his former wife. She, on the other hand, wanted to keep sticking pins in him to make him writhe. He'd done all the writhing he intended to do, though, at least on her hook. What Liv could do to him . . . He hadn't said anything to Sigvat about Liv. Was that because she'd wounded him less or because he had the feeling the fight would need her? He wasn't sure himself.

"If I didn't think you were important—" the Emperor ground out. Hamnet said nothing. He just waited for whatever happened next. If it was the dungeon, then it was, that was all. But if it wasn't . . . "Stop the Rulers, and there aren't many rewards big enough."

"By God, Your Majesty, I don't care about most of that nonsense. You know I don't," Count Hamnet said. "I just want people to leave me the demon alone. You, Gudrid, everybody. Is that too much to ask?"

"Frequently," Kormak said before Sigvat could answer.

The Emperor said, "You'd have all the privacy you want in a cell."

"True." Again, Hamnet left it there—but not for long. He couldn't help adding, "Till the Rulers get here, anyway."

Sigvat II made a horrible face. That worry had to be in his mind, too. "Give me what I want, Your Grace, and I'll do the same for you," he said. "I will keep Gudrid away from you while you fight the foe—you have a bargain there."

"Thank you, Your Majesty," Hamnet said. "And the rest of it?"

"If you beat the Rulers, I'll leave you alone," the Emperor said. "Before God, I will, and I'll see that Gudrid does, too. But if you don't—"

"Don't worry about it, Your Majesty," Hamnet said. Sigvat stared at him. He explained: "If I lose, chances are you won't get the chance to punish me. I'll be too dead for you to worry about it. Losing to the Rulers is its own punishment."

"Mm, yes, I can see how that might be." Sigvat smiled a thin smile. Hamnet Thyssen had a pretty good idea of what he was thinking. Whether Hamnet won or the Rulers did, the Emperor didn't lose everything.

Or he thought he didn't, anyhow. Hamnet doubted whether he'd thought things through—but Hamnet doubted that about Sigvat a lot of the time. If the Rulers won, the most he could hope for was to go on as their vassal. They were more likely to dispose of him and find another puppet—or to do without puppets altogether.

As far as Count Hamnet was concerned, Sigvat deserved that kind of fate. Whether the rest of Raumsdalia did might be a different story.

"Well, go on," the Emperor said. "God go with you. Good fortune go with you."

"Thank you, Your Majesty," Hamnet and Kormak said together. Hamnet went on, "Will the guards still have our weapons, to give them back when we leave the palace?"

"They will," Sigvat promised.

And they did, though the dirty looks one of them sent Hamnet's way suggested that he'd done some appropriating while Hamnet sat in his cell.

With a sword on his hip and a knife on his belt, Hamnet felt better able to face the world outside. He knew it was more likely to yield to such weapons than the heartless world of the palace was.

The Glacier lay a long way north, but he could feel it in the wind when he walked out. He stepped carefully; ice crunched under his bootheels at every stride. Yes, winter was here, sure enough.

"All you have to do now is keep your word and beat the Rulers," Kormak Bersi remarked.

"Yes, that's all," Hamnet Thyssen agreed. The imperial agent sent him a sharp look, scenting sarcasm. Hamnet hadn't intended any. He'd got out of Sigvat's dungeon. After that, wouldn't anything else be easy by comparison?

XVII

THE INNKEEPER WAS carving a roast goose when Hamnet Thyssen and Kormak Bersi walked into the taproom. "Oh. You two," he said, looking up from his work. "Your friends aren't here any more."

"Where are they?" Hamnet hoped he kept the alarm from his voice, but he wasn't sure. Would Sigvat do something really monstrous like releasing him while arresting Ulric Skakki and Audun Gilli and the Bizogots? Maybe the Emperor would think that was funny, not monstrous.

"They all went to what's-his-name's house a few days ago," the innkeeper replied.

Valiantly resisting the impulse to pick up the goose carcass and crown the fellow with it, Count Hamnet asked, "Whose house?"

"What's-his-name's," the innkeeper repeated, and Hamnet did take a step towards the steaming, juicy bird on its pewter platter. But then the man went on, "Old foof. White beard. Kind of a big belly. Throws big words around."

"You know this guy?" Kormak asked.

"Eyvind Torfinn," Hamnet said, aiming the words at the innkeeper and the agent both and so turning them into half a question.

Both men nodded. "That's him," the innkeeper said. "You know where he lives? You better, if you're after your pals, 'cause I sure don't."

"As a matter of fact, it's not too far from here, which is nothing but luck." Hamnet Thyssen paused. "Did somebody take my gear out of my room?"

"*Somebody* must have, because it's sure not there now," the innkeeper said. "Don't know if it was your pals, though."

"Thanks," Hamnet said dryly. Had Ulric or Audun or Liv remembered his sackful of chattels? Or had the innkeeper made them disappear? Count Hamnet couldn't imagine that the fellow would leave them around for some new lodger to find.

He went out into the cold again, Kormak Bersi at his heels. It wasn't much warmer than it would have been on the Bizogot steppe, if at all. The big difference was, it got cold sooner on the steppe, stayed cold longer, and rarely warmed up in between times. The Breath of God dominated winter there. It did the same here a lot of times, but not always. Here in Nidaros, other, warmer winds warred with it.

"So where is this foof's place?" Kormak asked, breath-fog streaming from his mouth and nose with the words.

"Here on the west side, on the higher ground closer to the palace," Hamnet answered. "His terrace looks out on the farm country that used to be at the bottom of Hevring Lake."

"This time of year, he's welcome to his stinking terrace," Kormak said with an exaggerated shiver. Hamnet Thyssen nodded. He wouldn't have wanted to stand around freezing his nose off, either. Kormak went on, "Well, we might as well go there. Can't very well get started if we don't."

"No, I guess not." Count Hamnet would almost rather have faced the Rulers in battle than gone to Earl Eyvind's home. The Rulers were honest enemies. Eyvind Torfinn was, or acted like, a friend. Facing Gudrid . . .

A grim smile spread across his face. It might not be so bad. He could tell her Sigvat wouldn't let her trouble him when he went north again. That was worth something, anyhow.

"Where exactly is this place?" Kormak Bersi asked after they'd wandered for a while.

"I'll find it," Hamnet said. And, after one more false start, he did.

Eyvind's house was almost as big as the castle Count Hamnet wondered if he'd ever see again. Hamnet knew the older noble had about as many servitors, too. And books took up the space servants didn't. Hamnet could read and write. He even enjoyed reading now and again. But Eyvind Torfinn's collection would probably take more than a year to read through, even if you read for a couple of hours a day. Hamnet had trouble understanding why anyone would surround himself with so many words.

And Eyvind's got Gudrid, too, he thought sourly. *That really means he has no time for words of his own.*

Kormak Bersi couldn't have known what was in his mind. The imperial agent set a mittened hand on the door knocker and rapped four times. Had he seized the brass knocker with fingers and palm uncovered, he would have left skin behind when he let go.

A panel above the knocker slid back behind a grate much like the ones on dungeon doors. Hamnet Thyssen and Kormak looked at each other, without any doubt sharing the same thought.

The eyes behind the grate widened. "You!" a male voice exclaimed. The panel slammed shut. To Hamnet's annoyance, the door didn't open. Instead, he heard running footsteps and that same voice shouting, "Earl Eyvind! Earl Eyvind! Thyssen's here!"

"Well?" Kormak said. "Is he going to let us in or drop boiling oil on our heads?"

Count Hamnet looked up. There was a murder hole above the entrance. Eyvind Torfinn and his servants could do that if they wanted to. Hamnet wasn't so sure Sigvat wouldn't thank them, too, even if the Emperor had turned him loose.

No boiling oil, no hot water, no heated sand came from above. A few minutes later, the door did open. Instead of Eyvind Torfinn's majordomo, there stood Ulric Skakki, the usual mocking grin playing across his lips. "Well, well," the adventurer said. "Look what the scavengers dug up and left on our doorstep."

"Is that an invitation, or shall we just go away?" Hamnet asked.

Ulric made as if to close the door in his face. Hamnet Thyssen made as if to draw his sword. They both grinned, and then stepped forward and embraced. Ulric also thumped Kormak on the shoulder. "You two may as well come in," he said. "I already bothered to open the door."

"Sorry to put you to the trouble," Hamnet said, and Ulric's grin got wider.

"If you are going to let them in, do it, by God," the officious servitor said from behind Ulric. "Think how much heat you're letting out standing there gabbing with the door open."

Hamnet and Kormak hurried inside. Ulric Skakki closed the door after them. Earl Eyvind's servant might have been grouchy, but plenty of people in Nidaros would have voiced the same complaint. Heat, in wintertime, was always a serious business, even for the rich.

"You'll take us to Eyvind?" Hamnet asked.

Ulric shook his head. "No, of course not. I was going to bring you to Gudrid. I'm sure you have so much to tell each other."

"That's not even funny as a joke," Count Hamnet growled.

"Well, maybe not," Ulric allowed. "You have my apology, for whatever you think it's worth."

"I'm sure it's worth its weight in gold," Hamnet said. Ulric started to nod, then broke off with a quizzical expression on his face. Kormak Bersi also looked bemused.

Earl Eyvind waited in the best-appointed study Hamnet had ever seen. It had a lot of books and a desk with a south-facing window. Few houses anywhere in the Empire had a window that looked north. The Breath of God militated against that. Several lamps and candles made the room bright even when the weather turned too harsh to leave the shutters over the window open.

Heaving himself to his feet, Eyvind Torfinn said, "Good to see you, by God."

"Good to be seen, Your Splendor." Hamnet Thyssen clasped Eyvind's hand. "And I think I have a lot to thank you for."

"My pleasure, Your Grace—please believe me," Eyvind said.

Kormak coughed. Hamnet introduced him to Eyvind Torfinn. "I also owe you a lot, Your Splendor," the agent said.

"Don't worry about it," Eyvind Torfinn said. "Don't worry about anything. Are you hungry? Are you thirsty? We can fix it if you are."

"His Majesty fed and watered us," Hamnet answered. "Now he's going to turn me loose against the Rulers. Amazing what getting an army pounded to pieces will do, isn't it?"

"Possibly. Possibly. I dare hope he would have let you go even absent a defeat," Earl Eyvind said. "I bent my efforts towards that end, I assure you."

"I'm grateful," Hamnet said, "and all the more so because . . ." His voice trailed away. He didn't want to talk about Gudrid with her current husband. He never had wanted to do anything like that. Just thinking about it made him acutely uncomfortable.

But Eyvind Torfinn understood what he didn't say. With some embarrassment, the older man said, "These things happen, you know." Did he mean his marriage to the woman who had been Hamnet's wife? Or did he mean that Gudrid had hoped Hamnet would rot in the dungeon? Or both at once? That would have been Hamnet's guess.

"Oh, yes. They do indeed," he said in a voice like stone. Were Audun Gilli and Liv sharing a bedchamber in Eyvind's home? How could they be doing anything else? *And where does that leave me?*

Alone.

He knew the answer. He knew it, and he hated it. Spacious though this place was, it would be far more crowded than an inn. And that would only make him feel more lonely, because he would be here without anybody. Next to solitude in the midst of a crowd, going off and fighting the Rulers seemed easy. While he was on campaign, he would have so much time to think, so much time to brood. He could hope he wouldn't, anyhow.

"Is that woman Marcovefa, the one who speaks the strange dialect . . . Is she really from a tribe atop the Glacier?" Eyvind Torfinn had naturally noticed her.

"Oh, yes." Count Hamnet nodded. "Do you understand her?"

"Not so well as I wish I did, but well enough. Some of the Bizogots who live near the western mountains talk the way she does," the scholarly earl replied. Ulric Skakki had said the same thing, but Ulric had lived among those clans. Eyvind, as far as Hamnet Thyssen knew, had just studied them. However he knew what he knew, he did know it.

"If you can follow her language, can you follow why her magic is so strong?" Count Hamnet asked.

"Well, I haven't seen much of it with my own eyes, you understand, so anything I know of it is at second hand," Eyvind answered. "I'd only be guessing, and my guess would be that her sorcery is strong because her folk don't have much else. If they need to do something up there, they have to do it with spells. I gather they don't know how to smelt metal any more. They have no crops. They don't even have large beasts to tame. What does that leave them but wizardry?"

"I had the same notion," Hamnet said slowly. "In a way, it makes sense. In another way, I wonder if it's too simple."

Eyvind Torfinn's shrug set his jowls wobbling. "It may well be. I said I don't know enough to be sure. We need more research, if we ever find the chance for it." He looked unhappy. "We have more urgent worries closer to Nidaros, I fear."

"You never tried climbing up to the top of the Glacier, either," Hamnet Thyssen said. "Even with the avalanche that made it easier for us, it's still nothing I'd care to try more than once."

"I believe you," Earl Eyvind said. "How does it compare to a stretch in His Majesty's dungeons?"

"I've never tried climbing the Glacier, Your Splendor," Kormak Bersi said before Hamnet could reply, "but I wouldn't care to do more than one stretch in a cell."

"I didn't care for even one," Hamnet agreed. "His Majesty is a great many things"—most of which he couldn't stand—"but an innkeeper he is not."

"Which, I have no doubt, is an understatement the size of a mastodon." Eyvind Torfinn smiled to show he'd made a joke. He was a good-hearted man. He was also a man who'd seen a dungeon cell from the outside but never, so far as Count Hamnet knew, from within. Despite that lack—or that luck—he did have a certain grasp on essentials: "Even if the Emperor did give you a meal, I daresay you'll be thirsty for something better than musty water."

"Yes, by God!" Again, Kormak spoke before Hamnet could. Hamnet didn't mind; he couldn't have put it better himself.

EYVIND TORFINN'S RECEPTION hall would not have been too small for the imperial palace. With all the Bizogots guesting at his home, he'd given one servant tapman duty. A couple of dozen Bizogots would be plenty to keep a tapman busy at all hours of the day and night, or so it seemed to Count Hamnet. With beer and wine and mead to choose from in place of fermented mammoth and musk-ox milk, the Bizogots might drink even more than they did up on the frozen plain, too.

Trasamund had a drinking horn—actually, a silver rhyton in the shape of a mountain sheep's horn—of beer in his hand when he saw Hamnet. "It is you!" the jarl boomed, rushing over to fold Hamnet into an embrace that made him think of a hug from a short-faced bear. "Ulric said Eyvind had got you loose, but Ulric lies the way most people fart—he can't help himself."

"I know some people who break wind through the mouth, but I'm not one of 'em," Ulric Skakki said with dignity. He sent Hamnet one of his crooked grins. "I hope I'm not, anyhow." His cup was smaller and plainer than Trasamund's, but he chose wine to fill it. He could rough it with the best of them, but he didn't when he didn't have to.

Liv was also there, and she came up to Hamnet, too. Taking both his hands in hers, she said, "I am glad to free you again. I wish you no harm, no ill—only the best. I am sorry we didn't end up fitting together the way you hoped. I hoped we could, too. Sometimes things don't work out the way you wish they would, that's all."

How was he supposed to answer that? It was gracious, and he believed it, but it still felt like a sawblade thrust through his liver. "Sometimes things don't," he agreed in a voice rough as shagreen. He squeezed her hands once, then let them go.

"That was well done," Ulric Skakki said quietly. Liv nodded.

For a moment, knowing how useless and how foolish it was, Hamnet hated both of them. "Well done or not . . ." he said, and made for the tapman. As he came up, the fellow raised a politely curious eyebrow. "Wine," Count Hamnet told him. "Whatever you've got that's sweet and strong."

"Coming up, sir," Eyvind Torfinn's servant said as he filled a cup. If Earl Eyvind was making his bountiful cellars available to his guests, Hamnet, like Ulric, aimed to take advantage of them. And wine was stronger than beer and ale and smetyn; even a determined drinker needed to pour down less to make the world go away.

Of course, the determined drinker would still regret it the next morning or whenever he finally sobered up. Right now, the morning seemed a million years and a million miles away from Hamnet Thyssen. The wine in his cup might not have been a great vintage, but it was sweet and it was strong. Hamnet wondered what the southern wine growers got that they thought worth as much as their marvelous elixir. *A poet could do something with that conceit,* he thought. No poet himself, he made do with savoring the smooth, blood-red richness as it slid down his throat.

"So what are you going to have to do for Sigvat to keep from decorating his dungeons again?" Ulric Skakki asked, sidling up to him.

"Nothing much," Hamnet asked. Unlike the tapman's a moment before, Ulric's elevated eyebrow was redolent of skepticism. "Nothing much, by God," Count Hamnet said again. "Just drive off the Rulers, that's all. They're inside the Empire, in case you haven't heard, and they've beaten the stuffing out of an imperial army and a bunch of imperial wizards. Believe it or not, that even got His Majesty's attention."

"And they said it couldn't be done!" Ulric said in mock—Hamnet supposed it was mock—astonishment. "He won't do anything to you if you don't manage it, either, I'm sure. Maybe cut off your fingers and toes one at a time and then start in on anything else that still happens to stick out. Like I say, nothing much. D'you suppose your balls'd count as one cut or two?"

"I hadn't worried about it—up till now." Hamnet spoke the last three words in as shrill a falsetto as he could muster.

He caught Ulric Skakki by surprise. The adventurer's laugh was high-pitched, too—almost a giggle. "*You're* not supposed to do things like that," Ulric said severely.

The others who understood Raumsdalian were laughing, too. Marcovefa chose that moment to walk into the dining hall. "What is the joke?" she asked. "Why do I always come in right after the joke?"

Some of that was in her own tongue, some in the regular Bizogot language. "Hamnet made it," Ulric said, and pointed to the newly released nobleman.

"Say it again," Marcovefa told him.

He did, in the Bizogot tongue this time. It sounded stronger in that language than it did in Raumsdalian. Hamnet wondered why that should be so, but had no doubt it was. Marcovefa laughed and laughed. Pointing to her, he said, "When I do go against the Rulers, I'll need you beside me."

She batted her eyes at him, for all the world like a coquette of the kind he couldn't stand. "Why, darling, I didn't know you cared," she murmured in surprisingly good, if still accented, Raumsdalian.

People in the dining hall laughed much harder at that than they had at Count Hamnet's joke. Ulric Skakki dropped his cup. Quick as a cat, he caught it before it smashed, but wine spilled on the floor. A servant scurried away and came back with a rag. Hamnet groped for an answer, even after the fellow was down on his knees wiping up the wine. Just then, he would sooner have embraced a rattlesnake than a woman, but he could see how Marcovefa might not appreciate that kind of reply.

"I want you for your magic, not for your—" he began, and then broke off again. His mouth seemed determined to land him in trouble whether he wanted to end up there or not.

"Twat?" Marcovefa suggested, in the regular Bizogot language—maybe she hadn't learned how to say that in Raumsdalian yet.

"Well, yes," Hamnet muttered, which brought on fresh gales of merriment from the Bizogots—Liv very much included—and Ulric Skakki. Where was Audun Gilli? Count Hamnet didn't see him, which spared him *complete* humiliation . . . but only by the tiniest of margins.

Or so he thought, anyhow, but then Marcovefa leaned up and forward and brushed her lips across his as if they were old lovers. "Don't worry," she said. "I promise not to give you anything you don't want."

"Ah, but will you give him everything he does want?" Trasamund bellowed. He thought his own sally was the funniest thing he'd ever heard, funnier than whatever had gone before. Hamnet Thyssen had rather a different opinion.

If he showed Trasamund he was angry, he lost. He saw that much. "I want to beat the Rulers," he said. "I want to drive them out of Raumsdalia. I want to drive them off the Bizogot plains."

"You do all that, and so many women will want to say thank-you with their legs open, you'll need a club to keep them off," Ulric said.

"Maybe not," Trasamund said before Hamnet could answer. "Maybe the sour look on his face will do it." He guffawed.

"You're your own best audience," Hamnet told him.

"Drive off Rulers? Not so hard," Marcovefa said. "Everyone makes big fuss about Rulers. Feh! This to Rulers." She snapped her fingers.

"The reason everyone makes a fuss about them is that they keep beating everyone," Ulric said. "It's a reprehensible habit, I know, and one from which they should be discouraged by any means necessary."

"What is *reprehensible*?" Marcovefa asked.

"Why, deserving of reprehension, of course," Ulric answered blandly.

"And what does *reprehension* mean?" Was her patience wearing thin? Hamnet Thyssen knew his would have been.

But Ulric went right on playing. "Reprehension is that which is reprehensible."

Maybe Marcovefa would have turned him into a newt. More likely, since there were no newts atop the Glacier, she would have chosen something like a pika instead. Before she could do anything she might—or might not—regret later, Hamnet said, "What Ulric is doing now is reprehensible. It deserves reprehension."

"Ah. I understand. Thank you," Marcovefa said.

Ulric Skakki sent Hamnet a jaundiced stare. "*You're* no fun."

"I wouldn't be surprised," Hamnet said. "But then, I've just come out of His Majesty's dungeons. The sport down there isn't everything it might be."

"Well, that's true enough," the adventurer agreed. "I didn't enjoy the stretch I put in under the throne room, either."

"You never told me you got jugged." Count Hamnet didn't know whether to believe him, either. Ulric had done a lot of things, but he hadn't done everything . . . had he?

"I never told you it snowed in the wintertime up in the Bizogot country, either. I never saw the need." He spoke with exaggerated patience. And then he went on to talk about what things were like in the dungeons. He'd been there; he left Hamnet Thyssen in no possible doubt about that. He knew more about what went on in the bowels of the imperial palace than Hamnet did himself. He knew guards by name and by habit. He knew those cells as if he'd lived in them for years. Maybe he had.

"How did you get out?" Count Hamnet asked when he finished.

"Same way you did," Ulric answered. "His Majesty found something where he thought I might be useful. As a matter of fact, it was that bit of business we did together six or eight years ago."

"You didn't tell me you were just out of the dungeon!" Hamnet exclaimed.

"You didn't ask me," Ulric said. "I'd washed most of the stink off, same as you did. I thought you'd get all sniffy if you knew I was coming up for air for the first time in . . . well, in a while, anyway. I'd say I was right, too."

Was he? Looking into himself, Hamnet thought he might well have been. "I'm sorry," the Raumsdalian noble mumbled.

"What? For being what you are? That's foolish," Ulric said. "Besides, you're . . . a little better now. And you've done a stretch yourself, which doesn't hurt."

Count Hamnet bowed. "Thank you so much."

Ulric Skakki also bowed, with a sinuous elegance Hamnet couldn't hope to match. "My privilege, Your Grace."

Before Hamnet could take the next step in the politer-than-thou dance, a servant came in and said, "His Splendor requests that I announce a meal is being served. If you will be so kind as to accompany me . . ."

All things considered, Hamnet Thyssen would rather have gone on sparring with Ulric. It wasn't that Eyvind Torfinn didn't set an elegant, even an extravagant, table. No, the problem was who would be sitting at it.

And, sure enough, Gudrid waited there when he walked in.

IGNORING HER WOULD have been rude, especially since he was a guest in her present husband's home. Glancing over towards Earl Eyvind, Hamnet thought the older noble awaited this meeting with more than a little apprehension of his own. *If there's a fight, I won't start it,* Hamnet decided. That being so, he bowed to Eyvind Torfinn and to Gudrid and took his seat without speaking to either of them.

Trasamund sat down to his left, Marcovefa to his right. Liv was some little distance down the table, between Ulric Skakki and a Leaping Lynx Bizogot Count Hamnet barely knew. Gudrid never failed to notice things like that. And of course she already knew Liv and Audun Gilli were sleeping together. Her mouth stretched into what looked like a smile of genuine pleasure.

"How does it feel to have lost another woman?" she asked.

"These things happen," Hamnet said stolidly.

"Oh, indeed." Gudrid's smile widened. "Anything can happen to anybody—once. If something happens to someone again and again, though, chances are it's his own fault."

You can't please a woman. She didn't shout it, not in so many words. She let the guests of her husband's generosity figure it out for themselves instead. And what she said might well have held a cruel barb of truth. But it was a barb that could also have stung her. Count Hamnet could have made some pointed gibes about her sport of infidelity . . . if he'd wanted to insult the man who'd got him out of Sigvat's dungeon. Since he didn't, he just shrugged.

Gudrid drew in another anticipatory breath. Hamnet Thyssen wondered how long he could go on giving mild answers if she kept baiting him. Not long enough, he feared. But Eyvind Torfinn beat Gudrid to the punch. "That will be enough of that, my dear," he said in tones that brooked no argument.

Gudrid blinked. She wasn't used to hearing such tones from her husband—or anyone else. "But he—" she began.

"That will be enough of that," Eyvind Torfinn repeated. "We are none of us perfect. Reminding one another how we fall short does nobody any good. And the Empire needs Count Hamnet, whether he is perfect or not. You may think what you please, of course, but I will thank you to stay courteous in what you say."

Servitors began bringing in the meal. Trays of mutton and spicy pork and goose filled the table. An edge sharper and more dangerous than the one on any carving knife filled Gudrid's voice: "And if I don't?"

If she intimidated Eyvind Torfinn, he didn't show it. Waving to one of the servants, he said, "My wife won't be dining with us after all, I'm afraid. Be so kind as to escort her to her bedchamber."

"Yes, Your Splendor," the servant said.

"But I don't want to go to my bedchamber," Gudrid said, which would surely do for an understatement till a bigger one came along.

"Will you mind your manners, then?" Earl Eyvind asked with surprising firmness.

"I will do and say whatever I need to do and say," Gudrid answered, as if no other reply were possible. Plainly, she thought none was.

"Rorik . . ." Eyvind said. The servant touched Gudrid on the shoulder.

She screamed at him, and at her husband. Hamnet Thyssen looked down at the tabletop. He'd seen Gudrid's temper kindle before. He'd been on the receiving end of it more often than he cared to remember. In a way, he still was. This fracas was about him, even if he didn't happen to be at the center of it.

Ulric Skakki yawned. "A little politeness would fix everything. Too bloody much to ask for, I suppose."

Gudrid didn't intend to be polite. She grabbed a knife. Rorik knocked it away from her before she had the chance to try to stab him. That made Gudrid screech like a dire wolf with an arrow in its rump. For his part, Count Hamnet didn't blame the servant one bit. His former wife didn't take kindly to being thwarted by anybody.

"You may stay . . . if you'll stay civil," Eyvind Torfinn told her. "Will you?"

Her eyes blazed. She wasn't about to forgive her husband any time soon, either. But she nodded and spat out three words: "Oh, all right."

Earl Eyvind beamed, which struck Hamnet as misplaced optimism. He kept his mouth shut, though. "Thank you, my dear," Gudrid's current husband said.

She answered with something low-voiced, something Count Hamnet couldn't quite make out. If Eyvind Torfinn did hear what it was, he affected not to. A certain amount of forbearance was an asset in any husband—or wife. The earl seemed to grasp that. Gudrid didn't, and probably never would. As for Hamnet himself . . . He felt he'd used all his forbearance and more besides, trying to stay married to Gudrid. Her opinion of that might have differed.

Gluttony seemed safe here. Gluttony, after the musty water and the small loaves of bad bread in Sigvat's dungeon, seemed all but obligatory. Hamnet might not have been able to match the Bizogots in his relentless pursuit of a full belly, but he did his level best.

Eyvind Torfinn reminded him of one of the reasons he was feasting so extravagantly, asking, "How soon do you expect to depart for the north?"

"As soon as I can," Hamnet answered. "As soon as His Majesty gives me orders I can show people, orders that let them know I really do hold command there."

Though Eyvind nodded, the cynical Ulric Skakki asked, "Will he give you orders like that in writing?"

"I don't know. I don't much care, either," Count Hamnet said. "If he does give me what I need, I'll go off and do my best with it. And if he doesn't, I'll go down to my castle instead—and wait for the Rulers to come to me."

"What does he say?" Marcovefa asked. Both Ulric Skakki and Eyvind Torfinn started to translate Hamnet's words into her dialect. Each waved for the other to go on. After a moment, Ulric did. Marcovefa listened, frowning, then said, "Does he really think they can do that?"

She spoke mostly in the usual Bizogot tongue. Hamnet Thyssen had no trouble following that. "You may think the Rulers are easy meat," he told her, "but, if you do, you're the only one who does."

"Too many *things* down below the Glacier." Marcovefa said that in her own dialect, but Hamnet had heard it often enough to have no trouble understanding it. Believing it was another story.

Hamnet Thyssen ate for a while. Eyvind Torfinn's chefs, as always, set a high standard. And, because Hamnet was just out of the dungeon, good food seemed even better to him. After a while, though, he looked across the table and spoke to Gudrid: "May I ask a favor of you?"

Her eyes widened in surprise not, he judged, altogether feigned. "What is it?"

"Don't ask His Majesty not to give me the orders I need," he said.

This time, the way she batted her eyelashes was much too familiar. "Why would I do that?" she cooed, as if she didn't know.

"To stop me. To make me go back to my castle. To make me fail," Hamnet said bluntly. "We both know that would make you happy. By all the signs, though, I'm more likely to fail if I do go up against the Rulers than if I don't. But if by some chance I don't fail, that will be good for the Empire. What happens to me doesn't matter much, not on that scale of things. What happens to Raumsdalia does."

Eyvind Torfinn nodded. So did Trasamund. So, rather grudgingly, did Ulric Skakki, who worried about himself ahead of most things. So did Liv, without the least hesitation. And so did Audun Gilli, although Count Hamnet made a point of not looking at him.

Gudrid? Gudrid stared at Hamnet as if he'd started speaking in Marcovefa's dialect. "Why on earth should I care what happens to Raumsdalia?" she demanded. "I care about what happens to me . . . and I care about what happens to you." The way she bared her small white teeth said she didn't want anything good happening to him.

Eyvind Torfinn took a sip of wine before speaking. The white-bearded scholar didn't usually have any idea how to control Gudrid. *As if anyone does,*

Hamnet thought. He feared whatever Eyvind said would only make things worse. Appealing to Gudrid's patriotism was like appealing to a dire wolf's sense of poetry. You could if you wanted to, but it wasn't likely to do you any good.

But all Earl Eyvind said was, "If you wish disaster upon your former husband, my sweet, the surest thing to do is let him go north and find it. That the Rulers have crossed the Bizogot plain in one campaigning season, that they have invaded the Empire, clearly shows anyone who stands against them is unlikely to stand for long."

His words held more truth than Hamnet Thyssen might have wished. Hamnet wanted to beat the Rulers, not to throw himself away as so many Bizogots—and, now, a Raumsdalian army—had done before him. Whether he could do what he wanted was a different question.

With Eyvind Torfinn's help, Gudrid saw that, too. She sent Count Hamnet one of her poisonously sweet smiles. "All right," she said, and then, "All right," again, her soft red lips and moist tongue giving the words a lewd caress as they escaped. "Sometimes the worst you can do to someone is to give him what he thinks he wants and then stand back and watch him ruin himself with it. If you want to play the hero going after the Rulers, be my guest. I won't tell Sigvat to stop you. I'll just laugh when you come back after you've made a fool of yourself. So will everyone else."

"I wouldn't be surprised," Hamnet said. "I'll have to do my best not to make a fool of myself, then, won't I?"

Gudrid's laugh was loud and rich. "But darling, we all know your best is nowhere near good enough, don't we?"

He shrugged. "All I can do is all I can do."

"This is true of all of us," Eyvind Torfinn said. "For myself, I think doing our best against the Rulers is more important than anything that has faced the Empire for many, many years. I am so convinced of this that, if I see anyone operating on a contrary principle, I shall feel compelled to change my will."

The Bizogots, even the Bizogots who spoke Raumsdalian, might have followed his words, but they didn't grasp the thought behind those words. Hamnet Thyssen did. And so did Gudrid. If she kept trying to turn Sigvat against Hamnet, Eyvind would cut her off after he died. Maybe she could get around that, but it wouldn't be easy. She looked daggers at him. He smiled in return, which did nothing to reassure her.

She put the best face on things she could: "If dear Hamnet wants to go north and kill himself, he's welcome to for all of me."

"Thank you," he said.

Marcovefa set a hand on his arm. "You do what you do. It will be all right. I will help," she said.

"Good. Thank you, too," he said.

Gudrid laughed again. "Your lovers get more barbarous every time, sweetheart. The next one will be a jungle ape."

"No, you taught me all I need to know about those," Hamnet replied. "Besides, she's not a lover—only a friend. Not that you would know much about friends, or what they mean." Gudrid bared her teeth at him. He thought his shot actually went home. That wouldn't be a first, but it didn't happen very often, either.

XVIII

S IGVAT II DITHERED two more days before sending Hamnet Thyssen the orders he wanted. Hamnet wondered whether Gudrid was trying to talk the Emperor out of it in spite of Eyvind Torfinn's warnings, or whether Sigvat simply disliked and distrusted him that much. The nobleman swallowed a sigh: either one seemed possible.

At last, though, a palace servitor fetched the required parchment to Eyvind Torfinn's home. Count Hamnet unrolled it to make sure it was what it was supposed to be. He didn't need Ulric Skakki to warn him against going north with a document he hadn't examined, a document that was liable to order any officer who read it to arrest him and kill him on sight.

The servitor only waited impassively while Hamnet read through the parchment. It was, in fact, everything he'd hoped for and more besides. A calligrapher had inscribed it in red and purple ink. It was bedizened with not one but three imperial seals, each stamped into wax of a different color. Sigvat II's scribbled signature at the bottom seemed almost an afterthought.

And it said everything it should have. It gave Hamnet powers just short of imperial to fight the invading barbarians "said to be known as the Rulers." All commanders in the north were ordered in no uncertain terms to subordinate themselves and their soldiers and wizards to him. Whether they would obey, and how well, might prove interesting questions. But Sigvat's orders seemed clear enough.

Ulric Skakki read over Hamnet's shoulder without the slightest trace of embarrassment. "What more do you want?" he said when he finished. "Egg in your beer?"

"I want to get moving," Count Hamnet answered. "Do you think the Rulers are standing still?"

"Tomorrow is soon enough, unless you think they're going to land on Nidaros with both feet tonight," Ulric said. "Do you?"

Part of Hamnet did—a large part, too. But he recognized that the Rulers wouldn't descend on the imperial capital before he could go out and face them. The Raumsdalian Empire was bigger than that. Odds were that the invaders remained in the northern forests. That would be strange country for them, and they probably wouldn't be able to push their mammoths through very fast.

"Tomorrow is soon enough," Hamnet agreed—grudgingly, but it was agreement all the same.

"There you go." Ulric set a hand on his shoulder. "Besides, who knows? Somebody else may go up against them before you get there. Probably will, in fact. If he loses, what will Sigvat think? That he needs you more than ever, that's what. And if he wins—well, so what? You're still out of the dungeon, and that's what really counts."

A lot of Raumsdalians would have held a decidedly different view of things. For them, a victory in which they had no part would have seemed worse than a thrashing. It would have marked the death knell of their ambitions. Hamnet Thyssen didn't feel that way, not least because he had few ambitions.

"Well, you're right," he said. Ulric Skakki knew him better than most, but looked surprised all the same. The adventurer had his own fair share of hope for himself, and naturally expected other people to have theirs, too.

A little later that day, Audun Gilli came up to Hamnet. "I will go north if you'll have me," the wizard said. "I want to do whatever I can against the Rulers."

There were ambitions, and then there were ambitions. Count Hamnet had hoped to live out his days happily with Liv. That wouldn't happen now. But did Audun deserve the blame because it wouldn't? Wouldn't Liv have taken up with someone else if Audun hadn't been one of the travelers in the north? Hamnet feared she would have.

"You can come," he said gruffly. "I don't love you, by God. Nothing could make me love you. But I won't sneak up to your bedroll and stick a dagger in you while you're sleeping, either."

Audun looked relieved. "Thank you, Your Grace!"

"For what?" Hamnet growled. "Now you've got a better chance of getting killed than you would have if I told you to go to the demons. So does Liv, for that matter."

"Do you really want to see her dead?"

"No, curse it." Count Hamnet's voice grew harsher yet; he hadn't imagined it could. Audun, for the most part, wouldn't have known a hint if it walked up and bit him in the leg. He took this one, though. Bobbing his head in an awkward gesture of thanks, he retreated in a hurry.

Part of Hamnet wanted to get blind drunk after that. He didn't, though, which went a long way towards proving how serious he was about setting out the next morning. He went to bed, if not sober, then close enough so that he wouldn't have more than a mild headache come the new day.

His bedchamber was as luxurious as any he'd ever known. A fireplace and two braziers held the cold at bay. His mattress was soft and thick, the furs that lay atop it even thicker. He had no excuse for not sleeping well.

But sleep didn't want to come. Count Hamnet lay in the darkness, staring up at the ceiling he could barely see. He muttered to himself. When muttering didn't do anything, he swore out loud. That didn't help, either. He groped under the bed till he found the chamber pot. After using it, he lay down again. Sleep still stayed away.

When it finally came, it took him by surprise. He drifted into a dream without realizing he was dreaming. He didn't remember much about it: only that it was one of those busy, complicated dreams that make waking life seem simple by comparison.

As he didn't realize when the dream began, he also didn't realize when it ended. He thought the weight pressing down on the bed next to him was something happening in his mind, not anything real.

Even when his hand touched warm, bare flesh, he turned that into part of the dream—a part that mingled sweet and bitter almost unbearably. But the soft, throaty laugh he heard then couldn't possibly have sprung from inside his own mind.

His eyes flew open. "Who the—?" he burst out. Liv, come to apologize the best way she knew how? Gudrid, come to torment him the best way *she* knew how? A serving girl, come to make sure he slept sound after all? No matter how kindly Eyvind Torfinn might mean that, Hamnet didn't want a stranger. To say he didn't want Gudrid proved what a weak reed words were. Liv . . . would hurt him more than she helped, though she might not understand that.

"Never mind who." The answer came in the Bizogot tongue, so it wasn't Gudrid or a servant. But it didn't sound like Liv, either. Who, then?

Knowledge smote. "Marcovefa?" Hamnet said. "Why—?"

"Because I want to. Do I need more reason?" A man would have said it like that. But Hamnet's fingers told him she was no man. She slipped under the furs beside him. Her fingers began to roam, too.

"How did you get in?" Muzzy with sleep, he knew he was a couple of steps slower than he should have been. All the same, he was sure he'd barred the door when he came in. He hadn't wanted company. He had it, though.

Marcovefa laughed again. "I am a shaman, remember? If I want to be someplace, I go there. If I want something to be mine, I take it."

"But—" Hamnet spluttered.

"Hush." Her mouth came down on his. That shut him up in the most effective way imaginable. He raised his arms to push her away, but they went around her instead. She twisted a little so that his hands found her breasts. She made a noise somewhere between a purr and a growl when he squeezed them.

The bed was wide. He rolled her over so that his weight pinned her to the mattress. His mouth trailed down from hers to her nipples. She sighed and pressed his head down on her. His hand found the joining of her legs. Her breath caught. As he stroked her, she opened them wider. She was wet and wanton, waiting for him.

"Here," she whispered. "I do for you." She twisted in the red gloom. Her mouth came down on him.

"Easy," he said as her tongue fluttered and teased. "Oh, easy. Or I'll—"

"So what?" She dove deep on him, so deep that she choked a little. That made her pull back a little, but she was laughing when she did.

More than a little of that and he would explode. He knew it, and Marcovefa had to know it, too. He didn't think she'd come here just for that, so he touched her cheek. She paused and made a questioning, wordless noise. "Let's do this," he said, pressing his weight onto her again. He slid in with just the slightest of guidance. They began to move together, as if they'd been lovers for years.

Again, he thought he would finish too soon to satisfy her. When his mouth slid down to her breast again, though, she murmured something in her own dialect. There he was, nearly at the peak of pleasure, and there he stayed, and stayed, and stayed, till delight turned almost painful. Marcovefa gasped and quivered beneath him, again and again.

"Now?" she asked at last.

"Now!" Hamnet said. They were both sticky and slippery with sweat, sliding together. He reached the pinnacle, and seemed to fall from it forever. Marcovefa shivered one more time.

"Good?" she inquired brightly.

"My God," he answered, and then, "Wait till I can see anything but fire in front of my eyes." She must have liked that, for she laughed again. The motion made him slide out of her.

"Maybe you sleep now," she said. Count Hamnet was inclined to think he'd sleep for the next month. This wasn't love—he'd known love twice now, and known it to turn on him and bite—but he'd never dreamt of so much animal pleasure. And then, mischief in her voice, she went on, "Or maybe . . ." That wasn't a complete sentence by itself, but what she did a moment later made it one.

After his sweaty exertions of a moment before, he hadn't thought he could rise again so soon. He hadn't thought he could rise again at all, not for days. But he surprised himself. Maybe—more likely—Marcovefa made him surprise himself. This time she rode him, less ferociously than he'd taken her. He didn't think she used any magic past that which any man and woman who please each other have. If he was wrong, he didn't much want to find out.

"There," she said when they'd both spent themselves again. "Is that better?"

"Better than what?" Hamnet asked, which set her laughing all over again. It was better than almost anything he could think of.

Almost. *If Gudrid truly loved me, and if she were truly faithful* . . . The thought flickered through his mind like heat lightning on a summer night far to the south of Nidaros. Then sleep *did* smite him, and the darkness in the bedchamber was as nothing next to the black welling up from deep inside.

WHEN HE WOKE the next morning, he thought at first he'd dreamt it all. That couldn't really have happened . . . could it? But he needed only a heartbeat's more consciousness to realize he wasn't alone in the bed. The thin, gray light leaking in through tight-drawn shutters showed Marcovefa asleep beside him, a small smile on her face. Her features relaxed in slumber, she looked improbably young.

His eyes went towards the door. Yes, it was barred. She might have done that right after she came in. She might have got out of bed after he fell asleep. She might have, yes. But he wondered whether it had ever been un-barred at all.

Marcovefa woke up a few minutes later. She looked confused for a couple of heartbeats, as if wondering where she was, and with whom. Then she grinned at Count Hamnet. "Good morning," she said.

"The night was better." He leaned over to kiss her. He half—more than half—hoped they would pick up where they'd left off, though he was any-thing but sure he could rise to the occasion.

But Marcovefa said, "We take care of one thing at a time. Now you are all right for a while, yes? So now we go and see what we can do to these Rulers." The invaders still didn't seem to trouble her, even if they had everyone else below the Glacier from Trasamund to Sigvat in something close to a panic.

Hamnet wondered if he ought to resent being lumped with a water wheel that had got out of kilter. Pride and the memory of pleasure warred within him, but not for long. He couldn't stay offended, not when he re-membered how she'd put him back in good working order.

Marcovefa slid out of bed, found the chamber pot, and squatted over it. Like the Bizogots, her folk needed less in the way of privacy than Raums-dalians did. She straightened up, still naked. Hamnet watched her in un-feigned admiration.

He looked around the room. He didn't see her clothes anywhere. Had she walked through the corridors of Eyvind Torfinn's house like that? Or—?

She fluttered her fingertips in a wicked parody of a gesture someone like Gudrid might have used. "See you at breakfast, sweetheart," she said—and vanished. Hamnet didn't think she'd made herself invisible. She'd really dis-appeared; a soft *pop!* of inrushing air said as much.

Could Liv or Audun Gilli apport themselves like that? Count Hamnet shrugged. He didn't know. He only knew he'd never seen them do it.

He used the pot himself, then dressed in the clothes Sigvat's servants had given him. They would do for winter wear, though they weren't ideal. He would have stewed in his own juices wearing them in a summer heat wave here. A slow smile—not an expression he was used to wearing—stole across his face. His juices had done considerable stirring in the night.

He found his way to the dining room. Eyvind Torfinn was there, eating sausages and duck eggs and drinking a hot infusion of herbs. Gudrid was there, too. So was Marcovefa. The two of them ostentatiously ignored each other. Hamnet Thyssen nodded to Eyvind Torfinn, then walked up to the cook. "I'll have what the earl's having," he said. "That looks good."

"Help yourself to the sausages, Your Grace," the man replied. "I'll give you your eggs in just a bit. Would you like two or three?"

"Three, please," Hamnet answered. The sausages were venison, their flavor enlivened with garlic and fennel. When he had his eggs—almost as fast as the cook promised—he sat down by Marcovefa. Catlike, she leaned against him.

Gudrid never missed a signal like that. One of her elegantly plucked eyebrows leaped. "This time, of course, it will be pure happiness," she said in a voice filled with vitriol.

"I doubt it," Hamnet answered. "It will be what it is, that's all."

Gudrid started to say something, then stopped with her mouth open. She must have expected him to come back with something like, *Of course it will.* His smile held a certain grim triumph. Sometimes getting the best of her even in tiny things felt more important than driving the Rulers beyond the Glacier.

Marcovefa pointed across at Gudrid. "She catches bugs, yes?" she said in the regular Bizogot tongue. Gudrid understood that well enough to close her mouth with a snap, and to redden in anger.

"Maybe we should all leave aside our quarrels, whatever they may be, until the happy day when the Rulers are defeated," Eyvind Torfinn said, also in the Bizogot language.

His wife understood that, too, which was not to say she agreed with it. As Count Hamnet's own thoughts showed, he wasn't sure he agreed with it, either. Beating the Rulers was his duty. Getting one up on Gudrid was a pleasure, and one he didn't enjoy nearly often enough.

At the moment, though, Gudrid's anger seemed more likely to be aimed at Marcovefa than at him. Gudrid had squabbled with Liv, too, and hadn't liked what happened when she did. Would she remember that angering shamans and wizards wasn't a good idea?

"With the Emperor's order in my hand, I want to go north as soon as I finish here, Your Splendor," Hamnet said. "And with me and the Bizogots out of your house, you should have peace again, God willing."

"May it be so." Eyvind Torfinn didn't sound convinced, and Hamnet had a hard time blaming him for that. Gudrid wasn't happy that he'd prevailed on Sigvat to open the dungeon. As far as she was concerned, Hamnet and Kormak Bersi could have stayed there till they rotted. She wasn't shy about making her opinions known, either. No, Earl Eyvind probably wouldn't have a happy time of it once his guests left.

Ulric Skakki walked into the dining room. He needed only a heartbeat to notice things there weren't much warmer than they would have been up on the Glacier. "Hello!" he said. "Have you called a truce, or shall I go back and get my sword and shield?"

"We have a truce," Eyvind Torfinn said, with perhaps more optimism than conviction. "Come on, my friend. Eat. Refresh yourself."

"I thank you kindly, Your Splendor," Ulric said. "Better grub here than I'll get up on the road, that's for sure. I may as well fill up while I've got the chance. Knowing Hamnet, he'll want to get moving as quick as he can."

"Your reputation precedes you," Gudrid murmured to her former husband.

"If you're very lucky, people won't say the same thing about you," Hamnet Thyssen replied. Gudrid bared her teeth at him. Eyvind Torfinn looked as if he wished he were drinking something stronger than his herbal infusion.

Ulric Skakki came back from the cook's station with enough food for three ordinary men. He was no Bizogot, but he could eat like one. He sat down and methodically started putting it away. Then Liv and Audun Gilli walked in. That might have made things even chillier, but Hamnet didn't think such a thing was possible.

Liv got a plate of food that rivaled Ulric's. Audun's eating habits were more sedate, or more typically Raumsdalian. *Do I want him along?* Hamnet Thyssen wondered. But that wasn't quite the right question. *Can I really stand to have him along?*

He looked over at Liv. She wouldn't come north if he told Audun to stay behind. Why should she, when the Rulers had already conquered the Bizogots? Next to that, why did she, why should she, care a copper for what happened to the Empire? But Hamnet knew he needed her wizardry, and Audun's, too. They hadn't beaten the Rulers, but had challenged them. And if they worked with Marcovefa . . .

If they work with Marcovefa, I'm stuck with them, he thought. Maybe, if he was sleeping with Marcovefa, seeing Liv wouldn't make him feel as if someone were sticking skewers into his marrow. He could hope it wouldn't, anyhow.

In strutted Trasamund. The Bizogot jarl had his arrogance back, however much it had suffered up on the frozen steppe. He waved to Count Hamnet, then went over to the cook and came back to the table with two large plates groaningly full of food. As he set them down, he growled, "Let's go north and kill all those miserable mammoth turds!"

"We will if we can," Hamnet said. "This ought to be our best chance."

"Nothing else matters. Nothing," the Bizogot said, and fell to eating as if there were no tomorrow.

"Nothing?" Gudrid murmured. Did she mean the way he was stuffing himself, or was she thinking of herself first as she so often did? She'd taken him into her bed almost under Eyvind Torfinn's nose. Was she reminding him of it, again right past her husband? She hadn't been that shameless even with Hamnet—or, if she had, he hadn't noticed at the time.

Whatever she was looking for from Trasamund, she didn't get it. "Nothing!" he said emphatically, his mouth full of sausage.

Marcovefa laughed softly. Did she know what was going on there? Had she heard, or perhaps somehow divined it? Hamnet Thyssen didn't know. Gudrid couldn't have known, either, but her baleful stare said she didn't like any of what she was thinking. Still, all she did was stare. She must not have felt like taking on another wizard just yet.

All the same, Hamnet was anything but sorry to be leaving Eyvind Torfinn's house.

BY THE WAY things looked, Earl Eyvind's stablehands were anything but sorry to see Hamnet and his companions go. The stables were enormous; Eyvind could afford not only the best but the most. Even so, feeding and grooming and caring for all those extra animals must have been a burden. The good-byes from the grooms and their assistants seemed most heartfelt.

Out through the streets of Nidaros again, this time zigzagging towards the north gate. The Breath of God was blowing. Maybe cities far, far to the south had streets that ran north and south. Nidaros didn't, and likely never would.

Fog puffed from Count Hamnet's mouth and nostrils every time he breathed out, but the wind took it and blew it away. He didn't like getting the Breath of God full in his face. Even here, a long way from the Glacier, it blew bitterly cold. So he thought, anyway. Trasamund and some of the other Bizogots smiled at the familiar blast. Someone—Hamnet thought it was Marcomer of the Leaping Lynxes—said, "This place is wonderful, but it was too stinking hot before."

"Some people don't know when they're well off," Ulric Skakki said.

"Like us, riding north?" Hamnet suggested. Ulric sketched a salute, yielding the point.

A caravan from the north was coming into Nidaros when Hamnet and his companions got to the gate. "What's the news?" Ulric asked. Hamnet supposed he would have thought of the question, too, but certainly not so fast.

The caravanmaster was a burly man with a gray-streaked black beard tumbling halfway down his chest. His face wore a scowl well, and wore one now. "The news?" he echoed. "By God, stranger, it's not good. There's some kind of Bizogot invasion or something up in the woods by the tree line, and I hear tell one of our armies took a demon of a licking."

He didn't have everything straight, but what he had was plenty to irritate the sergeant who was admitting him to the city. "Don't you go talking about our armies that way," the underofficer growled.

"What? Should I lie to this poor bugger instead?" The merchant pointed at Ulric. "If he gets it in the neck, do I want it on my conscience?"

"He won't get it in the neck, and you haven't got a conscience," the sergeant said. The caravanmaster let out an angry bellow. Ignoring it and reveling in his own petty authority, the sergeant went on, "What you have got is a demon of a lot of horses and mules that need inspecting. Who knows what you might be smuggling if you think our soldiers are no good?"

This time, the caravanmaster's howls threatened to shake down the icicles hanging like the teeth of a new portcullis from the gate's gray stonework. With the majesty of the imperial government on his side, the sergeant could afford to ignore those howls, too. And, since he was going to spend some time making the merchant miserable, he considerately waved Hamnet Thyssen's party of out Nidaros without asking for, much less examining, the order Hamnet had got from Sigvat II.

"Poor bastard." Ulric Skakki looked back towards the extravagantly unhappy caravanmaster. "Sometimes the worst thing you can do is tell the truth, you know?"

"Really?" Count Hamnet answered, deadpan. "I never heard that before."

The adventurer laughed out loud. "No, you wouldn't have, would you? Nobody in the dungeons would say anything like that to you, right? Neither would the Emperor, would he?"

"His Majesty has told me a lot of things," Hamnet said . . . truthfully. "I don't believe he ever mentioned that, though."

"No, eh? Somehow I'm not surprised." Even a free spirit like Ulric Skakki glanced back over his shoulder to make sure no one not from their party could overhear before going on, "His Majesty doesn't know enough about telling the truth to know it can be dangerous."

Hamnet Thyssen laughed then. He wondered why—it wasn't as if Ulric were lying. Of course, if he didn't laugh, he would have to weep or swear or ride back to Nidaros and try to assassinate Sigvat. Laughing was probably better.

But he confused Marcovefa. "What is funny?" she asked.

"Nothing much," Hamnet answered. "We're taking turns insulting the Emperor, that's all."

"Oh." But she frowned. "He deserves insulting, yes?" She didn't wait for an answer, but nodded to herself. "Yes, of course. So why is this funny?"

"You never met him," Count Hamnet said.

"Some people have all the luck," Ulric Skakki added.

Marcovefa's eyes twinkled. "Do you say I am lucky, or do you say he is lucky?"

"You're lucky you never met him—take it from one who has," Hamnet answered. Then, after a moment's thought, he went on, "Come to think of it, he's lucky he never met you, too, or he probably wouldn't be here any more." If Marcovefa could make herself disappear and go elsewhere, could she also do the same to someone else? Hamnet couldn't see any reason why not.

"If he is like that, why is he your chief—your, uh, jarl?" she asked.

Imagining the color Sigvat would turn if he heard someone call him a jarl made Hamnet laugh all over again. But the question deserved a serious answer, and he tried to give one: "Because his father and grandfather and grandfather's father ruled before him. Better a ruler from one family than endless wars to see who rules."

"Most of the time, anyway," Ulric put in.

"Most of the time, yes," Hamnet Thyssen agreed.

"Well, maybe," Marcovefa said. "Our clan chiefs go by blood, too. But we don't fight wars about who should be chief." She paused. "Most of the time, anyway." She did a wicked job of mimicking Ulric Skakki.

Hamnet believed her. "More things to fight about here," he said, which summed up the difference between a clan of hunters atop the Glacier and the Raumsdalian Empire in half a dozen words. Why would anyone fight to become a clan chief? Even if you won the job, what did you have that you couldn't have anyway? No one needed to ask that question of Sigvat II or any other Emperor. The palace spoke for itself.

Snow dappled the fields. Most of the trees had lost their leaves. The bare branches made them look like skeletons of their former selves. Crows and jays lingered, as they did in all but the worst of winters. Their cries were raucous in Hamnet's ears. Cattle pulled up grass the first frosts of fall had turned yellow and crisp. They weren't so shaggy as musk oxen, but they did have thick coats to ward off the Breath of God. Almost all of them grazed facing away from the wind.

Marcovefa eyed the cattle. She looked down at the horse she rode. She glanced over to a flock of sheep almost out on the horizon. "Even your beasts are *things*," she said. "So many. Too many, yes."

"We don't go hungry as often as you do," Hamnet said.

"Not here." Marcovefa touched her belly. Then she touched her heart and her head. "Here and here? Who knows?"

That made him grunt thoughtfully. He wasn't sure she was right, but he wasn't sure she was wrong. Did being desperately poor because of where you lived give you spiritual advantages? Marcovefa's magic argued that it did. Most of the rest of what he'd seen atop the Glacier suggested that the folk who lived up there were no more spiritual than they had to be.

It was a puzzlement. He owned himself puzzled. Past that . . . Past that, he would probably do better to worry about things he could do something about.

First among those was, what would Raumsdalian soldiers and their officers do when someone they'd never seen before started ordering them around? Count Hamnet knew he wouldn't find out right away. Except for the imperial guards, no large garrisons were posted in towns close to Nidaros. For one thing, those towns, lying at the Empire's heart, were unlikely to need large garrisons. For another, large garrisons not under the Emperor's direct control might give their commanders ideas, especially close to the capital. Most of Raumsdalia's soldiers, then, stayed near the frontier.

But the northern frontier, in particular, was not a place where garrisons had an easy time feeding themselves. The line where crops wouldn't reliably grow lay south of the tree line, which marked the border between the Empire and the Bizogot country. Without supply convoys up from the south, the soldiers would start to starve. (That was, incidentally, another way the Emperors could make sure their men stayed loyal and choke off rebellions.)

Hamnet thought about joining one of those convoys. But he didn't need long to change his mind. Yes, the wagons had large teams of big, stalwart horses drawing them. They wouldn't have gone anywhere if they hadn't. Even as things were, they were painfully slow. And that deliberate pace decided him against them.

Instead, his led the travelers off onto the side of the road and past the heavy wagons. The soldiers who rode as flank guards waved to him. He returned the courtesy. The Raumsdalians eyed the Bizogots with him with suspicion all the same. If the guards weren't alert, those barbarians might descend on the convoy. So it had to seem to the men with the creaking, groaning wagons, anyhow. He knew better, but doubted he could persuade them.

Trasamund summed it up in a handful of words: "We're wolves, by God. Of course the dogs don't like us." He sounded proud of his wildness, his ferocity.

Ulric Skakki raised an eyebrow. "What does that make the Rulers, then?"

Trasamund's answer was interesting, amusing, and highly profane, but not very informative.

Riding north seemed to speed up autumn's passage into winter, which would have come fast enough anyhow. The storms blowing down from the Glacier seemed fiercer and colder; more and more snow covered the ground, and the thaws between snowfalls grew shorter and shorter and finally stopped. Hamnet Thyssen was resigned to bad weather; the Bizogots were resigned to worse. As for Marcovefa . . .

"Yes, it's cold. So what?" she said when they camped one evening. She shared his tent as a matter of course these days. "We all know what to do about cold. We do it, and we go on. Why get excited?"

"Sometimes I think you're too sensible for your own good." Full of roast mutton, Hamnet didn't feel like getting excited—not about the cold, anyhow.

Marcovefa wrinkled her nose and laughed at him. "I can be as foolish as anyone else. But cold . . . just is. I lived on the Glacier, and on the mountain above it. I never got away from cold, not till I came down. I never knew about hot baths, for instance. Some *things* are good."

"Oh, yes." Hamnet nodded. The regular Bizogots rarely bathed, either. Getting truly clean was a luxury he cherished whenever he came into the Empire. If a copper tub and steaming water weren't some of the most important hallmarks of civilization, what was?

On campaign, he'd be dirty again. But so would everybody around him. After a while, he'd get used to it. He wouldn't be so rank as he would when he traveled up in the Bizogot country, and neither would the people he dealt with. For that matter, when the nose smelled the same stinks for long enough, it stopped noticing. He'd had plenty of experience with that in the dungeon, and before.

He'd also had plenty of experience making love with women who ended up breaking his heart. Somehow, he never got tired of it. What would Marcovefa do to leave him sorry he'd ever touched her? Something: he was sure of that. In the meantime, though, what she had to give was better than anything he could find anywhere else. Sorrow later? Probably—that seemed to be what happened with him. Pleasure now? Without a doubt.

"Thank you," he said after gasping his way to completion.

She laughed at him. "It takes two. Do you think you do not please me? Are you so much a fool?" She set his hand on her left breast. Her firm nipple and thudding heart said she had indeed kindled. "You see?" She laughed again.

"Yes," Hamnet said. Marcovefa might have told him something more after that. If she did, he didn't hear it. He plunged deep into sleep. Staying on horseback all day took more out of him than he'd expected. Maybe he was getting old. Maybe his time in the dungeon had drained him worse than he thought.

Marcovefa shook him awake in the morning. She seemed fresh and well rested, even if she'd fallen asleep after him. Was she using magic to lend herself strength and go without much rest? If she was, what price would she have to pay later? Count Hamnet wondered if she could do for him whatever she was doing for herself.

Asking her about it slipped his mind. He had a command here, one for which he was responsible. Bizogots liked sleep no less than anyone else. Ulric Skakki would have gone into hibernation for the winter if Hamnet gave him the chance. Hamnet was resigned to getting sworn at every morning, even if not enamored of it.

They started off later than he wished they would have. That happened every morning, too. He didn't know what he could do about it—he didn't think he could do anything.

It particularly galled him this morning because they were nearing the north woods. Somewhere ahead were the Rulers. He wanted to hit the mammoth-riders while they were still in among the firs and spruces. They would have trouble deploying in the woods—they were used to wide open spaces where no trees grew.

As usual, the gap between what he wanted and what he got yawned wide. He took no special notice of the first few men who rode past him, heading south as fast as their horses would take them. They might have been ordinary traders on business of their own. The odds were long, but they might have been.

But the fellow who still slung an imperial shield on his back . . . Hamnet Thyssen couldn't pretend he was anything but a fleeing soldier. "Where are you going?" he called. "What are you running from?"

The cavalryman's eyes showed white all around the irises, like those of a spooked horse. "Savages!" he said. "There's savages in the woods, and they're killing anything that moves!" He booted his horse into a weary trot and rode on.

XIX

GETTING ANY OF the soldiers fleeing from disaster in the woods to stop long enough to say exactly what had gone wrong up in the north was Hamnet's biggest problem. The men who'd escaped wanted nothing more than to put distance between themselves and the Rulers. They didn't want to talk: that slowed them down.

Some of them warned of mammoths. Some babbled about magic. None of that told Hamnet Thyssen anything he didn't already know. He finally had to capture a Raumsdalian soldier as if the man belonged to an enemy army, not the one Hamnet was going to command.

"Who the demon are you? What do you think you're doing?" the cavalry trooper demanded. He stared at the Bizogots who made up most of Hamnet's strength. Seeing that they were northerners, he went on, "Are you in league with the devils in the woods?"

"No, you idiot," Hamnet said. "The Rulers attacked the Bizogots before they ever got down here." *Not that I could make anybody pay attention to what was going on north of the tree line.* But the trooper wouldn't care about that. Hamnet went on, "I am Count Hamnet Thyssen. The Emperor has given me command in the north against the invaders." He flourished his orders without unrolling them. "Now who are you? Why are you running away?"

"I won't get in trouble?" the trooper asked warily.

"Not if you give me straight answers and stop wasting my time," Hamnet said.

"Well, my name's Ingolf Rokkvi," the rider said. "I was part of Count Steinvor's army. We heard the barbarians had done something nasty up near where the trees stop, but we didn't know just what was going on. We figured it was Bizogots kicking up their heels like they do sometimes."

"Oh, good," Ulric Skakki said. "That's the way to guarantee you win your battles—make sure your soldiers know exactly what they need to do."

Ingolf scratched his head. "Is he joking, uh, Your Grace?" he asked Hamnet Thyssen.

"I wish he were," Hamnet said, while Ulric snorted. Waving the adventurer to silence, Count Hamnet nodded to the trooper. "Go on."

"Well, I was trying to," Ingolf Rokkvi said. "We rode north up the forest tracks, looking for the savages. We figured we'd give them a hiding, and they'd run like they usually do, and then we could go home."

Trasamund and Marcomer and several other Bizogots growled at that scornful assessment of their prowess. Count Hamnet waved them to silence, too. His glare was enough to keep them from reaching for their weapons. He told Ingolf Rokkvi, "Go on," again.

"I will, if you let me," Ingolf said. "We were riding along, and all of a sudden the worst blizzard in the world blows up, right in the middle of the woods. You wouldn't think something like that could happen, but it did."

Hamnet glanced at Liv and Audun Gilli and Marcovefa. They all nodded. Liv and Audun looked worried, which meant they wouldn't have wanted to try a spell like that—Hamnet supposed that was what it meant, anyhow. Marcovefa looked amused, which could have meant . . . anything at all. "Then what happened?" Hamnet asked Ingolf Rokkvi.

"Mammoths happened, that's what!" Ingolf said. "By God, they did. Mammoths with soldiers on 'em. They were built like bricks, with big curly beards."

"The mammoths?" Ulric Skakki asked.

"The soldiers," Ingolf Rokkvi said reproachfully. "They speared us, they trampled us—you can't make a horse stand against a mammoth, on account of he's just not big enough—and they laughed while they did it."

"What happened then?" Count Hamnet asked.

"What do you think happened?" Ingolf's look told him he was short on brains. "We tried to get away from them. That's what you do when you haven't got a chance of winning, and we cursed well didn't. There was more horrible weather in the woods, and short-faced bears and dire wolves jumping out at us like they had no business doing, and all the time it was like we heard those savages laughing at us, like they thought we were the biggest joke in the world."

"Would you fight them again?" Hamnet asked.

Ingolf Rokkvi needed some time to think about that. "Maybe I would," he said at last, "if I thought we had some kind of prayer of winning. A lot of the ones who weren't on mammoths were on these funny deer, and they weren't anything special. A regular horseman doesn't hardly need to worry about 'em. But the mammoths, and the magic . . ." He scowled. "That's a pretty scary business."

"We can beat them. By God, we can," Hamnet said. Ingolf Rokkvi's scowl got deeper. He didn't believe a word of it. After what he'd been through, Hamnet had a hard time blaming him. A little desperately, the Raumsdalian nobleman went on, "We have a wizard who can match anything they do." He pointed to Marcovefa.

Ingolf eyed her the way a man will eye a good-looking woman, not like a soldier eyeing someone who might help his cause. "Well, if you say so," he said after a moment: he didn't believe a word of it.

His horse looked back at him and said, "Don't be dumber than you can help. She really can. She's not running from them the way you are, is she?"

That wasn't Marcovefa's style of magic. Audun Gilli enjoyed putting words in the mouths of things that didn't normally have mouths, or at least had no business talking. Audun looked innocent when Hamnet Thyssen glanced his way—ostentatiously innocent, as a matter of fact. Hamnet didn't love him and never would, but for the time being decided he wasn't sorry to have him along.

Ingolf's eyes almost bugged out of his head. "How did you do that?" he demanded of Marcovefa.

She really was innocent—of this, anyway. In her accented Raumsdalian, she said, "Is my fault if beast has more sense than you do?"

The cavalry trooper gathered himself. Hamnet had feared he might go to pieces—he'd been through a lot lately. But he didn't. "All right. I'll try," he said. "If I end up dead . . . I reckon the lot of you will be there beside me. Have I got that right?"

"Yes," Hamnet said simply. "The next town ahead is Kjelvik, isn't it? Does it have a decent garrison?"

"Not too bad," Ingolf answered. "I don't know whether they'll want to fight or bug out, though."

"We'll see," Hamnet Thyssen said. They all rode north.

THEY CAME ACROSS more soldiers fleeing the Rulers before they got into Kjelvik. Some of them they persuaded to turn around and resume the fight. Others, seeing a body of armed men coming their way from out of the south, rode around them no matter how far out of their way that took them. Hamnet didn't try to round up those soldiers; they were too far gone to be of much use.

Kjelvik sat on a low hill. There were no tall hills or steep slopes in the northern part of the Empire. The Glacier had lain here too recently, and had ground such things down under its immense weight. As Count Hamnet neared the top of the hill, he could look ahead and see the dark smudge of the north woods out on the horizon. He was getting close. So were the Rulers.

He got a less than overwhelming reception from the gate guards. "Who the blazes are you, and why are you coming the wrong way?" a sergeant asked.

Instead of answering with words, Count Hamnet displayed Sigvat's commission, all adorned with seals and gorgeous with ornate calligraphy. "What's it say, Sergeant?" one of the guards asked. "I can't read for beans."

"What? You think I can?" the underofficer said. "I went to work when I was a brat, same as most people. I didn't have the time to waste on my letters."

"This is an order from His Majesty, the Emperor," Hamnet Thyssen said. "It gives me command in the north against the new invasion of the barbarians."

"Right. And rain makes applesauce," the sergeant jeered. "Nobody in his right mind'd *want* to go fight these savages. They ride mammoths, I hear. *Ride* 'em—would you believe it?" Ingolf Rokkvi shuddered—*he* believed it, all right.

And so did Count Hamnet, who had also seen it with his own eyes. He growled, "Go get an officer—someone who actually can read. He'll tell you whether I'm lying or not, by God."

Grudgingly, the sergeant sent off one of his guards. In due course, the man returned with a young officer. "I am Osvif Grisi," he said. "What do you want, stranger? What do you need?"

"I want to drive the barbarians out of the Empire. I need Kjelvik's garrison to help me do it," Hamnet answered. Osvif gaped. Hamnet displayed his commission again.

"Is he a fraud, sir?" the sergeant asked. "If he is, we'll give him what-for like he wouldn't believe."

Osvif Grisi stared at the impressive parchment. He reached Sigvat's peremptory commands, his lips moving. Count Hamnet didn't think the less of him for that; he read the same way himself, as did most people who could read at all. The more Osvif read, the wider his mouth fell open. By the time he finished, his thinly bearded chin was hanging on his chest.

"Well?" Hamnet said.

The youngster's jaw shut with an audible click. He stiffened to a parade-ground attention. "Give me whatever orders you think right, Your, uh, Grace," he said. "I am at your service in all ways, as is Kjelvik."

"He's real?" Now the sergeant's jaw dropped.

"He's real, all right," Osvif said grimly. "If he told me to hang you from a pole off the battlements, you'd be hanging there now." The sergeant gaped. Osvif Grisi turned back to Hamnet. "What do you want from Kjelvik, sir?"

"Every soldier you can put on a horse," Hamnet Thyssen answered. "We're going to have to scrape together some kind of army to fight the Rulers, you know."

"I suppose so, yes." The young officer licked his lips. "I think you'd better talk to the town's commandant."

"Yes, I think so, too," Hamnet Thyssen agreed. "I've been trying to do that, and people keep getting in my way." He eyed the sergeant, who did his best to hide in plain sight. Maybe he imagined himself kicking his life away up on the battlements. Hamnet wouldn't have ordered him hanged, but he didn't have to know that. The noble nodded to Osvif. "Take me to him."

Kjelvik's garrison wasn't big enough to hold the walls for long against a determined foe. The keep wasn't strong enough to keep out an invader once he'd broken into the city. So Hamnet's professional eye told him, anyhow. The guards outside the keep's portcullis stared at the Bizogots behind him.

"I thought some different barbarians were loose in the north," one of them said to his friend.

"Me, too. Shows what we know," the other guard said. Then he noticed Osvif with Hamnet's party. "What's going on, sir?"

"This noble"—Osvif pointed to Hamnet—"is in charge of all defenses in the north, by His Majesty's command." That made all the guards spring to attention. Osvif went on, "I am taking him to Baron Runolf."

"Is that Runolf Skallagrim?" Hamnet asked. He hoped so—if the local commander was a man he knew, things would go smoother.

And Osvif nodded. "That's right. You've met him?"

"A while ago, but yes," Hamnet replied.

Runolf Skallagrim was about his own age, a little heavier, a little softer—a little happier-looking, if you wanted to get right down to it. "By God," he said when Osvif led Count Hamnet into his chamber. "Look what the hound dragged in!" As he rose to clasp Hamnet's hand, he went on, "What the demon are you doing here? Last I heard, you'd got jugged."

"That's old news now." Hamnet Thyssen displayed his commission.

Runolf looked it over. In due course, he nodded. "Well, that's better than sitting in a dungeon, I must say."

"Is it?" Hamnet asked bleakly. "In the dungeon, I don't have to worry about a mammoth stepping on my head."

"There is that," Runolf Skallagrim agreed. "So what do you want from me?"

"As many men as you've got, as many fugitives from the armies that have already lost to the Rulers as you can round up, and enough food for them to take north."

"You don't ask for much, do you?" Runolf said.

"If you've got three times that many men in your pocket, I'll gladly take 'em," Hamnet said. "Oh—any wizards in town? We need them, too."

"A supply train'll be hard enough to come by."

That was much too likely to be true. Kjelvik wasn't a town from which anyone in the Empire had expected an army to sortie. If Raumsdalia needed to move against invaders from a town this far south, they'd penetrated farther and done worse than anybody would have guessed possible. Well, so they had. "Do what you can, Runolf, please," Count Hamnet said. "I've met these Rulers before. They come from beyond the Glacier, and they're more trouble than you can imagine."

"Beyond the Glacier?" The garrison commander looked and sounded intrigued. "So those stories about a way melting through don't just come from merchants off the Bizogot steppe getting drunk and telling tales in taverns, eh?"

"No, they're true, all right. I've been up there. It's a different world. We haven't had anything to do with it since the Glacier walled it off, God only knows how many thousand years ago. But we do now."

Runolf Skallagrim grunted. "I *will* do what I can, Thyssen. And I think the first thing I'll do is set my men to rounding up the soldiers who've come south out of the woods. My bet is, we'll need a show of force before a lot of those buggers'll want to remember why the Emperor pays them."

"My bet is, you're right," Count Hamnet said. "Fair enough. Do that first. After they comb them out of the fields and the taprooms and the whorehouses, we'll see what we've got. Don't waste time on it, though. The way it looks to me is, we've wasted all the time we can afford, or maybe a little more than that."

THE SOLDIERS LINED up in front of Hamnet Thyssen and Baron Runolf were a sorry-looking lot. Some of them were obviously hung over. Some were still drunk. Several were wounded, though none seemed seriously hurt—a man with a bad wound wouldn't have been able to come so far so fast. They all glared at him. They knew he wanted them to fight the Rulers again, and they were anything but keen on the idea.

Most of them still had swords. If he hadn't had the Bizogots and some of Runolf's archers backing him, he wouldn't have been surprised if they tried to mob him and mutiny. His guess was that bad odds were the only thing holding them back.

"So you've met the mammoth-riders," he said.

"What do you know about it, you blue-blooded son of a whore?" one of the soldiers said. "Somebody told you they could do that, did he? Do you know what it *means*, though? Not bloody likely, not if you're coming up from Nidaros."

"I fought them half a dozen times, up on the Bizogot plains," Hamnet Thyssen said. He waved back towards Trasamund and the other big blonds. "So did they."

The soldier blinked and shut up. Another one found a bitter question: "Why the demon didn't you whip them? Then they wouldn't have set on us."

"We didn't because we couldn't." As usual, Hamnet used the truth, however unpalatable it was.

"How come you think you'll do any better this time, then, curse you?" the second soldier demanded.

"Because this time we have a wizard who can beat anything the Rulers throw at her." Count Hamnet waved to Marcovefa. She took a step forward and nodded to the soldiers as if they were first-rate fighting men, not the flotsam and jetsam of a campaign gone wrong.

"Another Bizogot twat—huzzah," the second soldier said, slathering on his scorn with a trowel.

Maybe he thought Marcovefa didn't speak his language. Maybe he just didn't care. If he didn't, he made a bad mistake. As Gudrid could have told him, angering a wizard you couldn't kill on the instant was commonly a mistake.

It was here. Marcovefa murmured to herself. The soldier developed a sudden, uncontrollable urge to disrobe. Once he was naked in front of his staring comrades, he acted like a jackass—literally. He brayed, got down on all fours, and started pulling scraps of dead grass up from between cobbles with his teeth. He also relieved himself like an animal, calmly and without shame.

Marcovefa murmured again. The soldier came back to himself—and cried out in horror as he realized what he'd done. Marcovefa suffered him to dress and return to the ranks with no further afflictions.

"Any other donkeys here?" Hamnet Thyssen inquired.

Nobody said anything. The unhappy survivors of one encounter with the Rulers looked apprehensively from him to Marcovefa and back again. Something like a sigh rippled through their ragged ranks.

Count Hamnet understood the sigh all too well. His nod was precisely calibrated between scorn and sympathy. "That's right," he said. "You can turn around and have another go at the barbarians—this time with a real chance of winning—or you can face us now. Which one looks like a better bet?"

Even after Marcovefa's magic, the question didn't seem to have the quick and obvious answer he'd hoped for. He knew what that meant: the Rulers had beaten the Raumsdalian army even worse than he'd feared. They'd made the men afraid of them, sure another beating lay around the corner.

But they also looked at the soldier who'd done such a humiliating impression of an ass. If that could happen to him, what was liable to happen to them if they tried to tell Hamnet no?

"We'll go, I guess," said a man with the look of a sergeant. "If the savages kill us, at least it's over with in a hurry." Most of the men assembled with him nodded; he'd summed up what they were thinking.

"We fought them again and again on the Bizogot steppe," Hamnet said again. "We lost more than we won—I won't tell you anything different, because I can't. But you can beat them. By God, you can! And we'll do it."

He didn't expect them to break into frantic cheers. A good thing, too, because they didn't—that kind of thing happened only in bad romances. A few of them looked thoughtful, which was about as much as he'd hoped for.

He turned to Runolf Skallagrim. "What do you think?"

"They'll march. They'll fight . . . some," the commander of Kjelvik replied. "If they win the first time out, they'll fight harder after that. If they lose the first time, they'll run away so fast, their shadows won't keep up with 'em."

"Heh." Hamnet hadn't remembered that Runolf had such a gift for pungent truth. Then he added the most he could: "We're better off with 'em than without 'em."

"You hope," Runolf said.

"That's right." Hamnet Thyssen nodded. "I hope."

HE'D COME INTO Kjelvik with a troop of Bizogots. He rode out of it with an army of Raumsdalians. It wasn't exactly the army he would have wanted, not when it was made up of garrison troops and men who'd already run away from the Rulers once. But it was an army, and it could fight. It could. Whether it would . . .

"We're going in the right direction," he told Ulric Skakki. "We're moving towards the enemy."

"So we are," the adventurer said. "If only we had to move father before we bumped into those bastards."

Runolf Skallagrim said, "What I don't understand is, why didn't the Emperor do something about these Rulers sooner?" He seemed glad to be out of Kjelvik. He kept reaching for his sword and pulling it halfway out of the scabbard, as if ready to go into battle then and there. If all the soldiers who followed were as eager as the baron, the Rulers really might have something to worry about.

"You'd have to ask His Majesty about that," Hamnet replied. "I really couldn't tell you." He didn't want to shout that Sigvat was a purblind idiot, even if that explanation made more sense than any other.

"Well, it's too bad any which way," Runolf said.

Count Hamnet nodded—that too was an understatement. The sky was gray and lowering, with clouds that seemed almost close enough to the ground to let him reach up and touch them. Snow swirled through the air— not a lot, but enough to compress the horizon to not much farther than bowshot. The wind blew out of the north. It didn't have the howl of the true Breath of God, but it was no gentle zephyr, either. The season felt like what it was: autumn well north of Nidaros, heading towards winter.

Sheep and cattle huddled in the fields, scraping up what fodder they could from under the snow. Army outriders scooped them up as they came across them. Outraged herders howled protests. Hamnet paid them for the animals the army took. That made them less angry, but didn't end all their rage.

Scowling down at the silver in his mittened palm, one shepherd snarled,

"Why shouldn't we pull for the stinking barbarians, when the soldiers who're supposed to be protecting us pull a stunt like this?" By the way he said it, Count Hamnet might have been paying him for the corpses of his family.

"Why? I'll tell you why," Hamnet answered. "Because the Rulers, if they come this far, will take your sheep, they won't give you even a copper, and they'll cut your throat if you complain, or maybe just if they spot you. That's why."

"You say so, anyhow," the shepherd growled, calling the noble a liar without quite using the word.

"Yes, by God, I do say so," Hamnet replied. "I've fought them before, which is more than you have. You don't know anything about them."

"I sure don't," the shepherd said. "But I know more than I want to about the likes of you." He spat in the snow at Hamnet Thyssen's feet and stumped off, his oversized Bizogot-style felt boots leaving equally oversized footprints behind him.

"Nice to know you've charmed the natives, isn't it?" Ulric Skakki remarked.

"We need the meat," Hamnet said. "He really doesn't know how lucky he is."

"And it's our job to make sure he doesn't find out, too." Ulric winked. "Aren't *we* lucky?"

"Speak for yourself," Count Hamnet said, which only made Ulric laugh. Annoyed, Hamnet went on, "If I were really lucky—"

"You wouldn't have me bothering you," the adventurer put in.

Hamnet Thyssen nodded. "Well, that, too, but it isn't what I was going to say. I was going to say, if I were really lucky, I'd have an honest-to-God army with me, not a garrison that doesn't know how to fight and a bunch of odds and sods who've already run away once and don't want to fight."

"I don't follow that at all," Marcovefa said. "Say in the Bizogot language, please."

"Why not?" Hamnet translated his own words.

The shaman from atop the Glacier rode up alongside him and kissed him on the cheek. "Sometimes you get what you wish for," she said, as if she were personally responsible for arranging it. No matter how much Hamnet looked around, though, he saw only the men he'd mustered in Kjelvik. They were better than nothing—but, as far as he was concerned, not nearly enough better.

On he rode. They might not have been enough better than nothing, but they were what he had. The storm got stronger. Now the wind did start to feel like the Breath of God. The snow swirled thicker. Just staying on the road towards the northern woods was anything but easy.

Another road, a broader highway, came up from the southeast to join the one Hamnet and his men were on, which ran almost straight north. If Runolf Skallagrim hadn't warned Count Hamnet the crossroads was coming up, he never would have known it. "Which road do we take?" Runolf asked.

Hamnet wanted to laugh, or maybe to cry. "You'd do better to ask some of the men who came south," he answered. "They have a better notion where the Rulers are than I do. And they have a *much* better notion where the Rulers are than Sigvat does, not that that's saying much."

Runolf's coughs sent steam rising from his lips and nostrils. They also suggested that Count Hamnet had said quite enough, or maybe too much.

Before Runolf could ask anything of the soldiers, Hamnet heard hoofbeats—lots of them—off to the right. He would have caught them sooner if the falling snow hadn't muffled them. He peered in that direction, but the snowflakes dancing on the north wind kept him from seeing much.

His first thought was that a caravan of merchants was coming to the crossroads on the other highway. That was close to laughable, too. The traders would be sorry if they got in front of his force and found the Rulers first. And they would slow him down if they blocked the road. He didn't want to have to swing out into the fields to get around them.

And then a peremptory shout came through the howling wind: "You there! Strangers! Clear the road for His Majesty's soldiers!"

"What?" If Hamnet hadn't been wearing mittens, he would have dug a finger in his ear to make sure he'd heard straight. When he decided he had, he shouted back: "The demon you say! *We're* His Majesty's soldiers!"

"D'you know what'll happen to you for lying?" In case he didn't, the still invisible man at the head of the—other army?—went into grisly detail.

"I'm no liar, you—" Hamnet Thyssen shouted back something even nastier. It seemed to shock the other side's herald into silence. Hamnet gestured to Runolf Skallagrim, Ulric Skakki, and Trasamund, and, a moment later, to Marcovefa. "Ride with me," he told them. He raised his voice and called "Hold up!" to the rest of his force.

He and his handful of companions trotted towards the challenge. He wasn't overwhelmingly surprised to find a party coming out from the other host to see who he was. An officer wearing the hame of a dire wolf as a head-piece shouted, "What do you think you're doing, interfering with His Majesty's army?"

"I told you—*we're* His Majesty's army!" Hamnet produced the orders he had from Sigvat II and thrust them at the other man. "Here. Do you read?"

"Yes," the officer in the wolfskin said angrily. He snatched the parchment away from Count Hamnet. Then fear filled Hamnet for a moment. What if Sigvat had reneged on his promises? What if this force had orders to ignore one Hamnet Thyssen, or to clap him in irons? If Gudrid had been working to get her way with the Emperor, it wasn't impossible. It wasn't even un-likely, as Hamnet knew all too well.

But, by the way the other officer's eyes widened, it hadn't happened. Hamnet blew out a fog-filled sigh of relief. "You see?" he said.

"I see," the other officer said unhappily. "You'd better come with me and show this . . . this thing to Count Endil."

"Endil Gris?" Hamnet asked.

"That's right," the officer said. "You know him, uh, Your Grace?"

"We've met," Hamnet answered. Endil Gris was a warrior with a consid-erable reputation for his wars against the savages who raided Raumsdalia's southwestern frontier. So far as Hamnet knew, Endil had never fought in the north before. Sigvat must have figured a capable general on one border would prove just as capable on another. Maybe the Emperor was right. On the other hand, maybe he wasn't.

"Come with me, then," the officer said, "you and your, ah, friends." His gaze lingered longest on Trasamund and Marcovefa when he said that. After a moment, though, he added, "You have some experience against these new barbarians, I've heard. Is that right?"

"Yes, it is," Hamnet answered. "Not happy experience, not a lot of wins, but experience. I gather that puts me one up on Count Endil?"

Instead of answering, the man in the wolf-hame only grunted. Endil Gris' army put him one up, or more than one, on Count Hamnet. Endil had more soldiers than Hamnet did, many more, and they were men with the look of regulars, tough and composed and ready—they thought—for what-ever lay ahead of them. Quite a few of Endil's men also had suntans that said they'd come up from the south with him. They couldn't have turned so brown on northern duty, anyhow.

Endil himself wore a black leather patch over his left eye. "Thyssen, by

God!" he said. "What are you doing here?" Even in mittens, his handclasp felt odd; along with his eye, he was also missing his right middle finger.

"Show him what I'm doing here," Hamnet told the officer in the wolf-hame, who still carried his orders. Reluctantly, the man passed the parchment to Endil Gris.

Count Endil held it out at arm's length to read it. Count Hamnet had to do more and more of that himself. When Endil finished, one of his bushy eyebrows leaped. "How the demon did you get the Emperor to appoint you god of the north? That's what this amounts to."

"Hamnet always did have a charming smile," Ulric Skakki said.

Endil glanced at him. "Skakki, isn't it?" As Ulric nodded, the veteran soldier went on, "I've heard of you, for good and for . . . well, for not so good."

Ulric Skakki nodded again, unembarrassed. "That's what life is all about, don't you think? I could say the same thing about you."

"I wouldn't doubt it." But Endil Gris gave his attention back to Hamnet. "You've got all the authority you need, don't you?" Before Hamnet could answer, Endil continued, "You've got it if I say you've got it, anyway. Otherwise, you're just a beggar with a bowl, looking for a handout anywhere you can."

How to answer that? If Hamnet tried to bluff here, he reckoned he would lose his man. Endil was not a man who gave way to bluffs; if anything, they enraged him. And so Count Hamnet shrugged and said, "Yes, that's about the size of it. His Majesty's right about one thing—I know more about the Rulers and how they fight than you do."

"You couldn't very well know less. I've never seen one of the buggers, not yet," Count Endil replied. "All I've heard about 'em is from people who ran away from them. So I was going to do the best I could, but. . . ." He shrugged and spread his mittened hands.

"I've seen them. I've talked with them. I've fought them. I've run from them, too. It's what you do when you lose," Hamnet Thyssen said. "But some of the forces I was with almost won, and I think we've got a wizard now who can stand up to anything they throw at us." He gestured towards Marcovefa.

"The Rulers, they are not so much of a much," she said in her curiously accented Raumsdalian.

Endil Gris' long, somber, mutilated face crinkled into an unexpected grin. "Nice to know somebody thinks so, anyway," he rumbled. "Everybody down in Nidaros was shrieking about how they ate us up without salt." He swung his good eye back towards Count Hamnet. "I'll serve under you, Thyssen. I think you've got a better chance of making this come out right than I do, and what else matters?"

Plenty of other officers would have made that question anything but rhetorical. To them, their chance for fame and glory came ahead of anything else. Hamnet thought Endil Gris was a man of a different, sterner, school. He hoped Endil was. If the one-eyed noble claimed he was, Hamnet couldn't afford to do anything but take him at his word. "Thanks," he said. "As long as we've got that settled, let's go after the barbarians and give them what they deserve."

"Sounds good to me," Endil said.

One of his aides had been listening with more and more agitation. "But, Your Grace!" the junior officer burst out. "This is *your* army! Are you going to let some . . . some stranger take it away from you?"

"Thyssen's no stranger," Endil Gris replied. "Why did we come up here, Dalk? To whip these Rulers right out of their boots, yes? If Count Hamnet can do that, I'll stand behind him, because I'm not sure I can."

"But—" Dalk didn't want to let it drop.

"Would you like to take it up with His Majesty?" Endil asked. "Would you like to go back to Nidaros and take it up with His Majesty?"

His aide recognized danger when it blew his way. "Uh, no, Your Grace."

"Very good. *Very* good." Count Endil was ponderously sarcastic. "In that case, would you like to salute Count Hamnet Thyssen and do everything you can to help him against these barbarians? That's what *I* aim to do, by God." He did it.

After a moment, so did Dalk. But rebellion still glittered in his eyes as he said, "May you lead us to victory, Your Grace."

Count Hamnet knew what that meant. He gave the unhappy Dalk a thin smile. "Don't worry about telling tales to the Emperor if I lose. He'll hear them from better men than you, I promise. And he pulled me out of the dungeon to do this. If he throws me in again, what have I lost? What has he lost?"

Dalk's eyes went big and round. "He . . . pulled you out of the dungeon?"

"I'd heard that," Endil Gris said. "I hoped it wasn't true. You're not the kind of man who ends up in one, except maybe for telling the truth."

"Well, you got the crime right the first time," Ulric Skakki said. "Such men are dangerous—and if you don't believe me, ask Sigvat."

"Enough." Hamnet held up a hand. "Only the Rulers get anything if we start slanging each other."

"You're right, by God," Trasamund said. "We Bizogots did that, and we paid for it." Dalk and Endil Gris both eyed him as if to say, *So what?* They didn't want to listen to a Bizogot. *Do they really want to listen to me?* Hamnet Thyssen wondered. *I'll find out.*

Then he realized Marcovefa had told him he would get a real army before he got it. How the demon had she known? How *could* she have known? *She's a shaman, that's how,* Hamnet thought. *A strong one, too, by God. Maybe we've got a chance in spite of everything.*

XX

HAMNET'S ARMY REACHED the southern edge of the forest before the Rulers broke out of it. The Raumsdalians rounded up more soldiers fleeing from the mammoth-riders. Count Hamnet wasn't sure he was glad to have them. He feared they hurt morale more than they swelled numbers. Some of them were eager enough to try conclusions against the Rulers again. More, though, babbled about barbarians spearing them from mammothback, and about magic shaking ground and twisting weather.

In summer, the forest—mostly pine and fir and spruce—was a dark green wave across the north of the Raumsdalian Empire. In the winter, snow cast a white veil of beauty over the same inhospitable countryside. The trees thrived where even oats and rye wouldn't grow, and went on thriving up till the ground stayed frozen the year around and the Bizogot plains began.

Within five minutes of Count Hamnet's ordering the army to halt before going into the woods, Ulric Skakki, Runolf Skallagrim, and Endil Gris all asked him the same question: "Are you going to go in there after them or wait till they come out and hit them on better ground?"

"That's what I'm thinking about," he answered . . . and answered . . . and answered. Suddenly, he tried to snap his fingers inside his mittens. It didn't work, but he still smiled. "Marcovefa!" he called.

"What do you want?" she asked.

"Can you find out where in the forest the Rulers are lurking?"

She nodded. "Yes, I think I can. They not belong here. They leave trail, show where they go, where they are."

"Do that, then, please," Hamnet said, in case she thought he was only asking a hypothetical question.

Marcovefa muttered to herself in the strange dialect the folk who lived atop the Glacier used. She rubbed her horse's ears—why, Count Hamnet couldn't have said, unless it was to touch something that did belong to this part of the world. After a moment, she pointed north and a little west. "They are there," she said in clear Raumsdalian.

Hearing her, Hamnet Thyssen had no doubt she was right. He looked to Endil Gris and Runolf Skallagrim. He would have been ready to argue with either one or both had they chosen to disbelieve, but they didn't. Each of them nodded in turn: her certainty brought conviction with it.

"How far?" Hamnet asked.

Marcovefa frowned and muttered to herself again. "A day's journey, no more," she answered. "But they are not standing still. They are heading this way."

She spoke in Raumsdalian once more. "How do you know that?" Runolf Skallagrim asked her.

Marcovefa's frown got deeper. She tried to explain, and she did go on using the imperial language, but what she said made little sense to Hamnet—or, he could see, to Baron Runolf or Count Endil. What did blue fringes have to do with anything? And why would there have been red fringes had the Rulers been moving away instead of forward?

"Fringes on what?" Runolf asked. "Their clothes?"

"No, no, no." Marcovefa sounded frustrated. "Their . . ." She couldn't find the Raumsdalian word she wanted, or even one in the regular Bizogot tongue. Finally, biting her lip in annoyance, she came out with one in her own dialect. That did neither Hamnet nor Runolf nor Endil any good.

"Their auras?" Ulric Skakki suggested, and went back and forth with her in her tongue for a few sentences.

She beamed. "Yes. Their auras. I thank you. The way their spirits rub against the fur of the world."

"The fur of the world?" Endil Gris still sounded confused, and Count Hamnet couldn't blame him, not when he was confused himself.

"I think someone who spoke Raumsdalian from birth would say, *the fabric of the world*." Again, Ulric did the interpreting. "Where Marcovefa comes from, there are no fabrics except felt."

Runolf Skallagrim asked a genuinely important question: "Do they know we're so close, with an army that's ready for them?"

"No." Regardless of how strange Marcovefa's sorcery was, she could be completely convincing when she wanted to. By Runolf's grin, she convinced him now. Count Endil also seemed satisfied. Even Dalk—whose family name, Hamnet had learned, was Njorun—nodded thoughtfully.

"We know where they are. They don't know where we are," Hamnet said. "What could be better? Let's go get them."

Nobody told him no or tried to talk him out of it. He always remembered that. The army was in good spirits as they rode into the woods. He always remembered that, too.

COUNT HAMNET ALWAYS liked going into the northern forests. He liked it all the better now that he had an army around him. The clean, spicy smells that came from the conifers fought the stink of soldiers and horses. The fighting men and their mounts didn't smell so bad as they would have in the summertime, but they smelled bad enough. Firs and spruces were better.

"Set scouts out ahead and to all sides," Ulric Skakki advised. "We want to surprise them. We don't want them surprising us."

"Yes, Mother, dear," Hamnet answered. Ulric laughed and stuck out his tongue. He didn't care if he annoyed Count Hamnet. He only cared about not getting ambushed—which, Hamnet had to admit, was reasonable enough.

Sending scouts up the road ahead of the army was easy enough. Sending them out on the flanks was anything but. The road, after all, was there to make travel easier. The horsemen trying to pick their way through the trees had a harder time of it.

Audun Gilli rode up alongside of Count Hamnet. The wizard still acted nervous and embarrassed around him—and still had good reason to. Nervous or not, he spoke up now: "I can't feel the Rulers anywhere ahead of us." Licking his lips, he added, "Neither can Liv."

"What are they doing?" Hamnet Thyssen asked Marcovefa. "Are they hiding themselves with magic?"

"If it's a masking spell, it's a good one," Audun said. "Better than any we use on this side of the Glacier."

Marcovefa's nostrils flared as she breathed in deeply. She might have been tasting the air, trying to find the flavor of the Rulers. She pointed ahead and a little to the left: the direction in which the road was taking the Raumsdalian army. "They are there," she said. "It *is* a masking spell, but not so much of a masking spell, not such a good masking spell." Turning to

Audun, she asked, "You not feel the . . . the *empty* moving along the road towards us? In the *empty*, that is where the Rulers are."

Audun started to chant a spell. Marcovefa gave him a different tune with words from her dialect. He imitated them as best he could. By the third try, his pronunciation was good enough to suit her. Instead of practicing the charm any more, he aimed it at the road ahead. His jaw dropped in astonishment.

"They really are there!" he exclaimed. "Or the emptiness around them is, anyhow." He gave Marcovefa an awkward bow in the saddle. "Thank you. I'll take this back to Liv, by your leave."

"However it pleases you," Marcovefa said indifferently.

That indifference pleased Hamnet Thyssen. How had Audun wormed his way into Liv's good graces, and then into her bed? By sharing magic with her, by learning spells he didn't know and teaching ones she didn't. Hamnet didn't believe Audun Gilli could teach Marcovefa anything. *What a shame*, he thought.

But he did ask, "If the Rulers use magic to look for us, they'll find us, won't they?"

"I have a small masking on us. Maybe it serve, maybe not. Better than their junk, though," Marcovefa answered. "Only a small one. Don't think we need any more. The Rulers too stupid even to think to look."

They weren't stupid, not to Hamnet's way of thinking. But they were arrogant. They always seemed to underestimate their foes. That could amount to the same thing. It could . . . if Hamnet could bring home a victory.

"Push the scouts forward," he ordered. "Does anyone know if there's a large clearing anywhere between the Rulers and us? If there is, I want to form my battle line there."

A couple of the men who'd run from the invading barbarians stirred. "There's a wide place in the road two, maybe three miles up," one of them said. "You're going to face those bastards anywhere, that's a pretty good spot." The other soldier nodded.

"If I remember straight, they're right," Ulric Skakki said. Had he been *everywhere* in the northern reaches of the Empire? Count Hamnet wouldn't have been surprised. And hearing him agree with the soldiers who'd been so unenthusiastic about going north again came as no small relief.

"All right. We'll do that, then," Hamnet said, nodding. He called to the trumpeters who directed the army's movements: "Blow *Forward!*"

The martial notes rang out. Count Hamnet urged his own horse ahead with pressure from his knees and with the reins. He reached down to make sure his sword was loose in the scabbard. It was, of course. He felt foolish for checking. But he wasn't the only man making sure his weapons were ready. When you'd go into battle soon, you wanted to be certain your tools wouldn't fail you.

He found the clearing where the soldiers and Ulric said it would be. It wasn't so wide as he might have wished, but it would do. He didn't think he would come across any better place to fight, anyhow. He put his armored lancers in the center, with horse archers on either wing. He also kept a reserve brigade he could rush to wherever it was most needed.

He was just getting his line the way he wanted it when a scout came galloping into the clearing. "They're coming!" the Raumsdalian shouted. "They aren't far behind me!" As if to prove him right, more frightened-looking horsemen emerged.

"Be ready!" Hamnet shouted. "We'll want to knock them back as soon as they start to deploy." He turned to Marcovefa. "Do they know we're here?"

"They know the scouts are," she answered.

His exasperated snort sent steam from his nostrils, as if he were a hard-running horse. "I know *that*," he said. "Do they know this army is here?"

She laughed. "Of course not, darling," she said. "I keep telling you and telling you—they are not very smart."

Maybe they weren't. Hamnet Thyssen wasn't so sure about that, but maybe they weren't. But they were very strong, or they wouldn't have come so far so fast. As arrogance could ape stupidity, so strength could do duty for wisdom.

More and more riders burst into the clearing. One was wounded, while another rode a horse with an arrow in the rump. Then a man on a riding deer trotted into the open space. All the way across it, Hamnet could see his leather armor and his thick, dark, curly beard—he was a man of the Rulers, sure enough.

Marcovefa proved right—he hadn't known a Raumsdalian army was on its way north. At the sight of so many soldiers drawn up in neat ranks, the enemy rider reined in frantically. Hamnet could read his thoughts—he had to get away and warn his friends.

"Loose!" Hamnet shouted. A good many archers had already strung their bows. Almost in one motion, they nocked and let fly. The arrows sang through the air. The warrior of the Rulers had time to throw up his shield, but it did him no good. The iron-headed shafts pierced both him and his riding deer. Together, they crumpled to the snow. Their blood streaked the clean whiteness and sent steam up into the air.

"Well, there's one of the buggers down," Runolf Skallagrim said. "He didn't seem so tough."

"No," Hamnet Thyssen agreed. "One by one, or even a few at a time, they're nothing special. But when you put a few of them together, or more than a few . . ."

For the next little while, the Rulers' outriders drifted into the clearing by ones and twos and threes. Plainly, their wizards had no idea an army awaited them there. The Raumsdalians started cracking jokes as they shot down the invaders. If the Rulers kept blundering into them in driblets, they could keep killing barbarians till they ran out of arrows.

But it wouldn't last, as Hamnet knew too well. A couple of warriors saw the carnage in the clearing soon enough to wheel their riding deer and bucket off to the north before the Raumsdalians could slay them. Before long, Marcovefa said, "They know, curse them."

"Now the real fight starts," Hamnet Thyssen said. Marcovefa nodded. The shaman from atop the Glacier would bear a lot of the burden on the Raumsdalian side. Hamnet bit his lip. That was a great deal to ask of anyone, and especially of a lover. Liv hadn't been able to shoulder such a weight, try though she did. The Rulers proved too strong for her up on the Bizogot plains. Hamnet had to hope the same thing wouldn't happen with Marcovefa here.

The ground trembled beneath his horse's hooves. The beast snorted and shied as a low rumble filled the air and then vanished again. Some snow fell from the branches of the trees lining the clearing.

"Just what we need," Kormak Bersi said: "a little earthquake right at the start of the battle."

"Somehow, I don't think that was supposed to be a *little* earthquake," Count Hamnet answered.

Marcovefa nodded. "They want to squash us." Her teeth flashed as she grinned. "They not get what they want." She looked towards the north. "Now they come down on us. They think we all—" She ran out of words, but gestured.

"Flattened?" Hamnet said.

"Flattened, yes. I thank you." Marcovefa smiled again, for all the world as if a forgotten verb were the only thing she had to worry about.

A rumble came from the north. More snow fell from tree branches on that side of the clearing. The ground seemed to shake again. This time, Marcovefa couldn't do anything about it, but Hamnet Thyssen didn't expect her to. With cries like horns full of spit, the mammoths with warriors aboard them thundered into the clearing.

"Loose!" Hamnet shouted once more, pointing towards the great beasts.

Hundreds of arrows hissed through the air. As the mammoths had up on the Bizogot plains, they wore armor of leather dipped in boiling wax. That kept most of the Raumsdalian shafts from biting, but not all.

Wounded mammoths' screams were even more blood-curdling than their usual cries. Some of the great beasts pulled riders off their backs with their trunks and dashed them to the ground, as if blaming them for the pain they suffered. And if they thought that, were they far wrong? Others broke formation. One or two trampled down the riding deer on either flank, smashing swaths of chaos through the Rulers' ranks.

But most of the mammoths kept coming in spite of the barrage of arrows. "Forward!" Hamnet Thyssen shouted. The Raumsdalian trumpeters amplified the command. Momentum of your own was the best way to meet a charge. *Even of mammoths?* Hamnet wondered. But by then his horse was already getting up into a gallop.

He knew he didn't want to try to withstand a line, even a disarrayed line, of charging mammoths on a horse that was standing still. He also knew men on horseback could beat men on riding deer. He'd seen that up in the Bizogot country. It ought to be even more surely true here, the Raumsdalians being better trained, better armored, and better disciplined than the big blond barbarians who lived north of them.

Nothing on this side of the Glacier could withstand a charge by heavy cavalry. Those big horses . . . suddenly didn't seem so big, when men on mammothback shot down at riders from above and speared them out of the saddle with long, long lances.

Still, the Rulers didn't have it all their own way—not even close. Count Hamnet slashed at a mammoth's leg, hoping to hamstring the monster. It didn't topple, but a squall of torment rewarded him. Another rider thrust his lance deep into a mammoth's unarmored belly. Even on so huge a beast, that was bound to be a mortal wound. Blood poured from it in great gouts. The mammoth sank to its knees, then rolled over on its side.

Something buzzed past Count Hamnet's head like an angry wasp. That wasn't an arrow—it was a slingstone. The realization made him want to duck. Especially if made of lead, those could be worse than arrows. Sometimes they sank into the wounds they created and disappeared.

You couldn't use a sling from horseback or mammothback or even, he supposed, deerback, not if you hoped to hit anything. Hamnet looked around till he spotted the detachment of enemy slingers, who had just come out of the forest and into the clearing, where they had the room they needed to set up.

"Get them!" he shouted, pointing their way. But a lot of enemy warriors stood between the slingers and the Raumsdalians. He looked around for Marcovefa. "Can you take out the slingers?" he asked her.

She didn't even know what they were. "I have other things to worry about," she answered. "Muchly magickings!"

Hamnet Thyssen hadn't felt any magic from the Rulers. Now he realized why he hadn't. Keeping their wizards busy was much more important than knocking out their slingers, who, in the big scheme of things, were no worse than nuisances.

So he told himself, not knowing how bad a nuisance could be.

But he had other things to worry about, too. An unhorsed—or undeered, or unmammothed—warrior of the Rulers cut at him. He took the blow on his shield and slashed back. His stroke caught the enemy warrior in the side of the neck. The warrior groaned and toppled, spouting blood.

"To me, Three Tusk clan! To me, Bizogots!" Trasamund roared. "Revenge is ours! Death to the Rulers!"

"Death!" cried his clansmates and the other Bizogots from clans all across the frozen steppe. "Death to the Rulers!"

They dealt out plenty of death, too. They steered clear of the mammoths, at which Hamnet Thyssen could hardly complain. But, big men on big Raumsdalian horses, they worked a fearful slaughter against the archers mounted on the Rulers' riding deer. The enemy warriors were brave enough and to spare; no one ever questioned the Rulers' courage. The horses towered over the deer, though, and gave the Bizogots a decided close-range advantage over their foes.

Shouting out his orders, urging his men forward on the flanks, and doing what he could to keep the mammoths from smashing through in the center, Count Hamnet began to sense a certain agitation among the Rulers, even if their courage did not falter. They were used to prevailing by strength of sorcery as well as strength of arms. Whatever they were used to, though, they weren't having their magical way today.

Off behind the enemy line to the right, Hamnet watched one of the Rulers who carried himself with even more arrogance than was usual for that arrogant breed screaming at four or five other men. They had to be wizards, even if they didn't deck themselves out in fringes like Bizogot shamans or in the fancy gowns Raumsdalian sorcerers sometimes wore. And, at the moment, they were mightily unhappy wizards, too.

One of them pointed towards the Raumsdalian line—pointed in Marcovefa's general direction, in fact. Hamnet Thyssen couldn't hear what he said and didn't speak his language anyhow. That didn't mean Hamnet didn't understand—oh, no. *They've got a wizard who's holding us up. That's what the trouble is.*

The enemy officer didn't buy a word of it. He did some more screaming. He did everything but jump up and down in the trampled snow. When screaming didn't satisfy him, he slugged the wizard who'd dared tell him the truth. He kicked him when he was down, too, then stepped away in magnificent contempt.

Hamnet watched the wizard slowly and painfully rise. He wasn't so sure he would have wanted to be that officer. High-ranking men who made their subordinates hate them suffered a startling number of unfortunate accidents. That was true among Raumsdalians and Bizogots, anyway. If the Rulers partook of ordinary human nature, it was probably so for them, too.

He glanced over to Marcovefa, who seemed to be enjoying herself in the thick of the fighting. "Maybe you should get back," he told her. "They know what you're doing. They'll try to get you."

"Let them try," she said gaily.

Hamnet Thyssen would have argued with her more, but Endil grabbed him by the arm and pointed to the closest mammoth. "Come on, Thyssen!" the other count yelled. "If we swing in behind that bugger, we can hamstring it."

"Do you think so?" Hamnet said, but he was already booting his horse forward alongside Endil Gris'.

He slashed at the mammoth's hairy column of a leg. So did Endil. The mammoth didn't crumple, as he'd seen one of the great beasts do. But it did scream in pain and lumber away from its tormentors. The warriors of the Rulers on top of the mammoth shouted in their guttural, incomprehensible tongue. They tried to get it to return to its duty. A mammoth was not like a man, though. It understood nothing of such notions. All it wanted to do was get away from what pained it.

"Not bad," Endil Gris said, and then, "Why do these curly-bearded maniacs ride deer instead of horses?"

"I don't think there are any horses beyond the Glacier," Count Hamnet answered. "I don't remember seeing any, anyhow. I suppose they tamed the best beasts they could find, that's all."

"You may be right. You sound like you make sense, anyhow," Endil said. "They aren't as good as horses, though. We can whip these bastards. How did they beat us before? We must have messed up."

"Magic," Hamnet Thyssen said. "They have better wizards than we do—or they did, till Marcovefa."

He looked around to make sure she was all right. She'd never seen a horse till she came down from the Glacier, either. She'd never seen any beast larger than a fox. She made a pretty good rider, though. And she had no trouble staying away from the Rulers—and, much more to the point, fending off the spells their wizards threw at her.

As long as Hamnet saw her well and unhampered, he could go back to the business of fighting the enemy without a worry. If he fell, Endil Gris or Runolf Skallagrim would take over and make about as good a general as he did. He was valuable to the Raumsdalian cause. Marcovefa was indispensable. He understood the difference. He hoped she did, too.

Not far away, Audun Gilli traded swordstrokes with a warrior of the Rulers on a riding deer. No one would even think Audun was a first-rate horseman or a first-rate swordsman. He was keeping the enemy fighting man from killing him, but that was about all. Hamnet Thyssen rode towards them. The warrior of the Rulers steered his deer away, not wanting to fight two at once.

Audun Gilli gave Hamnet a wry grin. "I didn't think you cared, Your Grace," the wizard said.

Count Hamnet couldn't even say he would be sorry to see Audun dead, because he could imagine plenty of ways he wouldn't. He could say, "I don't want anyone from the Rulers to do you in," without telling any lies, so he did.

"You'd rather do it yourself, if it gets done," Audun suggested.

"As a matter of fact, yes," Hamnet Thyssen answered. The wizard bit down on his lower lip. If he'd thought he would get some soothing hypocrisy, he need to think again.

Another slingstone buzzed past Hamnet. He pointed towards the dismounted men behind the enemy line. "Can you do anything about them?" he asked. "They're hurting us."

"I can try." Audun's quick spell was only a small one. It did no more than whip up snow into the slingers' faces. But that put them off—for a while, anyhow. He sent Hamnet a real smile this time—maybe the first one he'd given him since taking Liv away. "It's nothing big, and it works mostly because the strong wizards are all busy doing other things."

"It does what it needs to do, and no one's complaining—except those God-cursed slingers," Hamnet said. "If you stay up at the front of the battle line, try not to get yourself killed right away, all right?"

"I'll do my best," Audun answered. "Are you sure you mean it?"

"Right away, I told you," Count Hamnet said. "Liv wouldn't come back to me even if you did, so you may as well live—for now. We need you—for now."

"Would you want her back, since you've got Marcovefa?" the wizard asked.

That question probably deserved more serious consideration than it would get on the battlefield. "I don't know if I want her *back* so much," Hamnet Thyssen said. "I want not to have lost her in the first place, if you know what I mean. D'you see the difference?"

"I may. Yes, I think so," Audun Gilli replied. "I wasn't trying to steal her from you, you know. If she didn't want to go, she wouldn't have looked at me—not that way, anyhow."

Count Hamnet believed him. But what was meant to be reassuring proved more dismaying than otherwise. Gudrid had been ready to go, and she went. Liv had been ready to go, and she went, too. *Why* can't *I keep a woman? What will make Marcovefa decide it's time for her to leave?*

Those questions wouldn't get answered on a battlefield, either. The lull that had given him a minute or two to talk with the wizard ended. More warriors of the Rulers swarmed towards him on their riding deer. The mounts weren't everything they might have been, but the men on them were as fierce as short-faced bears. Hamnet had to fight for his life again, slashing with his sword, keeping his shield between his vitals and the enemy's weapons, and once smashing it into the face of a soldier he couldn't stop any other way. He picked up a cut over his eye that stung like vitriol and half blinded him as it bled. His sole consolation was that it could have been worse—it could have split his skull, and it almost had.

A slingstone thudded off his shield. He felt it all the way up his arm to his shoulder. Audun was fighting hard, too—fighting too hard to keep on harassing the slingers. Count Hamnet swore under his breath. Not keeping that spell on would get Raumsdalians hurt, but he didn't know what he could do about it. Audun Gilli was, he grudgingly supposed, allowed to keep himself alive if he could.

With a little luck, Raumsdalian horsemen would ride down the slingers before long anyhow. They were bending the Rulers on riding deer back and back on their flanks. If they could surround the enemy altogether, this whole army might get wiped out. Not even Sigvat II could complain about that . . . Hamnet supposed.

He couldn't worry about the Emperor, either. A warrior on a mammoth came much too close to skewering him with a long lance. He couldn't do anything about that but duck, hack at the spearshaft, and sidestep his horse to get out of the way. He shook his head, angry at himself. If you didn't pay attention to what was going on around you, you almost deserved to get speared.

Was Marcovefa paying as much attention as she should? This was her first big battle. Did she know enough to stay alive on the field? Where had she disappeared to, anyway? Count Hamnet stared across the field in growing alarm.

Spotting her, he sighed in relief. *That* was all right. But then, quite suddenly, it wasn't any more. He chanced to be looking her way when a slingstone caught her in the side of the head. It was a glancing blow. If it hadn't been, it would have smashed in her skull like a hammer smashing a rotten melon. Yet even a glancing blow proved quite bad enough. She swayed in the saddle and started to crumple to the ground.

"No!" Hamnet howled, a cry of despair both for himself and for the fight.

A Raumsdalian trooper held Marcovefa upright. If she did fall off her horse, she'd soon get trampled by friends and foes impartially. Hamnet spurred towards her, hacking past any enemy warriors who tried to stand against him. He saw them less as foemen than as obstacles like boulders and tree trunks.

"Hullo, Your Grace," the trooper said when Hamnet rode up. He was one of the men who'd run from the Rulers once and been forced back into the army at Kjelvik. "She got one right in the pot, I'm afraid."

"I saw it," Hamnet Thyssen answered grimly. He shook Marcovefa. Her limbs were as limp as a fresh corpse's. His thumb found her wrist. Her pulse still throbbed, and strongly. She lived, anyhow. He had a skin with beer in it on his belt. Holding it to her lips, he wished it were wine.

She choked, but then swallowed. Her eyelids fluttered. But she wasn't awake, not in any real sense of the word. Count Hamnet had no idea how badly she was hurt: he was neither healer nor wizard.

He hoped the Rulers didn't know how badly she was hurt. When she got knocked cold, what happened to the sorcery that held their spells at bay? Wouldn't it dissolve like mist on a hot day? How long would they need to realize that?

He got the answer faster than he wanted to. It wasn't quite a shout of triumph echoing across the battlefield, but it might as well have been. As soon as the enemy wizards found they could at last work unhindered here . . . they did. And the battle, which had inclined towards the Raumsdalians, swung the Rulers' way as well.

The trooper grabbed Count Hamnet's left arm, the one that wasn't steadying Marcovefa. He pointed into the cloudy sky. "By God!" he shouted. "Did you see that? Did you *see* it?"

Maybe because Hamnet was holding Marcovefa, maybe because he was too stubborn to yield easily to anyone's magic, he hadn't seen anything. "What?" he asked, his heart sinking.

"A teratorn!" the trooper cried. "Its claws almost tore my eyes out."

"Don't be ridiculous," Hamnet said. "There are never any teratorns on a battlefield till the fighting's over."

For a couple of heartbeats, the trooper looked doubtful. He knew that, too, once someone reminded him of it. But then he ducked and quivered. "Another one!" he yelled.

And Hamnet Thyssen saw it, too, and felt the wind of its passage, and smelled the stench of corruption clinging to its feathers. Was it there? Was it real? If he thought it was, if his senses told him it was, how could he doubt it? Who could guess what the wizards of the Rulers could do with no one there to thwart them?

Cries of dismay came from all over the field. Whatever the enemy's wizards were doing here, they were doing everywhere. Fear seemed to rise up from the ground like a poisonous fog and choke the flame of Raumsdalian hopes, which had burned so bright a moment before.

Desperately, Count Hamnet looked around for Audun Gilli and Liv and the wizards Endil Gris had brought north with him. They probably wouldn't be able to beat the Rulers' wizards—nobody but Marcovefa had done that. But they might slow down the enemy's sorcery and give the Raumsdalians a chance to do with weapons what they couldn't now with magic.

There was Audun, incanting as if his life depended on it—which was, no doubt, all too true. A puff of snow leaped up from nowhere and hit him in the face—almost the same trick he'd used against the Rulers' slingers. It wasn't deadly. But it made Audun cough and splutter and clap his mittened hands to his face to get snow out of his eyes. While he was busy with that, he couldn't chant or make passes. When he started again . . . he got another sorcerous snowball right between the eyes.

Where was Liv? Hamnet Thyssen couldn't see her, or the Raumsdalian wizards. He was sure they were doing all they could—Liv herself had her share and more of stern Bizogot courage. Whatever she and the Raums-dalians were doing wasn't enough. Even Hamnet felt despair and darkness rising inside him like mold crawling up a dank board.

Hoping against hope—the only kind of hope he had left—he shook Marcovefa. If only she would come back to herself, everything might yet be saved.

She moaned and muttered something, but didn't wake. For all he knew, her skull was broken. She might stay like this for days, or months, or years. Or she might die in the next few minutes.

"No, God," Hamnet whispered, as if God were in the habit of paying any attention to what he wanted.

He leaned over and kissed Marcovefa. The familiar feel of his lips . . . didn't do much. She murmured again. What could have been the ghost of a smile flitted across her face for a moment. Then it was gone as if it had never been. Hamnet Thyssen swore softly. He might have known his kisses held no magic.

"What's wrong, Thyssen?" Runolf Skallagrim cried.

"Our wizard's down, curse it," Hamnet answered.

"Then we're ruined!" Runolf was no coward, not without magic curdling his marrow. But he wheeled his horse and rode off to the south as fast as it would go.

All at once, the Rulers' riding deer seemed bigger and fiercer than Raumsdalian war horses. Rationally, Hamnet knew that couldn't be so, but terror drowned common sense. *It's only magic!* his mind yammered. It was magic, but it wasn't *only*. The mammoths seemed twenty, thirty, fifty feet high, and broad in proportion.

The Raumsdalian army melted away like the snow when spring finally came to the Bizogot steppe. It was flee or die, flee or be overwhelmed by what didn't seem to be phantasms at all. And once flight started, it took on a momentum of its own. Hamnet Thyssen was one of the last to leave the field. He brought Marcovefa away in his arms. Even he—or maybe especially he—knew a disaster when he saw one.

XXI

HAMNET THYSSEN AND what was left of his army made it out of the woods again. The one and only piece of good news he took from the lost battle was that the Rulers didn't press their pursuit. Maybe that showed how close they'd come to losing. If it did . . . well, so what? They hadn't lost.

And when would the Empire get out of the woods? Not soon, Count Hamnet feared. He'd had his chance to stop the barbarians, had it and failed with it. Now Raumsdalia lay open to invasion once more. He wouldn't get this army to fight again, not the way it had.

He looked around to see who'd lived through the battle. He didn't see Endil Gris, or Kormak Bersi, either. Where was Marcomer, the Leaping Lynx Bizogot?

Liv was here. She had a bandage on her forehead. A sword slash, someone had told Hamnet. Even though she wasn't his any more, he didn't like to think of that stern beauty marred. Maybe Audun Gilli knew a spell to hide scars or defeat them altogether. Hamnet could hope so, anyhow.

Trasamund was telling anyone who would listen about the slaughter he'd wreaked on the Rulers. All the slaughter in the world, though, wouldn't give him back his clan. He had to know that. Maybe the tale kept him from brooding about it . . . so much.

Silent as a snowflake, Ulric Skakki appeared behind Hamnet. The adventurer had a cut on his right arm, and one on his right cheek. He spoke out of the left side of his mouth: "She's awake."

"By God!" Count Hamnet said. "That's the first thing that's gone right in a while. How is she?"

"She asked the same thing about you," Ulric answered. "She wanted to come see you, but she's still too wobbly on her pins."

"I'll go to her." Hamnet hurried away.

Marcovefa sat on a wounded horse that had foundered and died. They'd laid her on the animal when they stopped here, to keep her out of the snow and in the hope that what was left of its warmth would help her. Maybe it had. Hamnet wasn't sure about anything any more—except that he was glad to see her with reason in her eyes.

"How are you?" He and she asked the same question at the same time. They both smiled. If his smile was as shaky as hers . . . he wouldn't have been a bit surprised.

"My head hurts." Marcovefa touched her temple very lightly, then jerked her hand away.

"I believe it," Hamnet Thyssen said. "A slingstone got you. I told you to move farther back from the fighting."

To his amazement, her smile got wider. "So you people say, 'I told you so,' too? Not just us on top of the Glacier?"

"We say it," Hamnet answered. "Sometimes we have reason to say it."

"Well, yes." She waved that aside as casually as if they'd been married for years. "What happened after I got hurt?"

"They threw magic at us. They threw fear at us. We lost," Hamnet said. "Why do you think we're down here? Without you . . . we lost. Without you . . ." He wondered how to go on. "Without you, it wouldn't have mattered so much if we won."

"I like you, too, but fight is more important now," Marcovefa said. Count Hamnet bit his lip, but he couldn't even tell her she was wrong. She looked around. "Can we fight more?"

"No," Hamnet said bluntly. "Even with your magic, I don't think we could make the men stand and fight again soon. The stone knocked you out. You didn't feel the fear the Rulers threw at us."

"I felt it. I held it off," she said. What that would have been like hadn't occurred to Hamnet Thyssen. Maybe he was lucky. Marcovefa shook her head very, very carefully. "Don't think I can do it again now. Head hurts too much. All scrambled up in there."

"I believe it. You almost got scrambled for good," Hamnet said. "This much over"—he held his hands maybe three digits apart—"and the stone doesn't hit you sideways."

"I know." Marcovefa looked unhappy. "I fight the magic to a standstill, and a stupid rock does for me. Not seem fair." Count Hamnet wouldn't have argued. Where was God while all this was going on? Probably on holiday at the Golden Shrine—there was no sign of him here. Marcovefa went on, "What do we do now, then?"

"Well, I suppose I have to send messengers back to Nidaros and let Sigvat know we lost." Hamnet sighed. "I'm really looking forward to that."

"You did everything you could. We all did everything we could," Marcovefa said. "We lost. It happens. Happens up on top of the Glacier, too."

"When the Emperor sends someone he doesn't like out to do a job, that fellow better do it," Hamnet Thyssen said. "If he doesn't, the Emperor will blame him. Otherwise, Sigvat would have to blame himself, and the next time he does that will be the first."

"As long as I don't get my head knocked, we win," Marcovefa said.

"But you did," Hamnet Thyssen answered. "And we didn't."

"DON'T DO IT," Ulric Skakki said when Count Hamnet chose a messenger to deliver the bad news.

"I have to," Hamnet said stolidly.

"No, don't," Runolf Skallagrim agreed. "We'll go back to Kjelvik. If we hold there, everything will look a lot better."

"How many of the towns in the woods held?" Hamnet said. "What does the Rulers' magic do to walls?"

"What will Sigvat do to you when he finds out you lost?" Ulric Skakki returned, which echoed Hamnet's thoughts uncomfortably well.

"Won't the wizard from the north hold those buggers off?" Runolf asked.

"Not for a while. She can't do anything much in the way of magic now," Hamnet answered. "She came too close to getting her head broken like a dropped egg."

"How long do we have to wait?" Runolf sounded suddenly apprehensive.

"No way to tell," Ulric Skakki said before Count Hamnet could reply. "You get hit in the head, you could be all right in a day or two, or you could go on having headaches and such for weeks."

"You sound like someone who knows what he's talking about," Hamnet remarked.

"And don't I wish I didn't!" Ulric said. "I've got clobbered more times than I wish I had—I'll say that. Probably why I'm the way I am today."

Hamnet, by contrast, had got hit in the heart too often. He reflected that he probably would again. Did you ever get used to such wounds? Could you? Liv hadn't hurt him so badly as Gudrid, but that wasn't because he'd got hardened in the intervening years. Far from it. The only difference was, Gudrid took a malicious glee in tormenting him, while Liv seemed sorry she'd decided she had to go.

Being sorry didn't stop her, of course. When did it ever?

Trasamund methodically cleaned blood from his sword and honed it against a whetstone to sharpen the edge and get the nicks out. He nodded to Hamnet. "We'll have another go at them," he said. "We almost licked 'em this time, by God."

"Yes." Hamnet let it go at that. He didn't want to lower the spirits of anyone who stayed ready to carry on. But he couldn't help thinking that a horse which almost escaped a sabertooth got eaten just the same.

And, no matter what Ulric said, Count Hamnet sent the courier off to Nidaros. Sigvat II needed to know what had happened up in the woods. For better or for worse—for better *and* for worse—the fate of the Empire rested in his hands. And after that . . .

Hamnet hunted up Runolf Skallagrim. "Tomorrow morning," he said, "we'll go down to Kjelvik, the way you said."

"About the best thing we can do," agreed the commandant of that town. "At least we'll have somewhere to fight from. The wall's in tolerable shape— you've seen it, for God's sake. And we've still got a lot of food in the granaries . . . and we'll be bringing back some more in the supply wagons."

"That was my next question," Hamnet Thyssen said.

How good were the Rulers at siege warfare? They were nomads like the Bizogots. He couldn't imagine them settling down around Kjelvik and building catapults and siege towers, the way a Raumsdalian army would. But, after a little thought, he could imagine them knocking down the walls with sorcery. How soon would Marcovefa be able to stop them if they tried?

Runolf had a different thought: "What if they just go on by us, go deeper into the Empire?"

"They wouldn't do that!" Hamnet exclaimed—by which he meant he wouldn't do that himself. But the Rulers? They might be a different story. So what if they had enemy soldiers behind them? If they were confident they could beat any force that came up against them, why would they worry? And wouldn't they have more warriors moving down into Raumsdalia off the Bizogot plains?

I'm full of cheerful notions today, Hamnet Thyssen thought. Nothing like losing a battle to bring such ideas bubbling to the surface like noxious gases from the asphalt pits of the far southwest.

Wounded men's moans did nothing to lift his spirits. He spotted Audun Gilli doing what he could to help some of the worst-hurt men with his magic. After a while, Audun looked up and nodded to him. The wizard looked weary, and who could blame him?

A yawn that surprised Count Hamnet told him how weary he was himself. He also realized how hungry he was. He had a couple of hard rolls in a belt pouch—they were even harder now than they had been when they went in there. Men were carving steaks from dead horses and roasting them.

If you were used to beef and mutton, horsemeat tasted like glue. If you'd eaten all kinds of strange things to keep your belly full, horsemeat wasn't half bad. Count Hamnet took out his belt knife and haggled a chunk off the haunch of an animal dead on its side in bloody snow. The meat, burnt on the outside, raw in the middle, wasn't good even of its kind. He ate it anyway.

Then he got a chunk for Marcovefa. She didn't show her usual wolfish appetite. That worried him. "Head hurts too much," she said. He grimaced. He couldn't do anything about that, however much he wished he could.

They slept Bizogot-style, with furs over them and snow heaped up to the north to hold away the Breath of God. The wind didn't blow too hard. It was as if even God had forgotten about Raumsdalia. And as for Hamnet Thyssen, he'd never spent a lonelier night in someone else's arms.

WHEN MORNING CAME, he asked for volunteers to go north and spy out what the Rulers were doing. He wondered if he would get any. More than a little to his own surprise, he did. "We're like fleas," one of them said. "A lot of the time, we aren't worth smacking." He grinned. He couldn't have been more than eighteen; to him, it had to seem more like an adventure, a game, than something where he could lose his life.

With the bulk of the army—with the bulk of what was left of the army—Count Hamnet marched south and east towards Kjelvik. He rode close by Marcovefa, in case she needed help staying in the saddle. Up till this summer, she'd never ridden, or even imagined riding was possible. She didn't look happy now—who with a nearly broken skull would have? But she rode.

And Kjelvik didn't seem particularly happy to see the returning soldiers, either. Fleeing men had got there before the army did, and had spread word

of the disaster it suffered. "Why did you go out there to lose?" someone
yelled at Hamnet Thyssen when he rode back into the town.

Were his bow strung, he would have shot the obnoxious, leather-lunged
pest. No one went out to lose a battle. Half the commanders who fought,
though, ended up with what they didn't want. Hamnet had wound up in
that unhappy number, even if not on purpose.

A stone in the house behind the heckler's head suddenly sported a
mouth. In a vicious, whiny imitation of his voice, it squawked, "Why did
you screw that broad next door?"

"What? I never—" But the local looked horrified. And the man standing
next to him, who was both larger and better muscled, looked first suspicious and then furious.

Hamnet Thyssen rode on before he learned how that drama turned out.
He looked around for Audun Gilli. When he spotted the wizard, he nodded
his thanks. He'd never thought he would do that, not after Audun took Liv
from him, but he did. Life was full of surprises, not all of them as nasty as
one would think.

The garrison cooks came up with meals tastier than charred horseflesh.
A bed in a room off the barracks made a better place to sleep with Marcovefa than snow-covered ground. A charcoal brazier gave the chamber at least
a little warmth.

"How are you?" he asked as the two of them sat down on the bed.

"Hurts," Marcovefa answered matter-of-factly.

Not tonight—I have a headache. Hamnet wondered if he was losing his wits
or just too tired to see straight. He'd seldom felt less lecherous. He might
want to hang on to Marcovefa through the night for reassurance—and
warmth, which was in short supply despite the brazier. Anything more
could wait . . . for the next year or two, by the way his eyelids sagged.

Sometimes things looked better after you woke up in the morning. This
wasn't one of those times for Count Hamnet. The brazier had run out of
fuel during the night, which left the room as cold as the inside of a snowball, almost as cold as the inside of Sigvat's heart. Hamnet still remembered
defeat much too well. And when he looked over at Marcovefa lying there beside him, the bruise on the side of her head was much too plain.

He lay quiet, letting her sleep as long as she would. Her eyes opened
about half an hour later. She smiled at him and said, "I need to piss."

"So do I," he answered. "I didn't want to bother you. How do you feel?"

"Not so bad," Marcovefa said, but she winced when she sat up and then stood. "Not so good, either." She used the pot first. As usual, she was much less self-conscious about such things than Raumsdalians, or even ordinary Bizogots. On that mountain up above the Glacier, privacy wasn't even a word. "What do we do now?" she asked as Hamnet got up and eased himself.

Lick our wounds, was the first thought that came to mind. "Try to find out what the Rulers are doing," he said out loud: it had the virtue of sounding better, anyhow. "See if we have to stand siege here."

"Can we?" Marcovefa asked—a much too pointed question.

"For a while, anyhow," Hamnet Thyssen said. "Till we're relieved, or till their magic knocks down the wall, or till your magic comes back. If yours comes back soon, we can last a lot longer."

She frowned in concentration, then shook her head, then winced again, regretting that. With a sigh that puffed fog from her mouth even indoors, she said, "Not there yet. Like my head all clogged up inside."

"You're lucky you really don't have a rock in there," Hamnet said.

"This is luck?" Marcovefa started to shake her head once more, but thought better of it. "With luck, the stone misses. With luck, we win the fight."

Hamnet had had those thoughts when someone told him something bad was really lucky. All it boiled down to was, *Well, things could be worse.* He supposed they could. That didn't make them wonderful the way they were.

"Let's go get something to eat," he said.

"Yes," she said, but the thought of breakfast didn't cheer her up, either. "Food makes me . . ." She couldn't find the word, but mimed puking.

"Nauseated," Hamnet supplied.

"Nauseated. Yes. I thank you," she said. "But I try to eat. I am a fire inside. I need dung to burn."

A plains Bizogot would have said the same thing. It still sounded odd in Hamnet's ears. "Come on," he said. "Let's see what they've got."

As in most towns where armies have suddenly arrived, breakfast was uninspiring. Oat-and-rye porridge with not enough butter or salt and a mug of sour beer didn't satisfy Hamnet's tongue. His stomach, though, quieted down. There was enough for the moment, anyhow.

Marcovefa ate without complaint, even though the food was strange to her. "You have so much," she said. "You get food, and you don't have to hunt for it even in wintertime. Do you know how lucky you are?"

Plains Bizogots said the same thing. They had enough themselves to appreciate how much more the Raumsdalians enjoyed, and to want it for themselves. Marcovefa's tone was different. Her folk had so little up there atop the Glacier, she might have come to the Empire from the dark side of the moon. She was beyond jealousy. Everything she saw surprised her.

She didn't always admire it: "Because you don't hunt so much, I see some of you sit around and get fat. You had better watch out. Such people are good only for roasting. Your foes will feast on you if you are not careful."

Count Hamnet's stomach did a slow lurch. He'd managed to make himself forget his prized shaman, his prized lover, had eaten enemy clansmen. No doubt those foes had also devoured men from her clan. Did that mean what she'd done was any better? *Maybe a little,* Hamnet thought.

And then she said, "If I ever catch the scut who hit me with that stone, I'll eat his liver without salt." A Raumsdalian would have meant it for a joke. An ordinary Bizogot would have, too, though a Raumsdalian who heard her might have wondered. Marcovefa was dead serious. And if she did find that slinger, he would be dead, too, dead and butchered.

Toward noon, a scout rode in. "They're out of the woods," he reported. "We skirmished a little, and then fell back."

"Are they heading for Kjelvik?" Count Hamnet demanded tensely. Could he stand siege here? If he couldn't, he would have to retreat *now.* If he did, Sigvat II would have one more reason not to love him.

But the scout shook his head. "No, uh, Your Grace. They're going southeast across country. You ask me, sir, they're heading straight for Nidaros."

"Can we strike at their flank, then?" Hamnet aimed the question more at himself than at the rider who'd just come in. Regretfully, he rejected the idea. His men had no spirit for another fight yet. And, without Marcovefa's sorcerous aid, they might as well have gone into battle without shields against an army of archers.

"What do we do if we don't hit them, Your Grace?" the scout asked.

The question was more pointed than Hamnet Thyssen wished it were. *Wait for the axe to drop* was the first answer that sprang to mind. He didn't come out and say that; he feared the scout would believe him. Worse, he feared he would believe himself. "I'll talk with the others," was what he did say, and that satisfied the scout, who didn't see—or didn't want to see— how little it told him.

When Count Hamnet gathered Ulric Skakki, Trasamund, and Runolf Skallagrim, none of them seemed eager to assail the advancing enemy. If Trasamund in particular held back, that told Hamnet the thing couldn't be done. And the Bizogot jarl did. "No point hitting 'em unless we hit 'em hard, and we can't right now, curse it," he said unhappily.

"Looks that way to me, too, I'm afraid," Ulric Skakki said.

"And to me," Runolf agreed. "If we're going to get squashed if we poke our noses outside the walls . . . well, then we don't, that's all."

Had Hamnet Thyssen had any great hopes of victory, he would have argued against the others. Since he didn't, he accepted their argument. Sometimes the best thing you could do was nothing.

He did send another courier down to Nidaros, warning that the Rulers were loose in the Empire below the northern woods and that he lacked the force to do anything about it. "Maybe a miracle will happen," he told Ulric. "Maybe the Emperor will send me more soldiers."

"Don't wait up expecting them, or you'll get mighty sleepy," the adventurer replied. "He'll probably yell for your head instead, for not doing enough with what he was generous enough to give you before."

"Yes, that thought crossed my mind, too," Count Hamnet said. "What am I supposed to do then?"

"Well, if you want to go to the chopper or back to the dungeon, you just do what dear, sweet, lovable Sigvat tells you to do," Ulric said. "If you don't, you do something else. If you don't feel like getting chopped, I'll go with you, for whatever you think that's worth. If you do, you're on your own."

Hamnet Thyssen set a hand on his shoulder, a gesture of affection and appreciation he rarely used. "Thanks. I'm not going to let Sigvat wreck me or the Empire, not if I can help it."

"You've got a chance to keep him from wrecking you," Ulric Skakki said. "If he doesn't wreck you, he'll have a harder time wrecking Raumsdalia, anyway. But you've got to worry about yourself first. You can do something about yourself. Right this minute, you can't do much about the whole bloody Empire."

The Empire was going to get bloodier. Count Hamnet couldn't do much about that, either, not till Marcovefa's wits unscrambled—if they ever did. *Congratulations,* he told himself. *You just found something brand new to worry about.*

He sighed. "Up till now, I've always put the Empire first. I still do, I guess, but. . . ."

"Yes. But," Ulric said. "One thing you still need to figure out is, there's a difference between the Empire and the Emperor. Raumsdalia can go on without Sigvat II, even if Sigvat's too cursed dumb to see that for himself."

Since Hamnet Thyssen hadn't seen if for himself, he maintained what he hoped was a discreet silence. Even if not just Sigvat but his dynasty perished, the Raumsdalian Empire *could* go on. Sometimes a truth was too obvious to be easy to see. Sometimes, in the woods, a mastodon was next to invisible. But then it would lift its trunk and trumpet, and everyone for a long way in all directions would know where it stood.

At least I know where I stand, Hamnet thought. That would have to do for now. "Who do you think hates me more right this minute?" he asked Ulric. "The Rulers or His Majesty?"

"Well, it depends," Ulric said judiciously.

"On what?"

"On whether your messenger has got to Nidaros yet."

"Oh." Count Hamnet weighed that. Then he nodded. "Yes, I'm afraid so."

"You're not afraid enough to suit Sigvat," Ulric said. "That's one of the reasons he doesn't like you." There was an understatement of almost cosmic proportions. Even the adventurer seemed relieved to change the subject: "How's your lady love?"

"About how you'd expect after almost getting her head smashed," Hamnet replied. He hesitated, then asked, "How's Liv doing?"

"She'll heal. She'll have a scar. It's a shame—she's a nice-looking woman. And no, in case you're trying to find some reason to come after me with a hatchet, I never slept with her. She is anyway." Ulric Skakki raised an eyebrow. "You don't need to ask me, you know. You could talk with her yourself. She's not like Gudrid—she doesn't aim to carve chunks off you every time she opens her mouth."

"I understand that," Hamnet said, as steadily as he could. "I still haven't decided whether it makes things better or worse." Even the glib Ulric Skakki had no quick and clever retort for that.

COUNT HAMNET WAS doing up his trousers as he came out of the garderobe when one of Runolf Skallagrim's junior officers spotted him. "Oh, there you are, Your Grace!" the very young subaltern exclaimed.

"Here I am, all right," Hamnet agreed. "And why does it make any difference that I happen to be here?"

"Because the baron needs to see you right away, sir," the junior officer said. "He's got six or eight men out looking for you."

"Does he?" Hamnet said with a marked lack of enthusiasm. That could only mean something had gone wrong. Two possibilities leaped to mind; he wondered which was the more appalling. "Well, I suppose I'd better go see him, then."

"Follow me, Your Grace." The youngster hurried off so fast, Hamnet Thyssen had very little choice *but* to follow him. He stopped in front of Runolf's door as abruptly as he'd sped away. When Hamnet came up a few heartbeats later, the fellow said, "Go on in, sir. I know he's expecting you."

"I'm so glad to hear it," Hamnet said. *What a liar I'm turning into in my old age.* He wasn't *that* old, but some days felt as if they added years. He worked the latch and went inside.

As he'd feared, a man with the look of an imperial courier waited with Runolf Skallagrim. "Morning, Thyssen," Runolf said, trying to pretend he knew Hamnet not at all well.

"It certainly is," Hamnet said, more or less at random. He inclined his head to the man who looked like a courier. "I don't think we've met."

"No, I don't think so, either. I'm Gunnlaug Jofrid," the man said. "I have orders to take you back to Nidaros."

Hamnet looked at him. "No."

"What?" By the way Gunnlaug gaped, Hamnet might have used a word in the language of the Rulers.

"It's a technical term," Hamnet explained, not unkindly. "It means, well, no."

"You can't say that!" Gunnlaug burst out. "His Majesty commands it!"

"Listen carefully. Watch the way my lips move. . . . No."

"But you can't disobey the Emperor," Gunnlaug Jofrid said, as if it were a law of nature.

"Oh, I can't, eh? I'm afraid we'll just have to see about that," Hamnet said.

"What will you do? Where will you go? Every man's hand will be raised against you, all over the Empire."

"Then I'll leave," Hamnet Thyssen said. "I've done it before. His Majesty won't be sorry to see me do it again."

Gunnlaug looked doubtful, to say the least. "That's not what my orders say. And how do I know you'll really do it, anyhow? How do I know you won't turn around and go somewhere and raise a rebellion? That would be worth my neck."

He wasn't wrong. He was, in fact, bound to be right. "Well, you can come with me," Hamnet suggested. "Then you'll be able to say you saw me ride up onto the Bizogot plain with your own eyes."

"You'd rather go up there than down to Nidaros?" Gunnlaug seemed to have trouble believing his ears.

"If I go down to Nidaros, Sigvat will either throw me back in the dungeon or kill me," Count Hamnet said. "If I go up into the Bizogot country, maybe the Rulers will kill me. But maybe they won't, too. And at least I'll be able to fight back. Any which way, I'm better off. Is that plain enough, or shall I get a stick of charcoal and some parchment and draw you a picture?"

"You're making fun of me!" Gunnlaug Jofrid's voice went shrill.

Hamnet looked at Runolf Skallagrim. "Nothing gets by him, does it?" Gunnlaug spluttered indignantly. Ignoring him, Count Hamnet went on, "Sorry this is awkward for you."

"I can see how you might not want to meet the chopper just yet—or any time at all, to tell you the truth," Runolf said.

"If you think I'm going to go to the back of beyond with you—" Gunnlaug began.

"The other choice is killing you right now," Hamnet Thyssen broke in. The courier shut up with a snap. Hamnet eyed Runolf again. "I didn't know I was so persuasive."

"Maybe I'd better stash the poor fellow in the guardhouse till you're ready to leave," Runolf said. "Wouldn't want him complicating your life even worse than it is already, would we?"

"This is an outrage!" Gunnlaug said. "An outrage, I tell you! When the Emperor finds out what you've done—" He broke off.

Had Count Hamnet the courier's boots, he would have stopped some time sooner. The snow wouldn't melt for months up here. A body that went into a drift wouldn't see the light of day till spring, and spring came late in these parts. Hamnet wondered whether he could afford to take the courier along. If the fellow kept trying to escape . . . Well, there was plenty of snow up in the forest, too.

"Do stick him in the guardhouse, Runolf," Hamnet said. "That will give me time to see who all wants to come along and to load pack horses. Easier than running off before we're ready."

"I'll take care of it," Runolf promised, and he did.

HAMNET RODE OUT of Kjelvik the next day. Marcovefa rode with him. So did Ulric Skakki. Audun Gilli and Liv came out side by side. Trasamund went along, as did a few of the other Bizogots. Most of the Leaping Lynxes who still lived stayed behind, though, judging their chances better inside the Empire than back up on the frozen steppe. Hamnet Thyssen had to hope they were wrong.

Also accompanying his band was Gunnlaug Jofrid. The imperial courier said, "Do you really imagine you can get away with this?"

"As a matter of fact, yes," Count Hamnet answered. "I can't believe Sigvat will send an army up into the Bizogot country after me. Can you?"

"He'd better not!" Trasamund rumbled. "He'd better not even think about it, by God! We'd swarm down into Raumsdalia and tear his precious Empire up by the roots if he tried. The very idea!" He snorted in disgust.

Ulric Skakki snorted, too, though quietly. An amused smile played over his features for a moment. Hamnet understood why: poor Trasamund had forgotten something. With the Bizogot clans shattered by the Rulers, the big blonds would swarm into the Empire only as refugees, or perhaps as vassals and hirelings of the mammoth-riders. The Bizogots' independent power would be a long time reviving, if it ever did.

The Rulers were still trickling down into Raumsdalia. Count Hamnet's band rode past several small groups of them even before it reached the edge of the woods. Hamnet led enough men to make the Rulers think twice about quarreling with him. He wasn't sure whether that pleased Trasamund or disappointed him.

Plunging into the forest again felt strange. Not far ahead lay the clearing where his army had battled the Rulers to a standstill . . . till that one unlucky slingstone took Marcovefa out of the fight and let the wizards from beyond the Glacier use the spells she'd blocked up till then.

She didn't remember much about what had gone on here. Hamnet doubted she ever would. He'd seen that loss of memory before in people who'd taken blows to the head. More often than not, it was a mercy.

Marcovefa didn't look at it that way. "I want to know what I did!" she complained. "I want to know what all they magicked at me. I want to know what I magicked at them. I know I was doing good—these Rulers are not so tough. But I want to know!"

"Maybe . . ." Hamnet Thyssen had to pause, because talking while he was gritting his teeth was hard. He made himself unclench his jaw and go on: "Maybe you could ask Liv and Audun Gilli. If anyone on our side knows, they're the ones."

Marcovefa kissed him. That made him glad he'd said what he had; he hadn't thought anything could. "I do that!" she said. She rode over to the

Raumsdalian wizard and the Bizogot shaman. Count Hamnet turned his head and looked the other way. He could suggest it, but he couldn't like it.

She was still talking with them when Hamnet's band came to the battlefield. Ravens flew away, croaking like big, black frogs. A short-faced bear looked up from a meal of . . . well, Hamnet hoped the beast was eating a dead warrior of the Rulers. The bear growled a warning at the newcomers. When they took no notice of it, it loped away, long legs carrying it off at least as fast as a horse could trot.

Marcovefa came back to Count Hamnet. *Yes, she does now—but for how long?* he wondered. Would he ever be able to get these doubts out of his head? She said, "This is where we fought?"

"That's right." He nodded.

"I remember the place. I remember the—the mammoths." She had to cast about for the word. "I remember the fear the foe threw. But even after I talk, I don't remember the fight." She slammed a fist down on her thigh in frustration. "I want to!"

"I don't know what to do about that," Hamnet said, in lieu of, *I don't think anyone can do anything about that.*

They pressed on to the north. A strange truce held whenever they passed bands of Rulers coming down into Raumsdalia. Once, a fellow who was pretty plainly a wizard stared at Marcovefa. Even in her damaged state, he knew her for what she was. When she bared her teeth at him in what was almost a smile, he flinched. The Rulers were made of stern stuff, whatever else you said about them; that didn't happen every day.

The trees began to thin out. The customs post at the tree line was a burned ruin. To the north, as far as the eye could see—and, Hamnet knew, far beyond that—stretched the snow-covered, gently rolling terrain of the Bizogot steppe.

"Here we are again," he said to Ulric Skakki.

"Never loses its charm, does it?" the adventurer returned.

"How can you lose what you haven't got?" Hamnet Thyssen said. Ulric laughed.

XXII

GUNNLAUG JOFRID RODE back towards the south. Count Hamnet didn't much want to let him go; he feared the courier would land Runolf Skallagrim in trouble. But the only other choice did seem to be slaughtering Gunnlaug, and Hamnet didn't have the stomach for it, not in cold blood.

"Don't worry. It will probably work out all right," Audun Gilli told him.

"Easy for you to say," Hamnet growled. "Runolf is a friend of mine. I don't like running out and leaving him in the lurch."

"I don't think you are," the wizard answered. "By the time Gunnlaug gets down to Nidaros again—if he ever does—how many Rulers will be between him and Kjelvik? With the worst will in the world, how much can Sigvat do to your friend?"

Hamnet Thyssen thought that over. His nod was grudging, but it was a nod. "Well, you've got something there," he said, and worried about it less. Too late now to do anything but what he'd done, anyhow.

"Now we find our fellow Bizogots, our fellow sufferers," Trasamund boomed. He seemed to have no doubts about what came next. "We fire them with our fury, and we lead them to victory against the accursed invaders."

He made it sound easy. Had it been easy, the Bizogots would have done it when the Rulers first swarmed down through the Cleft. Trasamund was always one to overlook details like that. Ulric Skakki said, "Finding enough to eat through the winter here ought to be interesting all by itself."

"We Bizogots don't starve," Trasamund declared.

"Except when we do." Liv had a better grasp on reality than the jarl did. Hamnet had known that for a long time. She went on, "Even with our herds, it isn't always easy. And we'll have to hunt without mammoths and musk oxen to fall back on."

"Dire wolves do it. So can we," Trasamund said.

"We can rob them, too," Ulric said. "What's left of a musk ox or a baby mammoth or one of the Rulers' riding deer that strayed will feed us for a while."

For a while, Hamnet thought. When the Breath of God blew hard from the north up here, folk needed more food than they did down in Nidaros, with fireplaces and braziers and double walls handy to hold cold at bay. You had to keep the hearth inside you burning hot, or else the Breath of God would blow it out.

Peering north, then northeast, then northwest, Count Hamnet saw . . . snow. No mammoths. No musk oxen. No riding deer. No geese or swans. No ducks or ptarmigan. No white-pelted hares. No voles or lemmings, either. He knew game of all sizes lived on, in, and under the snowdrifts, but finding any wouldn't be easy.

The horses would have to keep going, too. Unlike musk oxen or mammoths, they didn't always know enough to dig through the snow to find fodder underneath. Sooner or later—most likely sooner—the travelers would probably end up killing and eating the pack horses. Once the supplies they carried were gone, what point to fussing over them? He wasn't fond of horsemeat, but he wasn't fond of hunger, either.

"Come on!" Trasamund said. "Let's ride!"

He booted his horse forward as if he had not a care in the world. Up here in the Bizogot country, maybe he didn't. Whether he should or not . . . wasn't the same question. Count Hamnet urged his mount forward, too.

When he came north the winter before, he'd looked forward to running into people. The Bizogots guested strangers generously, knowing they might need guesting themselves one day before long. The Rulers, though, would be enemies no matter what. He made sure his sword stayed loose in its scabbard.

Nothing . . . Only snow and chill and rolling ground under the horse's hooves. Trasamund started singing a song about how splendid the countryside was. The jarl couldn't carry a tune in a bucket. He didn't care, but Count Hamnet didn't feel like listening to him.

"How are you?" Hamnet asked Marcovefa.

"I've been better," she answered. "My head still feels . . ." She made a face. "Things in there aren't right."

"A slingstone will do that," Hamnet said.

"But to knock out working magic?" She made another face, an angrier one. "It did that. I don't like it. I feel stupid."

"I can't work magic at all," Hamnet said. "Am I stupid?"

By her expression, the question was. "Suppose you go blind. Are you the same as you were before? I feel like I am blind in there." She carefully touched the right side of her head.

Liv pointed northwest and called, "A herd that way!"

Hamnet Thyssen saw nothing out of the ordinary when he looked that way. "How can you tell?" he asked. Even so simple a question hurt.

"Look at the air." Liv sounded as matter-of-fact as if they were strangers. "You can see the fog of all the animals breathing together." She pointed again. Once Count Hamnet knew where to look and what to look for, he could see it, too. That made him feel a little better, but not much. Liv went on, "I think they're musk oxen, but I'm not sure. The air doesn't look quite right." Hamnet couldn't tell the difference between fog from musk oxen and that from any other beasts. Could Liv, really? Maybe she could. The Bizogots had to learn such things if they wanted to go on living.

"*I* think they're musk oxen," Trasamund said. "I think we ought to slaughter one or two of them, too. We can use the meat. It will keep us going longer than the bread we brought north. Bread is all very well when you have no meat, but when you do. . . ."

Hamnet wondered who was watching that herd or flock or whatever the word was. If the outriders were Bizogots, there probably wouldn't be any trouble. If they were Rulers, there certainly would. His hand fell to his sword hilt again. He was ready for trouble, or hoped he was.

"Let's ride," Trasamund said once more. Nobody told him no. Ulric Skakki looked dubious, but Ulric looked dubious about half the time. He very often had good reason to look dubious, but Hamnet chose not to remember that.

Before long, the herd itself came into sight: a brown smudge on the horizon. The travelers hadn't gone much farther before Liv exclaimed, "Those aren't musk oxen!"

"I don't know what the demon they are," Trasamund said. Hamnet Thyssen still wasn't convinced they weren't musk oxen. But he had to believe the Bizogots knew better than he did.

Still, it wasn't a Bizogot who said, "They're riding deer, aren't they?" It was Ulric Skakki. He might look dubious, but he was also an adaptable man. Before long, Hamnet could see he was right here.

"What do we do?" Audun Gilli asked: all things considered, a more than reasonable question.

"I'm in the mood for roast venison," Hamnet said. His comrades bayed agreement.

"What if the Rulers have herdsmen with their deer?" Audun asked.

"Then in a little while they won't," Hamnet answered grandly. That got him more cheers. He began to string his bow. So did Ulric.

Sure enough, a herdsman rode out towards them . . . on a riding deer rather than a horse, which said by itself that he was a warrior of the Rulers. "You goes away!" he shouted in the Bizogot tongue, his accent and pronunciation terrible. "Goes away! Thises our deers is!"

"We ought to kill him just so we don't have to listen to him," Ulric murmured.

"Oh, we've got better reasons than that," Hamnet Thyssen said.

He and Ulric reached over their shoulders and nocked arrows at the same time. The enemy warrior seemed astonished that anyone on the frozen steppe would presume to disobey him. They'd both let fly before he even started to reach for an arrow. He hadn't finished drawing his bow before one shaft caught him in the chest and the other in the face. He slid out of the saddle and crashed down in the snow.

"Well shot!" Hamnet and Ulric shouted at the same time. Marcovefa pounded Hamnet on the back.

Another herdsman rode around from the far side of the flock to find out what was going on. Seeing his comrade down, he wheeled his deer and galloped off as fast as it would run.

Liv pointed at the deer and murmured . . . something. Suddenly, though the deer seemed to be running as hard as ever, it was hardly moving at all. The warrior of the Rulers beat it and cursed it, none of which did him any good. When the invaders had no shaman with them, they were vulnerable to Bizogot magic. Hamnet had seen that before.

The warrior leaped down from the ensorceled riding deer as the travelers drew near. He must have seen he had no hope for escape, for he charged them with drawn sword. Trasamund dismounted and met him blade-to-blade. "The Three Tusk clan!" the jarl cried.

He beat down his foe's guard with a few fierce cuts. The killing stroke almost took off the enemy fighter's head. The warrior of the Rulers staggered, blood gushing from a wound he couldn't hope to stanch. After a few lurching steps, he crumpled, the sword slipping from his fingers.

"If only there were one neck for the lot of them!" Trasamund cleaned his blade in a snowdrift.

"Would make things simpler, wouldn't it?" Ulric Skakki said. Hamnet Thyssen nodded.

The riding deer shifted nervously, half spooked by the shouting and by the stink of blood. But the beasts were more nearly tame than so many musk oxen would have been. The travelers had little trouble cutting several of them out of the herd and leading them downwind so the smells of their slaughtering wouldn't frighten the others so much.

"Maybe we ought to use them for pack animals and slaughter the extra horses," Audun Gilli said. "They fend for themselves better than horses do up here."

"But we can ride the horses if we have to." Trasamund was a staunch conservative. "We don't know how to do that with them."

"And they are beasts of the Rulers," Marcovefa said. "Maybe, if they stay alive, Rulers can use magic to track them."

Audun pursed his lips. "Yes, that could be," he said. "I should have thought of it myself."

And so they slaughtered the deer, wrapped the meat they wanted to take in the animals' hides, and loaded it onto the pack horses. Then they pressed north, up towards Sudertorp Lake and what had been Leaping Lynx country. But the Leaping Lynxes, these days, were as shattered as Trasamund's own clan.

"What can we do up here?" Hamnet said. "What hope have we got of putting a piece of this clan and a chunk of that one together and making an army that can stand up to the Rulers?"

"I don't know," Ulric answered. "But I do know Sigvat can't put you in a dungeon up here, so that leaves us ahead of the game right there. Or do you think I'm wrong, Your Grace?" He used Hamnet's title of respect with irony.

"I only wish I did," Hamnet said. They rode on.

MARCOVEFA LOOKED AT the snow. She frowned in concentration, and maybe in a little pain, as she whistled a strange tune in a wailing, minor key. Then she muttered to herself. "That's not right," she said.

"Try it again," Hamnet Thyssen told her. "Your magic's bound to come back to you sooner or later, isn't it?" He fought not to show his fear.

"Well, I hope so. I don't want to be mindblind the rest of my days," she answered. *Mindblind* wasn't really a word in Raumsdalian, which didn't keep Hamnet from understanding it—and from understanding that he wasn't the only fearful one here.

Marcovefa eyed the drifted snow again. She nodded to herself, as if to say, *I can do this.* Then she whistled again. The tune was almost the same as it had been before—almost, but not quite. Hamnet couldn't have defined the difference, but he knew it was there.

Suddenly, a vole popped out of the snow. It stared at Marcovefa with small, black, beady eyes. Then, as if recognizing her as one of its own kind, it scurried towards her. Her smile blazed brighter than the weak northern sun. She stopped whistling. The vole let out a high-pitched squeak of horror, almost turned a somersault spinning around, and scooted away.

She let it go. As she turned to Hamnet, her eyes shone with triumph. "There!" she said. "I did it! I called the vole to me!"

"Good," he said. "Would you hunt that way up on top of the Glacier?"

"Sometimes I would, if I had to," she replied. "But you see? I did a magic! Not a big magic yet, but a magic! My head is not ruined, not for good."

"God be praised for that," Hamnet said gravely. "Do you suppose you can call mammoths the same way when you get better?"

He was teasing her, but she took him seriously. "I don't know. I never try anything like that up on the Glacier. No big animals up on the Glacier, not except for people." She bared her teeth. Maybe she was teasing him back. Or maybe she was remembering the taste of man's flesh. Then her grin faded. She touched the side of her head, still swollen and bruised. "I have myself back again. I have my self back again." She made Hamnet hear the pause in the middle of the word.

"Good." He could imagine what that meant to her. And he knew what it meant to the fight against the Rulers. Without Marcovefa, there *was* no fight against the Rulers . . . unless Sigvat could somehow mount one. From everything Hamnet had seen, that struck him as unlikely.

She whistled again. Another little furry head popped out of the snow-bank. Another ensorceled vole started towards her. This time, she took it in her hands before relaxing the spell. Count Hamnet wondered if the vole would die of fright. It didn't—it just twisted loose and ran away.

"Not an accident. Not a happenstance," Marcovefa said happily. "I can really do this."

"Good," Hamnet said. "If any of the Rulers stick their heads out of the snow all of a sudden, we know just how to take care of them."

Marcovefa laughed. Hamnet was joking, and then again he wasn't. She'd worked magic, but she hadn't worked strong magic. If this was the most she could do, how could she stand against the Rulers? And if she couldn't stand against the Rulers, what was the point to anything?

"Suppose we meet the Rulers in the ordinary way," Hamnet persisted. "What can you do then?"

"Whatever I have to do, I can do," Marcovefa replied.

That was encouraging, or it would have been had Hamnet had more confidence in it. But he didn't want to show Marcovefa he had no confidence; if he did show her that, wouldn't it hurt *her* confidence? And confidence that she could beat the Rulers was one big advantage she enjoyed over both the Bizogots and the Raumsdalians. She'd always thought she could, and she'd been right most of the time—till that slingstone made her wrong at just the wrong moment.

"Voles," Hamnet Thyssen muttered.

"If I see any mammoths hiding in the snowdrift, I am able to call those, too," Marcovefa said brightly.

"Oh, *good*," Count Hamnet said. Marcovefa couldn't always tell when he was being sarcastic. This time, she noticed, and thought it was funny. Hamnet went on, "Suppose they aren't hiding there. Suppose they're just . . . mammothing along. Could you call them then?"

"Mammothing? Is that a word?"

"It is now."

"I don't know if I could or not," Marcovefa answered. "I tell you this, though—I want to find out."

"So do I," Hamnet said. If she could call mammoths the way she called voles . . . Well, what good would it do the Rulers to ride them, if they wouldn't go where their riders wanted them to? Sometimes mammoth corpses got buried in floods or cave-ins and frozen underground for years or even centuries, then came to the surface again. Some of the people who found them that way thought they lived like moles and died when air touched them. How much of a difference was there between moles and voles?

If you were a vole or a mole, a lot. Otherwise?

"I have my magic back," Marcovefa said. "Nothing else matters." Count Hamnet was inclined to agree with her.

COMING UP TO the steppe before, Hamnet had passed smoothly from one Bizogot clan's territory to the next. As often as not, riders near the edge of one clan's lands—or the fierce dogs they had with them—would let him know when he'd come within the bounds of a new jarl's domain.

Now the Rulers had shattered the arrangements that prevailed for so long. In a broad swath down the center of the frozen plain, the invaders had beaten and broken up the clans that had roamed there for so long. The Rulers had commandeered as many of the herds as they could lay hold of, but others still wandered with no one to protect them from lions and short-faced bears and dire wolves . . . and from hungry Bizogots as much on their own as the musk oxen and mammoths and horses were.

Chaos and banditry, of course, spread far beyond the clans the Rulers had actually broken. Refugees and fugitives went where they would, went where they could, and turned their swords and bows against the Bizogots already holding those grounds and herds. Some of the clans the Rulers hadn't touched got smashed to pieces by their own folk . . . and then they spread disorder farther yet.

In the midst of such madness and uncertainty, a knot of hard-bitten travelers who weren't afraid to fight had no trouble gathering a following. Men who wanted to hit back at the invaders but saw no way to do it on their own were glad to join people who did have a plan.

"How does it feel, being most of the way towards a king?" Ulric Skakki asked Hamnet after they'd collected a pretty fair beginning to an army.

Hamnet rolled his eyes. "How does it feel, being out of your head?"

"I enjoy it most of the the time," Ulric said easily. "Now answer my question."

"I'm not a king. I'm not a jarl, either. I'm barely even a general," Hamnet Thyssen said. "If Trasamund wanted that slot, he could take it. I wouldn't say a word. This is his country, not mine."

"That's why he's standing back and letting you have it," Ulric said. Before Hamnet could tell him he was crazy again, Ulric went on, "Up here, he's just another Bizogot—and just another Bizogot who's lost to the Rulers. But you, you're—"

"Just another Raumsdalian who's lost to the Rulers," Hamnet broke in.

Ulric Skakki shook his head. "You're a foreigner. You're interesting. You're exotic. You carry hope."

"And other diseases," Hamnet Thyssen said.

"Ow!" Ulric wasn't easy to wound with words, but he flinched then. Gathering himself, he said, "Well, the Rulers would agree with you."

"Bugger the Rulers. Bugger 'em with a pine cone," Count Hamnet said.

"That's what we're here for," the adventurer reminded him.

"I know," Hamnet said. "We're going to have to hit them. If we don't, the Bizogots will decide we're good for nothing. They'll ride off and leave us, and then—"

"We *will* be good for nothing," Ulric Skakki finished for him. "Well, the world has been telling me I'm good for nothing for a long time. Maybe it's been right all along. You never can tell."

Hamnet Thyssen glowered at him. "We haven't got much of an army here. If we strike at the Rulers and lose . . ." He shook his head. "If that happens, we're ruined."

"We wouldn't be way the demon up here if plenty of people didn't already think we were ruined," Ulric said. "So far, we've hurt the Rulers here on the steppe. We've killed their men and slaughtered their animals. And have they hurt us? Have they even touched us? They haven't, and you know it."

Reluctantly, Hamnet nodded. He did know it, but knowing it brought no reassurance. "Pinpricks," he said. "We've given them pinpricks, and they haven't bothered noticing. But they will if we hit them hard."

Ulric Skakki set his mittened hands on Hamnet's shoulders. "You can stay invisible, or you can make a proper enemy. The way it looks to me, those are your only choices. And you can't do both at once. So which would you rather?"

"What do you think?" Hamnet asked.

"Well, I hoped I knew," Ulric Skakki answered.

"You do," Hamnet said grimly. Ulric nodded and stopped bothering him, one of the more sensible things the adventurer ever did.

FOR ALL THEIR bold talk, Hamnet and Ulric didn't lead their growing band across the frozen top of Sudertorp Lake, the way they'd gone north the year before. They'd almost died the year before, too, when magic from the Rulers cracked the ice and nearly spilled them into the freezing water.

Maybe Marcovefa could have shielded them from a repeat of that fright. She seemed sure her sorcery was close to full strength. All the same, Count

Hamnet didn't want to test her before he had to. And, despite the confidence she showed, she didn't seem eager to test herself, either. Ready, yes, but not eager.

"When the time comes, I will do what wants doing," she said. "Till then Well, each day I am stronger. Each day my head is clearer."

"That's what I want to hear," Hamnet said.

"I do not say it because you want to hear it. I say it because it is true," Marcovefa told him.

"All right. Good." He didn't want to quarrel with her. He looked across the rolling, snow-covered landscape. With no trees, the Bizogot steppe grew boring in winter. "I wonder if the Golden Shrine is anywhere near here. If it is, you'd probably heal right away if you went inside."

"We knew of the Golden Shrine up on top of the Glacier, too," Marcovefa said. "We thought it was up there—somewhere up there. Sometimes we went looking for it, but no one ever found it."

"When your ancestors first went up atop the Glacier, they already knew about the Golden Shrine," Hamnet answered. "Most folk say it's the oldest thing in the world. Some say it was there before the Glacier first came down from the north. Eyvind Torfinn believes that, I think."

"He is a strange man. He has no magic in him, but he is wise. I did not think that could be, but it is." Marcovefa paused. "He is wise, except for the woman he chose. She is pretty, but. . . ."

"You know she was mine once," Hamnet said.

"I know she was wed to you once, yes. But she was never yours. Gudrid is only Gudrid's."

"Well, yes," Hamnet agreed. "But I didn't know that then, and I paid for the lesson." Gudrid was even prettier in those days, too, which made the price dearer—or at least seem dearer to a man who was younger himself.

"The Golden Shrine . . ." Marcovefa seemed willing not to talk about Gudrid, which suited Count Hamnet fine. "We say you find it if you don't expect it. If you look for it, it is never there." Her grin was impish. "We must have looked for it. It was never there for us."

"We say the same kinds of things about it," Hamnet agreed. "I didn't believe it was there at all till I learned of the lands beyond the Glacier. Now I think maybe there is such a thing. But it is where it wants to be, not where we want it to be. Does that make any sense at all?"

"More than you know, maybe," Marcovefa said.

Before Hamnet could ask her what she meant, a scout came galloping back. "We found them!" he shouted. "We found the stinking mammoth turds! Now let's go kill every cursed one of them!"

The Bizogots who formed the bulk—formed almost all—of Hamnet's army roared like the predators they were. Everyone thundered forward. Hamnet didn't much want a battle just then. He had one anyhow. Now he had to try to lead it. If he didn't, one thing seemed plain: the army wouldn't be his any more.

THERE WERE THINGS the scout hadn't said. How many enemies waited ahead? Were they ready to fight? For that matter, Count Hamnet wondered whether his own army was ready to fight. They'd run from the Rulers often enough before. Only one way to find out . . .

"I see 'em!" Trasamund bellowed. So did Hamnet Thyssen: a line of men on riding deer, with the bigger lumps of mammoths anchoring the center of their line. They were ready, then.

"Try to stay out of slingstone range!" Hamnet shouted to Marcovefa.

She gave back what was anything but a military salute. Then she blew him a kiss. He wondered what it meant. He wondered if it meant anything. He'd find out—probably sooner than he wanted.

Sooner than he wanted, he found the Rulers had at least one wizard with them. Snow leapt up from the ground. It took the shapes of wolves and of the fierce great cats from beyond the Glacier—*tigers*, the Rulers called them. Count Hamnet thought they were illusion till one of the snow tigers tore the throat out of a scout's horse and then killed the Bizogot, too.

If Marcovefa couldn't do anything about that . . . Would the magic beasts break up the Bizogot charge by themselves, or would they terrify the Bizogots into turning around and fleeing? They weren't far from scaring Count Hamnet into turning around.

But then they all burst into puffs of steam. Marcovefa laughed in delight. Hamnet thought that was joy at having her power back. He was delighted that she had it back, too.

"Give them something to remember you by!" he yelled.

Marcovefa laughed again. "Oh, they will remember me!" she said. Maybe it was her joy that made her do what she did next. All the Rulers' riding beasts—deer and mammoths alike—seemed to go into heat at the same time, and into a more fiery heat than any they knew in their proper mating season.

A mammoth interested in rutting with another mammoth was a

mammoth rather spectacularly not interested in carrying warriors of the Rulers into battle. The same held true for riding deer. Bucks butted at one another and locked antlers. Does pushed their way towards the males, ignoring the riders trying to push them towards the Bizogots.

Some of the enemy fighting men could still use their bows. Most seemed at least as distracted as their beasts. The Rulers had no hope fighting with swords and spears. Those required cooperation between warriors and mounts, but they had none.

Only a few slingers made life difficult for the Bizogots. The band Hamnet's men had come across didn't seem to be an army on campaign, as the one down in Raumsdalia had been. It was probably a clan's worth of men—if the Rulers used clans. The Bizogots broke their line with ease. Why not, when their own animals had broken it?

Hamnet sent horsemen straight at the slingers. He couldn't do that so neatly as he would have with Raumsdalian soldiers. The Bizogots didn't obey for the sake of obeying, as trained troopers would. But when he pointed at the slingers and shouted, enough Bizogots took the hint to do what he wanted done. They charged.

One slingstone hit a horseman in the face and knocked him out of the saddle. But the slingers couldn't fight cavalry at close quarters. A few who held their ground paid for it. The rest broke and ran, and the Bizogots rode them down, too.

Seeing them run told Hamnet Thyssen what a victory he'd gained. Far more even than Raumsdalians, the Rulers were disciplined warriors. Losing to men from the herds—their contemptuous term for anyone not of their folk—was the worst disgrace they knew. Fleeing from the herds . . . He wondered if they'd so much as imagined such an enormity.

He pointed Bizogots at the Rulers' wizards, too. More snow beasts sprang against them—maybe those were this clan's sorcerous specialty. If so, it did them no good. Marcovefa boiled these monsters out of existence, as she had the others.

Then Count Hamnet got to enjoy the spectacle of wizards running for their lives. Running helped them no more than it had the slingers. Not even a wizard of the Rulers could aim a spell as fast as an archer could aim an arrow. And shrieks of agony disrupted the harsh gutturals of the Rulers' language.

The enemy commander kept on roaring commands from mammothback till his mammoth, consumed by erotical lust, plucked him off with its trunk and threw him down, hard, onto the frozen ground. Then he shrieked, too, a shriek that ended with horrible abruptness as a mammoth foot descended on his chest. Hamnet Thyssen was close enough to hear ribs snap and crackle and pop, close enough to watch blood splash out to stain the snow. He looked away. He also rode farther away, lest the mammoth decide he and his horse stood in its way, too.

After their leader died, a few of the Rulers tried to surrender. That went against everything the iron-souled invaders were supposed to hold dear. Count Hamnet had seen it happen before even so, in the invaders' rare defeats. The urge to live could corrode even the sternest discipline.

But the Bizogots' lust was up, too: theirs for blood hardly less than that of the Rulers' beasts for coupling. Hamnet and Ulric Skakki both shouted that some of the enemy should be spared. Trasmund shouted the same thing, which surprised Hamnet—was the jarl finally discovering what a good idea staying practical could be?

Much good it did him if he was. His fellow Bizogots paid no more attention to him than they did to the foreigners among them. More blood dappled the white of the frozen steppe. And then it was over: there were no more Rulers left to kill.

Even Trasamund seemed pleased. "By God, this'll give the musk-ox buggers something to think about," he boomed, looking around the trampled field. The iron stink of blood filled the frosty air.

"Well, so it will," Ulric Skakki said. "And the first thing they'll think about is how to do in the bastards who did this to them."

That struck Hamnet Thyssen as being altogether too likely. But battle fever thrummed in his veins, too, and he said, "Let them try! As long as we've got Marcovefa, they don't stand a chance."

Ulric mimed a slingstone glancing off someone's head. Then he mimed a slingstone catching someone between the eyes. Hamnet glared at him, not because he was being foolish but because he wasn't. It could happen. It almost had. But it hadn't.

"We can hurt them now," he said. "We can hurt them badly, maybe even stop them from getting down into the Empire."

"Hurrah!" Trasamund said sourly. "What good does that do my land? What good does that do my folk?" His wave encompassed the whole of the Bizogot country.

"If no more warriors or wizards of the Rulers can get down into Raumsdalia, maybe the Empire will be able to deal with the ones who are there now," Count Hamnet said. "That weakens the enemy everywhere, not just in the south. It's all one big fight, you know."

"Ha! Easy for you to say." Trasamund wasn't convinced.

"Last summer, the Bizogots didn't think it was one big fight," Ulric Skakki reminded him. "They tried to take on the Rulers clan by clan—and look what that got them."

Trasamund glared at him—again, not because he was wrong but because he was right. "You are an impossible pest," the jarl growled. Ulric bowed in the saddle, as if at a compliment. That made Trasamund no happier.

Hamnet Thyssen looked around one more time, now to make sure Liv was all right. She wasn't his any more, but. . . . *But what?* he asked himself, and found no good answer. He knew too well he would have done the same thing were Gudrid on the field, even though she might hope he died in battle.

There was Liv, binding up a wound on Audun Gilli's arm and chanting a healing charm over it. Catching Hamnet's eye, she nodded gravely to him. He made himself nod back. Unlike Gudrid, Liv plainly wished him no harm. That helped, but not enough.

He forced himself back to matters he could do something about. "We'll plunder them," he called, not that the Bizogots weren't already tending to that. "We'll plunder them, and we'll slaughter their riding deer—"

"And I, by God, will ride off on one of their mammoths!" Trasamund shouted.

And, to Hamnet's amazement, he did. After Marcovefa let her spell lapse, the mammoths and deer soon calmed down. A woolly mammoth let the Bizogot jarl clamber aboard and guide it along. Trasamund whooped with joy and pride. He was a boy with a new toy—a toy that could kill him if he got the least bit careless, but he didn't worry about that, not then.

Count Hamnet didn't worry about it, either. For once, he didn't worry about anything, and wondered why not. His gaze slid towards Marcovefa. She grinned back at him, then eyed an enemy corpse and reached for a knife, as if to butcher it. She was only half joking, if that much. Hamnet didn't care. Savage or not, cannibal or not, she gave him hope. And when you had hope, what else did you need?